UNWANTED

ALSO BY CATHERINE M. WALKER

Unwanted (Emergence, 1)

Sacrifice (Emergence, 2)

Defiance (Emergence, 3)

Shattering Dreams (The Being Of Dreams, 1)

Path Of The Broken (The Being Of Dreams, 2)

Elder Born (The Being Of Dreams, 3)

NEWSLETTER

If you'd like updates of my progress, promotions and advance notice of when the next book comes out drop by my website and join my newsletter.

www.catherinemwalker.com

UNWANTED

EMERGENCE
BOOK ONE

CATHERINE M. WALKER

ISBN: 978-1-925776-13-3 (eBook)

ISBN: 978-1-925776-14-0 (Paperback)

ISBN: 978-1-925776-15-7 (Hardcover)

https://www.catherinemwalker.com

 Created with Vellum

Not only Unwanted, but the whole Emergence series nearly ended up, disregarded and never to be seen by anyone else again. A few people helped kick Unwanted over that last hurdle. Thank you:
Abigail
Alexandria
Betsey

CHAPTER
ONE

It took time to set up a village this way, but grateful villagers were easier to manage, than those taken by force. It was a tactic the Warlord had used with great success in the other villages that had been taken. Their enemy could always be relied on to attack a target as fat as this village, and while he and the Warlord's forces would always fight the Sylannians, the Warlord might as well get a double advantage from the fight. This way, they got to defeat their enemy and welcome a grateful, willing new village to expand the Warlord's domain.

Michael ruthlessly suppressed his twinge of guilt. People would die needlessly tonight. Not that the villagers would ever know his own warband, the Unwanted, and indeed all the Warlord's forces in this region, surrounded their village. Watching, waiting for the Sylannians to attack the helpless villagers before the combined warbands would ride in to save them. But he couldn't really complain. Nor could he blame the Warlord. This was, after all, his own battle plan.

More of them would die and suffer if we weren't here at all, Olivia said.

None of them would die if we'd killed the Sylannians when I first received word of their presence, Michael said.

They would. The Warlord wants this village. There's usually more than one stupid person thinking they can fight us, Nathanial said.

Michael nearly snorted in amusement as his long-time friends and second-in-command for the Unwanted echoed some of his own thoughts. He pulled his attention back to the village. He'd always found the stillness in the hours before dawn eerie. The villagers, totally unaware of what was about to befall them, slept on. The only disturbance to the quiet night was the fighters around him: the creak of leather as they shifted position, the sound of their breaths, the slow, deliberate scraping of a sword being withdrawn from a sheath, the snort of a horse nearby. All of it sounded harsh and overloud to him, a herald that screamed the presence of the warbands to any who would listen. Yet he knew the soft lap and flow of the river masked even the inadvertent noise of hundreds of the Warlord's fighters while they waited for the assault to begin.

At least, that was all he would hear if he relied on his normal senses. But with the power of the veil to fuel his perception, he could also hear a steady, rhythmic ripple that disrupted the normal flow of the river. It was a sound he recognised. Despite the hour and the fact that he couldn't see them, boats travelled on the river towards the village. Now, those in the boats were close enough he could hear the thoughts of the people in them, and while he couldn't speak the language, he recognised it: Sylannian.

As the Sylannian boats drew ever closer to the village, he sent his othersight out, almost seeming to fly over the village towards the jetty. The shadowy outlines of the invaders, with the muted glow from the power of the veil they held, came into focus. He didn't have to count their number. Sentries out in the vast, interconnected river system had already counted them and reported back to him. Six long wooden boats, each patterned with the same colours its occupants wore, each filled with forty people. In that odd way of a Sylannian raiding force, this attack force comprised all female soldiers, except for one Sylannian male. As the enemy drew closer to Michael's position at the edge of the village, he no longer had to rely on the veil to sharpen his senses. He could hear the slap of wood on water. A faint splash as the oars broke the surface of the river, followed by a ripple as they passed, pulling them closer to the jetty.

Stand ready, he ordered. *Remember, the Sylannian male will be fighting somewhere in their midst. Kill the male and their whole attack will fall apart, making them much easier to kill.*

Michael sent his mind out, checking on each of the leaders of the other squads around the village, making sure they were all where they were supposed to be. He kept his eyes on the village, tensing as he saw the faint outline of six boats pull up to the shoreline, followed by the slap of booted feet running on the wooden jetty. Flames lit the darkness as the Sylannian raiders set boats along the water's edge alight, their way of preventing anyone following them after they'd taken what they wanted and fled down the river. It was quite effective. Or it would be if the Warlord's forces weren't here. As the shadowy figures of the Sylannian raiders flooded into the village, a crack of splintering wood, a meaty thunk and a shriek shattered the early morning silence. It was the sound they were waiting for. The Sylannian attack on the village had commenced, yet still they waited. Michael gritted his teeth. Images, sounds, smells flooded his mind on replay from a time when the screams and flames were consuming his own city.

Everyone ready? The Warlord's strong mental voice demanded attention.

We're in position, Warlord. Awaiting your order, Michael said.

Michael drew his sword, not bothering to check the position of his people first. He didn't have to. All the members of his own warband would be formed up exactly as he'd trained them to. Calm flooded him as he waited for that one word they all knew was coming.

Attack!

The Warlord's command rang in his mind, unleashing the combined fighters on the unsuspecting raiders and villagers alike. Michael dropped his mental barriers and sucked as much of the power of the veil into himself as he could hold. Exhilaration pulsed through him as the chill of the veil washed through him. He knew his eyes and those of the Unwanted glowed with the power they now held. The veil fuelled all of his people, making them stronger, faster; heightening their reflexes and senses. He ran from the trees, Olivia on one side of him, Nathanial on the other, his people streaming behind them as they entered the now-seething village to engage the Sylannian forces in battle.

Switching to his othersight, he could see the bright sparks of the lifeforces of the Unwanted and the other members of the Warlord's troops, each burning brightly, fuelled by the power they held. Then the duller, muddy pulsing of the villagers and the Sylannian raiders alike. Viewed like this, they were indistinguishable from each other. Although neither he nor any other member of the Unwanted would have difficulty distinguishing this enemy. The Sylannians all wore their odd, colourful garments that were as effective as his own fighting leathers while they were alive and fighting, but reformed to mere silk when they died. Michael could tell from the low-level power that pulsed sluggishly in the Sylannians they were none of them any stronger than the average person.

Michael noted the distinct bright glow of the Warlord leading another unit as they spurred their horses towards the docks. The Unwanted might only have a third of the number of soldiers of the other warbands, but he and his people were stronger. Much stronger. The Warlord fell on a group of Sylannians attempting to retreat to their boats, dragging the few captives they'd managed to grab with them as they fled. A flash in the dark wrenched Michael's attention back to see a dagger carving a path towards his neck. He flinched, raised his sword, and lunged desperately out of the weapon's path. Suddenly steel rang as a blade bearing the glowing symbol of the Unwanted along its length intervened. Michael ignored the wash of cold air as Olivia sucked in more power and struck an enemy to his right. The veil shimmered in response as a disk of pure power took shape. Olivia braced herself and thrust the shield forward. The Sylannians directly in front of them staggered as if someone had hit them with a physical force.

Michael, pay attention! A small mental slap accompanied Olivia's voice.

Michael ignored his friend's exasperation to concentrate on the fight at hand. Everyone else could take care of themselves. He spun his own shield of power and shunted it up to deflect an enemy's thrusting daggers and delivered a sharp jab into the Sylannian's neck.

Reinforcing the strength of his arm and sword with the veil, he parried to deflect his opponent's weapon. His opponent hesitated, eyes wide, as she tried to copy how he was using the veil. He lunged and slashed at his enemy. There was a slight resistance as his blade met the Sylannian's armour. He grunted in effort as his blade flared and sliced through her protective clothing. She staggered, one hand pressing to her stomach, and fell back. Michael ignored his fallen opponent to concentrate on the next one.

Michael heard a faint sound through the veil, like air being sucked through a pipe, as the Warlord drew in large strands of the power that wove around them all. An explosion shook the ground, vibrating through the air, causing Michael to stagger. Elemental fire leapt into existence on the Sylannian boats, casting a blue glow across the battlefield. The heat from the elemental flames rolled over him, fuelled by the veil—not even water would stop it.

The distraction proved fatal for the Sylannians. There was no such thing as honour in the Warlord's ranks. Michael launched himself at another enemy whose back was to him and cut her down with a slash. Ignoring the spray of blood, he pushed forward, showing no mercy. He lunged with his sword, running through another Sylannian as she spun to face him. He inhaled, as he and the Unwanted were suddenly in a pool of calm, surrounded by madness.

That's one Sylannian battle group down.

Unless I miss my mark, that was the Warlord who set the Sylannian boats alight over near the pier. He's battling with the second, Olivia said.

Aiden's team has a third Sylannian battle group under control over near the far huts, Nathanial said.

The members of Michael's warband were quickly checking the fallen and dispatching any remaining enemies. He drew on the veil and switched to his othersight to assess the ebbing life-force of the fallen.

These won't survive. We can finish them later if needed. Let's keep moving. Michael spoke only to the members of his band.

He sensed more than saw them nod, before they drew power and ran further into the village, seeking the other Sylannian battle groups. As Michael drew nearer to the centre of the village, the sounds of battle increased. They all picked up their pace towards the screaming and rounded the corner to find a group of villagers trapped by two Sylannian battle groups. Michael reached out with his mind and drew in more of the strands of the veil, almost shuddering as the energy flowed into him. He could see other strands of the pure energy being absorbed into the members around him and they used the veil they'd consumed to propel themselves forward. The village blurred as they surged into the town square. The villagers were fighting with anything they could get their hands on; Michael simply fell on the Sylannian raiders from behind. Half of the enemy fell to the blades of the Unwanted before the Sylannians fought back.

The villagers seemed to take heart at the relief the Unwanted offered. People attacked with an assortment of axes, brooms, kitchen utensils, and even a couple of short swords. It was comical, yet somehow they pulled it off. The women of the village held a defensive line in front of their men. One of the village men yelled, charging forward, only for a thrust of power from one of the other villagers to pull him back.

"Stay back, Father! It's you these hellions want," a young woman shouted as she lunged, her sword slipping past her opponent's guard.

Michael swore as the final Sylannian battle group swarmed in from the side. Despite the additional numbers the fighting technique of the enemy became frenzied. Michael struck out and a Sylannian slumped to the ground, bringing the sole Sylannian male into sight. Michael reached out with his power, wrapping tight bands of the veil around the man and pulling him towards him. The bound man's eyes widened in fear and he desperately battered against the hold Michael maintained on him. Michael braced himself and lunged, thrusting his sword out as he wrenched his captive towards him. The man grunted as Michael's blade slammed through him and Michael released his hold, letting the body topple to the ground. On the death of the male, in his othersight Michael saw the fine tracing of power that spun like a web from the Sylannian male to all the Sylannian woman shatter. As those mental bonds that bound his enemy fragmented, the fluid and structured fighting of the remaining Sylannians disintegrated and became frenzied attacks on anyone around them, including their own fighters.

The Sylannian male might be dead, but they still had a fight to finish. A flash of metal to his left caught Michael's eye and he twisted to fend off a sword that was striking for his own heart. A blast of power from Olivia sent several of the Sylannians toppling back.

Perhaps we should have waited for one of the other warbands to assist before jumping into the middle of this, she observed as she fought off an attacker next to him.

Michael had to concede Olivia's point. Being outnumbered by about four to one were long odds, even for them. He lost himself in fighting, drawing in power and battering down the enemy. Utilising the power he held, he pushed a couple of the Sylannians away to give himself a little breathing space, only to see them cut down from behind as another team finally joined the fight. Michael accounted for two more of the enemy, grinning in appreciation as the local woman he'd seen fighting earlier ran through a third. He almost stumbled when there were no more Sylannians for him to kill.

For a moment, there was stillness. A stark, shocking silence. Then the wailing started, interspersed with the groaning and weeping from the injured.

TWO

As the early morning light dawned, the eerie blue tinge caused by the elemental fire on the water dispersed. At least it appeared that way to Michael. That blue glow, which showed up in his othersight, marked the fire as being fuelled by the veil. To normal eyes, it would appear as any other fire. Tony, the leader of the other team that helped them defeat the last Sylannian battle group, joined them.

He doesn't appear too happy, Nathanial whispered.

Oh, I noticed. Do you think we're in trouble? Olivia asked.

I think we are. Now, shut up and let me apologise to the man, Michael said.

"Warleader, it's hard to protect you if you keep leaving us behind." Tony glared at him.

"Sorry," Michael muttered, then plastered a smile on his face. "Then again, that is why we practiced this manoeuvre."

"Helps work out the problems," Olivia said, her tone cheerful, as if they weren't standing in the aftermath of a battle.

"Next time we'll try to remember to drag you lot with us," Nathanial said.

"Thank you. I'd appreciate it. The Warlord would not be happy with me if anything had happened to you," Tony growled.

"Nothing did. You and your crew appeared at just the right moment." Michael tried to put as much sincerity into his voice as he could. It helped that it was true, and the other warband really had shown up when they'd needed them to.

I forgot they were meant to be watching over us, Olivia said.

Me too, Michael replied.

At a subtle gesture from Nathanial, he turned and saw a group of soldiers heading his direction. Even surrounded by fighters bristling with the glow of power and weapons, the figure of the Warlord was unmistakable. He wore authority like a glove as he strode across the village towards the Unwanted, causing the villagers to stare. More than one stepped back as they sensed the approaching threat. The Warlord and his people had been stronger in the veil than others around them and that was how the Warlord had originally risen to dominance, defeating the others who'd claimed the title of Warlord —including his family. He and his people used their gifts to enhance their fighting abilities to a level far beyond what others had tried before. The Warlord gathered those with great talent in the veil to him in those days. He still did. The Warlord's eyes glowed with the remnants of power he hadn't released, as Michael guessed his own did. Michael didn't miss the glitter in the Warlord's eyes as they swept the now calm village. Not all of it was due to holding onto the veil. The Warlord loved a good fight. Particularly a battle he'd just won so conclusively. With a negligent wave of his hand, the Warlord extinguished the blaze on the water. Michael barely stopped himself from rolling his eyes at the theatrics. The Warlord always liked everyone to know that he was the one with all the power.

Seeing motion from the other side of the square, Michael tensed, then relaxed as he saw Aiden making his way from behind the protective ring of his own team. Aiden's second-in-command, Derick, was at least competent, which was probably the only reason the Warlord's true-born son survived. As Aiden sheathed his sword, Michael noted it was still clean. Not so much as a speck of blood marred Aiden's face, hands, or fighting leathers, either. To all appearances, he could have just walked out of his tent after a good night's sleep. Then again, it would have shocked him to see anything else. It was Aiden's people who took care of the actual fighting. The Warlord had handpicked all of them, although at least half of them were men and women Michael had refused to have in the Unwanted even if they'd had the talent. Originally, the job of making Aiden appear competent, and keeping him alive, was a task the Warlord had asked Michael to fulfil. Their father had explained that Aiden to all appearances would be the leader of the warband while in reality, Michael would be the one in charge when fighting actually occurred. It was an *honour* he'd refused. A decision which, thankfully, the Warlord had accepted. Michael pointed out while he and Aiden had been raised as brothers, they did not get on. If he were forced into constant company with the man who'd effectively become his foster brother, he'd probably end up running Aiden through out of sheer irritation. The Warlord had sighed, conceding the point. Michael couldn't understand how the Warlord could have fathered such a son.

As the Warlord's party drew closer, Aiden leant against one of the wooden posts that held up the roof of the outdoor communal area. Michael barely restrained himself from laughing. Aiden always liked to maintain the appearance that he was at ease. At least after the messy fighting part was over and done with. Michael turned back to his own people.

"Check the enemy. Finish any that still live," Michael ordered the now-idle soldiers.

Michael almost winced at his own bored tone. They'd done this so many times. Dealt death to the enemy even though they no longer posed a threat. They'd learnt, early on, that if a Sylannian was breathing, she was a threat. Particularly if she could get her hands on a blade. Sylannians were good at mindgifts, at insinuating themselves into the minds of others to get what they wanted. At least they were when they weren't fighting and dying. So, they usually killed them all.

The members of his band didn't question his order, they just dispersed, most of them retracing their steps to where they'd begun their battle with the Sylannians. Aiden moved to stand aloof to one side, his intention to ignore the orders clear. The Warlord's son had fumed when his father had nominated Michael as warleader, arguing with the Warlord that the role should be his own. The argument might have been successful if Aiden had displayed any competence at warfare at all.

The fallen were scattered on the cobbled square, their blood seeping into the ground between the stones. He could distinguish, without too much effort, those who were already dead from those who weren't by the way the muddy red glow of the veil deserted the body, leaving behind an empty shell. Not wanting to leave the clean-up to his men, Michael strode across the intervening space where a few of the enemy still lived. Two of them were upright and being detained; two were lying on the ground. Nathanial grasped the arms of one of the Sylannians, his face impassive. Over on the pier more of the Warlord's people loosely surrounded another of the enemy. Finally, he turned to the Sylannian moaning on the ground and the local woman trying to treat her.

Michael knelt beside the injured Sylannian. He gestured for the villager who was trying to heal her to move back as he drew his long dagger from his belt. The villager looked at him over the body of the Sylannian, confused for a moment, then her eyes fell on the dagger he held. Michael waited as the villager raised her eyes to meet his own. As she opened her mouth to protest, Michael shook his head, and the protest died on her lips. While it stood her in good stead that she could show compassion to her enemy, they had their orders. Michael lashed out with his blade, plunging it into the Sylannian's chest, ending the injured woman's life between one heartbeat and the next.

The villager who'd been trying to help the Sylannian backed away, her hand pressed against her mouth. He'd seen and felt such fear before. People who were afraid of what he and his people would do to them now that the immediate threat no longer existed. Michael smiled grimly and dismissed the healer from his mind. Not far away, bending over another injured enemy he recognised the woman who'd yelled at her father to retreat during the fight. He switched to his othersight and saw the bright red glow of the power she held within her. She had been strong enough in the use of the veil to pull her father out of harm's way. The fact she was still conscious after such effort showed abilities above the norm. He walked over to the villager and the injured enemy. Her dark brown eyes met his, then turned to the Sylannian he'd just dispatched just moments before. She bowed her head, dark brown hair obscuring her face for a moment, before she stood and backed away. This one was strong and smart. He moved towards the Sylannian, knowing delay wouldn't help.

Put your weapon away. Let me go. The captured Sylannian whispered in his mind, a wave of compulsion intertwined in her words.

Michael raised his blade, shielding himself against the Sylannian as her questing mind tried to find a way to influence him. These Sylannian raiders hadn't possessed extraordinary physical powers, but they were excellent at their mind tricks. Fortunately for the warbands, it was difficult to manipulate another's mind while fighting a battle. The ability to overpower another's mind, was different to using the veil to make yourself faster or stronger or to spin shields. One was purely a mental ability while the other manifested physically. The physical abilities were skills the Unwanted excelled at.

Unfortunately for this Sylannian, he was good at both and much stronger than any of them. His blade plunged down.

"Hold your blade!"

Michael froze at the command from behind him, his weapon hovering above the woman's neck. Relief filled her eyes. Little did she know, her fate at the end of his blade would be far kinder and quicker than any justice meted out by the Warlord. Michael withdrew his blade and moved to one side, the female villager effectively shielded behind him as he did so. Hopefully, his energy would mask the woman's power.

With the aid of the contact between them, Michael could communicate with her mind. *If you value your freedom, don't move, do not draw the attention of the Warlord. Allow the power you hold to disperse, slowly.* The woman behind him tensed, and he sensed her confusion as her emotions and internal monologue about him leaked from her mental shield before she complied.

Stupid. If he wanted to kill me, he obviously would have done it already. Not like he isn't capable of it. Powers, he's strong.

The Warlord strode forward and went down on one knee beside the injured Sylannian. All the members of the warbands stiffened; they didn't like the Warlord getting within striking distance of the enemy now the fight was over. Not even an injured one. As the Warlord leant forward and grabbed the Sylannian's arm, hauling her head and shoulders off the ground, Michael felt a wave of confusion from the villager behind him. Her muttering mental monologue invaded his mind.

What is that brute of a man doing?

Hush, girl, the Warlord might hear you, Michael replied. But despite himself he stiffened as the injured Sylannian gasped in pain and he averted his eyes as the Warlord licked his lips.

"Well, you're comely enough. I'm sure you'll be glorious sport when you're healed." The Warlord's voice held a note of appreciation.

The Warlord abruptly let go of the Sylannian and there was a crack as her head smacked onto the cobblestones, causing her to moan. The Warlord stood, gesturing to some of his people who strode forward to stand guard on the injured Sylannian.

"Warlord, are you sure allowing one of them to live is wise?" Michael said.

"You worry too much."

"Need I remind you of what happened with the last Sylannian you took?"

"Unlike the last one, I will make sure my mind is firmly shielded against her. I will not allow her an opportunity to slide a dagger between my ribs." A cold smile spread across the Warlord's lips. "Or to try and urge me to kill myself. This one will be locked back up before I fall asleep."

Michael stiffened and deliberately raised his head to stare at the space over the Warlord's shoulder, so the groaning woman was out of his vision. Olivia's hand rested on his shoulder squeezing it gently.

Careful, my friend. They need to believe you still have a heart, but too much, and it won't add up with the warrior they just saw save them, Olivia said.

Huh, a game to make everyone believe I have a heart while the

Warlord has none. This is deception, just to perpetuate the rumour of his ruthlessness. To spread fear in our enemy and dissuade our own people from rebellion. While still giving someone more sympathetic to appeal to if something really is wrong. It will get him killed one day. I'd rather we just kill them outright than play these games. Michael turned to bring Nathanial and the Sylannian he still restrained into view. *Your prisoner is up next in this little game.*

I wish the Warlord would stay on script; the Sylannians were all meant to die except the one near the pier, Nathanial replied.

The Warlord turned to stare at the Sylannian that Nathanial still held. "I don't think I need two of you, though."

With a cruel smile on his lips, the Warlord strode towards Nathanial and the Sylannian prisoner he held and in a fluid motion, drew his blade and slashed it across the Sylannian's neck.

Nathanial simply raised his shield the moment before the Warlord's blade struck, preventing the blood that sprayed everyone from getting on him, then sighed and let the lifeless prisoner drop. A yell from the pier drew his attention to one of the guards on the ground and the third of the prisoners jumping into the fast-moving waters of the river. Michael could hear the Sylannian channelling the veil to propel herself as far down the river as she could.

That went well, Nathanial said.

Better than the last time we tried to set up for one of them to escape, Olivia said.

Hopefully the Sylannian who just escaped will get home to tell tales of their defeat at the hands of the cruel barbarians, Michael said.

They ignored the Warlord who was swearing profusely as he strode over to yell at the guards who'd let their prisoner escape.

"Not that you deserve it, but someone check that fool's injuries and make sure he doesn't die," the Warlord snapped.

"Warleader. What do you want us to do with this one?"

Michael regarded the wounded Sylannian the Warlord had ordered them not to kill. A detail stood guard on her, and knowing the Warlord as he did, his father had probably forgotten about her them moment he turned his attention elsewhere.

"Restrain her and place her in the back of a cart to be taken back to the stronghold at Yalleska," he said.

Michael dismissed the fate of the Sylannian as the men carried her away. It was likely she'd die from her injuries—both the ones she'd sustained during the battle and when her head had smacked into the ground. If she was unfortunate enough to live, she'd rot in the stone cells in the bowels of the stronghold at Yalleska. Although he was certain rumour would fly from this place that the captive was destined to end up in the Warlord's bed. Just as the Warlord intended, even though it was one of the few atrocities the Warlord had never committed. Michael felt the villager behind him stir, felt her outrage.

Would you have your family, your village, slaughtered? Olivia's mindvoice was soft as she addressed the other woman.

From the moment he'd first raised his war banner, the Warlord had ruled through his reputation of fear and cruelty. Not afraid to get his hands dirty, he'd risen to prominence by being bigger, meaner than anyone else. By being willing to put anyone to the blade to ensure his own position. Back then, unlike todays staged drama, if the Warlord made a threat, you could be certain he would follow through. In all his years, since the Warlord had claimed Michael's life and consigned him to the path of war, he'd never witnessed such absolute brutality as in those first few years riding under the Warlord's banner. If he was honest with himself, he'd carried out a great many of those horrors himself. He was the sword the Warlord used with admirable efficiency. The Warlord was a different man today to the one who'd set Michael's home of Vallantia in flames all those years ago. Not that many guessed the effort the Warlord went to in order to maintain his brutal reputation.

Olivia came to stand near him, without seeming to pay attention to the villager behind him, she simply drew more power, adding her own strength to her personal shield. Between them, with the energy they were both drawing, the woman behind them would be virtually invisible to the other-sight of anyone who might think to check. They couldn't help the Sylannian woman — not that Olivia cared to any more than he did—but perhaps they could spare this one. At least, that was what the woman behind them and her fellow villagers would believe, for now.

Michael pushed away some very uncomfortable thoughts, his guilt at the part he played in this deception. Particularly since this one was his own, not the Warlord's. Yet he knew with certainty that this villager who was stronger than normal in the veil would have a much better life believing he'd saved her than she would riding with the Unwanted.

THREE

Aiden stood on the steps of what passed for an inn at this village his father had just taken into his domain. It was provincial and without the benefits of the major towns he was used to. He wondered when they would finally leave this hovel, and when he could, after patrolling a few more villages in his father's domain, go back to the stronghold at Yalleska.

"Need anything?" Derick asked.

Aiden turned to his captain and waved the man off. "I can't imagine anyone here is less than grateful. Relax while you can." Aiden made an effort to smile.

The crew he led had started out as his father's people. He'd spent time observing both Michael and Olivia and, to some extent, his father. They managed to attract loyal people. So, he'd tried to do the same with his own people. As much as it had pained him, the effort had paid off—they'd become his. They all understood the Warlord wouldn't live forever. When his father died, they realised he would be the next Warlord and they would be rewarded for their loyalty. Much like that core group that surrounded his father were now.

Movement caught the corner of his eye and he turned to observe as Michael was moving from the centre of the troops he led. The vaunted warleader was seemingly unaware of the attention and adoration he garnered as he ducked behind one of the buildings. This was a pattern Aiden had noticed at the raids in other villages. At some point Michael would sneak off alone. Aiden scowled. The Unwanted lazed about as they always did after a battle; by the looks of it, half of them weren't even up yet while others, who'd fought just as hard, ran around performing camp duties. They even had one of his father's personal warbands pandering to them, instead of protecting his father like they were meant to.

His father insisted Aiden treat Michael as his brother. At first, it had been fun to have a little brother, but at some point his attitude towards his so-called little brother had changed. He'd realised Michael was a threat to him and his own eventual rise to Warlord. Michael always got respect, no matter what he did, regardless of whether he'd earned it. He'd even heard his own father call Michael *son*. When Michael wasn't being formal, he called the Warlord *father*. Aiden glared at Michael. The problem was, his father and Michael meant it. They thought of themselves as father and son.

Aiden was attracting attention from some of the locals, word had gotten around the village he was the Warlord's son, but he ignored it as he caught sight of Michael disappearing into the forest. "I wonder what you are up to, brother," Aiden whispered.

Keeping his gaze on the tree line, he walked across the camp deliberately, careful not to walk in the same direction as Michael. If any of Michael's loyal followers saw him trying to follow their beloved band leader, one of them would try and stop him. Olivia, currently sitting with the Unwanted, certainly would. Aiden scowled. He hadn't needed a *sister* foisted on him, either.

It was only when he reached the forest's edge that he realised he'd made a mistake. There wasn't a path. Gritting his teeth, he drew the veil and thrust it ahead of him. He pushed past stray branches and vines as he forced his way into the cover of the trees. As he shoved one branch out of his path another snapped back towards his face, his eyes widened, and he tried to duck reflexively. A sharp edge scraped the exposed skin of his neck, he swore but resolutely kept stumbling forward. He finally stopped, taking a moment to suck in air, swiping at the sweat that stung his eyes as he reassured himself that no one could see him. He reached up and brushed his gloved fingers along his neck and saw the blood on them.

"Damn you, Michael," Aiden muttered.

Even when he wasn't around, the man had a way of making him appear incompetent. His skin crawled. As the hairs on the back of his neck rose, he scanned his surroundings but saw nothing out of place. Aiden continued, doing his best to ignore the branches that seemed to reach out and snag at his shirt, arms, and legs. Yet he couldn't help but think of the ease with which Michael seemed to melt into the forest. Even when there was no evidence the warleader used the veil to forge a path for himself, he'd never returned from one of these excursions covered in foliage or with bloody skin.

Aiden's foot caught on a root and he flung his hands out as he lurched forward. Branches snagged and dragged at him as he fell. On impact with the ground, air exploded from his lungs. To make the indignity worse, he landed face-first in a small stream he hadn't been aware was there.

With an inarticulate growl, Aiden thrashed, grabbing at the surrounding branches to help pull himself upright. Drenched, he glared at the offending forest around him, only somewhat mollified when he realised he couldn't see or sense anyone. If he couldn't see them, they probably couldn't see him. He brushed at the dirt and assorted foliage that had attached itself to him and couldn't help but feel aggrieved as the water seeped into his leather boots. He tried to use the branches to pull himself up the bank, only for his feet to slide out from underneath him and dump him in the mud. Eventually he managed to stand and strode along the path that ran beside the small stream until he heard voices.

Aiden froze, his teeth clenched. He'd always recognise Michael's voice. The other was female and one he didn't know. He'd almost forgotten why he'd come traipsing out here in the first place. Unable to sense anyone else other than the three of them he realised they were all well away from the village. With care—Michael was extremely sensitive to those manipulating the veil—Aiden expanded his awareness, focusing on the voices. He turned towards where he sensed the others were standing.

Aiden ground his teeth as he observed that bright spark that was Michael. With an effort, he unclenched his jaw. Then he turned his attention to the other person, bringing her into focus. Aiden gasped and took a step back.

"I've got you now, brother," Aiden whispered.

A slow, predatory smile spread across his lips.

FOUR

This tiny village in the middle of nowhere had little to recommend it. Despite what the locals might think. Certainly, it was bigger than those around it, which was why his father had picked it. Yet while the areas closer to the river and the dock had cobblestone streets and a few stone dwellings, the village deteriorated out of the centre. The bulk of the village consisted of rudimentary wooden huts. There was a single two-storey building off to one side with a vast open area out front of it.

This place apparently attracted traders not only from outlying villages but also travellers from outside realms, and it boasted an inn. The easy river access made it an attractive venue. Not that he was an expert on such things, but Aiden guessed the river was broad enough and deep enough for some of the bigger barges to dock here. Still, given the sleepy nature of the village it surprised him that anyone would bother to come here. The inn housed a few rooms on the upper floors and an open common room below serving food and drinks. Right now, his father had taken over the largest of the rooms on the upper floor. The men and women of the warbands had spread out, camped where the traders normally put up their temporary stalls.

A smile returned to Aiden's lips. Not even being here in this poor excuse for a village was enough to sour his mood. This time he had Michael right where he wanted him. Aiden kept his head high and tried to smooth out his limping gait as he pushed open the wooden door to the inn and made his way through the common room. His father's people gazed at him idly. Their eyes tracking his limping progress yet dismissing him all the same.

What happened to him?

Probably came out the worse for wear, fighting with a local.

His father's people had meant him to hear their commentary, but Aiden didn't give them the satisfaction of a reaction. He might not have Michael's proficiency at mindspeech but he wasn't that bad. Grabbing the handrail, he carefully walked up the stairs to the second floor, doing his best to ignore his protesting ankle. Even here, in an inn with one entrance and his father's people filling the common room, there were still guards. Two stood duty at the end of the hallway outside the room his father had taken. One turned to stare at him as he drew to a halt outside the doors to his father's rooms, feeling his face heat as the guards pointedly ignored his presence.

"Are we really going to play this game today?" Aiden couldn't help his sharp tone.

He took in the bored, disinterested expressions on the faces of the guards. Silence stretched without either of them showing any signs of being even slightly uncomfortable. Gritting his teeth, Aiden shuffled back and leant against the wall. This was a game he was acquainted with. These men would not let him in until his father gave permission, even if his father was sitting inside doing nothing at all. His father was aware he was out here. He could sense it.

It didn't take long, just enough time for him to know he was being made to wait on purpose. One of his father's guards finally jerked his head at the door.

"You can go in now."

Aiden stared at the guard. He hadn't even overheard the communication that must have occurred between his father and his men. That meant his father was familiar enough with his guards to deliberately exclude him.

Pushing off the wall, he couldn't help the limp. He stumbled and flushed at being caught out as less than physically competent. The muscle-bound guard caught him, firm hands wrapping around his arms just before he fell, steadying him.

"Thanks."

As the doors opened he disregarded the guards and limped towards his father. It wasn't hard to pick out the Warlord, even if he hadn't been his son. Not just because his father was the only one left in the room, as everyone else beat a hasty retreat but because he dominated any room he was in. This man was everything Aiden was not, to the point that sometimes Aiden wondered at his parentage. The Warlord was big, well-muscled and lean, despite leaving most of the actual fighting to Michael these days. Aiden shared the same dusty blond hair, he supposed. His father wore his fighting leathers, weapons still strapped around his waist, even here in the luxury of his rooms. Everything about him screamed threat, even here where he was supposed to be relaxing.

The Warlord. The words whispered unbidden in his head. He almost winced at the betrayal of his own mind; even he thought of this man as *Warlord* rather than *Father.*

His father's eyes raked over him and his face heated. He

really should have taken the time to clean up before coming into his father's presence. The disapproval was palpable.

"Dare I ask what got you into this state?" His father walked from the window he'd been standing at and took a seat.

"I went for a walk in the forest, it's a little wilder out here than I realised." Aiden noticed his father did not invite him to sit.

"You'll clean up before dinner, I hope?" His father's lip curled into a sneer as his eyes took in his whole muddy and dishevelled appearance.

"It's just as well I went for a walk; I ran into Michael but thankfully he didn't see me," Aiden said, watching his father for a reaction.

"I doubt he'd approve of the mess you've managed to get yourself in from a simple walk, either," the Warlord commented.

"Father, he was with a woman from the village," Aiden said.

"What? You've taken to sneaking around and watching while Michael beds a woman now?"

"No! He was with a woman, but—"

"Couldn't find anyone who suited your tastes?" Disgust dripped from his father's voice.

"Michael has betrayed you," Aiden said, desperately trying to get the conversation back on track.

His father stilled before turning his head to face him fully. The Warlord's face was expressionless. Aiden froze under the Warlord's regard, wondered how the conversation had spiralled out of control. He shuddered as a blast of cold washed over him, indicating his father had just drawn in the veil. It was the only warning he had before his father's power buffeted him and he staggered back a step. He gasped as a stinging blow hit his face as his father's sudden anger spiked.

"Whatever brought you to that conclusion?" The Warlord's tone was quiet, devoid of humour.

"The village woman. She's strong in the veil. Very strong. He can't have failed to notice." He paused. "Michael has hidden one of strength from you." The words almost rushed from his mouth but he couldn't help it.

He straightened, triumphant. His father would tolerate many things, but a traitor was not one of them. Instead of acting as Aiden expected, his father threw back his head and laughed.

"You fool."

"Father, I know what I observed in that clearing," he said, hating the note of desperation that carried clearly in his voice.

"Did you ever stop to wonder how we are usually a step ahead of the Sylannian invaders?" The Warlord stared at him.

Aiden could feel the contempt rolling off his father in waves. "We have hundreds of our people patrolling the river. Michael just gets lucky..." he trailed off as his father raised his hand.

His father stood abruptly and stalked towards him. Aiden barely kept himself from stepping away. He wondered how such a big man could move with such deadly grace.

"Your brother saves them from me. Or so they think. At that point they become remarkably grateful." His father's use of the word "brother" was deliberate.

"What?"

"They become our lookouts. An early warning system spread throughout the tributaries and villages."

Aiden felt himself go pale as his father's words sank into his mind and he realised his mistake. The feeling of triumph he'd experienced moments before fractured, the pieces jabbing into him, causing him to wince in pain at failing. Again.

"I didn't know—"

"Obviously. It isn't a mistake that Michael is my warleader. He would never betray me. He's like the son I never had." The Warlord twisted the words so they stabbed just so.

Aiden gasped as his father's words seemed to echo in his head. He'd known his father preferred Michael over him, his own flesh and blood son, but until now the Warlord had never disowned him. He bit his lip to stop it trembling, the faint metallic taste hitting his tongue as he drew blood. Aiden concentrated on the pain in his lip, and purposely looked towards the empty space to one side of the Warlord. His father would take too much satisfaction that his words had struck into him like barbs.

"I'm sorry. I didn't know." Aiden stumbled back as his father's power buffeted him, pushing him towards the door. "He's not your son, Father. He and his Unwanted are dangerous, why can't you see that?"

"I trust Michael. He has ridden with me since he was thirteen. You aren't a child anymore, Aiden. Can't you see why I made the effort to ensure both Michael and Olivia were treated fairly?"

"He's the son you wished you had and she's the daughter you've never had. Both more like you than your only child?" Aiden's words were laced with bitterness.

"They're both strong in the veil." His father sounded he was explaining to a child.

"That's why they're dangerous. You should have killed them both," Aiden said.

"First there was Michael, then Oliva, then Nathanial. Now there are enough of their kind to fill a warband."

"It's not even a full squad, but yes, there are more just like Michael." Aiden frowned as he stared at his father and swallowed. "I don't understand."

"Isn't it obvious that more like them are appearing in the

world? If I killed them, what of the next ones like them? Then the ones after that, then the ones I don't find? Who takes out those people when they come to take what's mine?" His father's eyes glittered, gaze boring into him.

"But Michael—"

"Is mine, even he thinks of me as his father now. Just as Olivia is my daughter. Through them, the Unwanted follow me faithfully. They will stand between me and any threat." The Warlord shook his head.

"You think there are more like them?"

"We're at war, Aiden. Try to think, if people like Michael and the Unwanted have been born and lived past puberty in my domain, they are probably appearing elsewhere as well. Now, get out, and try to be nicer to your brother and sister. When I die and your brother takes over as Warlord, your survival might depend on him liking you." The Warlord turned and walked towards the window on the far side of the room.

Aiden paled, his breath coming in short, sharp breaths. "You, you can't mean to make him Warlord? I'm your heir."

"Then perhaps you should start behaving like it. If you want to be considered my heir, you have a great deal to prove." The Warlord turned his head, his eyes flat and cold. "Michael is my son in every way that matters. He's shown himself to be loyal and competent, which is why he's my warleader. You have been nothing but a disappointment."

Aiden stumbled back at each word his father uttered, feeling like his father's fists were pounding into him. He wanted nothing more than to flee his father's presence and started to turn.

The Warlord halted him. "Oh, and Aiden?"

"Yes, Fath—" Aiden stopped, his mouth dry as his father's cold eyes seemed to pin him to the spot. "Warlord?"

"Your brother isn't the young, inexperienced boy who

made the mistake of trusting you. If you go against him, you wouldn't have a chance—he'd kill you. At this point, I'm not completely certain I'd stop him."

Aiden turned, his hands fumbling on the door latch, wrenching it open as he fled his father's presence. Not even mocking laughter followed him, just the wave of the Warlord's contempt.

FIVE

Aiden kept his head up as he walked out of the inn, ignoring the milling soldiers as he walked over to where Derick and his own crew congregated. He kept his face blank as some heads turned to follow his progress. There was no doubt those on guard duty outside the door to the Warlord's room yesterday had spread word of their argument. Derick's face was calm as he approached and passed the reins to his horse. Aiden placed his foot in the stirrup and mounted without bothering to check his gear. Not that he needed to. Derick always ordered some members of his team to pack up and prepare for him. A creak of leather over to one side caused him to look over just in time to see Michael and the Unwanted mount their horses, all perfectly in sync. He sneered as whispers jumped from villager to villager at the feat. They were so easy to awe. Aiden's brow furrowed as he glared at Michael. His face flushed as the Warlord's words repeatedly whispered to him, 'Michael is my son in every way that matters'.

"Aiden."

Aiden pressed his lips together in an effort not to snarl as he stared at his father's favourite, his so-called brother.

"Aiden!" the Warlord snapped.

Aiden jerked upright and swung his head around to stare at the Warlord, only realising he could hear his father's voice because he was right there, calling his name.

"Father?" Aiden was proud his voice didn't waver as he urged his horse forward, closer to the head of his father's warband.

Aiden's heart sank as the Warlord's attention shifted to Michael before turning back to him.

"You'll ride with the Unwanted until further notice."

"But, Father—"

Even as the words left his mouth and before his father's face suffused with anger, Aiden realised it had been a mistake to question the Warlord's authority. Cold blasted over him a moment before a fist of power slammed into his stomach and breath exploded out of his lungs. Aiden groaned as he hit the unforgiving ground, his horse dancing away.

"That wasn't open for debate, Aiden," the Warlord said.

His father's cold fury rippled through the air between them; rage prickled his skin, wrapping around him and seeming to stifle the air he tried to breathe.

"Yes, Warlord." Aiden's reply was barely a whisper.

Aiden groaned in pain again as he rolled over and boots hit the ground nearby.

"I didn't give you permission to help him," the Warlord snarled.

"Warlord," Derick said.

Aiden marvelled that his captain's voice sounded calm even in the face of the Warlord's fury. He pushed himself onto his knees. An oppressive shock and fear hung over the village like the heaviness of a thunderstorm as he staggered to his feet.

His skin crawled in the stark silence. Everyone stared at him. He licked his lips, spotting his horse being held by one of his people nearby and he walked over and snatched the reins, jerking on them as his horse snorted and tried to dance aside. As the beast stilled, Aiden grabbed the saddle, placed his foot in the stirrup, and gritted his teeth as he hauled himself back up. He breathed in, grateful that none of his ribs protested. Riding would have been a misery if they had. It was going to be bad enough with all the aches and pains he felt already.

Although he couldn't hear the exchange Michael and the Warlord appeared deep in conversation, but the warleader turned when he felt Aiden's gaze on him. Aiden's spine stiffened as he realised it wasn't just his brother who was observing him. It was all the Unwanted. The faces and minds of the Unwanted were just as blank to his senses as Michael's. Not even a flicker of emotion or a random thought came from them, although he did not doubt at all that they were as displeased by this development as he was. Aiden glowered at them; in any other company except this one, he'd be considered exceptional when it came to mindgifts. Aiden urged his horse forward, angling to take a leadership position in the Unwanted. He smirked as irritation flashed on Michael's face.

"You will obey your warleader in all things, Aiden," the Warlord said, his voice rumbling across the distance and the threat rippling through the veil, causing the breath to catch in Aiden's throat. He halted his horse, hating that his shoulders hunched automatically in response.

"I don't think you're ready to ride as a scout, Aiden," Michael said, and motioned with his head back towards the centre of the ranks formed up behind him.

Aiden clenched his jaw and glared at Michael. He opened his mouth to reply but, feeling the weight of his father's eyes on his back, he restrained himself. The ranks of the Unwanted shuffled until a gap appeared in their midst. His face heated as he realised Michael had communicated with his people, and he hadn't even perceived a whisper. It would seem like such a simple thing to others, to him it demonstrated how powerful they really were. Aiden wrenched the reins to one side and swore as his horse shied, dancing sideways in response. He gripped tighter with his legs, hauled the reins back and guided his restive mount into position among the Unwanted, who seemed to absorb him effortlessly into the centre of their ranks. Aiden gazed between his horse's ears, not wanting to meet anyone's eyes.

"Derick, form up behind my ranks," Michael said.

Despite himself, Aiden's head snapped up. Michael couldn't help but show off his ability to do whatever he wanted without his father saying a word. Aiden turned to catch a glint of what he could only described as satisfaction in the Warlord's eyes.

"Try to teach him to have a spine, Warleader," the Warlord said.

Aiden refused to react as he knew his father wanted him to. Instead, he simply returned his gaze to the backs of the riders in front of him but his brain raced. If his father wanted proof he could get on with Michael, then he'd prove it. His father just had to believe it, even if Michael didn't. Aiden was barely aware as the Unwanted shuffled around him, and two of the warleader's strongest people, Nathanial and Callan, ended up on either side of him. No doubt picked by Michael to monitor him.

Even though not a single order was given, the Unwanted surged forward. His own mount followed the horses around him without him having to spur the beast on for once—even that ungrateful beast adding to his humiliation. Aiden ground his teeth; he was being unreasonable, but he didn't care.

CHAPTER

SIX

A bloodcurdling cry rose from the invaders as a flash of deep maroon and cream silk in the rear of the opposing Sylannian line moved to join the battle. Khaliun was close enough that she could see the flare of black hair as the woman and those who surrounded her joined the battle. Sun glinted off the dual blades she used in lightning-fast combinations with deadly precision. Khaliun closed her eyes, holding in the curse she wanted to let loose. She'd seen this pattern in battle before. The appearance of the enemy who wore the maroon and cream colourings with that woman fighting in their midst heralded the loss of the battle. Those who wore maroon and cream never showed up until they were about to win.

Khaliun scanned the grass plains below as her tribe took a moment to rest the horses. To the uneducated eye, the battle line would seem to surge and heave to little purpose. Yet that layman would be wrong. The different clans fought in separate sections. While some manoeuvred their horses, multiple clan groups merged and fought against the enemy. It was a coordi-

35

nated effort. The ability to fight the way they did was their strength; it was their weakness. They could fight separately in their own small tribes with their co-leaders coordinating their own people. Or multiple tribes of a clan could merge and fight as a combined unit, or even several clans could combine efforts. She could feel the concentration of her co-leader Tarkhan as his power surged, manoeuvring the horses of one clan below to the aid of another. It was one of the skills that he excelled at. Hers was mindspeaking.

Their horses had given them a certain advantage, particularly in the early years. Those they faced hadn't seen their like before. Unfortunately, these invaders had arrived via the river and conquered the bulk of the rich and lazy river clans before they'd even realised they were being attacked. Those who numbered among the rich river, grass, and hill clans had shunned Kallith Clan for generations. Yet when word of this war had reached them, an emergency conclave of all the co-leaders of the barrens reached a unanimous conclusion. Leaving non-combatants in the safety of Kallith, their oasis deep in the heart of the barrens, the bulk of their fighters rode out to aid their fellow clans. Having to fight for their existence in the barrens, they hadn't gotten lazy like the others. They were better fighters, yet it still wasn't enough. The strangers outnumbered them by a seemingly inexhaustible number. It didn't matter how many they killed, more took the place of the fallen.

That bloodcurdling cry rang across the battlefield again, with the splash of maroon and cream as it moved inexorably through the battle lines. Tribe after tribe fell as the wave crashed over them. Khaliun closed her eyes, her mind screaming denial.

We've lost this battle. We need to retreat. Tarkhan's pain echoed her own.

She was about to reply when she glimpsed a knot of riders fighting desperately off to one side. These weren't the random fighters from a clan she was barely familiar with. They were riders of a fellow tribe from the barrens. Erden and Orghana, with their tribe members surrounded by enemies. They were fighting for their lives, although from her quick assessment, they held the upper hand. Her eyes widened as another wave of the invaders, hard on the heels of those in maroon, swept in. One of those groups headed straight towards the amassed tribes of the Kallith Clan. She reached for her bow and arrows and swore profusely when she remembered the quivers attached to her saddles were empty.

Rest is over, our own need an escape path. Khaliun spurred her horse.

She outpaced her tribe, taking them by surprise, but trusted they'd follow. Not that they needed further instructions after she sent them the image of Orghana and Erden's tribe surrounded and fighting for survival.

Let's not get sloppy now! Tarkhan snapped at some of their riders who'd fallen out of formation.

Khaliun opened herself to the veil and sensed each member of her clan that rode with her. The thundering of hooves came sharply into focus, the screams of humans and horses alike, the clash of each sword and every death fading to the background. They had one goal: ride down their opponents and win an escape route for their friends.

Erden, Orghana, we're incoming, just stay alive.

Khaliun drew her sword just before they ploughed into the enemy line, showing no mercy for the Sylannians they trampled over. She lashed out with her sword and used the veil to shunt her opponents aside. Too many of her people fell to Sylannian blades. Right now, she didn't have the time to mourn the losses. They had a job to do and if they didn't do it, she was certain that they would fall to the invaders. Khaliun swung her sword, ignoring the wet spray across her face that soon mixed with the heavy dust hanging in the air. Dealing in death was a messy business, and she had no intention of letting any of these Sylannians live.

Khaliun, you lot took your time getting here. Erden's tone was light and bantering despite being embroiled in a fight.

Sorry, there was this minor issue of all these Sylannians in the way.

Oh, is that why you came—jealous? Orghana chuckled.

As she drove her horse forward, another attacker fell, his skull crunching under the hooves of her horse. Despite the circumstances, Khaliun grinned, glad to make it through to Erden, taking the time to cut down another woman who charged her.

These must be new. Tarkhan's horse reared, hooves striking out, slamming into the forehead of a Sylannian who rushed at him.

Was it their stupidity when facing off against a mounted attacker that gave it away? Orghana asked.

They still outnumber us, and there are more coming. Time to leave, Khaliun said.

She wheeled her horse around, wincing at her abrupt tone. While she had the right to command her own tribe, it was another matter to order around the members of another tribe, particularly other tribe leaders.

Do you need to warn the others or was it just us in a predicament? Orghana asked.

As the members of the two tribes formed up around her, Khaliun gritted her teeth and spurred her horse forward. They'd only had a slim chance of holding off the invaders in this fight. She hated having to flee, they'd battled and conceded so many territories in this war, but she had to acknowledge the truth: the lands of the Yannar Clan were lost. The river lands had fallen long ago and now they'd lost the last remaining grasslands. Khaliun opened her mind just a little further.

Retreat. We have lost this territory. We'll reform at the rendezvous point. Khaliun sent the mental equivalent of a bellow across the battlefield.

The invaders would hear the order as well, but it couldn't be helped. She ground her teeth in frustration. Seeing one attacker looming before her, Khaliun screamed her frustration and, with one vicious strike of her sword, took the woman's head off. Ignoring the blood, churning dust, and mayhem around her, she led her fellow clansmen away from what had been one of their few remaining territories.

SEVEN

Tarkhan was ill at ease with the wait, despite the rocky surrounds that made him feel more at home than the undulating grass lands they'd been fighting in. The longer those few of them who'd extracted themselves from the invaders remained here, the higher the likelihood of discovery. Their enemy would find this refuge, the ravine that ran between the grasslands, hills and barrens, soon enough.

"Relax, Tarkhan. The enemy intends to stay in the lands they are conquering. They have followed the same pattern every time they've attacked. They take land, then pause long enough to consolidate their hold on their new territory."

Khaliun's tone was heavy and despite her words, she was no more at ease with this wait than he was.

"Sorry, didn't realise my emotions were leaking," Tarkhan said.

"You're not. I just know my co-leader."

Tarkhan couldn't help but grin in response, his shoulders relaxing incrementally as she sent a wave of soothing at him. It was hard to ignore Khaliun when she put her mind to it. She was one of those rare people born with such great strength to survive. They'd found none of her equal in all the clans. So, he didn't believe her warning at all.

"We've lost this war," Tarkhan said as he stared bleakly at the sheltering cliffs around them.

"There is still our oasis, Kallith, in the heart of the barrens, and Hallaran, the lake in the hills. Both are still free of these people," Khaliun said.

Tarkhan looked at her. They had been co-leaders for a very long time. Her tone was uneasy. She knew Tarkhan was correct. Even if she wasn't ready to admit it. Khaliun was too good a leader. Too good at commanding and fighting, even if it was a skill they'd mostly picked up because of necessity. He ducked his head, considering his next words.

"When the grasslands leaders apprised us of this conflict in the lands of the river clans, none of us could have known the devastation the invaders would wreak on our homelands," Tarkhan said.

"How could we? We'd never encountered them before," Yangir said.

"There are so few of us left." Orghana drew closer, refusing to meet anyone's eye.

"We can hold them back—"

"No. We can't." Tarkhan unclenched his hands, which had curled into fists at his side, reminding himself it was the situation he was angry at, not his fellow leaders.

"We can't just give up." Khaliun's eyes flashed.

"Our job as leaders is to lead. We need to see that our people survive. It's not our role to lead them to their extinction because we refuse to accept the truth!" Tarkhan snapped.

Tarkhan scanned the other tribe leaders as they gathered closer. He couldn't help but notice that they were all leaders of Kallith Clan who'd made it to the rendezvous point. None of the Yannar Clan had joined them in their retreat. Finally, Erden cleared his throat and Tarkhan swung his gaze over to the man.

"I agree." Erden held up his hand, his forehead wrinkled.

"Just because we had to ride in and pull you from danger —" Khaliun spat.

Enough, Khaliun, I know you hurt. I feel it. We all do. But it's time for us to retreat, Tarkhan said.

As Khaliun tensed, hands clenching into fists, Tarkhan sprang from where he had been lounging and positioned himself between Erden and Khaliun, grabbing her shoulders. Not that he thought she really would resort to violence but fighting, even the verbal kind, was the last thing they needed.

Tarkhan ignored the uneasy silence around them and concentrated on Khaliun. While he'd done his best to make sure the comment was private, he had the distinct feeling that the others had caught what he'd said. It was a problem with mindspeech. Sometimes you shared far more than you intended. Of course, some of that might have been because he wasn't as good at mindspeaking as Khaliun. She stared at him, not saying a word, but he sensed the complex array of emotions from her. Images flicking into his mind one after the other, overwhelmingly of their most recent battle. Loss hit him, followed by a sense of failure. So much so it nearly caused him to double over, as if he'd taken a sharp blow to the stomach.

So many of our people have died. I failed. Khaliun's voice rippled with pain.

No. We did not seek this fight, he said.

We only fail if we don't accept the truth. Erden stood and crossed the distance between them, before placing a hand on her shoulder.

We fail if we allow what remains of our people to die, Tarkhan said, allowing her to sense his own pain at this decision that very much mirrored her own.

Tarkhan felt Khaliun crumbling, her anger fading as fast as it had risen, and gave way to Erden, who wrapped his arms around her.

Orghana made eye contact with him as she tapped the ground next to her with one hand. Her eyebrow rose slowly as he hesitated, checking one last time on Khaliun and Erden. Broadening his own perception a little, he smiled. Khaliun had expanded her own mental barrier to shield them both. Orghana rolled her eyes towards the sky, shaking her head.

You possibly averted a lovers' tiff, she whispered in his mind.

Tarkhan choked back a laugh. Despite the circumstances, his mood lightened. At least, it did for a moment. He'd learnt to cherish those moments, however briefly, when the world seemed right again. Feeling a hand on his shoulder, no pulse of emotion, just simple comfort, Tarkhan took a steadying breath. His eyes met Orghana's and in them was understanding. Tarkhan brought himself back to their current problem as he realised the silence, other than the whisper of the wind though the grass, was complete. He found his fellow tribe leaders of the Kallith Clan in a ring around him, waiting for his response. Even Khaliun and Erden had finished their private conversation and were facing him.

"We need to lead what remains of our people," Tarkhan said, breaking the silence.

"What do you suggest?" Narantuya asked.

"Ulagan and Tuya were going to ensure the old trade path through the Heights was clear and stocked in case we needed to flee. It's time. We'll take the cold path up the Heights and beyond," Tarkhan said.

"If they follow us?" Yangir asked.

"We go in waves. I'll be tail guard," Tarkhan said.

"Not alone, you won't." Khaliun's eyes flashed.

"What about the Hallaran Clans?" Orghana asked.

"What of them? It's not like they helped us in this fight." Yangir shrugged, his tone dismissive.

"Why should we care?" Erden asked.

"Because they are of the People, they are Clan!" Silence settled at Tarkhan's pronouncement.

Tarkhan's power flared as he glared around the gathered tribe leaders. The tendrils of emotions filtered through him, laced primarily with obstinance, anger, hurt, and embarrassment.

"Could any of us truly leave our own to face the invaders alone?" Orghana asked.

"You all go, gather supplies and forge a path in the Heights. I—"

"We." Khaliun's tone was firm.

"We—" Tarkhan smiled tightly at his fellow leader. "Will retreat via the Hallaran Lake and warn them of what we plan."

"Whether or not they join us, our consciences will be clear," Khaliun said.

"We'll follow the path you've set," Tarkhan agreed, the matter settled.

"We'll mind the non-combatants of your tribe who remain at Kallith Oasis," Erden offered.

Tarkhan and Khaliun stared at each other for a moment before they came to a silent accord.

"Take our fighters, who are here with us as well." Khaliun held up her hand as the other tribe leaders protested. "We'll be safe enough. They can ride rear guard and protect your retreat. Chono and Delbee may refuse to help, but I doubt they'd harm either of us."

"They will be like our own." Orghana reached out and squeezed his hand.

"Return through Kallith's heart before heading to the Heights," Erden said.

"We'll wait for you there as long as we can," Orghana pledged.

Tarkhan was relieved both he and Khaliun were in agreement. It had hurt a part of him to find themselves in opposing camps. Even if it was the role of co-leaders to come to the same problem from different angles, to determine the best solution to keep their tribe and their clan safe. Finally, they turned their attention back to their fellow clan leaders and nodded, accepting their path forward.

EIGHT

Isabella noticed something had distracted her friend and followed her gaze. She groaned, seeing the object of Sonja's attention. Damien. Increasingly of late, he was the subject of speculation not only from Sonja, but from some of the older women in the village as well. Never mind such admiration seemed contradictory to the other primary emotion directed at her brother. Fear. They feared Damien's presence would bring the Warlord down on them all. She regarded her brother as she tried to see what others saw, that managed to push away their fear, even for a moment. Tall, blond, and muscled, the hard work of hunting and swordplay was paying off. Sonja's eyes were sparkling.

"I know he's your brother, but, oh my, he's filled out nicely since last season." Sonja giggled.

"I really don't know what you see in him. He's irritating," Isabella growled.

Sonja laughed, throwing her hands up in mock disgust. "How is this fair?"

"How is what fair?" Isabella frowned.

"I'm two years your senior, yet I can still be mistaken for a boy if I'm wearing trousers. You haven't even noticed that perhaps boys aren't as irritating as all that and look at you. Unlike me, you have curves in all the right places." Sonja pouted.

"You're only a year older and I, well, Mother said I've developed a little early." Isabella's face heated.

Her mother had said much more than that. She'd warned her to be careful and said it was a sign she'd be too powerful, just like Damien. An unspoken fear lingered in her, a nagging worry that she'd be a risk to everyone in the village, just like Damien was. She didn't think it would help to tell them they were correct; her powers were like Damien's. They'd worry. So, for now, it was a secret she shared with her brother. It's not like she could have hidden it from him. She wished her body hadn't betrayed her the way it had. She'd much rather Sonja's flat chest and boyish figure. As much as she tried, her clothes did nothing to disguise the fact that she'd developed breasts, a waist, and hips.

Sonja laughed and wrapped her in a fierce hug. "Never mind, Isa, you'll wake up one day and suddenly see boys a whole different way." Sonja's voice rippled with amusement.

"I don't see how. In case you hadn't noticed, there aren't too many boys around our age here in the village," Isabella grumbled, despite the fact she wasn't interested in boys at all.

"Don't turn around, but the baker is watching you again." Sonja's face screwed up.

"He's always watching me," Isabella whispered back.

It seemed every time she was in the village of late, the baker watched her. Although not as openly anymore. Not since she'd seen him with his hand down the front of his pants a few months back, watching her through half-lidded eyes as he moaned. Isabella shuddered; he was old enough to be her father. No one else in the village seemed to have noticed anything out of order that day, except Damien.

Damien had flung himself at the baker, beating the other man with his fists. She'd overheard more than one adult in the village mutter, in the weeks after the incident, that the baker was lucky Damien hadn't been carrying any weapons. It had been Damien's mentor, Owen, who'd hauled him off the nearly unconscious older man. Damien had been unapologetic about the altercation and refused to say what had prompted it. Her father had just gazed at Damien. She guessed immediately that they'd been engaged in a conversation, excluding her. Whatever her brother had said, it had made her father press his lips together, and his anger spike. As they'd both turned to regard her, she'd known it had been about her and about how the baker had leered at her.

After it happened, her parents shooed Damien out of the house, ordering him to burn off his anger chopping wood. This, despite the enormous pile already neatly stacked at the side of the house. They'd sat her down and insisted on having an extremely embarrassing conversation about relationships between men and women. About babies and how to use her own powers, like most women, to keep herself from getting pregnant. Even though she'd already been taught about this, her mother and father had gone through it in excruciating detail.

Her mother still supervised her every month as she sank into a trance and sent her senses inward. Under her mother's instruction, she would draw on that store of energy within her, then seek that tiny spark that she recognised as the small egg inside herself and destroyed it. Her mother also made her practice manipulating her flow. Her mother didn't want her daughter to grow up being one of *those* women who practiced little, if any, control over their own bodies. Isabella couldn't imagine ever seeing a boy the way her mother and father spoke about, much less ever wanting a relationship or agreeing to have a child with one of them. Of course, that might be because of the lack of boys her age, and her brother certainly didn't count. She hadn't talked with her parents about the way the baker continued to stare at her. She was just being silly. It wasn't like the baker had ever touched her, but something about the way the older man was always there, staring at her, made her skin crawl.

Isabella hadn't admitted that once her mother had guided her mind to show her that first time how to recognise the egg inside herself, she didn't need the constant practice to learn to use the store of the veil that resided in her. She kept that secret to herself. Instead, she dutifully practiced her breathing and manipulating the veil that lived within her. She didn't admit that she really didn't need to practice locating and manipulating the energy within her. Damien had been teaching her for years, after she'd seen him pull a band of the veil into himself. She'd promptly copied him and reached out with her mind to draw the almost insubstantial silver-grey strand towards her. She hadn't realised she was seeing the veil that appeared all around her with her mind, not her eyes. Damien had told her it wasn't normal to see the wispy strands of the veil that were everywhere in the world around her. Let alone be able to reach out with her mind and draw it into herself to replenish that bright store within her as much as she wanted. When regular people like her mother used their powers, for even the smallest thing, they had to wait until the energy inside them replenished gradually. It left other people sluggish and tired to use even a tiny amount of power to accomplish minor tasks.

Isabella rolled her eyes as she noticed a small half-smile on her friends lips, as Sonja's attention was wholly captivated by Damien again. Isabella's face heated again as she caught the whiff of desire and heat from her friend. Increasingly, she found the feelings and random mutterings of others intruded on her. While she might not see boys that way, it was obvious Sonja did. It seemed it wasn't only her brother who had changed over the last season.

Eyes sparkling, Isabella used her friend's distraction to her advantage. Sonja had but a moment to notice as Isabella gathered water from the river and drenched her. She launched herself at her spluttering friend as they both plunged into the river.

CHAPTER

NINE

Damien gripped the axe loosely in one hand. As he leant casually against the tree, he sipped some tiscan tonic his mother had made for him. Unlike when he'd been a child, he no longer had to mask the slightly bitter taste with juice. As he put the stopper back in the small bottle he noticed there was only a mouthful left. He seemed to go through more and more of the tonic of late. He slipped it into his vest pocket, making a mental note to brew up another batch. His mother would panic if she became aware of how much he was consuming to hold his powers in check. He reached for his water can sitting nearby and took a long swallow to chase away the aftertaste.

Laughter pierced the air from the river causing him to smile. The discarded buckets and children playing and splashing was evidence that they'd abandoned their afternoon chores.

Nausea washed over him. It was the only warning he had before a bout of veil sickness hit him. Damien doubled over in pain and a gasp tore from his lips. Every muscle in his body

51

contracted. As his vision started to flicker, he staggered, disorientated as the clearing he could see with his eyes was overlayed with thick bands of energy. It poured into him in increasing amounts. He tried to reinforce his mental shield, to regain control and stop the veil that rushed into him in greater quantities than he could hold or manipulate. As he lost his battle to regain control, the world around him faded. A pall of grey surrounded him as if a curtain stood between him and the world. His breath caught as the feeling of the veil intensified. It sparked and flickered around him, small bolts of energy striking at him. The squeals of childish laughter receded, replaced with the random internal mutterings and obervations of others ricocheting in his mind.

Come on, Betsey, into the paddock.

That door needs fixing.

Should turn him out.

Then, a hollow ringing—a noise picked up by his ears, not his mind. Even in his current state, he could tell the difference. An almost absent part of him noted he'd dropped his water flask. He was locked in place unable to move as if the veil held him in its embrace. Thick bands of the veil surged, swirling and flowing into him. Sweat prickled his skin and his entire body trembled as the pure power of the veil poured into him. Every fibre of his being was on fire, and he screamed. The real world receded further, the surging power and pain demanding his attention. A small corner of his brain wondered if this time, the veil sickness would kill him.

Boy will be the death of us.

Somehow, he was aware they had directed the spiteful mindvoice at him. His mind seemed to take up the chant, the words repeating over and over again.

Death. Death. Death.

"Damien, come on, now, calm down. Let go of the veil."

Damien gasped as bolts of power hammered him. He spun, power flying out from him like a fist and slammed into the man who'd startled him. Damien sagged in relief as the power left him, falling to his knees as his body trembled in reaction. He wrestled with himself, trying to push himself back from the void, from the place that crackled with power, a power that sang to him. He stared blankly at the man his powers had struck where he slumped against a tree. A name seemed to hover on the edge of his mind. He should know this man, but he couldn't tease the name from where it hid. Energy licked around him and through him. His mind blank. He stared, wondering where he was. He recognised the shuddering intake of his own breath as he realised he not only didn't know who the man was, he didn't know who *he* was.

Damien, listen to me. Let the power go.

As the man reached out a hand, the energy within him gathered, poised to strike. *Damien.* The name struck him as familiar, and he wondered if that was his name. Then another person placed herself between him and the world. The clamouring mindvoices retreated as she grasped his forearm.

Damien.

He stared into blue eyes so much like his own. He paused again, wondering how he knew his own eyes were blue. Slowly, she was pulling him back to the world, energy flowing like a stream from him to her. She soothed the pain that flared through him. As the agony receded, awareness returned. Damien. He remembered now, his name was Damien.

Isabella, he said.

He recognised her now; Isabella was his sister. Damien gasped, and the veil fled him as quickly as it had filled him a moment before. Leaving him feeling depleted. Empty. His mind was sluggish as he stared at the man he'd struck. Owen. The name seemed to dredge up from the depths of his mind.

The man he'd been about to kill was Owen, his mentor. He sagged, curling up on the ground. Didn't care who might see— he didn't have the energy.

Sorry, Owen, Isabella.

He winced as even his whispered mindvoice caused his head to ache even more. Exhaustion weighed him down. He opened his eyes only to wince at the light.

"Come on, Damien, let's get you back to your house and a bed," Owen said.

I'll be fine.

"You'll be more comfortable sleeping this off in bed," Isabella said.

Damien groaned and rolled onto his knees, wondering when his little sister had become so smart. He paused as the nausea rose and the world spun and lurched around him. Every part of him ached, a sense of wrongness hanging over him. Isabella was correct, of course, they both were. He wondered, yet again, why he alone suffered with the veil this way.

"Go on, everyone. Get back to your tasks," Owen ordered.

Damien ignored the fact that he'd caused a scene. Again. He had no choice but to allow Owen to help him up and leant heavily on his mentor. He made no pretence that he could stand by himself.

"He'll bring the Warlord down on us all with such displays!"

Damien cracked his eyes enough to see Mark Miller, the baker, glaring at him. He recognised that spiteful mindvoice now. As far back as he could remember, he'd known the baker feared him, though he'd never really understood why. Although after he'd caught what the man had been thinking about Isabella, the act the baker had been caught at while he watched her, Damien had given the man good reason to hate him. If that poor excuse of a human ever tried to hurt Isabella,

Damien swore he'd kill him — if his father or Owen didn't do it first.

"Enough of your nonsense, Mark. He's still a lad."

"Bah! He's almost an adult…"

"A lad who isn't responsible for being prone to attacks from the veil. You know as well as I the visiting healer said the lad was suffering from veil sickness. Now go," Owen growled.

Damien's mentor tensed as though Owen were bracing for a fight. That left Damien wondering if he'd be able to stand by himself if his mentor abandoned him to fight the baker. If he'd had the energy, he would have laughed. A fight between Owen and the baker was no contest at all.

Owen hadn't been born here, in the village, but had come here after the rise of the Warlord. He kept his past to himself but he'd set up the defences around the village, including the early warning system on the river. It was a simple measure comprising ropes and bells that were lowered across the river after dark that would raise a racket if approached, but none other had come up with the idea before Owen set it up. Unlike many of the villagers, his mentor had been trained in using the blades he carried. Owen would have won any fight, hands down, and his mentor didn't need the ever-present blade he wore to kill a man like Mark Miller.

Damien's breath shook as his vulnerability hit him. Now the veil had gone, he couldn't sense anyone in the village, let alone what they were feeling. When the veil had withdrawn, it had done so completely. He was as helpless as a newborn right now, or perhaps worse. He couldn't even perform the smallest task.

These recent attacks were new and unpredictable, and increasingly hard to recover from. People said he might die from veil sickness. At times like this, he was afraid they were correct.

CHAPTER
TEN

Jaclyn stood atop a hill with an overview of the settlement below. There was little chance those below would observe her. In the heat of the day, those of the clans slept. She wondered if this place would finally bring the death her brother wished for her. She and her family had fought the trader clans for what seemed like a lifetime. It had cost her many Sylannian lives, but they had gained so much land. The islands of her homeland were groaning under the weight of their population. Not only could the lower caste families of Sylanna spread out here, but there was also plenty of space to produce food and other resources as well. The People had been rich with the land. She'd done what many before her could not: conquered this place piece by piece. And now she'd nearly won this war. Once she took the Hallaran Lake, the hills region and all the tribes of the Hallaran Clan that called this place home would be hers. Those formerly of the trader clans conquered at the start of this war told her there was only one more sector to take after this: the Kallith Clan in the sector the locals called the barrens. She'd been told that area would prove problematic to take.

Jaclyn frowned and pushed consideration of future battles aside. This sector had proven unlike the river lands and the grasslands, where they'd often faced sudden hit-and-run raids. Here in the hills there had been no one to fight as her family and sister houses swept across the sector. Not a single member of any of the tribes of Hallaran had even been seen in this new territory and so far she'd taken it without a fight. Inexplicably, they all appeared to be here at the Hallaran Lake, in the heart of the hills. That had given her pause. Tactically, she didn't understand why they were here. There were no fortifications that she could see, although she conceded the lake did give them a constant supply of fresh water that in turn enabled them to grow crops. But that would only be an advantage if the Hallaran Clan could hold off her own forces.

"Is this a trap?" Ricardo asked.

"If so, it is a remarkably bad one." Jaclyn didn't take her eyes off the oasis below.

There were a lot of low, single-storey structures clustered on one side of the lake. She'd learnt that those buildings housed the tribe that remained in residence each season to tend the crops that were grown here. On the other side of the lake there were fruit-bearing trees and beyond the orchards, crops were grown. Normally there would only be one of the tribes that made up Hallaran Clan in residence, but even she could see there was more than one tribe here at the lake. The circular tents constructed of hides thrown over wooden frames, with a metal chimney jutting out from the centre billowing smoke, spread out behind the regular buildings. All the tents bore the branded symbol of a lake that alternated with the symbol of an animal in a band that ringed each tent. Different tents had different animals—where the symbol of the lake signified they were of the Hallaran Clan, the stylised animal marked which tribe of Hallaran the occupants belonged to, so that tents with matching symbols were grouped together. The tents that sprawled up the hill behind the main buildings certainly explained where the missing tribes of the Hallaran Clan were.

"These all appear to be Hallaran tribes," Ricardo mused.

"Before, there have always been signs of the tribes of the other clan groups," Myra said.

"In particular, where are those of Kallith?" Jaclyn scanned the massed tents below for some sign of them. "They've been present at every battle for years."

She'd learnt to recognise the markings of those of the barrens. Once they'd swept over the river clans all those years ago, the other clan groups had joined the fight. Of those she'd learnt to recognise the warriors of Kallith. They were fierce opponents, one and all, each bearing the tattoos of the warrior class on their face and arms. The hit-and-run tactics with wicked arrows that rained down on her own forces not only slowed this conquest but had cost the lives of many of her fighters. It was just as well that replacement daggerwives were something she had an abundance of. For all that the clans had plenty of space by comparison to her people, their population was low. She guessed there were more people living on her island court back in Sylanna than the People had in all the clans combined.

As a cool breeze sprang up, the whisper of the loose panels of her spidersilk robes blended in with the rustling of the long grass. Probably not the safest form for them to be in given they were on a war footing, which accounted for the disapproving expressions of some of the lesser wives around her who kept their spidersilk in its armour formation. Of course, her spidersilk gown could return to its hard armour shell in a moment, and she still wore her daggers. No self-respecting scion of the ruling class in Sylanna would be seen without them, let alone a daughter of the Monarch House.

This place would fall much more easily than the other two areas. Soon, this war would be won, and she could return to the Court of a Thousand Islands. This land would give the lower caste families a new place to live in with a strong workforce to serve them. Crops could be grown and animals tended, as well as precious ore used to make their fighting blades and more. There were riches in the barrens, or so she'd been informed.

"Commander?"

Jaclyn didn't turn from her study of the lake below. "Yes?"

"Our patrol has captured a man who claims to be a leader from the settlement below. He's asking to speak to you." There was a note of surprise in the daggerwife's tone.

Jaclyn turned, her eyebrows rising. "He asked for me by name?"

The daggerwife blushed. "No, Commander. He asked for whoever was in charge."

"Do we think he is one of their leaders? The others we've taken haven't proven to be cooperative." Ricardo was clearly sceptical.

Jaclyn reached out and took Ricardo's hand. "Who knows, husband? Perhaps we should find out."

Jaclyn walked towards her own tent with Ricardo and primewife Myra. Jaclyn breezed through the entrance to her command tent as the minor wives pulled back the canvas partition that served for a door on her approach. They had added to their number since leaving the Court of a Thousand Islands, with sister houses and the lower caste families arriving to aid in this war. She had deemed it prudent to place more layers around Ricardo in this foreign land. Although not all risks were because of the clans they fought. It wouldn't be the first time one of the lower sister houses attempted to raise their own standing by disposing of houses above them in station. Or for her dear brother, the king, to arrange for the death of her and her family while they were here in these lands. It would be an unfortunate tragedy of war, of course.

Jaclyn settled in the low chair. The only concession to local habits was the pile of cushions that certainly made the chair more comfortable. Ricardo settled next to her, while Myra stood slightly behind with her hand on his shoulder. The other wives walked across the room to join them, carpets softening the footfall of their boot-shod feet. The spidersilks worn by the daggerwives were in their hard-shell armour form and their blades were prominent. None would take a chance with one of the untamed clansmen near Ricardo. Or Jaclyn herself, the firstwife of their family.

When they were settled, the flaps opened to admit a group of daggerwives and a man, bound and collared with silk. The spidersilk was useful for so many things. The origin of the spidersilk was a closely guarded secret, with the giant silkspiders who spun their webs of the silken strands being endemic to the Thousand Islands that formed Sylanna. It held the veil within its strands, allowing it to be soft or hard, and was stronger than any metal. It took an affinity for the spidersilk to trigger it to reform, an ability no one outside her homeland seemed to possess, making it ideal to restrain their captives.

Those holding his bindings pushed him down onto his knees, careful to make sure he wasn't within striking distance of Jaclyn.

"Who are you?" Myra's voice was clear and slightly bored.

"Chono; I'm the co-leader of the clan in residence this season at Hallaran." The man kept his eyes on the ground

"Does your co-leader know you are here?"

If this man's co-leader was aware of this, then he wouldn't be here alone. She would be here kneeling beside him. Jaclyn had learnt a great deal about these people and their customs during this conquest. A concentric swirling tattoo on the left side of his forehead, spilling onto his temples, marked him as a leader. His co-leader would bear the mirror image of the tattoo on the right side of her face. Their habit of marking up those of prominence in their community with tattoos had proven quite handy for identifying them.

"No. I've been taking rides alone in the evening for the last month. She thinks it's to clear my head. I've been expecting your forces. I want the best for my people," Chono said.

"What is it you think is best, Chono?" Ricardo regarded the clansmen.

"I can give the Hallaran Clans to your keeping, with as few deaths as possible." Chono licked his lips and his eyes rose from their examination of the floor. "I can make sure I disarm anyone inclined to fight, to make it easier on your people."

"How would you do this?" Myra was clearly sceptical.

"The tribes of Hallaran Clan are here to discuss our fighting strategy. It is custom for everyone to disarm when entering the meeting house. I'll call a meeting to discuss our defences in the morning. I'll invite our best fighters to consult, making sure they, too, are contained and disarmed." Chono broke into a sweat.

Jaclyn let the silence linger in the tent, watching as Chono knelt in front of her before she finally stood. The daggerwives tightened their grip on the silken ropes that bound the man as she approached. A hushed whisper of power flowed from one of his keepers and, at her urging, the collar wrapped tighter around his neck. She leant over and cupped his cheek, tilting his head up.

"What is it you wish in return, Chono?" Jaclyn could sense his desperation and fear.

"Reports say some of the younger men you take, the ones with more power, are given to your women. That they have some authority, easy lives. I have little power, but I can give you the tribes of the Hallaran Clan, surely that is worth something?" Chono responded.

Jaclyn let the silence stretch between them before she smiled. "Very well, Chono. We will remove your collar, for this one night. You will go back to your clan and surrender them to us tomorrow. You will then accept your collar again, calmly, willingly, as an example to your clan. Then, I will reward you as you have requested. You will be assigned as a possible breeding male to some of my people."

"Thank you," Chono said.

"Don't mistake this, Chono: we will remove your collar for this one task. You are ours already. If you cannot deliver as you have promised, we will punish you." Jaclyn regarded the pathetic man kneeling in front of her without a hint of empathy. It didn't do for those they enslaved to believe they had more worth than they did.

Chono's smile faded. "I can't guarantee those in the meeting place won't fight, but they won't be armed."

"You said they disarm. Where do they store the blades?"

"There's a rack to the right of the doors, it's the only entrance."

Jaclyn turned and walked away from him, returning to her seat. At her gesture of dismissal the daggerwives holding Chono's bonds hauled him to his feet and led him from her presence.

ELEVEN

Delbee walked from her hut, or rather, the hut that was temporarily hers, as one of the custodians of Hallaran this season. For now. The thick stone walls kept it relatively cool during the day. The breeze caused the grass to ripple and cooled the air as it blew across the lake.

"Delbee, come, I've called council to discuss our response to the invasion," Chono's thin voice called.

Despite her best efforts, Delbee's spine stiffened. When the combined clans of Hallaran had voted for co-leaders of her tribe, they had chosen her for her fighting spirit. It was almost as if they'd had foreknowledge of what was to come. Unfortunately, in their esteemed wisdom, they'd also selected Chono to be her co-leader. A more spineless, self-serving man could not be found in all the lands that the People called home. They'd believed his passive nature would offset her fire, making them perfect co-leaders. Nothing could have been further from the truth.

"What is the point, Chono?" Delbee didn't bother to face him.

"My strategy has kept all the tribes of the Hallaran Clan intact," Chono almost whined.

"At what cost?"

"Our people are alive," Chono said.

"No. The People—our people—are dying."

"If the warriors of Kallith couldn't swing the fight in the favour of the river or grass clans, how do you presume we could?"

"Our numbers may have been the difference between death and life. There is no honour in withdrawing to our sanctuary while other clans die," Delbee spat at him.

"Don't be obstinate. Just come to the meeting hall," Chono pleaded.

Delbee closed her eyes and took a deep breath, trying to calm herself. She longed to be out with the fighters helping to defeat the enemy. Yet co-leaders had to agree to a course of action. Or they were meant to. In this, she and her co-leader could not find common ground and Chono had acted without her knowledge to call on the tribes to attend an emergency meeting. If only the other tribe leaders of Hallaran Clan hadn't heeded Chono's call. If only the other tribes had ridden to the aid of the other territories. As it was, all the tribes of Hallaran had come. By tradition, that handed the power of the individual tribes of Hallaran to the tribe in residence at Hallaran Lake, which this season as the leaders of the clan in residence, it was her and Chono. For reasons known only to himself, Chono refused to budge from his position that the fight the other clans were involved in was not their own. Chono insisted they needed to stay here, safe at Hallaran Lake. So, they sat here, while outside their lands other clans of the People fell, one after the other, to the invaders.

"You know my opinion. There is no point to these endless discussions you call with the other leaders." Delbee turned her back on Chono, striding across the camp towards the children's compound.

A shot of indecision, fear, and panic from her co-leader caused Delbee's step to falter and she nearly turned around, but gritted her teeth and kept walking away. She sensed when he finally withdrew, panic still weighing heavily on him. Delbee decided to continue with her original plan for her morning and spend time with the children. After Chono's talks were over, she'd find out why he panicked. As much as his indecision and extreme caution frustrated her, they were still co-leaders and she needed to help him face whatever it was he feared. Even if he was just concerned the others might continue to argue with his determination to stay here in the heart of Hallaran. Even here at the Hallaran Lake, word had filtered back, or it had in the early years of the conflict. Those who'd called the river region home had fallen, and the conflict had moved inexorably to the grasslands. No news had filtered their way since they'd withdrawn here. From what she knew of the fighting in the early days, it didn't seem like a war. It was a fight for survival.

Delbee acknowledged those on guard who stood on duty and opened the door to the children's compound, murmuring her thanks to the guard who followed her and took a position just inside the door. It made her sad, such a measure was a sign of the looming dangers. As the doors shut behind her, she closed her eyes and breathed in the coolness that wafted over her, soaking in a moment of peace. Taking a deep breath, she allowed her worries to recede into the background. Even if only for a moment.

"Mother!"

Delbee smiled, opening her arms to her children who extracted themselves from their lessons with the other children. They were almost too old for such behaviour, but that day wasn't here yet. She hugged them, pushing the chaos that was her world aside and wanting nothing more than to make sure their world was safe—though even hiding here would only buy them so much time. Delbee shook herself, pushing her dark considerations aside and turned her attention to her children as the custodians called the other children to order, urging them to pay attention to their lessons.

"Show me. What have you been working on?" Delbee walked with them to the inner hall.

Here she could see they had been working on their weaving skills along with the other children. She smiled at their work. Neither of them displayed any talent at all in the artisan skills. Their aptitude for working with leather to produce saddles and bridles was passable but it was just as well others were good at fashioning clothes, otherwise they'd have nothing to wear. While both had shown an interest in metal- and woodwork in the past, neither was very good at it. They took after her more than their father. Still, as any diligent child of the clans, they each cross-trained so they would understand the path others trod. She considered it important for those who excelled on the warrior path. Delbee made a mental note to request a foster period for both the children with one of the tribes of Kallith. Her smile faltered slightly as it occurred to her that none of them might live through this war to see it happen.

Delbee smiled at the custodians of the children's compound, about to ask how the children were progressing with their other lessons but a sudden pull as someone—many someones—utilised the veil made her spin around. Moments later, glass shattered and wood splintered, sounding like an explosion.

It had come from the direction of the meeting house.

"Get the children back to the rear," Delbee snapped to the custodians.

Drawing her blade, she ran towards the door, several of the custodians and the guard on duty by her side and similarly armed. They'd barely made it to the door before she heard and sensed a rush of power just before the door and windows splintered inwards. She staggered under a shower of glass.

The invaders had arrived at Hallaran.

TWELVE

Damien rolled over, wincing at the light that filtered through the cracks in the shutters. His mind was idle, fatigue weighing down on him. The fatigue wasn't unusual, but being awake if it was still before midday was. At least since his episodes of veil sickness had increased this last season. Damien concluded it must be dusk, since these days if it was early morning it took his father to wake him and drag him out of bed. He couldn't remember the last time he'd woken up in the early morning of his own accord. Damien groaned as his memory of his last veil sickness episode flooded back. While his parents and the visiting healer referred to it as a sickness, to him it felt more like he was being burnt from the inside, his body melted and reforged.

He remembered he'd been halfway through his afternoon chores for the day, which meant he hadn't completed them, and groaned again. That would annoy the elderly task master who assigned them each day.

Without consciously thinking about it, he could feel the

veil, as if a tap had turned on, allowing it to flow into him. It was cause for both relief and trepidation. It was hard to admit to his family, but it was just never quite right when he couldn't touch the veil. They'd told him that to ward off the sickness he should try to minimise how much he utilised the veil. They said if he lost himself in the power he could die, just as others with abilities like his had before him. Yet of late, the longer he spent trying to keep from using the veil, the sicker he'd feel. Until he lost control. Then it was the opposite of everything they told him. He couldn't pinpoint exactly what triggered his attacks, but regardless of whether or not he refrained from using his powers, the veil sickness incapacitated him when it hit. His tonic didn't seem to help the way the healer said it would, neither did abstaining from his abilities, if anything lately the attacks were getting worse. Even more concerning were the moments during and when he was coming out of an attack, when he didn't recognise anyone around him or even know who he was. He hadn't admitted this recent development to anyone. It was something that no one else would understand.

Damien didn't feel a burning need to get up and his parents generally didn't bother him after one of his attacks. His skin prickled with the touch of a seeking mind. A powerful mind like his own—and it wasn't his sister. This was the touch of a stranger. Eyes flaring open, he gasped and sat upright. He shuddered. The hair along his arms stood on end. There was no one in the room with him, but he was being watched. He could feel the weight of them through the veil as more eyes joined the first. Hundreds of eyes gazing at him. He'd perceived nothing like it before, even if he recognised instantly what was happening. He'd never encountered anyone else with power even remotely like his own, except for Isabella. Even his sister wasn't as powerful as he was right now. The presence wasn't his little sister playing games—he'd recognise Isabella's use of the veil instantly.

Damien closed his eyes, blocking everyone out for a moment, his senses ranging further afield, towards the clamour he'd heard in his mind, seeking the power he'd that had drawn his attention. As he travelled, he identified the small, well-kept homes, the commons and meeting hall. He flew over the fields and followed the one road out of town. He focused on the flare in the veil that had attracted his attention. A bright glow, brighter than anything he'd perceived before, pulsing with an energy that none here in the village possessed. None, except possibly he and Isabella. He paused his questing mind as the mindvoices of the strangers came into focus sharper than those of his fellow villagers.

Did you feel that?

Can't we just camp out?

Does it have to be at this place? It's barely a village.

Enough! We'll stay here overnight and re-provision.

Damien held his breath as he distinguished the voices of multiple others and he realised their attention was drawn towards him. As he focused on the brightly glowing mass, he realised his impression of hundreds of eyes earlier hadn't been his mind playing tricks on him. If there were only a handful of people, he'd be able to distinguish individuals by the veil that glowed within them. He sharpened his focus, drawing closer, and gasped as the lifeforces separated into the outline of ghostly figures. The power wrapped around these strangers and through them; it burnt brightly within them as if they were creatures of the veil. He'd never seen these strangers before, but there was no doubt in his mind that they could only be one group: it was whispered those that rode within the Warlord's ranks were insanely strong in the veil. No others were ever described this way, with both fear and awe. It was the Warlord.

Damien fled back to himself. He flung the blankets aside and bolted from his bed, knowing they had little time. From the clatter of dishes and hushed conversation, his family was in the kitchen. Damien surged forward, wrenching his door open, and bolted down the hallway into the main room, barely aware that he'd used the veil. His mother, father and Isabella stared at him, shock radiating from them. He grabbed Isabella's hand, hauling her unceremoniously up, causing the kitchen bench she'd been sitting on to topple over, clattering on the stone floor.

"Son, what—"

His father stopped abruptly as Damien cut him off. "The Warlord, it can't be anyone else. They're on the road into town and will be here soon."

Isabella, it's time to hide. Just like we practiced, Damien said.

"Wait, talk sense, Damien, there's no one out there, let alone the Warlord," his mother said.

"They're on the road into town. They'll be here soon." Damien felt the weight of their disapproval but persevered. "I know I'm not meant to use my abilities, but I couldn't help it. I woke up and I could sense them."

"Now, son, you had one of your turns. There's no one out there, you probably just had a nightmare—"

The sound of hoofbeats drumming on the hard-packed road outside in the otherwise quiet village caused his mother to stop talking and her face drained of colour. She turned to the window, his father at her side, and eased the shutters open to peer outside into the increasing gloom.

His father turned. "Go, hide."

Damien led Isabella to the back of the house. He released her hand and stooped to grab the edge of the rug on the floor and threw it back. Kneeling, he willed the edge of the loose floorboards up, slipping them aside to reveal the lined bolthole they'd dug under the floor. He held out his hand to Isabella once more and she slipped her hand into his without a word. Damien helped her ease into the hiding place, ensuring she was comfortable before he reached for the floorboards.

What's happening? Isabella's mindvoice was hushed.

Damien reached out and brushed the tear from his sister's cheek, instantly feeling guilty for the fright he must have caused her. He flashed her the image of the figures that burnt brightly with power. She gasped, a hand pressed to her mouth. She knew what that meant.

It will be all right. Just as we practiced. Damien willed Isabella to comply. *Withdraw into yourself. You are not here. Take yourself into the grey place.*

Tears welled up in her bright blue eyes. *But what about you?*

Damien closed his eyes briefly. *It's too late for me. They know I'm here, but they don't know about you. Promise me you'll stay in our secret place, in the grey, until you detect me leaving?*

Isabella sobbed, her hands immediately pressing to her mouth to stifle the noise.

No! Isabella wailed.

You will stay hidden here, in the grey. They'll take me and you'll be safe.

No, hide, you'll be safe too, Isabella said.

If he crawled into the hiding hole as well, it would doom them both. Damien stared into Isabella's eyes, using all the compulsion he could exert.

Damien watched as tears welled in his sister's eyes, but sighed with relief as she bit back a sob, and faded from sight. He'd discovered the grey place years ago when he'd been trying to hide from the task master after he'd burnt the food in the communal kitchen. While he didn't know precisely where it was, it was power. When he went there, others couldn't see him. Isabella was the only other person he'd been able to teach that trick to, even though she was a couple of years younger than him.

Satisfied, he slotted the floorboards carefully back into place, then pulled the rug back over them. He walked over the spot, straining to hear if the boards would give a tell-tale creak, but breathed a sigh of relief when they did not.

As he rushed back to the front of the house, he heard running and slamming doors nearby. He paused long enough to pick up both his father's sword and his own, plus a large bush knife from the rack in the side cupboard on his way through the kitchen. By now he could hear the clatter of hooves, the jingling of halters and the grumbling of men. His father and mother were still at the window, peering out at the strangers, but as Damien approached, his father flipped the curtain back into place. He grabbed his sword from Damien with a simple nod, and slid the belt around his waist. His mother took the bush knife from him, her lips narrowing at his sword.

"You will say here, Damien," she ordered.

"Mother, they—" Her hand rose, fingers pressing against his lips.

She pulled him in and hugged him. "Stay here."

"I'll not let you both be hurt because of me."

"I agree with your mother. Stay put. We'll deal with these strangers," his father said.

"They already know I'm here," Damien said.

"Not another word, Damien. You'll stay put."

The look his father gave him was stern, his lips pressed in a firm line as he gestured to the back of the house. No matter how useless hiding would be, he ducked his head, it was no use arguing with his parents. They just wouldn't listen to him.

Damien stilled, listening without trying to draw power. If he drew the veil right now, it was certain to attract unwelcome attention, even though he suspected it was too late. He slowed his breathing and listened to the indistinct voices outside. He recognised one as the Speaker for their village. Damien had a momentary pang of sympathy for the man. Usually he was just the mouthpiece for the village, dealing with the traders and other groups who passed through. He settled disputes between villagers and made sure everything was in good order. The other voice was unknown to him, but it was deep and demanded attention. The conversation didn't take long before there were more sounds. He could process them without having to use his powers, although it was difficult to stop himself. It was so much easier to lift conversations and images from people's minds. Boots struck the ground as the strangers dismounted. The steady clop of horses being led away in the direction of the animal pens. He gathered they were setting up camp in the centre of the village. Whoever was in charge was likely taking over either the meeting hall or the Speaker's own cottage. Perhaps both. In the commotion, there was one distinct voice.

"Strange, Speaker. For such a large village, there are no children about." The deep, rumbling tone had an edge to it.

"... dangerous times... Warlord..."

If it had been possible for Damien to hold even more still than he already was, he would have. He'd been correct in his guess. It was the infamous Warlord. The one that sacked villages as easily as he saved them. For a price. So the rumours indicated.

"Ah, but you are safe now. My soldiers are here." A faint hint of mocking was clear in the Warlord's rumbling tone.

"Of course, Warlord. It is late, the children are all indoors. It is custom here."

The order from the Speaker was clear. All of them were to stay where they were. Closing his eyes, Damien shuddered. There were horrible rumours of what happened to women and girls that the Warlord took a fancy to. He was determined that Isabella would not meet such a fate. Everyone said that the Warlord took those with power.

Damien's resolve settled. He'd give himself up, become one of the Warlord's feared killers. He'd rather that than allow Isabella to suffer at the hands of the Warlord. Damien sent his power in a thin, guided stream towards his sister. The compulsion he sent was simple.

Stay hidden!

He was relieved as he sensed her nod, although her lips trembled. Satisfied that she agreed to stay where she was in that grey place. She'd be safe there.

At least safe enough, until the Warlord claimed him and took him away.

THIRTEEN

Jaclyn hid in the shadows thrown by a tree at the rear of the meeting house. With a small pulse of power, she made the individual panels of her spidersilk robes form around her legs, arms, and torso. It hardened, encasing her in effective battle clothing. She ignored the other inhabitants in the camp who yet hadn't realised their fate. Others had the duty of taking and containing them with as minimal loss of life as they could. Of course, they had found during this conflict that the clansmen, with few exceptions, were not remarkable fighters. As it was, they killed the outer sentries quietly, with no alarm being raised. Then Chono led a group of men and women into the meeting house, just as he'd promised. It remained to be seen if Chono had told them the truth and really would have all their fighters unarmed and detained, or if he was trying to lead them into a trap. Either way, she was confident they would absorb the Hallaran Clan into the Sylannian kingdom before nightfall.

They had discussed their approach to the meeting hall after

Chono had departed the previous evening. It was apparent that even if those inside were surprised by the attack and disarmed, her own forces couldn't all go through the same door. Particularly since, if Chono hadn't deceived them, these were the leaders and fighters of the Hallaran Clan. While the meeting hall had only one large entrance at the front, windows lined the walls, giving them multiple entrance points to enable them to surround those inside.

She reassured herself that the daggerwives of her sister houses were in place around the settlement at Hallaran Lake to take the clan members who weren't involved in the meeting with their leaders and best fighters. Jaclyn nearly laughed at the notion. Best compared to what? Liliana, the head of the daggerwives of her own house, was nearby, her fellow cohort spaced in teams of four around the meeting house. Jaclyn, Ricardo then Myra were all in place, each lined up outside a window. Each with their own protective detail, intent on keeping their charges safe. It was Liliana's job to spearhead the assault on the meeting house. All the pieces were in place.

Go!

Jaclyn pulled on the veil, feeling Myra and Ricardo do the same as, on command, Liliana and her cohort sprinted forward. Jaclyn concentrated her power into a flow of energy around Liliana as she ran, then punched it through the window right as Liliana leapt. The explosion resounded around the oasis as all the windows burst inwards, shattering in time for Liliana and the daggerwives to dive through, daggers in hand. It was the signal for the sister houses to launch their own attacks.

Jaclyn ignored the screams and shouts that rose from her attack. She waited for that tell-tale stillness that would herald the end of the battle. On this occasion, she guessed it would occur just moments before Liliana called her into the meeting house. After she'd checked with the other daggerwives that their own attacks had gone as planned.

Finally, after what seemed like an agonising wait, there was that stillness she'd been waiting for.

Commander, the village has been contained, Liliana said.

Jaclyn smiled. Liliana had proven to be an able leader of the daggerwives in this conflict. She'd risen through the ranks after her predecessors had died. She was like a diamond that adversity had polished to show its true aspect.

Jaclyn barely waited a breath for her own protection detail to move before she followed, making her way around the building towards the shattered door.

I almost wish this had been a full battle, Myra sighed.

At least that way, we could have fought as well. Ricardo's grumpy tone made her smile.

Jaclyn kept her face impassive as she entered and paused, aware of Myra on one side and Ricardo on the other as the daggerwives who'd come with her flowed around the room to join their fellow wives. The members of the clan who'd had the misfortune to be inside this building were subdued on the ground. Collared and bound by the team that had come through the doors.

A clanswoman screamed, causing Jaclyn to spin as the captive was suddenly free of restraint and lunged towards her. Jaclyn's focus narrowed. She drew her blades as both Myra and Ricardo drew their own. Before she could take further action, Liliana had propelled herself from the opposite side of the room, her blades striking the woman down. As the blood sprayed, Liliana barely paused before launching herself at the daggerwife who'd let the clanswoman loose. The woman desperately swung the collar at Liliana that should have contained the clanswoman. Ducking under the hardened collar as it swung towards her head, Liliana lunged forward, blades striking the woman with the efficiency born of the battlefield.

Husband, First, Prime, are you well? Liliana asked.

We are well, Liliana, Myra assured the daggerwife.

That's the closest my brother and his wives have come to succeeding in an attack against us. He must be getting desperate, Jaclyn observed.

Our thanks for your timely action, Ricardo said.

Jaclyn glanced at Myra. They were both familiar with that tone from their husband. She had no doubt that Ricardo had decided that Liliana would join him in his bed tonight. As she had been doing for months now. If Liliana wasn't already pregnant, she would be soon enough. This was yet another thing she was exceedingly lucky with. Ricardo often made superb choices.

Jaclyn drew her attention back to those contained in the meeting room. Blades still drawn, as the room stilled.

She studied Chono, backed into the corner, eyes wide. Two daggerwives were in front of him, daggers drawn, protecting him against any potential threat.

"We're secure, Commander."

Jaclyn sheathed her daggers then turned to Chono, where he still cowered in the corner.

"Come here, Chono." Their captives turned their heads as she spoke. Chono licked his lips then walked towards her, the only one unshackled. Several of his clansmen snarled and lunged, only to be incapacitated by their bonds.

Finally, Chono stood before her. Jaclyn held out her hand and smiled as one of her people handed her a plain, grey-blue strip of spidersilk. She wrapped it around his neck and sent a small pulse to it, hardening it into a collar.

"Well done, Chono. You have served me well. I will reward you, as I promised." She stroked his cheek.

The two women assigned to be his guard placed themselves between Chono and the others, making it exceedingly clear that Chono was now one of theirs.

FOURTEEN

Damien took controlled breaths, neither actively pushing the power from him nor blocking it. Just allowing it to flow around him without trying to control it. From the moment he'd woken up this morning, he could sense the surges of power being utilised by the Warlord's people. It was a noticeable increase from the normal activity of the village. The strength of the outsiders was breathtaking. Even the usage was distinct, somehow.

"They're just like me," Damien whispered.

Guilt flooded Damien. The most prominent emotion he could feel from the villagers was fear, yet he sat wondering what it would be like to ride with the warband. The opportunity to learn the full scope of his power was an enticing option. It was the first indication he'd had that the price of his strength in the veil might not mean an early grave. Although the cost of joining these people was said to be his soul. To become a cold-blooded killer at the direction of the Warlord was too much. But the threat of the Sylannian raiders was real. Why else had Owen set up the simple but effective ropes with bells that were lowered across the river at night? Any who tried to come upon them that way would make enough racket to wake the village.

Even without his powers, he could hear the villagers making their way into the meeting hall. He'd argued with his parents again this morning, trying to reason with them. He told them he would rather give himself up than allow them or his sister to be harmed. They wouldn't hear of it, and he was ashamed to admit it was his fear of becoming a monster like the Warlord's people that held him in place. He had to admit, even if only quietly to himself, his emotions went from one extreme to the other. Alternating between being horrified and intrigued by the idea. The idea of becoming a killer weighed more heavily on him than the possibility he might die of veil sickness. The mood that had settled on the village was sombre. Still, he detected a hint of defiance. Most of the villagers, not just his own family, seemed inclined to defy these outsiders who'd ridden into their midst.

Damien concentrated, blocking out all sound: the wind, the rustling of leaves, the call of the birds. He concentrated on hearing the words that carried across the space between his home and the meeting hall. Sweat prickled his forehead. It was the first sign he had that he was trying too hard not to use the veil.

He could feel their minds searching for him. See the thin tendrils of the veil guided by people questing, the coolness of their touch making him shiver as it brushed him. They were aware he was here, somewhere, but unless he was actively using his abilities, they wouldn't know where.

Biting his lips, he shuddered as a touch brushed him again. His breath escaped his lips, ragged even to his own ears. This person who searched for him was strong. He could feel the stranger urging him to draw his power, as if they somehow guessed exactly what he was doing to avoid detection.

Give up, boy, the Warlord said.

Damien stiffened, his breath exploding from him as the words echoed in his mind. But if the Warlord was certain where he was, his soldiers would have dragged him out by now. Damien determined to ignore the taunting voice.

He stilled as other snatches of conversation from the meeting hall carried to him on the wind.

"… no, we can't…"

Damien frowned. That was the Speaker.

"… it's our duty to protect the children…"

The task master might be old, but his voice was firm.

"… bah… he's nearly an adult…"

The baker was easily identifiable by his spiteful tone.

"… nearly is not the same…"

Damien smiled as he recognised Owen, his mentor, who at least spoke up for him.

"… kill us all for one…"

Again, the hateful baker urging the others to give him up.

An explosion of noise caused Damien to jump before he realised it was just the rap of a staff on the wooden floors of the meeting hall. It was as clear as if he were standing in the room with them. The crack resounded around the village in counterpoint to the sudden silence. The voice that issued was unnaturally loud.

"Let me make this easy for you." There was a harsh edge to the Warlord's voice as he spoke to the villagers in the meeting hall.

I know you are here. We sensed you when we approached the village.

Damien stiffened as the Warlord double-talked. Speaking aloud to the adults in the hall while also whispering in his head.

"Accede to my demands or my men will torch your entire village."

The silence that settled was deafening.

The destruction of your village will be your fault.

"Then I'll just take those of you I deem will aid my cause into service."

I won't just take you. I'll take the useful women, children and men. Then leave the rest to die.

"You can't threaten us this way. We'll decide in council and answer you when we're ready, Warlord. Or should I more appropriately address you as Paul Olenna, Speaker of Yalleska? We are equals you and I, both Speakers of our respective villages." The defiance in the Speaker's voice was clear.

The resultant gasps told him he wasn't the only one shocked at such blatant defiance. Everyone knew the Warlord did not use his name and regarded no one as his equal. He'd killed for less than the disrespect their Speaker had just shown.

"Burn the crops!" The Warlord's words were clipped and harsh.

Damien stiffened as an image flashed in his mind of men and women lowering burning torches to the village crops. A burst of power aided the ensuing flames to spread quickly.

It's in your hands. You. Or all that you love will be destroyed.

In his mind's eye, the crops in the village fields burst into flames. He leapt from his bed and ran from his room, then burst out the front door with such force it slammed against the wall as he ran out into the village common area. Flames and smoke were twisting up into the sky from the village crops, just as he'd seen it in his mind. Damien drew power and lunged with his hand outstretched.

He wasn't sure what he did or how he did it. Power flowed from him across the village crops; thunder rumbled from the sky and a sudden deluge fell from roiling black clouds, even though the moment before the sky had been a clear, perfect blue without a cloud to mar it. Now it was only the crack of lightning that lit up the dark that shrouded the village, pushing back the gloom to reveal the Warlord's people at the perimeter of the village crops. Another bolt of lightning followed the first. Damien gasped as the burst of light revealed he was now surrounded by the Warlord's people. All were dressed in black and brown fighting leathers inset with bands of silver that shone with the veil. All bore the crest of a sword plunging into flames on their chests that flickered as if the flames were alive. They regarded him without expression. Without a trace of fear. He smiled sardonically.

Why would they fear him?

These were the men and women that the horror stories were about, the embodiment of rumours that were whispered from village to village. They didn't fear anyone. They caused fear.

He raised his eyes to meet those of the man in front of him, to find them glowing with power. It made him wonder if his own eyes glowed. These were experienced fighters. Damien stiffened as one man stepped forward, his hand outstretched.

"It will be all right, lad. You'll ride with us and, in return, we will leave your village and family in peace." The man addressed one of his cohort. "Aiden, I'll take this one into my ranks. Advise your father that we have him while we get ready for the ride out of town."

A fleeting, sullen expression passed across the face of the one called Aiden as he turned and stalked away. Damien stared at the back of the sullen man as he walked towards the meeting hall.

Damien licked his lips, trying to push down his panic. He didn't really care about who the sullen man was but it gave him something else to think about, even if only for a moment, other than what he'd done and the situation he was in now. Damien dragged his attention back to the man in front of him.

"You'll leave everyone alone? They were just trying to protect me," Damien said.

"Your village will be fine, boy, as long as you do as the Warlord commands."

Damien swung his gaze back to the first man who'd spoken to him and caught an expression on his otherwise impassive face. He shook his head. It couldn't have been what his first impression told him it was. Yet there was a back part of his brain that told him that the fleeting expression on the older man's face was pain.

Hearing a cry and the drum of feet running towards him, Damien swung his attention around to his mother and father running towards him from the meeting hall. Damien squeezed his eyes shut, going cold as his mother ran, wailing at the top of her lungs, begging them not to take her baby boy. He went to go towards her but found himself blocked by the powerful strangers that still surrounded him.

"I won't try to run or anything. Just—" Damien took a trembling breath. "Just let me say goodbye to my parents."

The man who'd first spoken watched him for a moment and finally the people blocking his path melted back at a wave of the man's hand.

FIFTEEN

Michael waited until the lad settled uneasily on a spare horse with its lead rope tied to the saddle of his. Not that the horse would do anything but follow his. The uneasy seat Damien maintained showed he was far from an experienced rider.

I'll make them pay for this.

The threat of retribution caught Michael's attention. Interestingly, it wasn't from the parents, but from someone else. They merged with other random mindvoices and, given the Warlord didn't demand they find the individual responsible for the traitorous desire, he gathered he was one of the few who caught it.

Steady, the Warlord will order you killed and the lad will still ride out of town in my warband, Michael warned the stranger.

Michael made sure he stayed nonchalant, his face bored, as he felt the stranger's startled response. Even more interesting was the boy's reaction. Even though Michael had narrowed his mindvoice to the stranger's, the lad stiffened. He'd overheard the communication. Michael might not know who the man was, but it was clear Damien did.

Damien is just a boy. The Warlord will pay for this. I'll make sure of it.

I'll do my best to take care of him. Michael replied. *The Warlord makes no idle threats. He is just as likely to kill you if you resist.*

Michael didn't change his posture, but he swept their party for signs anyone else had caught the exchange.

Owen, I'll be fine. Protect Isabella! Damien said.

Michael nearly winced as Damien broadcast his message to anyone who was paying attention with the talent to hear it, rather than narrowing it down to a personal communication. Although now, at least he had a name for the stranger who'd been threatening retribution. He was hoping it was only their proximity to Damien that allowed him to not only hear the communication, but to catch the image of a young girl who shone with power. It took Michael a moment to work through what his recruit was thinking and feeling, but he finally worked out that Isabella, the girl Damien had pictured, was Damien's sister. He nearly gave himself away with a shudder as the fear that Damien had for his sister hit him. He hoped the lad didn't sense his acknowledgement that the Warlord would probably insist they go back for the girl, never mind her age.

Enough, Damien. Shut it down.

Damien stiffened at his instruction, but to Michael's relief the lad's mind suddenly shuttered, becoming opaque. The boy would have to learn control, and fast, if he wanted to survive in the Warlord's service, and he hoped the Warlord hadn't heard that last message Damien sent. If she was half as powerful as Damien seemed to be, it was inevitable she would end up riding with them.

He glanced at Olivia, who rode nearby. *You caught that?*

Of course. I don't think the others did, though. Olivia was, as always, calm. It seemed a part of her nature that, no matter what was going on, she remained unruffled and considered.

This one is strong.

Olivia's mindvoice was grim. *So, it seems, is his little sister. We can all be grateful the Warlord didn't sense her.*

We'll have to keep dropping in to check on her. If she turns out half as strong as her brother, she'll need guidance.

Nathanial, riding nearby, scanned the silently watching villagers before replying. *There certainly isn't anyone left in the village who'd be able to help her.*

Hopefully the Warlord won't be back. She should be safe enough for now, Michael said.

We seem to collect people to protect, Olivia said.

Michael sensed his friend sigh, even if she didn't allow it past her lips. It was a sentiment he couldn't refute. The number of people that drew on his time only seemed to grow.

Why does everyone insist on treating me like a child? Damien muttered.

Michael traded glances with Olivia at the sulky tone of the lad. Not that Damien had meant the question for either of them. It was more like he was muttering to himself. Except unlike a normal person, when they might only hear an occasional word and fragmented sentences, with Damien, they caught the whole thing. Still, the lad was welcome to sulk if it made him feel better, particularly since he didn't volunteer to ride out of town with them—as long as he paid attention when they tried to teach him better control.

Settle, lad, concentrate on not attracting the Warlord's attention. Michael relaxed with effort into his saddle.

More than you already have. Olivia's exterior had returned to her normal nonchalant self, although her tone was bantering, flicking an image of Damien dousing them all in water to protect the village crops.

As Damien's horse snorted, Michael nearly laughed at the panic on the boy's face. Damien stared at the horse as if he expected it to bolt on him.

Try to not make a spectacle of yourself by falling off the horse, either. Michael grinned.

The lad did not know the life he was walking into. Oh, the Warlord was aware the boy was strong, after Damien's display when he was forced out of hiding it could hardly have been missed. But he doubted the Warlord suspected how strong Damien was. Even with the sudden storm Damien had raised, Michael judged the Warlord had dismissed the accomplishment. People often did things in stress, fear, and pain that they couldn't replicate later. Otherwise, the lad would be in the Warlord's custody. The Warlord would want to assure himself of the boy's loyalty before he let loose one who was that strong. Still, Michael took a hint from Olivia's tone. They'd stressed the lad enough with all that had happened to him and the unknown that he was heading into.

SIXTEEN

Jaclyn patrolled the sprawling habitation with its combination of permanent buildings and tents. In these early days of conquest, it was vital to make sure they contained those exhibiting behaviours that suggested they would be a problem. They kept adults occupied so they couldn't foment dissent, and they started indoctrinating the younger villagers to their new way of life. They had separated some out and sent them to other territories they had firm control over.

It was important to be seen. The way her command unit patrolled gave the impression their numbers were far higher than they actually were. Thanks to Chono's betrayal, the clan's fighters and leaders had been contained already. Those left had lost their will to fight.

With a unit of daggerwives around her, Jaclyn finally made it back to where her people camped. She had to admit the lake nestled in the rolling hills that made up this sector was rather pleasant, particularly with the slight breeze. She breathed a sigh of relief as she walked back into her own command tent.

She yearned to be back in her court, in the heart of the Thousand Islands. Back in civilisation. There was one more sector of the clans to be taken, and this conquest would be complete.

That would begin as soon as she was certain this sector was fully under her control.

As the inner door opened, Jaclyn frowned as an underwife approached and handed her a sealed communication. Jaclyn turned the missive over and at the sight of the seal the message bore, she barely kept herself from grimacing.

"First, we received a communication from the king."

As much as she wished it was otherwise, communications from her homeland, in particular her brother, still found her. Although she wondered how long this one had been chasing her across this land. It was relatively easy to get the messages from the king's court to their base in the Riverlands—the first sector she'd conquered and secured. It took somewhat longer now to get from that base to wherever she and her family were. Jaclyn eased open the seal and scanned the message it contained as Ricardo entered the room, hand in hand with Liliana.

"What does your dear brother command of us?" Ricardo was under no illusions regarding her brother's role in sending them to this hostile land to get rid of them.

The fact the king's power play had not only failed but failed spectacularly must be galling for the king and his wives.

"Samuel has issued our recall. We are to return to the Court of a Thousand Islands."

"It will be good to see our children again," Liliana said, a small smile spread across her lips. "It is too early for any announcements, but First, I bear an unborn child of the house. So I might have been forced back, anyway. It will be good to be with you all during this time."

As a smile bloomed on Ricardo's lips, Jaclyn strode forward

and placed her fingers gently on Liliana's abdomen. Slowly, cautiously, she reached out with her powers, feeling Ricardo do the same. In her othersight, she could just see that small, glowing spark that meant new life. Jaclyn and Ricardo shared their wonder and delight as they sensed the boy child they would welcome to their house.

"All of you, out," Jaclyn said, waiting for the rustle of silk to stop as the daggerwives and underwives left them in privacy.

She ushered Liliana to the couch and eased her onto it, Ricardo joined her, wrapping Liliana in his arms.

"You must take it easy, particularly in these early months, Liliana."

When Jaclyn, then Myra had each borne a boy child, her brother's eyes had glittered with malice. With so few men born to their people, such an occurrence brought a family great power. So, when she'd birthed a second son, powerful families had taken notice. It brought Jaclyn's house into line with the Monarch House. Some believed it put them ahead of the Monarch House, since the number of wives attributed to the Monarch House was substantially higher. Having three sons in her house made Jaclyn a threat to the Monarch House. A fourth wouldn't help one bit. Her loving brother, and more importantly, his wives, had already been hoping Jaclyn and her family would die during this campaign, neatly ending the threat to her brother. When Samuel's firstwife and primewives found out that Liliana was pregnant with another boy child, and they would find out, their days were numbered.

"I know the risk this brings to our house. I'm sorry, but I'm not," Liliana said, smiling.

"We will protect our house." Ricardo's voice was soft as he held her, but with an undertone of steel.

"Ricardo, Myra, and I have discussed this day. We've already drawn up plans to make sure our house and our children survive the blades of Samuel's wives." Jaclyn smiled. "Now, rest. I will have the daggerwives and underwives begin preparation for our return to court."

Jaclyn shared a troubled look with Ricardo as she stood and went to issue her orders. She needed to track down Myra.

SEVENTEEN

Tarkhan growled in frustration as he observed Hallaran from where he was lying on top of a hill. He scanned the camp once more, looking for *something*. His horse moved restlessly, feeling his unease. Members of the Hallaran tribes moved around the camp, horses were corralled where they should be. Nothing was out of place. Other than that all the Hallaran tribes seemed to be camped here at the heart of their ranging lands. It certainly explained why they'd encountered none of the Hallaran tribes at their usual haunts as they rode here. Despite the normalcy, something had him on edge.

Gritting his teeth, Tarkhan nodded at Khaliun who waited patiently for him to finish his scan of those below. He crawled back from the top of the hill before standing and remounting. His gut clenched as he urged his horse forward and they continued their way down towards the settlement. Chono and Delbee were the custodians of Hallaran Lake this season. Before the war, representatives from the leaders of each clan met several times a year to discuss business and negotiate everything from trade to disputes for the benefit of the People. So, while he didn't know either of them well, he was as familiar with them as any of the other co-leaders of a tribe not from their own clan.

I know this was my idea, but something feels off. Tarkhan wished he could articulate what was wrong.

Relax. We'll discuss the plan with Chono and Delbee. They either agree and flee our homeland with us. Or they'll decide to hide here until the invaders overrun them. Either way, we warn them that the tribes that form the Kallith Clan are withdrawing, Khaliun said.

I'd feel better if they'd sent people to help fight against the horde. Tarkhan grumbled.

You know Chono isn't much of a fighter. It's probably just as well it was the duty of his clan to act as custodians this season, Khaliun reasoned.

While his co-leader's advice made sense, he couldn't shake the uneasy feeling. He'd volunteered to make his way across the Hallaran Clan's territorial region to warn them of the departure of the remaining clans. He'd agreed with Khaliun that they should range wide, checking for the tribes of Hallaran as they rode. They both recognised the risk of the delay but had deemed the extra step worth it. Right now, he was regretting it. Although he had nothing to pin down the source of his agitation.

You're right. It's just... I don't know. Something has me on edge.

Chono came into sight as they pulled up to the meeting house. The settlement at Hallaran Lake was one of the few permanent establishments that the tribes who traditionally claimed these lands took turns rotating through and main-taining.

Chono grinned, although a faint worry showed in his eyes. "Tarkhan, Khaliun, well met. What brings you here?"

Tarkhan dismounted and tied his horse's reins to the nearby post, snagging Khaliun's reins as she dismounted and securing her mount as well.

"Chono, we have news of a decision from Kallith Clan that impacts the tribes of Hallaran Clan." Khaliun's tone was grave.

Tarkhan scanned his surroundings, his eyes narrowing as his unease spiked again. He shook himself and returned his attention to Chono.

"It sounds serious. Perhaps you'd both like to come into the meeting house? I'll get refreshments and you can share your news." Chono turned and led them to the meeting house.

"Thank you, Chono. We wouldn't be here if it wasn't important." Tarkhan tried to keep his tone light.

He turned to the side and withdrew his weapons from his belt, placing them on the rack made for that purpose. Khaliun joined him and did the same. It was an old custom that stretched back further than anyone actually remembered. Although Tarkhan suspected that in some long-ago time, discussions at the meetings between the various clans got heated, blades drawn, and people died. Now the custom was so entrenched, it was something one did automatically, without having to be asked or think it through.

Chono waited until they were ready before he led the way to the cushions in the centre of the room. Tarkhan followed, frowning as he sat down. Something was different, but he couldn't quite place what it was.

"You didn't bring your tribe with you?" Chono's eyebrows rose. "I'm sure my clan would love to show them the hospitality of Hallaran."

Khaliun shook her head. "No, they return from the battlefield to the barrens with the other tribes of Kallith Clan. It was our duty as leaders to inform Hallaran of the decision reached by the leaders of Kallith Clan, but there was no need for us to put our fellow tribe members at risk."

There was a moment's silence as Tarkhan traded glances with Khaliun. It was a breach of tradition, once in the meeting house, to talk business before they drank and broke bread together.

"Where's Delbee? Our news is grave and your co-leader will need to hear it," Tarkhan said.

Chono's smile became fixed. "Oh, she's tied up right now."

Tarkhan frowned, but the door opened. Tarkhan tried to smile and relax as the clanswoman brought in a tray. Her demeanour was stiff as she walked towards them, hands shaking as she placed the tea and the plate of sweet breads and fruits on the low table between them. It didn't reassure Tarkhan in the slightest to see Khaliun's calm demeanour had cracked slightly as she stared, her eyes wide. Neither of them expected the tea and food to be prepared so quickly, ritual or otherwise, particularly given their arrival had been unexpected. It was also a breach of tradition to conduct the guest rights ritual before Chono's co-leader Delbee was present. Tarkhan attempted to make his smile genuine. Shaking himself, he thanked the woman before turning his attention back to Chono.

Chono picked up the teapot and poured tea into the cere-monial bowl. He placed the pot down and picked up the bowl, sipping the liquid it contained, his eyes meeting theirs over the rim.

"I welcome those of Kallith into the heart of Hallaran. From now to the moment you depart for your homeland, your safety is mine to care for. You are of Hallaran." Chono's tone was solemn.

Tarkhan reached out and grabbed the bowl and main-tained eye contact with Chono. The ritual words fell from his lips without any need for him to think of them: "I accept your pledge and swear I will uphold the safety of all of Hallaran as I do those of Kallith." Tarkhan lifted the bowl to his lips and sipped the fiery liquid, it scalded his lips, tongue, and throat as he drank. A reminder of the punishment that lay in the future of any who betrayed guest rights.

As Tarkhan passed the bowl back to Chono their figures brushed, and he caught the sense of anticipation mingled with satisfaction from his fellow leader. The sensation ceased as Chono drew the bowl back to his lips and sipped the scalding liquid again.

"As I hold those of Kallith in safety, you are now of Hallaran. Speak freely and know that you are safe." Chono passed the bowl to Khaliun.

Khaliun accepted the bowl and sipped the contents. "We are all the People before we are Clan. I accept your pledge of guest right."

Tarkhan relaxed a little as Chono placed the bowl back down on the low table and passed the platter to him, he gravely selected a sweet bread, taking a bite as tradition dictated. When they'd partaken in the guest custom, Tarkhan relaxed into the cushions. He stared at Chono, who had what he could only think of as a pained expression on his face. Finally, Tarkhan took a breath. While it was unusual to brief another clan with only one leader present, it was time to pass on the warning they had come here to give.

"We did what we could, fighting to support one clan after another, but they all fell to the invaders. They must be perilously close to Hallaran Lake now. Have you had any news?"

As the silence stretched, Tarkhan glanced at Khaliun, then back at Chono. Part of him was still mulling over the fact that all the tribes of the Hallaran Clan were in residence. A fleeting glimpse of pain crossed Chono's face.

"I'm afraid I have, my friends. You shouldn't have come here." Chono stood, retreating as the doors to the meeting house slammed open.

Tarkhan stood, turning towards the door. Sylannians poured into the room, the silks from their robes flaring, then wrapping around them to form a solid shell. Tarkhan groped for a blade that he no longer wore. He charged at the line of the enemy in front of him and found himself swept off his feet. His breath expelled as he was slammed into the stone floor, with multiple people pinning him down. He gasped for breath and tried to heave them off, twisting and straining, but stilled when one woman held a blade to his throat. Her dark eyes stared into his own as he froze.

"Shh... there now, calm down. We don't want to hurt you."

One of the other Sylannian invaders wrapped a piece of silk around his neck. A whisper of power brushed over him as other lengths of silk wrapped around his wrists and waist. He took a deep breath, trembling with nerves. Snarling, he flung himself up, his fist striking towards his captors. A breath of the veil gave but a momentary signal before what appeared to be nothing but silk hardened and tightened, restricting his air. He gasped for breath as the band tightened around his throat. The silk around his wrists drew taut and dragged his arms back behind him, the bands cutting into his wrists. He turned his head to one side and saw the strange silk around his neck, wrists, and waist ran to rings on the walls. As he stilled, the band around his neck loosened and he sucked in air.

He finally realised what was different about the meeting hall: there were normally tapestries hanging on the walls, suspended by the rings. Hallaran was proud of their tapestries and always had some on display. As the enemy carefully withdrew, he threw himself at them, only to gag as his collar cut off his air again. Tarkhan gasped and slumped to his knees. He went to grab the collar around his neck but bound as he was, he couldn't reach it.

A Sylannian stalked to him. His head jerking back as her hand stroked his face. Her fingers tracing over the tattoos that heralded him as a leader of Kallith. He shuddered as her fingers traced the wolf eyes of his warrior tattoo.

"You will learn, my wolf warrior of Kallith, as the others have. Stop fighting. You will only hurt yourself." A satisfied smile curled his enemy's lips. "That isn't something we allow. You're far too powerful. You are one of the lucky ones: it will be the breeding house back in Sylanna for you."

These Sylannians hadn't been as kind to his co-leader. She'd gone down under their blades and was now bound like he was, but in her case, they'd drawn blood and she was unconscious on the floor.

Fingers wrapped around his jaw and wrenched his head around until he could see nothing but dark brown eyes.

"Don't worry about your friend. She killed one of ours. We can't allow that to go unpunished. Before we're done, she'll beg to die, but she'll spend her life in servitude."

He throttled down his panic. He could sense Khaliun still lived, and panic wouldn't help him or her. He saw Chono off to one side with three of the dagger-wielding women around him, seemingly comfortable and at ease in their presence. As he watched, one Sylannian wrapped a collar around Chono's neck. Tarkhan's eyes widened as he saw the silk twist as if it was a living thing.

"Traitor!" Tarkhan spat at him.

Chono shook his head. "I did what was best for my clan and our people. We are a part of the Sylannian kingdom now. Give them what they want, Tarkhan. It's not so bad. You will have a life of comfort. I will see that the Kallith Clan are treated fairly."

Anger flooded him and Tarkhan lurched forward only to collapse, gasping for breath as the collar cut into his throat. His vision darkened as he lay wincing, a Sylannian's mindvoice urging him to sleep.

EIGHTEEN

The collar tightened around Tarkhan's neck as he strained his bindings once more, desperate to glimpse Khaliun. She hung in bindings like his own, bound between stakes as the cruel sun beat down on her. It was a stark contrast to his own confinement. He, at least, was in one of the mud brick cells built to house those who'd broken clan law. It was basic, with no rugs or tapestries, but he had a cot to lie on. Tarkhan grabbed the collar that bound him in one hand and the silk rope connected to it with the other, wrenching at them to gain his freedom. When that failed, he tried to pull the metal loops that were fastened to the wall. But as he fought, the bindings around his neck, wrists, and waist grew tighter and tighter. He'd learnt the Sylannians didn't have to be present to activate the bindings they'd placed on him. The cloth was pliable but hardened and restricted his airflow if he fought his bonds. He'd pass out if he pushed it too far, and when he woke, he'd find himself washed and in the cot with his bindings soft.

Thinking about the Sylannians touching him while he was

unconscious made him shudder. Worse, they chipped away at his mind, trying to insinuate themselves in his head. His skin crawled, and he forcefully turned his mind away from that possibility. Tarkhan swore. If this hadn't been the meeting place of the Hallaran Clan, there wouldn't be any solid buildings made of mud bricks to hold him, let alone a cell. If this had been one of their normal tents, he and Khaliun would likely be free.

Tarkhan slumped onto his bed and forced himself to relax. It didn't take long for the bindings to become soft as silk again. He took a long, slow breath and drew in the veil. Reaching out with the power, he probed and tested the silk. He allowed his mind to sink down, seeking the whisper of the veil right on the edge of his awareness. He could almost hear it, like a low, melodic hum. It was singing a song he couldn't quite understand. It confused him and caused him to lose concentration when he tried to use the veil. Last time his captors had manipulated the bindings, he'd ignored the mesmerising song of the silk and keep his mind focused on their use of power. He had little else to do, locked in here as he was, so he spent much of his waking hours trying to understand how they communicated with the bindings and got them to do what they desired.

As fear threatened to overwhelm him, he ruthlessly pushed it aside. This time, he had to get free. Concentrating, he closed his eyes, a line appearing on his forehead as he mimicked what he'd seen the women do. Music had never been his strong suit, but he modulated the veil, sending patterned vibrations into the silks that bound him. He willed it to unbind him. The whispering response from the silk answered him, causing him to freeze, a moment passed that seemed like an eternity before the melodic hum of the silk changed and came into focus, it sang to him even if he didn't quite know the words. Then it slithered from his throat, wrists, and waist. His breath caught in his throat, before he carefully sat up then leapt away from the bed. He scrambled back against the wall, staring at the silk pooled across the sleeping cot and trailing onto the floor. Now it seemed to be an innocuous grey-blue lifeless puddle, rather than that veil-imbued stuff that had trapped him.

One careful step after the other, he walked forward. He reached out, his fingertips brushing the swath of grey-blue silk. He concentrated, sinking down to that almost inaudible hum and realised he could still hear a faint whisper from the silk. A gasp escaped him, and he jerked his fingers back. It was like a caress from a living thing. He reached out again and slowly gathered the silk to him. If nothing else, he could use it to strangle anyone he encountered. Staring out the window, he couldn't see anyone.

He regarded the simple wooden door. Being a holding cell, the bolt was on the other side. While he could have used the veil to punch though the door, it would be loud and would send shock waves through the veil that might rouse people from their midday nap. He'd rather they slept on.

He pushed the filaments of power through the door. The change in the vibration of the veil told him he'd reached the metal bolt beyond the wooden door. A tremor ran through him as he concentrated, urging the tiny amount of power he controlled to wrap around the bolt. It was difficult since he couldn't actually see the bolt. His mental grasp fumbled more than once. Finally, the bolt slid back on the door and he scrambled as far back as he could into the corner of his cell. The fear he'd been trying to deny rising to the forefront of his mind.

He hated that his breath caught in his throat. Even though it was his power that slid the bolt back, part of him feared it was his captors coming back to get into his mind once more. Tarkhan pushed his fear aside and eased the door open. He let his eyes adjust to the unfiltered light before stepping out and pulling the door closed behind him. He was already crossing the yard towards Khaliun when he remembered the bolt was loose from its casing on the cell door. Eyes narrowing in concentration, with a mere breath of power, he slid the bolt carefully into place.

With care, he extended his awareness beyond the square, it would give him some warning if he was about to be discovered. Ignoring the heat that beat down on him, he jogged lightly to where Khaliun hung from her bindings between the posts. He grabbed her and supported her weight as she moaned softly.

Shh, Khaliun, it's me. I know you hurt, but you must try not to make a sound while I get you loose.

I'll try, Khaliun said.

He lowered his awareness once more until he could perceive the whispering silk. Tarkhan ignored the little niggling whisper in the back of his head that Khaliun's bindings might not respond to the same pattern as his. Tarkhan sank into a semitrance, relief washing over him as the whispering melodic hum of the silk still sang to him. The vibrations of power he sent in reply cut through the song of the silk and he nearly sighed with relief as it loosened and rippled, fluttering to the ground. Tarkhan adjusted his grip on Khaliun, dropping to one knee. He balanced Khaliun against his body and collected the silk. Satisfied no one else was nearby in the quiet camp, he gathered Khaliun into his arms and stood. He could feel the effort she was exerting to keep herself silent, to not let the pain she was in leak out to any paying attention. He wrapped his power around her, bleeding off some of her pain, and sent soothing pulses to her. While he had little healing talent, he could do that much.

Tarkhan was careful not to jar his friend and cause her more pain as he made his way towards one of the buildings, but as he was about to turn the corner to the horse yards, his awareness screamed at him. He froze before lowering Khaliun to the ground in a pool of shade thrown by the rock wall. Eyes scanning his surroundings, his lips compressed as he desperately searched for a weapon even though logic told him he wouldn't find a sword in the open. The invaders were a lot of things, but even if they had been in his homeland long enough to start napping during the day, they weren't that stupid.

Finally, he unslung the length of silk he had looped across his body. He doubled it over several times and twisted it to form a cord. Keeping to the shadow thrown by the wall, he walked to the corner, one careful pace after the other. Tarkhan paused at the edge of the wall across from the horse yards. One guard leant against a tree, close to his position. The guard had her back to him, facing towards the yard and the hills beyond.

Stalking forward, Tarkhan flung the loop of the silken cord around her and wrenched his arms back sharply, tightening the loop around her throat. A sudden intake of raspy breath abruptly cut off. She flailed and her hands clawed at her neck, then she tried to lash out and strike him. He wrenched the silken rope even harder until the neck snapped, before she collapsed. He eased the Sylannian's body to the ground and took a moment to catch his breath. It wasn't an honourable way to kill, from behind like that, but right now, he wasn't feeling all that accommodating. He hefted the body over his shoulder and then dumped it behind one of the large feed bins, out of sight from the rest of the village. Almost as an afterthought, he leant down and took her dual blades. Their curved blades were much longer than daggers, but shorter than his sword. Slipping the blades into his belt, he turned and inspected the horses.

He quickly separated out their own horses. Not that Khaliun could ride unassisted, but extra mounts to swap out would increase their speed. He quickly gathered what supplies he could find, filling the water bottles they'd both kept in their saddlebags before making his way back to Khaliun.

Some children remain in the longhouse, Khaliun's mindvoice whispered in his head as soon as he contacted her.

Khaliun, I understand, but we barely have the chance to flee ourselves.

No. We must try, Khaliun insisted, her mental voice shaking in intensity. *We pledged to hold those of Hallaran as our own. Chono broke guest rights but our fellow clan members did not. It is our duty to protect them.*

Tarkhan ducked his head, before he shook his head and stood. *Stay here. I'll see what I can do.*

While the village was still quiet, other sentries would be out. Although he knew from what he'd seen in the brief glances out the cell window, the enemy had been sending the villagers of Hallaran to one of their other territories. The Sylannians had told him he'd be going as well, in one of the last caravans out as soon as they were sure he wouldn't try to escape. A half-smile spread his lips. Theirs was a vain hope. He was no Chono. Tarkhan jogged across the camp. He took a moment to wrap one length of silk around his forearm and drew a blade. With care, he sent his power questing through the door. Not sensing anyone on the other side, he opened the door and entered, relieved when the emptiness of the dark interior proved his senses had been correct. As he eased, the door closed behind him. His eyes caught sight of the dark stain on the floor. Blood. People had died here and while the Sylannians had removed the bodies and obviously tried to clean, they hadn't done a good job.

Tarkhan stiffened as fear from someone else washed over him. His hyper-alert senses told him there were two people beyond the closed door that led to the boys' sleeping quarters. He pushed the door open.

A woman, one of the Sylannians, was leaning over a young man restrained on the bed, her hands on his temples. He recognised what she was doing. They'd tried to insinuate themselves into his mind as well. Tarkhan respected the young man. He might not be old enough to bear his clan tattoos or those of the warrior caste, but he deserved them for withstanding the Sylannian's efforts.

The Sylannian was so intent on breaking into her victim's mind she didn't seem to know he'd entered. He jerked her head back by her hair and drew his stolen blade across her throat. He twisted her aside as blood spurted from her wound, holding her as she struggled weakly. When she slumped, he lowered her carefully to the floor. He quickly wiped the blade, placing it on the edge of the bed. The young man's eyes were wide, his breathing ragged, but he didn't cry or scream.

Shh, we have little time. Tarkhan held his fingers up to his lips.

The young man turned his head, eyes sliding over to the dead Sylannian as Tarkhan reached out with his powers, releasing the youth from his bindings.

Thank you. The boy took in his tattoos. *You're of the Kallith.*

I am. I and my co-leader came to warn your people, but we came too late, Tarkhan said.

He sized up the young man as he stood. Unless the Sylannians had taken him from the single male quarters and placed him here, he was still underage. Tarkhan took the blades from their fallen enemy and handed them to the young man.

Some of the younger children remain, the boy told him.

Tarkhan understood what the lad didn't say: he wouldn't leave without trying to rescue the other children.

I've only ever seen two others in the children's compound.

Tarkhan reached out and squeezed the lad's shoulder, sending reassurance, then turned and sent small filaments of power into the room beyond the door, testing for other Sylannians. Finally satisfied no one else was up he ran lightly through the outer room, his senses ranging ahead of him. It was useful that the oldest of their villages throughout all the clan territories were laid out along similar patterns, but it was both a strength and a weakness. On the one hand, their attackers would have been familiar with the basic layouts of their most common buildings. On the other, it meant his surroundings were familiar. On his way through, he grabbed a long metal poker from the fireplace then went to the room where he could sense two people sleeping and carefully forced the bar between the handle, door, and frame. While he could go through the door and kill their enemy while they slept, he couldn't bring himself to do it.

Tarkhan entered the children's dormitory, his eyes widening as he realised there weren't just younger children in here, but older clanswomen as well. The older women seemed to be on tethers that were longer than the children's, long enough to allow them to tend them. He held his finger up to his lips, as those in the room stirred, grateful he was still wearing his traditional hide clothing and his tattoos clearly identified him as a warrior of Kallith and a leader of a tribe. Taking a moment to concentrate once more, he sent the vibrations to the silk that bound all in the room. He was shocked when the silk responded quickly, each time he interacted with it the strange communication he had with it seemed to get easier.

Quickly, we don't have time. Straight to the horse yards, we'll saddle up and leave this place.

The older women leapt from their cots, gathering the young children to them. As his charges filed out of the room, he breathed a sigh of relief. He closed the door of the dormitory and ran into the back of one of the older tribeswomen who'd paused in the hallway. She sent a wave of power into the room, one pervasive whispering word at the Sylannians within the room.

Sleep, the older tribeswoman urged, that one word laced with compulsion.

Tarkhan's eyes widened, and he shut his mouth abruptly. There was no way those in the room would wake up any time soon. The woman's eyes crinkled in amusement at his astonishment, although there was a hard edge glinting in the depths. She turned and followed the others towards the door.

The boy he'd rescued turned and handed the older women one of his confiscated daggers. The older woman grasped the dagger in her hand and urged the boy out the door to follow the others. The older woman turned with a flicker of a smile, patted him on the hand. Her reassurance washed over him.

Hush, fighter of Kallith. We couldn't get past those bonds. Those of us set to watch the children might be past childbearing age, but we have our strength.

Even though it had seemed like hours had bled away in the children's enclave Tarkhan noted the sun had barely moved, it was still high in the sky. He ran through the village, retracing his path back to his co-leader. As he rounded the last corner, he was relieved to see Khaliun was where he'd left her. He knelt at her side, fatigue drowning him. His own injuries weren't as severe as Khaliun's, but they were sapping his strength. All this activity, as well as his excessive use of the veil, hadn't helped. Still, right now wasn't the time to fall prey to that fatigue. He could sleep and heal later.

I'm sorry, Khaliun, I know you're hurt. We need to get out of here.

Tarkhan gathered her into his arms and strode across the yard to his horse, which stood patiently where he'd left her. Two of the older children came over with a block mount. Two people assisted Tarkhan in placing Khaliun on the horse. They steadied her while Tarkhan mounted behind his co-leader. He thanked the woman who passed the reins to him. They mounted their horses expertly and led the way around the pens, out of camp. The other women and children riding in a string behind them without a word. Tarkhan waited until the last of his charges had ridden out of the pens before urging his horse forward.

CHAPTER

NINETEEN

Now that the camp had sprung up in an orderly fashion Michael sat on a log near the fire. While it might not be a main travel route, by the looks of it, this clearing had been used for camping before.

"So, what did you do to earn our father's displeasure this time?" Michael asked Aiden. "It must have been spectacular, given his punishment."

"Who knows?" Aiden grimaced. "You probably know more than I do."

"He didn't speak to you about riding with us before this morning?" Olivia asked.

"I didn't know anything about this little arrangement. You were there. I found out at the same time you all did," Aiden said as he reached forward to grab a mug from a pile in the centre and filled it up from one of the flasks.

"You must have done something to draw his displeasure." Michael stared at Aiden flatly.

"Now we are all stuck in each other's company until father says otherwise." Olivia sighed.

Michael didn't have to turn around to know that their latest recruit, Damien, stood uncertainly just out of the glow caused by the firelight.

"Damien, stop lurking." Michael accepted the mug Olivia handed him.

"Join us," Olivia said.

"If you sit where we can see you, we know you're not running off back home," Nathanial said.

Michael chuckled. "I'd have to send Nathanial to fetch you back if you did something that stupid. Sit."

Damien had wandered closer and sat hesitantly on another log as Nathanial gestured to a spot near where he was sitting.

"I wasn't considering running off," Damien said.

Michael gazed at Damien, assessing his soft reply. He noted the old-but-serviceable sword Damien wore at his waist and the obviously well-worn hunting leathers. The few meagre possessions his mother and father had pressed on him, including the sword, would do. At least for now, until they could fit his latest recruit with more appropriate gear.

"Can you use that blade?" Michael asked.

"Better than my cooking. They wouldn't let me anywhere near the communal kitchens back home." Damien blushed.

"We'll start your training when we reach Callenhain." Olivia handed Damien a drink.

Michael guessed Olivia had given their latest recruit juice, since from the wailing of his mother he wasn't of age yet. Although Michael judged the weeping about him being just a child was a bit of a stretch. Anyone would have believed the lad was a babe being ripped from his mother's arms.

"When will we get to Callenhain?" Damien's eyes didn't leave his drink.

"Tomorrow, all going well."

"Unfortunately for you, your village was just on our way," Olivia said.

"It was too small for the Warlord to care about," Damien said.

Michael's eyebrow raised at that observation, and he traded glances with Olivia. Damien's comment wasn't a question. It was a matter-of-fact statement. Rather astute for a someone raised in a small village.

"Technically, Ranlith was within the traditional boundaries of Callenhain. When the Strafford Warlord surrendered to the Warlord, that included Ranlith," Olivia said.

Michael sipped his drink, then added, "We just didn't bother to ride through until now."

Callan sat on the other side of Damien and raised his mug. The chatter of the individual conversations stilled. Each member raised their own mug in response, all eyes tracking unerringly to Damien.

"Welcome to the Unwanted, brother," Callan said.

"Unwanted," Michael intoned, along with everyone else.

A thin strand of the veil sprang up, flaring and racing between them, connecting them all. The final filament of power was thin and stretched as it reached out to Damien. Damien wasn't really one of them yet. Michael smiled as the lad seemed stunned, a hint of confusion rolling off him.

Damien raised his mug and sipped along with the rest of them. Michael could almost hear the cogs of his mind processing what had just happened.

"Unwanted?" Damien asked.

"It's who we are. What we are," Nathanial said.

"To everyone except each other," Callan interjected.

"You need to understand. When we return to your village —and we will return, eventually—your family, your former friends, will reject you," Olivia said.

"No, they wouldn't do that." Damien shook his head.

"They will. It's happened to us all," Michael said.

"You will be viewed no differently to the rest of us," Nathanial said.

"No. Or at least, my family wouldn't. Neither would Owen." Damien hunched over and kept his gaze on the ground. "But I didn't really have any friends there."

It was clear to Michael that even if the lad didn't want to articulate it, he couldn't help but be aware that many in the village hadn't trusted him. How could he not? With his abilities, he would easily have picked up the distrust and fear from most of the other villagers.

Nathanial turned to Damien. "Didn't you always feel like an outsider?"

"Were you told to hide your power?" Callan asked.

"Not use it. To hold the veil at bay, even though to do so made you feel sick," Nathanial said.

"They didn't believe you, though. They just kept giving you the same advice." Callan's tone was bitter.

"My family loves me." Damien fixed his eyes on his boots, his jaw clenching.

"You were an outsider even before we came to town. Feared by some, I'd warrant, given your strength," Nathanial said.

"We're an aberration, Damien. Of all the people in the Warlord's domain. We are the strongest in the veil," Olivia said.

"You must have realised you could do this," Callan said, as a ball of glowing light appeared, floating in the middle of the table.

"Or this," Olivia said, a surge of power sending a bowl through the air at Michael's head.

A shimmering barrier flared to life, and the bowl shattered, raining down on the table.

Along with the physical aspects of our abilities, you have strong mindgifts. You can mindspeak individuals or groups over distance, listen in on conversations that you shouldn't be able to, influence others' minds.

Michael saw Damien flush as he remembered overhearing the conversation he'd been having with Olivia as they rode out of the lad's village. He suppressed a wince. He could tell exactly what Damien was thinking about because his mind shields were shocking.

We're going to have to do something about that almost-non-existent mind shield, Olivia said, before turning her gaze back to Damien.

"Most have abilities of one sort or another, but not all of them," Olivia said.

"Certainly not to the power level we do," Nathanial said, then shrugged. "Some people may have rudimentary skills in the other areas but have a strong affinity for a particular skill, like healers, or the smiths with an affinity for metal."

"You knew you were different from everyone else," Michael said.

He watched Damien carefully as the lad's shoulders hunched, his forehead creasing as he shook his head. On the subject of his family, his mind was still spiky with stubborn disbelief. Michael could hear his internal monologue. Damien clung to the hope his village wouldn't reject him. His situation was different.

More like he was trying to convince himself what he was fearing wasn't true.

Michael sighed and dropped the topic. Damien would learn in his own time. Eventually the boy would die and in his place would stand a man who was a member of the most feared warband in the Warlord's domain.

There was no return after joining the Unwanted.

TWENTY

Tarkhan woke as dawn spread across the plains. Swearing softly, he rolled over and climbed to his feet, scanned the horizon in the direction of Hallaran, where he knew pursuit would come from. He drew in the thin tendrils of the veil's power and allowed it to carry his consciousness further afield. Reaching out with his senses, he tensed as among the small herds of animals he caught the unique spark of people, much closer than where Hallaran was located. He didn't have to see them with his eyes to recognise they were Sylannians and it gave him hope they were still a way off. Still, they didn't have time to waste, their travelling pace was slower than those who pursued them and they had a long way to go.

He'd hated stopping the night before but he had to admit, the rest had probably done them some good and they had a little time, even if it wasn't much. Tarkhan turned to check on Khaliun, but some women were busy changing the dressings on her injuries. He wondered if they ever slept. He could see with his othersight the small pulses of healing energy they were sharing with his co-leader. Their healing gifts were weak, but every bit would help and it was more than he could do, since it was an ability that had passed over him entirely. It was likely the Sylannians had identified anyone who possessed a strong healing talent among the Hallaran Clan and already sent them to their homeland.

Feeling a hand on his arm, he withdrew his awareness back to himself to find one of the rescued women.

"Come, we don't have many supplies, but we have enough to have tea and bread before we break camp again," the woman said.

"I fear we don't have time. Pursuers are following our trail."

"You'll have tea, and you'll eat. You won't do us any good if you fall out of your saddle, faint with hunger," the woman growled at him, hands on her hips.

Tarkhan couldn't help but grin and held up his hands. "All right, but we can't take long."

"Good. Everyone else, including your co-leader, has been tended to, so it's just you now," the woman said.

The woman led him to where their meagre supplies were spread out on a handy rock shelf. As much time as he'd spent in the saddle, it still surprised him how much could be shoved into saddle bags. What astonished him even more was where his charges had found the supply of dried meat, fruits, and nuts. He picked up a strip of dried meat and gnawed on it, his stomach growling in response. He smiled as the woman poured some tea into a pot and topped it with water from a water bladder. Tarkhan's skin prickled from a light brush of the veil as the woman assessed his own abilities. She looked at him expectantly.

Tarkhan grinned. Using a small pulse of power, he heated the water in the kettle until steam was curling from the spout. She left the kettle to one side while the tea steeped and went about the camp, bossing around the children and other women to pack their sparse camp and get the horses ready. Tarkhan helped himself to the dried fruit and nuts while everyone else moved with purpose, preparing to mount up and continue their flight to their last remaining territory. He'd just grabbed another strip of meat when she finally poured some tea into a mug and offered it to him. It was a pleasant surprise to see no leaves in his tea. Tarkhan half-stood to leave until he caught the woman's disproving glare. Sighing, he sank back down and meekly sipped his tea, savouring the last mouthful before tucking a selection of some of the dried food in his belt pouch for later.

"Thank you. I didn't realise how hungry I was until I started eating."

"They wouldn't have fed you much. Easier to break into your mind if you're weak with hunger," the woman observed.

"How do you know?" Surprise made him stiffen.

"They had me working in the camp kitchens. There were some, like you, who didn't get fed much. When they came out of confinement, they were changed." A flicker of sadness passed over her face.

"Come on, let's push on. I'd rather not have us fall back into the Sylannians' hands. Not sure I could withstand their attentions again." Tarkhan shuddered.

Pushing his unease aside, he crossed their small camp to where Khaliun rested. They'd found her a thin blanket from somewhere and she had a vest bundled up as a pillow. One of the older children led his horse towards the rocky ledge he'd used as a table. Tarkhan smiled sadly. These youngsters should be playing and carefree. Instead, they'd been born into a time of upheaval and loss.

"I wish I could let you rest more, but we need to get going," Tarkhan said softly.

"I know. They are coming after us." Khaliun's eyes rose to his own. "Don't let them take us again."

Tarkhan squeezed his eyes shut and took a breath. He could feel Khaliun's fear, pain and sadness all seeming to war inside her over what had happened.

"I won't," he vowed.

When he picked her up, her pain was instantaneous, transferring between them both. It increased his own fatigue and he gritted his teeth. He smiled grimly, blocking her attempt to stop the transfer between them. As his pain level increased, hers decreased. He might not have the healer's gift, but this was something he could do.

Please, Tarkhan, don't. You need to fight if they catch up to us.

If they catch up to us, we're dead. We need to stay up and keep moving to Kallith. We'll stay in the saddle longer this way.

Tarkhan ignored her protests and carried her to the rock ledge. The older boy steadied him as he stepped onto it, then leapt up himself to help place Khaliun on the horse. The others steadied her while he mounted the horse himself. He was grateful for his battle archery training that meant he could keep Khaliun upright in the saddle while guiding his mount with the pressure of his legs instead of using the reins. But even with Khaliun's horse to swap out with, they were slower than their pursuers. The only advantage he could see was that before nightfall they'd be heading into territory he was familiar with.

TWENTY-ONE

The hairs on the back of Tarkhan's neck stood on end, but he refused to turn and check behind him. Instead he kept his eyes resolutely on the trail. A familiar giant rock spur jutted up and out like a broken finger—a boundary marker for the outer edge of Kallith Oasis. He spurred his horse into greater effort. The horse snorted but responded, breaking into a canter.

"Keep going, past that rock spur, follow the trail and don't turn back!" Tarkhan yelled at the survivors of Hallaran on the trail ahead of him.

The drum of hooves sounded behind him, seeming to get louder by the moment. Their luck had run out just after they'd resumed their journey. On one of the regular stops to rest the horses, he caught sight of dust and a black speck on the horizon behind them. Even though they tried to keep ahead of the Sylannians, their enemy had almost closed the gap.

Leave me behind. Pain laced Khaliun's mindvoice.

No. We went into Hallaran together. We get home together or not at all.

As he expected, Khaliun shifted against him, and Tarkhan tightened his grip on her. His co-leader was too weak to take matters into her own hands, which was something he could be grateful for. As stubborn as Khaliun was, she would have fallen off the horse, hoping it would delay the Sylannians long enough for the rest of them to get to safety. As it was, a slight movement was all she could manage. Of course, the unused straps from one of the spare horses which secured her to the saddle would also hamper that effort even if he hadn't been paying attention.

The breath caught in Tarkan's throat at the whistle in the air behind. He prevented himself from reflexively ducking in his saddle but a light brush of feathers against his cheek caused him to swear as arrows sped past him, their shafts splintering as they crashed harmlessly into the rocks. As the last of his small group rounded the bend ahead, he smiled grimly.

I'm sorry, Khaliun said.

Don't be.

They're too close; we won't make it.

I know, but hopefully, those we freed will make it to safety.

We might be lucky and take a couple of them with us.

Tarkhan drew the dagger he carried in his belt as he signalled his horse to turn to face the enemy. He instantly realised his mistake as a wave of satisfaction from Khaliun flooded his mind. Her own body was now between him and the Sylannians—she was effectively a shield between their enemy and him. Frowning, he signalled his horse to turn again, to head back towards the spur.

Sorry, my friend, hold on to the saddle, let the horse do the work, Tarkhan said.

Before she could answer, Tarkhan threw himself from the saddle. He couldn't help the cry of pain as he crashed into the rocky ground, air exploding from his lungs. As horses thundered closer, he searched desperately for his weapon. Seeing his dagger a short distance from him, he scrambled forward, fingers closing around the hilt. With a battle cry on his lips, he jumped to one side and grabbed the reins of a horse, wrenching its head down as he plunged his blade repeatedly into its rider. As the horse scrambled for footing, legs failing as it crashed to the ground, he pushed himself away, rolling desperately out of the way. He bared his teeth and screamed again as the Sylannians reined in their horses to face him, several leaping out of their saddles. Tarkhan glared at his enemy and raised his blade. They would take him, but he was determined to kill as many of them as he could.

A hollering cry resounded in the rocky hills and Tarkhan's eyes widened. The drumbeat of hooves followed the cry and clansmen rode full tilt down the rocky slopes from all around him.

"Tarkhan!"

That call caused him to draw in his power and thrust it at his attacker, grinning tightly as the Sylannian staggered back in surprise. Hearing drumming hooves, he spun and leapt, timing it perfectly to land in the saddle of the horse that had been led to him by his fellow leader, Orghana. As Orghana ploughed through the milling Sylannians, she braced herself before lashing out with her boot-shod foot, smashing it into the face of the enemy closest to him. The Sylannian spun on impact, with an audible crack as her neck snapped and she slumped to the ground.

With the reinforcements from Orghana and Erden's tribe easing the pressure, he wheeled his horse around and charged yet another Sylannian. Grinning fiercely, he rode down an unsuspecting attacker from behind, then heard a whistle and pushed his power above him in a thin shield. A flight of arrows streamed past him and slammed into the enemy, their bodies slumping. His horse danced sideways as Tarkhan assessed the skirmish, his eyes narrowing as he spied a knot of Sylannians attempting to flee. With another battle cry, Tarkhan spurred his horse, knowing that Orghana rode on his other side. They separated at the last minute, and with perfectly timed sweeping strikes, they took off the heads of the two Sylannians.

Tarkhan leapt from his horse, tackling the Sylannian male who crashed to the ground under the impact, his blades falling from his grasp. The Sylannian's eyes glazed as Tarkhan hauled him to his feet.

"Why?" Tarkhan roared at the almost senseless man. Not waiting for a response, Tarkhan screamed and, with a sudden, wrenching snap, broke his enemy's neck, letting the lifeless body fall to the ground.

With the death of the Sylannian male, the few remaining invaders fell quickly to his clan members, as if the fight had suddenly gone out of them. As abruptly as this fight started, it ended. Tarkhan closed his eyes momentarily, listening to the soft breeze.

"Leave their bodies to rot. Their flesh can feed the birds. They deserve nothing else." Orghana's voice was harsh.

Tarkhan opened his eyes and spun only to find his horse, unconcerned, grazing nearby. He grabbed her reins and climbed back into the saddle.

"Mount up; those of you without horses, double up!" Erden called.

"I didn't expect I'd survive this day," Tarkhan said.

"I nearly died when you turned around to face those who followed you." Orghana's eyes travelled over him from head to toe as she spoke.

"We had it planned. All you had to do was get to the spur." Erden threw a dirty look in his direction.

"I was so focused on keeping us all moving I didn't check." Tarkhan flushed, it wasn't like him to be so unaware of his surroundings. "Khaliun and the others of Hallaran tribe?"

"Relax. They're being led back to Kallith Oasis. Let's get you back there before you disgrace the name of a warrior of Kallith and fall out of your saddle," Orghana scolded, although there was a hint of a smile on her lips.

Tarkhan snorted, then gritted his teeth as pain shot through his ribs, alerting him to the new assortment of aches he'd gained. Not that his restraint fooled Orghana, who simply fell in beside his horse as the rest of the tribe formed around them and they headed up the trail towards home.

TWENTY-TWO

Jaclyn took a deep breath, closing her eyes as a waft of air with a hint of moisture from the nearby river washed over her.

"It seems like a lifetime since we've been in this level of humidity," Ricardo said.

"I feared we'd be engaged in this war forever and never feel it again."

What do you think is behind your brother's recall? Ricardo mused.

It wasn't really a question, but Jaclyn answered anyway. *Perhaps we didn't die soon enough.*

She scanned the now-bustling riverside town. It was unrecognisable from the small, ramshackle meeting place that had stood here when she first claimed the settlement for Sylanna. There had only been one central stone building, along with a bunch of smaller dwellings, as was the clansmen's general practice. Given locals had used this as the staging point for many of their trading missions, there were tents sprawled around haphazardly. In the intervening years of this campaign they had rebuilt the dock along the river front, since the original had been destroyed, and erected buildings for trade, storage and living, which had become the entry point for shipping supplies to and from Sylanna. The Court of a Thousand Islands was beautiful, yet it was food, or rather the lack of it, and dwindling land that had first driven them to invade the trader lands.

The former locals, the collared, scurried about their business, dressed in basic earth-toned robes that had been common among the non-combatants before she'd taken over. Only those who had followed the warrior path had worn their hide armour and that was now strictly forbidden. Interspersed among them, recently resettled Sylannians from the overcrowded islands of their homeland were distinct from the locals in their flowing silk garments, with the only uniformity being the dual daggers worn at their waists. The custom amused her. It wasn't like most of these from the lower caste families could use the weapons they carried effectively.

"There are more of our people here than I imagined there would be," Maya said.

"Lesser families, hoping to improve their standing in this new land," Ricardo observed.

"Clear the path!"

Jaclyn saw a daggerwife, horse dancing to one side, a hand on her blade. Beyond the woman a flutter of nondescript brown robes was followed by cursing and a dull thud as the former clansman fell to the hard-baked dirt road. Jaclyn caught his dark eyes as he sat up, carefully wrapped packages scattered around him. Jaclyn ignored him and turned her attention back to the path ahead.

A large multi-storey building, right on the edge of the riverbank, loomed ahead. Graceful arcs, spires, and intricate designs carved into the woodwork marked it as alien to the clans. A wall surrounded the place, guards on the gates and at strategic points, keeping vigilant watch on all who approached. A slight chill washed over Jaclyn, then the whisper of sound just before the gates swung open as the guards used the veil to open them. It would have been much easier to open the gates by hand, since those who'd used their powers to perform the simple task would need to rest now, but it was a small deception intended to make the locals think her people were much stronger than they actually were.

Jaclyn relaxed back into the saddle as they passed through the outer gates into the courtyard of what was her home here in these lands. Even though neither she, Ricardo nor any of the inner circle of her family had spent time here after they had secured this territory.

"The gardens have grown so much," Liliana said.

Jaclyn's mood lightened, this garden sanctuary behind their walls was nothing like her home but compared to the harsh environment of the battlefield it was luxury.

STANDING in the middle of the reception area, the intruders were hard to miss. A splash of colour against the muted tones of the polished wooden floors and walls. A group of women, tall, beautiful, their silken robes draping expertly with the slight flutter caused by the soft breeze coming from the windows. Shutters opened so the backdrop of the river beyond contrasted and framed them perfectly.

Beautiful, yet bland in their uniformity.

At the centre, a man and a woman stood. Jaclyn's eyes immediately picked out the thin band of cream and maroon thread in a spiderweb pattern on the edges of the man's light grey robes. She was certain they deliberately chose the rather dull colour to offset the banding. The cream spiderweb band meant he was related to her and to her brother, the king. Although given the sparseness of the thread, only remotely.

I wonder where your brother dug him up from? Ricardo mused.

Who knows, I guess this is to be the new overseer when I depart.

The barest hint of a smile touched her lips. If Ricardo didn't recognise the man, then he was remote indeed, likely from one of the lower caste raised above their station. In male circles, the number of those with rank were few enough they were all acquainted with each other. In contrast to the stranger's robes, her own silks were a solid maroon with the cream spiderweb pattern decorating the entire robe. The complicated tracing of cream thread through the royal crimson showed she was a daughter of the Monarch House and the king was her brother. She'd survived the purge when the new king had taken the throne and she had just as much claim to the Throne of a Thousand Islands as her brother did. However, the immaculate display that greeted them made her conscious of the fine coating of dust that prickled her sweaty skin. It itched.

Jaclyn wondered idly how many hours their underwives had spent grooming them. All for this one moment.

Ignore them. Jaclyn kept her pace steady, ignoring the group arrayed to block her path to the sanctuary of the inner rooms.

She didn't have to say more. Her family flowed around her and Ricardo, moving with an efficiency born of years of fighting a war in this foreign land. There was an inrush of power and the chill of the veil as it washed over her. She didn't draw the veil herself; she didn't have to. The silent tableau shattered as the intruders found themselves shunted out of her path when an invisible fist of power slammed into them. The pretty, decorative things sprawled on the floorboards to either side of her as she mounted the stairs. Splashes of green, red, yellow, and pink formed an unwilling honour guard as she and her family mounted the stairs, gazing straight ahead, not acknowledging the discourtesy, the challenge offered by a minor family.

They should be grateful they even survived this day.

It was soothing, hearing the lapping water of the river after so many years inland, fighting with the clans. She'd spent glorious moments in the inner sanctum playing with the children before the underwives ushered them off to nap. Even though she was safe here, part of her was always on guard, her power reaching out, brushing the minds of any who approached her sanctuary. Jaclyn didn't turn from the window as the whisper of silk and soft footfall behind her indicated someone had entered the room. With her replacements occupying the house as well, they were all on edge, so it could only be a member of her own family. Neither she nor any of her fellow wives trusted anyone her dear brother would send to replace her.

"Yes, what is it?"

"First, the new overseer would speak with you."

Jaclyn contemplated withholding her consent, but now that she was bathed and wearing clean silks, she was feeling much more amenable. With the whispering touch of her mind, her silks reformed around her into armour.

"Show them in."

Myra came to stand beside her and she smiled. Trust the primewife to scan for any threat that might approach.

It's so nice to hear the water again, Myra commented with a complicated burst of emotions, peace, longing yet threaded through with caution.

It seemed she wasn't the only one looking forward to

seeing their home again, even if they were also dreading what would come at them next. Footfalls behind her on the wooden floors indicated the daggerwives of her house had entered the room.

"Commander, so good to see you—" The voice behind paused as the speaker laughed. "Then again, I suppose that is a title that no longer belongs to you, Jaclyn."

"Not quite yet. Not until I depart this place." Jaclyn kept her gaze on the water.

"I tried to see your children when we arrived, but the underwives of your house wouldn't let us into the enclave. The king was most concerned when they disappeared from the court." His voice held an edge.

Jaclyn spun, allowing her anger to carry across the room to the interlopers who'd dared to show familiarity. Who'd dared issue a threat, no matter how masked it was by fake concern towards her children. A scrape of metal bore testimony to the fact that Myra had drawn her deadly blades.

"You forget yourself." Her voice was clipped, threaded with menace.

The man who'd spoken stepped back, his eyes wide as he fixed on Myra's blades. Trembling, he sank to his knees, pressing his forehead to the floor.

"Mistress, forgive me."

"You may think you have my brother's favour, but he is far away, and I am here," Jaclyn said.

"I meant no harm, Mistress."

"My children are safe from the likes of you, and their loving uncle."

"The king entrusted me with checking on their welfare, he—"

"My brother would not shed so much as a tear if I or my children died."

"The king trusted—"

"The king trusts no one. You're disposable. It's why he sent you here," Jaclyn snapped.

Jaclyn was aware her family had flowed into the room, surrounding her, all of them armed. Her anger flowed through to them, infecting them all with the common purpose of protecting themselves, protect their family. The new overseer's wives sprang to their feet, hands drawing daggers. The scrape of steel resounded in the room as her family drew their blades.

Jaclyn's heart froze as Ricardo strode into the room. His power surged, ethereal fingers curling around the grovelling overseer, flinging him against the wall. In a blur of motion, Ricardo was on her replacement, his blade pressed against the other man's throat. The daggerwives of her house surged forward in response. At the clear threat to their husband by the dagger being held against the new overseer's throat his wives froze. She could almost feel their panic.

"We will be gone from this place soon enough. If you seek to harm Jaclyn, any of my wives, or our children, king's favour or otherwise, I will end you."

Ricardo growled, power flaring around him, emphasising his rage. In another burst of power fuelled by his anger, Ricardo flung the new overseer out of the room. The other man's wives soon joined him as Ricardo wrapped them in his power, shunting them back to join their husband. The walls shuddered as the door slammed shut.

Jaclyn walked forward and wrapped her arms around her husband, resting her head on his back. A tear rolled down her cheek, but she ruthlessly pushed aside her feelings and sent a sharp probe into Ricardo's mind. She and Ricardo gasped as a sharp spike of pain went through them both as she renewed that old bond between their minds. One that she hadn't used since shortly after arriving in this land.

"Calm, Ricardo, please. You cannot take such risks when we return to court."

Jaclyn pushed down her panic, her breath catching as the image of Ricardo, dead on the polished wooden floors of the Court of a Thousand Islands, flashed in her mind. Ricardo was her husband, her life. The act of living if he died was unthinkable. She stroked his temple, expelling a shaky breath as she detected the steady pulse of life within him.

"I know we return to court. I promise I will try not to risk myself," Ricardo replied.

"The Court of a Thousand Islands is not as safe as these lands, husband," Jaclyn said.

"I've felt more alive since we came here to these lands, since you've allowed me more freedom. Please don't make me forget," Ricardo whispered.

"I'm sorry, husband. I must take control of your mind once more." Jaclyn squeezed her eyes shut. "If others back at court discovered you were an uncontrolled male, the king would rule we were a threat to the security of Sylanna. That would allow the Monarch House to hunt us all down and kill us with impunity."

Ricardo sank to his knees as she cradled him in her arms. Feeling herself drowning in his eyes, she tilted his head and kissed him.

"I won't make you forget unless I must. I'm sorry, husband." Hating herself for reverting to old habits at the first hint of a threat, she took control of his mind, forcing calm on him.

Tears traced down Jaclyn's cheek. She much preferred the Ricardo they'd discovered out here in this foreign land. Without the constant need to shield and protect him from the blades of rival families, she and Myra had stepped back from managing him. They'd continued to protect his mind, of course. He was a man and, like most Sylannian men, was susceptible to those around him.

There was no resistance from Ricardo as she re-established her control of his mind. Only acceptance laced with sadness. He was a Sylannian male of high birth; he'd been protected most of his life. Every thought, every action controlled to keep him from harm—from himself, from others—except for these last few years here in the trader lands.

Battling with herself, with her own fear, Jaclyn pushed his mind just that little further. Not to make him forget these last few years and the freedom of mind she'd allowed him, she'd promised she wouldn't do that, but to passively accept her will.

"We will return and deal with whatever my brother thinks up to throw at us. None will harm our husband or children." She allowed her determination to flow from her to all her family. The familial bonds that bound them all thrummed to life with a common and deadly purpose.

TWENTY-THREE

Michael relaxed incrementally as they approached the gates of Callenhain. Parents might still rush their children indoors to hide—there was always a level of distrust and fear. Fortunately, Callenhain had been a part of the Warlord's domain for long enough that its population had become used to them. It probably helped that they had lived relatively peaceful lives within Callenhain's walls. Largely thanks to the Warlord and his men. While he was used to a certain level of distrust and fear, it would be the first time Damien would experience it. More than one strong mindspeaker had been driven mad from the press of so many random voices intruding on their minds.

Nathanial, Callan, keep Damien with you, and in the centre when we reform, he instructed.

On it, Warleader, Nathanial replied.

He's never dealt with the sheer weight of minds against his mental barriers before. This could get messy, Olivia warned.

Let's see how he goes.

Michael spurred his horse forward. They galloped ahead,

splitting with half their people following him and the other half following Olivia as they went around the Warlord's units and took point. Seeing the relaxed formation the Warlord's people still had, he grimaced. Right now, even a semi-competent enemy would have a decent chance of getting close enough to threaten the Warlord's life.

Tighten up around the Warlord. Now, Michael snapped at them.

Yes, Warleader. A feeling of embarrassment flowed from the leader of the Warlord's protection detail.

The other leaders had taken their people and peeled off each time they reached a crossroads. Either leapfrogging over the group, doubling back the way they'd come, or heading along a path that would take them back through the heart of the Warlord's realm. It was common practice for them to patrol as widely as they could. That just left his own band with the addition of Aiden's and the two that had ridden out with the Warlord when he ventured out of Yalleska. Even though it was a little out of his way, their proximity to Callenhain and being able to goad the former warlord of Callenhain was too good an opportunity for the Warlord to pass up. At least he gathered that was why the Warlord hadn't already peeled off to return to his stronghold at Yalleska.

Callenhain was a sprawling, sleepy riverside town, yet Michael opened himself to the veil. Thin strands sprang into his vision, stretching between the Unwanted. He didn't expect to need the extra boost pooling their collective power gave them but it was ingrained habit and Olivia's family estate was on the other side, so they might as well get this initial show of force over with.

They were close enough to the gates that Michael could see the faces of locals, traders, and travellers arriving late from the city. The bored guards on the gates clearly weren't interested in checking the arrivals in a timely fashion. They seemed to move in slow motion as the warbands thundered down on them. Then those on foot scattered, caravans urged their draught horses on, pulling them to one side. Those on horseback who didn't move soon enough found their horses skittish and dancing sideways.

Shield, Michael said.

That one word caused the veil to shimmer, interposing itself between them and the people outside the gates. Puffs of dust sprang up. Squeals sounded from those not fast enough as they fell, thrust aside by the shield that interposed itself ahead of them.

Nathanial, Callan, slow us down, Michael ordered.

Their collective strength drained as Nathanial and Callan exerted themselves. While he couldn't see it from his position, he felt the power spring out. Connecting, not with them, but the horses they rode. Collectively, the horses slowed, timed to the will of Callan and Nathanial. It was small details that impressed and intimidated people far beyond the skill utilised to perform such acts.

Michael relaxed back into his saddle as his horse slowed to a walk, right on cue, as they went through the gates of the main walls that circled Callenhain. He kept his gaze steady, focusing down the road, trusting his people on either side of him. His role was to ooze strength and confidence.

After all this time, it was a role he performed well. The spikes of recognition and fear hammered into him, the thudding of booted feet on the cobblestones, doors slamming, yet he ignored them. It was laughable, in a way. He had no interest in the average man, woman, or child. Neither, these days, did the Warlord—unless he pointed out the individual. If he did that, they weren't mundane.

Reinforce the shield on your mind, Damien, Nathanial instructed.

Callenhain is much bigger than your tiny village. If you don't shield properly, it will drive you mad, Callan said.

Michael sought Damien's mind. Each member of the Unwanted was a steady pulsing energy, except one at their heart: Damien. His energy flared and stuttered, his mind under assault by the press of people he'd never encountered. Michael swore. He recognised the fitful flaring of Damien's powers.

Damn it, the lad is spiralling into a transition attack, Olivia observed.

So it seems, and not an easy one, Michael said.

I wouldn't have expected another one so soon after his last. Concern threaded through Olivia's mindvoice.

We both know transition is impossible to predict, Michael said.

Michael drew more of the veil into himself and strengthened the bond between himself and Damien.

Michael, that's too risky! Olivia swore.

Michael ignored Olivia's concern. His second-in-command drew more of her own power, throwing an extra shield around his body and mind while he was distracted.

Damien, let me help you. If you strengthen your mental shield, it will help cut down the external chatter of others.

Through the strengthened connection he and Damien now shared, Michael sensed the prickly edge of Damien's mind. As he feared, his recruit was becoming lost, already struggling to recognise the difference between himself and the oppressive multitude of minds that clamoured for his attention. Michael could interpose a mental barrier on Damien that would cut down the incessant chatter of others, but it would do nothing to help Damien keep his own barriers in place next time—and there would be a next time. Michael swore as the veil swirled and surged into Damien, who stiffened in pain at the further onslaught.

"Next time can take care of itself," Michael muttered, then expanded his power to surround Damien, drawing him into his own protective mind barrier.

The effect was immediate and Damien almost wilted in relief, although his mind was still in turmoil. Michael's eyes widened as bolts of power leapt from the threads of the veil that swirled all around them and hammered into his recruit. The veil flared and sparked around them before it arced through both of them. He reacted almost instantly, merging his mind with the lad's, taking the excess power, bleeding it off and passing it to the network that connected them all. An extra barrier flared to life around Damien. Although this shield was to protect everyone else if his powers went out of control. They didn't need this section of Callenhain burnt to the ground.

Feeling a battering at his mind, Michael winced. It was an unconscious action, but Damien's mind was fighting his.

Nathanial, get ready to catch, Michael ordered.

Being good with mindgifts and being able to manipulate people's minds was one thing Michael guessed he could thank his mother for. There were occasions it came in useful, even if he hated using his abilities this way.

Michael used the connection he'd made and dived into Damien's mind. For that moment, between one breath and the next, Damien's mind almost screamed in panic, lashing out in all directions. As Michael seized control, he forced Damien into a deep sleep. He remained connected to Damien long enough to know that he'd slumped and been caught and supported by Nathanial. Shuddering, Michael broke the connection between them, his own mind reacting to the shock of the connection, then the sudden severing of it as he relaxed back into his saddle, allowing Olivia to take the lead.

That was foolish, Olivia chided.

Michael winced as the chastisement seemed to echo in his head, but couldn't help the faint smile that spread on his lips.

I know, but he was about to lose control at the worst time possible. Powers, he's strong.

It worked, but I think we need to get him to a bed, Olivia said.

If I'm not mistaken, that's the first place our warleader will go as well. Nathanial's tone was dry.

Enough fussing. I'll be fine. Michael tried to put the reassurance he didn't feel into his voice.

Pick up the pace, let's get this show done with, and then get to the estate. Olivia's tone was firm.

On Olivia's order, the pace of the entire warband increased. There was no disagreement from any of them. There was time for a show to impress the locals, then on other occasions to get within the safety of the walls of the estate to tend their own.

Olivia stared up at the imposing outer walls of the Strafford estate and, for the first time in her life, she was relieved. Unable to help herself, her eyes slid over to Michael. With a breath of power, she reached out to her friend, just enough so she could feel that low ebb of energy that pulsed sluggishly within him. She could sense Michael was exhausted, and he kept himself on this side of consciousness by sheer willpower alone.

Hold on, my friend. Once I get you inside, you can allow sleep to take you. Olivia kept her communication on a tight band so no one else would overhear.

As they rode through the portcullis and into the inner courtyard, Olivia barely waited for her horse to come to a halt before she dismounted. She went straight to Michael and reached up with both her hands and power to steady him as he half slumped from the saddle. Olivia spared a moment to check on their problem child, seeing Callan and two others gently easing his unconscious form out of the saddle.

"Callan, get Damien into the barracks. Someone is to be with him and keep his mind shielded at all times until he recovers," Olivia ordered.

"Of course, I'll take the first shift myself," Callan said.

We need to get Michael behind closed doors. He's barely conscious, Nathanial said.

Olivia waited until Nathanial had joined her before they gently assisted Michael out of his saddle—without their aid he would have ended up unconscious on the ground in the cobbled courtyard.

"You two, with me." Olivia barely glanced at the two members closest to her before turning to face the estate. "I hate this place."

Olivia straightened her shoulders and resolutely guided Michael towards the broad stone stairs that led to the large double doors.

"I'm sure the Straffords could have made it bigger if they tried really hard." Nathanial's tone was bland as he supported Michael from the other side.

Olivia regarded the sprawling four-storey estate house and grunted. "I think they were trying to outdo the Rathadons' family estate in Vallantia. Every time a Rathadon warlord added an extension to their estate, a Strafford warlord would hear about the building spree and try to outdo it."

"Ah, the good old days. Where the ruling class could still build a bigger and better dwelling, while those that were beholden to them starved," Nathanial said.

Olivia kept a light touch on Michael's mind as they negotiated ascending the stairs, assuring herself that Michael remained conscious. A thrust of power sent the double doors back, the crash as they impacted with the stone walls echoing in the reception area. The Strafford family guards who'd been stationed on the doors took in five of them bearing down on them and wisely stepped out of their path.

As they reached the stairs that led to the upper floors Olivia groaned. There was no way Michael was going to climb to the top floor.

"You two, give us a hand. We're going to have to carry him," Nathanial said.

"I'll be fine..." Michael whispered.

Olivia ignored Michael's faint protest. While Michael hadn't taken serious hurt from Damien's loss of control, right now he wasn't in any kind of condition to think straight.

"Just stay awake until we get you into a room," Olivia said.

With the help of the two band members that had followed, she and Nathanial made their way up the broad staircases. They made it almost to the top before their luck ran out and her mother appeared on the landing of the top floor.

"Why, Olivia, what's happened?" her mother asked.

"Nothing to be concerned about. Michael just needs to rest," Olivia said.

Her mother turned and issued instructions to the servants who'd been staying clear of them all. Olivia glared at her mother, torn between gratitude and irritation. A couple of the household staff scurried up the hallway ahead of her and flung open the doors to a room down towards the end. Olivia sighed. After all these years, it wasn't like she needed help to find the rooms that were put aside for her, Michael, and the Warlord when they paid a visit. Thankfully for her own peace of mind, the occasions when she was forced to stay here were few and far between. Olivia ignored her mother, who fussed and wrung her hands as she accompanied them. Nathanial grinned as he rolled his eyes. Thankfully, getting Michael into the room and laying him on the bed proved less problematic than getting him all the way up here in the first place. As Michael sighed, his eyes closing as he lost his fight to stay conscious, Olivia turned.

"Out, all of you." Olivia snapped. "No one is to come in here without my authority."

"But Olivia—"

"That includes you, Mother." Olivia stared flatly at her mother, not caring in the slightest as the woman wilted at the harshness of her tone. "Michael needs rest. He's hardly likely to get much of that if you are in here trying to fuss over him."

Nathanial, at his diplomatic best, walked forward and gently took her mother's arm, guiding her from the room. Olivia sighed with relief as the door closed, blocking out prying eyes. She turned back to Michael and saw a shimmering physical shield surrounding her friend. While they had greater strength in the veil than regular people, it exacted a cost. They tended to sleep longer than normal people. Sometimes they were forced into a sleep like state, as was the case with Michael now, that they had little ability to control or avoid for long. It was a secret the Unwanted went to great lengths to guard.

TWENTY-FOUR

Tarkhan didn't dare relax as they rode into Kallith Oasis; he feared if he did so even minutely, he'd fall from his horse. Although seeing his home lake released a tension that had been with him since the fighters of Kallith Clan had ridden out in defence of the other clans of the People. Somehow, he felt it should be different after all these years, yet it was a relief that it was the same. The clouds and surrounding mountains were reflected in the crystal-clear water of the lake. Rock huts were off to one side. Finding rock for buildings was one thing they hadn't had trouble with as it was something they had in abundance in Kallith. Although crops were a little more difficult in the barrens than in the other sectors. They produced enough to eke out a living but made far more from the mines and horse herds that ran on some of their lower plains. Trying to traverse his homeland was a little trickier than the rolling hills of Hallaran or the river or lake clans. As the Sylannians had found out when his fellow clansmen had ridden down on them, unseen until it was too late.

Tarkhan pulled to a halt in the open space in front of the meeting hut, grateful he wouldn't have far to walk. Taking a breath, he hauled himself off his horse with none of the effortless grace a lifetime spent in the saddle typically imparted. Finally, Tarkhan walked into the large meeting hut with the other leaders and, with the doors shut firmly behind them, he walked across and slumped back into a pile of cushions. He covered his face momentarily as relief and shock warred within him. He'd held himself together by sheer willpower, knowing Khaliun and the women and children were all depending on him. Tension was thick in the hut as their fellow leaders wondered what had happened to them.

Yangir and Narantuya walked in, obviously filled in by the others as Yangir went straight to Khaliun's side who was resting on cushions nearby. Yangir's breath hissed as he cut away Khaliun's vest and top and the injuries they hid were revealed. Tarkhan, feeling gentle hands touch him hesitantly, drew his hand away from his face as Narantuya knelt on the cushions by his side.

"I'm all right. They didn't hurt me." Tarkhan was exhausted but that was nothing a good sleep wouldn't cure.

"You were pain-sharing with Khaliun; you know prolonged use of that ability also hurts you." A healing pulse from Narantuya washed through him.

"Throwing yourself off your horse the way you did probably didn't help, either. If I know you're hurt, Narantuya certainly does," Orghana said.

Tarkhan flushed, but it was futile trying to deny Orghana's words, let alone Narantuya's. Narantuya's healing ability was different to his—she didn't share his pain, she simply healed him. Although there was nothing simple about her healing talent. While healing fatigued her, it didn't hurt her. He didn't bother to contradict Orghana's assertion.

"Chono betrayed his people; he betrayed us. Khaliun killed one of theirs before they took her down. They strung her out in the heat and tortured her."

"Chono did this?" Yangir paused in his ministrations to Khaliun, his eyes flashing in anger.

"He didn't wield the blades, but he was the willing bait in the trap."

"If we didn't have our own people to think of, I'd take a war group and kill him," Erden grated.

"I wasn't sure Khaliun would live." Tarkhan sighed and gave in as Narantuya continued to treat him.

Tarkhan tried to relax as Narantuya, with Orghana assisting her, made quick work of taking his shirt off by cutting it with sharp knives. Both women fussed over him, and he had to concede wherever Narantuya's talent brushed, deep aches receded and muscles unknotted. While his keepers had cleaned him when he hurt himself, they hadn't really healed him. Along with a lack of food, the pain from his injuries had been a way to weaken his mind so they could breach his mental barriers.

Finally, Narantuya and Orghana helped him sit back up, carefully binding his ribs in a fresh bandage and assisting him in pulling on a loose shirt. He did not know where it had come from or whose it was, but he was grateful for it.

Not finished yet, they piled up more pillows and pushed him back into them. He chuckled, then winced as his ribs let him know they weren't happy with laughing just yet. Tarkhan relaxed; his fellow leaders would fuss over them both, regardless of the protesting.

"That's all I can do for today. I'll tend your ribs tomorrow," Narantuya said in a soft voice.

Tarkhan was content to rest as Khaliun was still being treated by both Erden and Yangir. Her injuries were far worse than his own. Thankfully, Yangir had more than a touch of the rare healing talent and wasn't sparing himself. Tarkhan could almost see some wounds on Khaliun's flesh knit under Yangir's hands.

Finally, Yangir sat back, sagging slightly, his exhaustion apparent. Erden helped Khaliun slip a shirt back on, then leant back on a pile of pillows and pulled her into his arms.

The sight made Tarkhan smile. Their relationship was one reason their respective tribes had been close more often than not. It didn't appear like Erden was letting her go anytime soon.

"Thank you for your care and sorry for making you wait. How are our exodus plans coming along?" Khaliun asked.

"No need to apologise, Khaliun. Treating and easing your injuries comes first," Yangir said.

"We can't stay here. Those pursuing us are dead, but I fear others aren't that far behind us." Tarkhan struggled to sit up, only to have Narantuya and Orghana push him back onto his pillows.

"We have sentries out. I have ordered them to leave some nasty little surprises for any other enemies who might come after us all." Orghana's tone was fierce.

Reassurance and comfort ran through him from Narantuya, who lay beside him, her hand resting lightly on his shoulder. Tarkhan took a breath, allowed what she offered to work, as all his muscles relaxed.

"What of our exodus plans? Where are they up to?" Khaliun asked again.

"Ulagan and Tuya's people left shortly after you set out for the Hallaran Lake. They've been busy these years we've been fighting. They scouted ahead, laying the trail and setting up a temporary sanctuary in the Heights. Half my clan has already followed with extra supplies, which they'll leave in stockpiles with markers alongside the trail up the Heights," Yangir said.

"We left our clan in Ulagan's care and came back to guide you all." Narantuya said.

"Has any contact been re-established with the people who live on the other side of the Heights?" Tarkhan asked.

Erdan shook his head. "No, not yet."

"I know we have no choice, but those people on the other side were fractured with stories of a warlord who conquered village after village. We could trade one evil for another." Erden toyed with the edge of the cushion near him, pulling at a loose thread. "It's why we stopped trading there all those years ago, even before the war with Sylanna."

"Yes, there were stories about the vicious nature of their warlord, but there are no stories of our own trading caravans being set upon," Khaliun said.

"Ulagan and Tuya confirm they believe their scouts have found some territory for us." Yangir licked his lips, looking from one person in the meeting hall to the other. "It's away from the villages of the people who live over the Heights."

"I know it's a risk, but I'd rather our people have some chance rather than none. We will go as planned." Tarkhan met the eyes of the other leaders of Kallith in the silence that followed his statement. The leaders of the warriors of Kallith traditionally held responsibility not only for the safety of the Kallith Clan but all the People. Even if it was an authority they rarely used, it was his and Khaliun's responsibility.

"We'll start the evacuation after this meeting," Orghana said.

Tarkhan pushed down the pain that threatened to overwhelm. Opposite him Khaliun's eyes and emotions were a mirror of his own. The fact that the collective Hallaran Clan fell to Chono's cowardice was heartbreaking.

They were talking about leaving behind everything they'd ever known. Even for people who'd been nomadic in their past, this was a difficult thing. These lands had always been their home. They might have roamed far from them, but they were still home. Losing their fellow clans, even those they didn't get on with, was a blow. So many of their people were dead or had been taken in a senseless war.

Tarkhan deliberately pushed aside his dark thoughts. For tonight, he'd let someone else be the strong one. He rolled over into Narantuya's arms, accepting the steady stream of uncomplicated comfort and shelter she offered.

Samuel sat on his throne, glaring at the people near the balcony. Normally, he would have been in his element, surrounded by his wives and the heads of the other houses, all of whom would do their best to gain his favour. He was the king, after all. He remembered his triumph when he and his wives had swept through the court, killing his mad mother, father, and his father's wives. Disposing of his siblings at the same time to ward off any threat they possessed—although his mother and father had already started killing his siblings. That glow of achievement as he'd sat on his mother's throne had been fleeting. He still remembered the next moment too, when the people in the court had moved and he'd seen her: Jaclyn. His sister had somehow survived the purge and taken Ricardo as husband. That had been a betrayal; he and Ricardo had been friends.

He'd spent the intervening years trying to remedy that oversight. Yet she neatly side-stepped his every attempt to put her in situations that would lead to her untimely death. This was his court, yet the power had shifted. He could see it. Now that his sister was back there were those who courted her favour over his. Her blood was as pure as his own, no taint of outside blood, and of direct monarch descent. Jaclyn's house was also proving its strength by birthing sons and conquering other lands to bring them into Sylanna, which gained them much needed land and resources.

Sending her to fight the traders to take the land and people for their own, expanding his kingdom, had been intended to achieve a few things. The first of which was the death of his sister and the destruction of her house. How could he possibly have known she and her house would prove able leaders to head that conquest? That she would not only survive, but also be credited with taking the land, and in the process, become even more popular than she had been to start with.

"How does she do this?" Samuel hissed.

"Calm, husband." Chelsie lay a hand on his arm.

"I meant her to die, not live and succeed." Samuel slumped, aware he was behaving petulantly but didn't care.

As Fiona entered the court, walking across the room to join them, he smiled, reaching to grab her hand and pulled her close.

"How did that task I gave you go?" he asked.

"A squad of the daggerwives should be attacking as we speak." A predatory gleam glinted in her eyes.

He observed his sister surrounded by her admirers on the other side of the audience room, and frowned. Something tugged at the edge of his awareness that he couldn't quite put a finger on.

~

Samuel breathed in sharply, his eyes widening imperceptibly, and he swallowed. It was always disconcerting to come back to himself, to be in control of his own mind and body again, rather than under the firm influence of his wives. He wasn't entirely certain walling off a small piece of his consciousness, all those years ago before he accepted Chelsie as his firstwife and she'd taken control of his mind, had been a good idea. If anything, he feared it was bringing on the madness his people suffered even sooner. Samuel was certain, even more than he had been before he'd become a husband, that the mate bonds caused the affliction. In the Monarch House, it was even worse. He had hundreds of wives, each with a mate bond tying his mind to theirs. A web of connections between all their minds with him at the centre. It was increasingly difficult to know who he was; if an idea was his or that of one of his wives. The mate bond was a tradition so bound in their history it was hard to change, so he'd tried to subvert it. Admittedly it worked, to an extent, this small piece of the man he'd been had escaped manipulation by his wives. It just wasn't quite as he imagined it would be.

Although she was older, than he felt she should be, he realised he was staring at Jaclyn. He was torn between being appalled that his sister and her husband were back here at court, and relief that they were both still alive. Being in such proximity to his wives when he came back to himself was never a good thing. He always feared they'd find out they didn't have full control of him and remedy that oversight. But Jaclyn still lived. He'd spent many years working at pushing her away and keeping her as far away from the court as he could. Samuel did not know why he'd recalled Jaclyn from the war in the trader lands, but he must have. He was the king, after all. That meant his wives had grown impatient waiting for Jaclyn to die in the trader lands and come up with a new scheme. He just didn't know what it was.

Samuel paled as he realised he must have been under for a

long time, to him it seemed like only the other day he'd ordered Jaclyn and her family to conquer the trader lands. It had been far longer. These moments of awareness seemed to become rarer. Time had passed, yet he had very little memory of the intervening years. He wondered if it was seeing Jaclyn here in court that had triggered his return this time. It sent a small part of him into a happy place to know she'd survived the worst he and his wives could throw at her. He'd known, absolutely known, that if any of his siblings would be able to not only survive but thrive, it would be her. He fixed a smile on his face as he realised Jaclyn's presence in court had distracted his wives. It was the reason they hadn't noticed that little inner spark that was him, aware and functioning. If he'd had the luxury of time, he would have wallowed in self-pity. He stared at Jaclyn. He had to get her out of the court again. If she remained, it would allow his wives too many chances to kill her.

"Pity we can't put that barbarian warlord and his people to good use to kill her off," Chelsie said.

Samuel smiled, as an idea came to him. He vaguely remembered something about a warlord who, despite everything, had put an end to their attempts to get a foothold in the lands they'd claimed.

"Now that we've recalled her from the conquest of the trader lands, why can't we just send her against the barbarian warlord?" Samuel was careful to make sure his real motivation didn't show. It wouldn't do for his wives to discover he wanted Jaclyn and her house to survive.

"You know we took the commander rank off her for a reason," Chelsie said.

"Of course, but we could just send her to conduct raids."

"It could just end up making her more popular than she already is if she succeeds."

"She's bound to run out of luck eventually. Besides, without the rank of commander to protect her, she only has control over her own house." Samuel smiled coldly, as he gazed at Jaclyn. "Perhaps the barbarian warlord will do us a favour and succeed where the traders failed."

A cold smile spread across Chelsie's lips. "You're right. We can just keep sending her against them, raid after raid. She's bound to die, eventually."

Samuel kept his gaze on his sister. Somehow, he had to manoeuvre events to make sure they appointed Jaclyn as commander again. Still, one small step at a time. First, he had to ensure he could get her out of the court. Then he could work on manipulating things to give her the extra protection being appointed commander of the Sylannian forces gave her. If only he could stay in his own headspace long enough to achieve all these things. Still the first step of getting his wives to agree to send Jaclyn away from the court again had been achieved, so he'd take the small victories where he could get them. The evening seemed a lot better. He stood, walking across the room. The lesser families gave way as he made his way unerringly towards his sister.

CHAPTER

TWENTY-SIX

A breeze blew down the hallway from the shuttered windows that ringed the court. Jaclyn resisted the urge to reform her silks into armour and, instead, allowed her gown to flutter against her skin. Jaclyn gazed across the court at her brother, Samuel, surrounded by his wives.

He's up to something. Ricardo's mindvoice was laced with suspicion.

Jaclyn didn't have to ask which particular *he* her husband was referring to. Jaclyn sent a soothing pulse into Ricardo. Not that Samuel wasn't always up to something. It just remained to be revealed what his next attempt to destroy her house would be, and whether they and their entire family would survive it. Of course, that didn't mean she was sitting around, blindly waiting for her dear brother to kill them all.

"Jaclyn, I'm surprised to see you here."

"What, and miss the opportunity to see you after all this time?" Jaclyn's heart froze, waiting for the response that would

156

detail what her loving big brother had in store for her and her family.

"Ah, I'm so sorry. My messengers must have missed you," Samuel said.

"The barbarian lands are proving problematic." Chelsie's eyes glittered with malice.

"After all your success, why don't you conduct some raids over there?" Samuel's expression was distinctly smug.

"We're sure you will accomplish great things." Fiona's smile widened as she sent a tight message, her mindvoice cutting. *Don't worry, we'll take good care of your daughters. And your sons.*

Jaclyn didn't give herself the luxury of reacting. Of course, she doubted he'd sent a messenger at all. King he might be, but Samuel was small-minded and petty. It wasn't enough for him that he had power. He took every opportunity to prove it to everyone around him—as long as his wives surrounded him. Samuel wouldn't confront anyone if he didn't have the ever-present threat of at least a dozen of his wives baring their wickedly sharp, curved daggers.

"What, miss this opportunity to bid you farewell Samuel?" Jaclyn smiled pleasantly. It irritated Samuel and his wives that she could address him as an equal rather than use your majesty. "Of course we came."

Dark brown eyes, much like her own, glinted. Jaclyn allowed her smile to widen just a little more and was rewarded as Samuel's lips pressed together and his eyes glittered. Chelsie's hand rested on his arm and the spark died from Samuel's eyes, his anger subsiding. Jaclyn eyed her brother. He'd grown soft. A far cry from the man who'd wrested the leadership of Sylanna from their mother. With his black hair unbound and trailing down his back, flawless olive skin, if he hadn't had the silk billowing pants on underneath the flowing top, she'd mistake him for a female. Then again, probably not. Sylannian women were much tougher than the men. Samuel's wives weren't an exception to that rule.

Jaclyn transferred her gaze to Chelsie, wondering if she had been managing her husband a little too much. It was common practice, particularly in the upper ranks of Sylannian houses. Yet there was a fine line between modifying behaviour to protect them from themselves and having the husband lose himself. Their husbands were too valuable to risk. Without their husbands, there would be no children; with no children Sylanna would die.

I wonder if it is really my brother that rules, or his wives, Jaclyn wondered.

You think they've gone too far? You think they court madness, as your mother and her fellow wives did with your father? Myra asked.

We were friends, once. Samuel wasn't always petty. There was a time he dreamed of changing Sylanna for the good of us all, but I think his wives are treading a fine line. He is not what he was. It was clear Ricardo was troubled.

Given the topic, Jaclyn resisted the urge to soothe Ricardo. Being back at court was causing her old habit to rear its head. Guilt swelled as she realised she was no better than Chelsie. She'd seen her mother, and her fellow wives and husband, descend into madness, the bonds between their minds too tight, their minds merging to the point they didn't know who they were anymore. It was a known problem of the mind bonds they forged. The madness had prompted her brother to usurp the throne.

"You won't take the children with you this time. The barbarians are not like those from the trader lands. I'll take good care of them here." Samuel's smile didn't reach his eyes.

Once again, Jaclyn refused to allow her brother to see the

impact his words had on her. No matter that she'd expected nothing less from him and his wives.

"From everything I've been told about the barbarians, I wouldn't dream of taking the children into harm's way." It surprised Jaclyn her voice showed no hint of emotion.

"Good. We can't possibly risk your children. Make sure you are on your way by the end of the week. Enjoy your last few nights in civilised company." With one final triumphant grin, Samuel turned and swept away with his wives surrounding him.

"Of course, Samuel."

I think we need to get back to our court. Ricardo's tone held a hint of worry.

Taking a breath, Jaclyn relaxed her hold on her husband's mind. She'd made the promise to herself, long ago, after seeing her mother's house descend into madness, that she'd leave her husband free will. It was proving much harder to do, to abandon custom, than she'd ever dreamed it would.

Jaclyn left her brother's court with her family around her. She kept her pace steady, not wanting Samuel to know that he and his wives had caused her to fear for the safety of her family.

It didn't help that Ricardo had obviously picked up on the same thing.

Joy poured directly into her mind from Ricardo, causing Jaclyn to gasp. A subtle burst of communication letting her know he realised she'd refrained from turning his mind away from worry. He recognised the instant she'd relaxed her hold on his mind and withdrew again. As she'd done when they'd been in the lands of the traders. Instead of causing her concern, she realised it brought relief and happiness to her as well.

TWENTY-SEVEN

Tension drained from Olivia as she walked into the barracks where the Warlord's people bedded down while they were in Callenhain. In normal circumstances, she would rather be out with them, but the Warlord insisted she stay in the castle itself. To be honest, it was easier to be in the estate house since she'd made a point of checking on Michael several times during the night. Michael was housed in rooms just down from the Warlord's own, which were, of course, on the top floor of her family home. Heads turned as the troops tracked her progress through the barracks.

"Olivia, the warleader?" the man sitting on the edge of his bunk asked.

"I insisted he stick to his rooms and rest today, but he's fine." Olivia smiled reassuringly.

Actually, he was quite willing to be confined to his rooms for the day. Not that she needed to mention that point to anyone. It meant he could avoid her family and everyone else and abdicate responsibility to her for the day. The perfect excuse to gain a moment of privacy, which was a rare thing in the life they led. Of course, she'd made sure it was their own guarding his door and keeping everyone out under her orders.

Nathanial, where's our latest recruit? Olivia asked.

She doubted Damien was still asleep and suffering any more than Michael was, at least not at this hour. Unlike Michael, he would not be spending his day lazing about. Those of higher-level ability going through "transition", as the Unwanted called it, or "veil sickness" as commoners referred to it, had different reactions. The uncontrolled power that surged through them incapacitated some, while others barely noticed a change at all—other than a gradual increase in their abilities. There was one thing that they all had in common: the more active those going through transition were, the easier they seemed to cope.

Meal room. Just finished eating, Nathanial replied.

He's recovered well today, I trust? Olivia turned and walked across the common area, skirting around the scattered chairs. With an almost negligent thrust of power, she pushed the double doors open.

As expected, he has. How's Michael? Nathanial's tone held a note of concern.

He's fine. Enjoying a rare respite from duty, by my order. Olivia waited; she could feel Nathanial considering his next words.

Good. I can't remember the last time he had some time to himself, Nathanial said as he excused himself from the group he'd been sitting with in the corner of the meal room and joined her.

Olivia checked the meal area and found Damien sitting off to one side. She could sense he was contemplating what he should do next. She smiled. That was an issue she was about to solve for him. Olivia took it as a good sign Damien was wearing his old worn hunting clothes with his sword in place on his belt.

"Glad to see you're dressed appropriately."

"I don't have much else." Damien blushed as he suddenly seemed to find his empty mug entirely fascinating.

Uh oh. I think our newest recruit is smitten. Nathanial's chuckle sounded in her mind.

He's a little young, Olivia mused.

Nathanial turned to her, his eyes sparkling. *Is that a mutual interest I detect?*

That's enough out of you, Olivia growled.

Olivia decided to ignore Nathanial who was grinning unrepentantly at her. She sighed as his grin widened. She shook her head, pushing his comment aside. Yes, Damien would be a very good-looking man, but as of now, he was still young in more ways than one. He had a great deal of growing up to do, and besides all that, he was their recruit.

"You won't need much else. We'll get you outfitted, but our master armourer is in Vallantia. It will be some time before we get there."

"I'm used to these." Damien shrugged.

"They'll do for now."

"Trust me, they are more suited than what I was attired in when I fell into this life. My clothing, if you could call it that, was suitable for bed sport and not much else, and I had handled nothing sharper than a butter knife," Nathanial said.

Damien's eyes widened as he stared at Nathanial. Shock was the only feeling she sensed coming from him. That was the other thing they were going to have to work on: he leaked constantly. In their line of work, it wasn't a helpful trait.

"Come on, it's time to see if you can actually use that sword you carry." Olivia turned, not waiting for Damien's response.

Nathanial fell into step without comment. A chair scraped behind her and the soft footfall of boots on the stone floor gave away that Damien followed as they left the meal room.

"I can," Damien said from behind her.

While confidence filled his reply, she could sense his underlying trepidation. She caught Nathanial's eye, her eyebrows rising. He rolled his eyes.

Try to be his friend, the one he goes to if he has a problem.

Might be easier for you. Nathanial chuckled.

Perhaps, but his crush will get in the way, she replied dryly, feeling a wash of amusement from Nathanial.

"If you at least have the basics down, it will make things easier. Our fighting style is a little different, but don't worry, we'll train you," Nathanial said.

Olivia could feel it as Damien contemplated what he'd been told, then turned his mind to his next concern. She waited. It didn't take long before he got the courage to speak up.

"Michael, the warleader. Is he all right?" Damien asked.

"Michael is fine." Olivia turned to him and smiled.

Damien's smile faltered. "I woke up here. Everyone was saying I lost control, and the warleader got hurt. I don't remember what happened."

Olivia reached out, placing a hand on Damien's shoulder. "What's the last thing you remember?"

"Yesterday...?" Damien paused, uncertainly.

"Yes, we arrived here yesterday," Olivia said.

"We were on the road, a wall and gates loomed up, Callenhain I guess..." Damien swallowed, his breathing became shallow. "Then I was confused. I couldn't keep everyone out of my mind—"

"Easy, it's all right." Olivia reached out and tilted Damien's head up, meeting his eyes. "Transition hits us all differently. Blackouts are not common, but not unheard of either. You did nothing wrong."

"Is this the first time you've had a blackout?" Nathanial asked.

"No, the last couple of times I had one of my attacks, I blacked out." Damien flushed. "Transition? Is that what you call it? In Ranlith they said it was veil sickness."

"It's the same. Many die. I'm guessing your elders told you that part?" Olivia smiled reassuringly. "Take heart. All of us in the Unwanted have been through it and survived."

"Why is it happening?"

"Increasing amounts of pure energy channel through your mind and body. Believe it or not, you are the one sucking the veil into yourself, at greater levels than you can currently control or use. Normal people die, but people like us don't." Nathanial shrugged. "We don't know why, just that it happens."

"As best we can guess, it's like puberty. You're changing physically and mentally, growing into your abilities. Once your powers levels settle, you'll be fine." Olivia shook her head, aware Damien wasn't the only one in the common room listening intently to the discussion. "Dwelling on transition won't help, either. Come on, it's time we gave you something else to concentrate on other than when your next transition attack is going to occur."

He will not have an easy time of it, Nathanial said.

So it seems; best we keep him busy.

Olivia walked out the final set of doors and crossed to the centre of the training grounds, drawing her blade as she did so. Nathanial took a position opposite her without having to be told. She gestured to a position a safe distance from Nathanial.

"We will demonstrate the drills I want you to practice. Watch this first run through, then mirror Nathanial's sword strokes on the second run." Olivia instructed.

Olivia tried not to smile as Damien's anxiety went up

another notch and turned to Nathanial, who indicated he was ready. In some ways, what they were about to do was harder than actual battle: performing each move precisely in a coordinated effort. Actual battle was an instinctive, rapid-fire flow of movement. Unfortunately, no one really reached that stage without first learning the hard way. Practicing enough that the instinctive move was the right one to counter your enemy.

She slashed her blade down in a slow, controlled move. Nathanial grinned and responded with a block before answering with his own strike. They traded blows slowly, in a carefully choreographed sequence. Deliberately keeping their display controlled, every stroke perfectly executed. When the sequence was over, they both halted, took a step back, and flipped their blades at each other with a slight bow of their heads. One blade master acknowledging another. Olivia almost smiled at the disappointment coming from Damien in waves. She took that as a good sign. The drill they'd performed was familiar to him.

Nathanial breathed in, then faced Damien and flipped his blade into a ready position. Damien, despite his distinct feeling of disappointment earlier, reeked of nervousness conveying a flavour of uncertainty as his own movement was clumsy compared to the one demonstrated by Nathanial.

"Just shadow the movement of my blade as best you can," Nathanial instructed before turning his attention back to Olivia.

Olivia flipped her blade in response and launched back into the drill they'd just performed, taking care to keep every move slow and precise as Damien attempted to copy Nathanial's moves against an invisible partner. She'd rather be launching into battle than this agonising dance. Yet in its own way, it was the repetition of what she'd lived and breathed since she'd been a child—if somewhat slower and without the addition of what made the Unwanted the force they were. There was more than time for Damien to learn that addition; first they needed to learn if he had the basics of blade work. Olivia was satisfied Damien hadn't been boasting about his abilities with the blade as Damien shadowed Nathanial's blade strokes during their drill. She called a halt and moved aside.

"Nathanial, if you could partner up against Damien?" Olivia asked.

Nathanial waited as Damien took her place opposite his new training partner. Damien was even less confident now that he had someone to drill against but on the plus side, he didn't appear entirely panicked, as those who'd never trained with a sword often did.

"Ready?" Nathanial flipped his blade in salute.

"Repeat the drill we just ran through, slowly," Olivia instructed.

She was impressed. While Damien might not be up to their standard, he definitely had the basics down. His weapons trainer had been good, given the small village they lived in. It made her wonder at Damien's former tutor's background. He hadn't leant to instruct the blade to this level living his entire life in that sleepy little village.

Nathanial corrected only a few moves using sloppy form by the expedient of slapping his opponent's arm or side with the flat of his blade. A signal that had this been an actual fight, it would already be over.

"Again, this time faster," Olivia said.

Damien took the instruction in his stride, his brow creasing as he went through the drill again at a faster pace. Damien winced as Nathanial's blade lashed out, slapping him on the side. As the doors of the training ring opened, Olivia glanced over as more of their people came in. The newcomers paused just inside the doors and she acknowledged them, signalling permission for them to enter the training grounds, but otherwise kept her attention on her recruit.

"Hold," she ordered. "Well done. You're holding onto yourself too tightly. For now, I want you to open yourself to the veil as you train. Don't do anything with it. Just allow it to flow through you."

"I'll warrant you'll feel better if you do," Nathanial chimed in.

"You'll run through that drill every day. Once you've got it down, we'll move on. Go practice on the pell." Olivia watched as Damien went off to do as instructed, radiating more confidence than he'd exhibited at the start.

"He's not too bad, all things considered. That was an advanced drill we went through." Nathanial stepped to her side, sheathing his blade as he did so.

"A lot better than I expected."

"His control of the veil is woeful. That will really need some work," Nathanial said.

"Let his mind rest for another day, then start him on some basic mind control drills. He needs to at least be able to shield his mind from others." Olivia was more concerned by Damien's lack of skill in that regard than she was about his blade work.

"It's not that unusual. He's obviously had far more practice with the blade than with the veil."

"You're right. It's not like he would have had anyone capable of training him properly. It's surprising enough that his mentor seems to have been competent in the blade," Olivia acknowledged.

As more of their people entered the training grounds Olivia sighed and did the rounds of those training, keeping a careful eye on them. She offered corrections for sloppy technique occasionally, which was met with acceptance. It stood those who'd chosen to get some training in well. It wasn't every day they had grounds like these to train in. At a guess, most of those not needed for duty were off sampling some of Callenhain's delights. Besides that, while she was out here, it meant she had a legitimate reason to avoid her family. Olivia sighed, wishing she could come up with an excuse to get her out of the dinner this evening.

TWENTY-EIGHT

Olivia stared at the dress in the woman's hands. It was flouncy. An atrocity of lace and frills in a deep forest green and silver, the traditional colours of her family line. If it had been a more elegant gown, she might have acceded and worn the thing.

"I am not wearing that monstrosity," Olivia said.

"I'm afraid you have no choice, miss. It's the only dress we have for you to wear at such short notice." The maid sniffed.

"Actually, I do have a choice." Olivia stripped off her weapons as she walked through her rooms.

She wasn't a total barbarian; she'd wash all the grime and sweat off before she appeared as ordered. An audible sniff sounded behind her.

"Miss, give me a moment; I'll hang your gown and assist you with your bathing."

Olivia stifled a sigh. The woman normally served in her brother's rooms. It wasn't just her body language that gave away that she'd rather not be performing this duty, it was her inner dialogue, or at least the bits she unwittingly projected.

When combined with her emotions and occasional flickering image she also insisted on throwing out there, it was clear the woman believed it was beneath her to be relegated to serve a woman who was no better than a common thug.

"I've been bathing myself for a very long time. Go. I'll manage somehow to get myself ready." Olivia couldn't help but laugh.

"But, miss, all the bows up the back of your gown, you'll never be able to tie them by yourself," the woman declared.

Olivia turned her head towards the maid, trying to remember that the woman wasn't responsible. She was only doing her job. All of this came from her family.

"It's all right. I told you, I'm not wearing it. If you leave now, you can say I threatened you. I'm sure my loving family will believe it. My dress standards, or lack of them, will be my fault." Olivia stripped off her uniform and flung them on the bed as she stalked past it.

Olivia strode into what her family called the bathing chamber. A converted closet that had an oversized elongated barrel filled with water. Personally, she'd hate to be walking in the courtyard below when the house staff drained the water. She would rather bathe in the river, but since that wasn't an option, the water could at least be hot.

Drawing the veil as she walked up the wooden stairs, she sent a stream of power into the water. Steam curled from the bath as she eased into it. Despite herself, she relaxed and placed the dagger she carried on a shelf within reach. She sighed, and with a small thread of power, increased the temperature. It was funny how it was the small things that made her appreciate being strong in the veil. Her family probably ordered the poor servants to complete what would be for them the exhausting task of heating their water.

OLIVIA SMILED at the servant as she took a goblet from his tray. Although her smile was only on the surface, she'd obviously done a good enough job of pretending to be relaxed and happy to be here since the man blushed. It didn't seem to matter how much time had passed since she'd been that unwanted child, she still found it unsettling to be here.

She contemplated the great hall and those who graced it. They were very pretty. Callenhain had certainly flourished under the Warlord's rule. The scions from the wealthy families stood around, while her mother and father simpered and fawned over the Warlord. Hearing a whisper of voices, Olivia turned towards the doors just as they closed behind Michael. She smiled; he'd also declined to wear anything other than his accustomed fighting leathers with his ever-present sword in place at his waist.

Thank you, Olivia said.

You didn't see what they'd left for me to wear. Michael's mind-voice conveyed a shudder.

Olivia barely held back her laughter at the image of the ensemble he sent her. It seemed lace was all the rage in Callenhain. His shirt had had a lace collar that ran down the front of it and lace cuffs that trailed out of the sleeves of a jacket made of stiff yellow fabric with matching breeches. Much like the men were wearing here in the court. Then again, taking into account what the other women were wearing, the dress her mother had left for her wouldn't have been out of place.

She still wouldn't have been seen dead in the thing.

Those present stared at her when they thought she wouldn't notice, disapproval spilling from them. She was the wayward child they'd thrown out who'd had the audacity to survive. Yet none of them dared comment. She'd had the gall not only to survive but to be valued by the Warlord and become one of his feared warriors.

"Really, Olivia, you couldn't dress appropriately? Even just this once? I know they left a gown in your rooms."

Baren's pompous tone was easily identifiable. Olivia kept her expression in check as her younger brother joined her. Time had not been his friend. He'd grown fat and lazy in the wealth Callenhain enjoyed.

"I'm not sure I'd describe it that way, Baren. Why pretend to be something I'm not? I ceased to be a child of this house the day your loving parents threw me out through the city gates." Olivia winced at the bitter undertone that laced through her words.

"Come, sister, surely, we can all put the past behind us?" Baren laughed.

A small group of simpering men and women who'd accompanied Baren tittered on cue.

"I have moved on, so I don't even feel the need to pretend I like you. Even Aiden is more useful than you."

"Ouch. Now that must hurt, Baren. My dearest sister Olivia despises me." Aiden sauntered up to her other side. "You see, that's what brothers and sisters do sometimes. We can say nasty things to each other. But I'm not about to stand here and let an outsider do so."

Olivia almost stared at Aiden in shock. He was correct, of course. She despised him, as he did her. It had almost been instant since the moment they'd met. At that point, she hadn't even been aware he was the Warlord's son. She'd just known they wouldn't get on. Of course, it made sense that Aiden viewed her and Michael as rivals for his father's attention. It hadn't made her like him any more. Not even the Warlord's insistence on treating them as his own children had remedied the distaste she held for Aiden.

"I think the days that this house could dictate how Olivia dresses have long passed. You most assuredly do not have the right to do so, Baren." A cold wash of the veil preceded Michael's arrival.

"After all, you haven't faulted Michael's dress," Aiden noted, his eyes glittering.

Olivia smiled as sweat beaded her brother's forehead. Baren might have been certain he could challenge her with impunity, but obviously when faced by Michael, he wasn't as confident. Olivia nearly laughed that it was Michael that her brother feared more rather than the Warlord's true-born son, Aiden. Then again, perhaps he was more perceptive than she gave him credit for.

"I didn't mean any disrespect. I just assumed you might like to be civilised…" Baren trailed off, licking his lips, his face going pale as his gaze sliding from her to Aiden then Michael, before resting back on her again.

"We're in civilised company? Really?" Olivia took in the grand hall and everyone in it, her eyebrow rising.

"Now, children. What have I told you all about being nice?" the Warlord's gravelly voice intervened.

"I'm not sure that is a lesson I remember, Father," Olivia said.

Her parents were walking towards them as she spoke. Her mother paled and her father's face flushed red. She could feel their outrage. All because she'd called the Warlord father. How either of them believed she would consider them her parents after all this time was beyond her. While she had never been as close to the Warlord as Michael, he was still more her parent than either of these two pretending outrage. She also knew, without a doubt, the Warlord wouldn't throw her out of a gate to appease anyone. He would flatten an entire city and everyone in it for her.

"Olivia, it's so good to see you!" Her mother's voice dripped with fake sincerity. "You really shouldn't keep her away so much, Warlord."

As her mother opened her arms and stepped forward in what Olivia could only imagine was an attempt to pull her into an embrace, Olivia stepped back. Her mother's smile faltered, laughter dying on her lips as no one joined in, her face flushing.

"Really? I got the distinct impression, given the way you treated Olivia, that you couldn't wait to see the back of her. At least Michael's birth parents fought for him. As pointless as it turned out to be," Aiden almost purred.

What is with Aiden tonight? Olivia was incredulous.

No idea. It's moments like this I could almost like him, Michael admitted.

Aiden waylaid the passing servant and co-opted him into refilling their glasses.

"Here's to the unconventional family we've become." Aiden half turned, ignoring Olivia's parents, and raised his goblet.

Olivia raised her goblet, knowing that Michael and the Warlord did the same. Her parents stood, their backs stiff, then, with a barely perceptible hesitation, raised their own goblets and sipped.

"I'm sure you'll excuse them. I've tried to raise them all as my own flesh and blood. They spend so much of their time on the road and in battle. Comfortable surroundings like these aren't a common occurrence." The Warlord's smile widened as her parents hastened to agree with him.

Not that she could imagine them doing anything else but agree with the Warlord when he was right there in front of them. While he'd put aside his accustomed fighting attire for the evening, he certainly wasn't wearing one of the atrocious lace shirts all the other men seemed to wear. By not conforming, he stood out. As did Aiden, she had to admit, who had dressed in a similar fashion to his father. Both a warning that dangerous people weren't all ugly or deformed. Indeed, the Warlord was probably one of the most dangerous people here, but he was also one of the most striking.

"Well, it's all turned out for the best, I'm sure," Baren said.

"Of course, you would see it that way. Particularly since, unlike Olivia, you weren't the one bundled up and tossed out of the gates at the Warlord's feet." Michael's voice was as expressionless as his face.

Her father took a large swallow from his goblet. "So, is there anything you need from me on this visit, Warlord, or are you just calling through?"

The Warlord held out his glass. A servant scuttled over and filled it for him. Those in the court shuffled as he took a sip. All the while the Warlord's eyes never left her father's.

"I'm hearing some disturbing rumours."

Her father smiled brittlely. "Rumours, Warlord?"

"Whispers of traders who've reengaged with the flesh trade."

As the Warlord's gaze travelled around the assembled peerage, more than one member blanched. Her father's face drained of colour.

"I... I'll have my people investigate. I'm sure it's just a wild story."

"For your sake, Speaker Strafford, I hope so. I'd hate to think that filthy trade has been occurring right under your nose, unopposed."

Her father took a step back, his hand rising. "I'm sure it can't be true, Warlord. Everyone knows the penalty for dealing with the flesh trade is death."

"I should hope so, but for the penalty to be a deterrent, my Speaker, in the second largest trading centre in my domain, needs to be enforcing it rather than turning a blind eye." The

Warlord's tone became chilling as he gazed flatly at her father. "You don't want me to have to come back here to investigate a second time, Speaker Strafford."

In the frozen silence that followed, the Warlord passed his empty glass to a servant and, gesturing for them to follow, turned and walked to the doors. Olivia dipped her head to her parents and turned to follow in the Warlord's wake with Michael and Aiden falling in on either side of her.

Did you know about that little detail?

No. I guess now we know why Father insisted he needed to pay a visit here before returning to Yalleska.

As they walked down the hallway towards their rooms, the Warlord paused, turning to them. "Michael?"

"Yes, Father?"

"Join me."

Michael nodded and, with a parting glance at Olivia, followed the Warlord into his rooms. It would take an idiotic person to start up the slave trade again. It was one of the few absolutes the Warlord had.

TWENTY-NINE

Michael followed the Warlord into the palatial sitting room, with plush rugs on the floor, paintings on the walls. There was a giant window that during the day gave a stunning view out over the grounds to the forest beyond, with the city in the distance off to one side.

"Take a seat." The Warlord gestured to a couple of high-backed leather chairs positioned to take advantage of the windows. The Warlord poured two drinks from a decanter placed on the low table between them.

Michael bit back a sigh and sat. The Warlord's half-smile gave away that he had caught Michael's unease at his surroundings. He'd been hoping this would be a quick request ordering him to investigate the rumours surrounding the re-emergence of the flesh trade. Then he could go back to his rooms or out to the barracks to check in on his people. Michael took the indicated seat and picked up the amber liquor that had been poured for him and took a sip. The sharp, bitter-sweet liquid filled his mouth then warmed his throat as he swallowed.

"You've never been comfortable in the trappings that match your birth." The Warlord gestured around the room.

"My brothers, perhaps, but this hasn't been my life." Michael took another sip of his drink, then smiled in appreciation. This was one trapping of his birth he could appreciate.

"I judge you'd best get used to it. This is in your future," the Warlord said.

Michael's eyes widened, and he tried not to choke. He didn't attempt to hide his reaction.

"How can I assist, Warlord?" Michael guessed there must be something more than a discussion about his parentage.

"How did it go with the girl?" the Warlord asked.

Michael frowned; Kara was not really on his Warlord's mind. Particularly after the discussion surrounding slavery in the ballroom. Michael sighed and settled back into his chair; the Warlord obviously intended this to be a full debriefing. He didn't normally ask questions about the people chosen for the task of maintaining their sentry and communication network.

"She understands the importance of the role and is grateful enough for me sparing her and not dragging her away from her village."

Silence stretched between them for a moment as the Warlord considered his words until he finally spoke again.

"Aiden is still a snivelling little coward who hides whenever he can get away with it." The Warlord's tone held an edge.

"His basic nature will not change."

"Given how often your warband rides into battle, I hope some of your courage will rub off on him," the Warlord grumbled.

"Aiden has a spine, as long as there is someone else to do the dirty work when the fighting starts." Michael relaxed as the Warlord laughed.

"You realise he came running to me to report you as a traitor?" The Warlord's lips twitched.

Michael snorted in amusement. "I wondered what he was up to sneaking around in the forest."

"You realised he had stumbled upon you and Kara?" The Warlord's eyebrows rose.

"Of course. Even when he thinks he is being subtle, Aiden is clumsy in his use of the veil."

"In all this time, he hadn't worked out how our sentry network was set up."

"Ah, is that what prompted you to dump him on me?" Michael did not bother to try and hide his exasperation.

"Well, nothing else has worked." The Warlord gazed at him. "Aiden and your brother by birth have something in common."

"What? They are both incompetent and hate me?"

He'd long come to terms with his mixed feelings towards the Warlord and his position of trust. Aiden hadn't been wrong: the Warlord, for all intents and purposes, had become a father to him—if a somewhat harsh and occasionally abusive one. The Warlord treated him more favourably than he did his own son, a circumstance Aiden had never forgiven. While the night the Warlord had taken him into his ranks was burnt into his memory, Michael didn't hate the Warlord. He'd spent more time with the Warlord, fighting for him and in his company, than he ever had with his real father or mother. It wasn't fear of what the Warlord would do to his family that caused him to stay. Not anymore.

"I can't change the past, son, nor will I apologise for it." The Warlord's sharp eyes regarded him. He picked up the bottle of liquor and held it out. By the Warlord's comment, he'd obviously been leaking some of what he'd been thinking. The Warlord always seemed to elicit a response from him.

Michael closed his eyes. It wasn't the first time the Warlord had called him son or implied that Aiden was as much his brother as his own flesh and blood. It was a tricky dance they played. Warlord to warleader. Father to son. Even though they shared no common ancestor, he had to admit that bond was there between them. He took a breath and shook himself, then held out his glass, watching as the Warlord, his father, filled his glass for him. He hadn't realised that he'd finished the first drink.

"We are under attack by Sylanna. That was as true back then as it is now. My family not only stood aside from their duty to protect the people, they didn't help you when you stepped up. They stood in your way," Michael said. "I understand the why of what happened, Father, even if I didn't back then."

"How's our latest recruit?" the Warlord asked.

"Still coming to terms with the situation. We've started his training. That will distract him, at least. We have arranged a gentle nag for Damien to ride, rather than the baggage animal he's been on." This was at least a much safer topic and distracted him from contemplating how similar he was to the Warlord.

"How's his blade work?"

"I'm told it's surprisingly good, given he grew up in the middle of nowhere," Michael admitted.

"You think that was his trainer? The one vowing vengeance when we left his village?"

Michael realised he shouldn't have been surprised that the Warlord had picked up on the threat.

"I'd bet on it. He's reasonably strong in the veil. I'll check in on him and see if I can recruit him when we end up back there."

The Warlord stared out the window for a moment. "What about Damien's skill with the veil?"

"His powers are fluctuating. He's of that age. Once his abilities finally settle down, I wager he'll be one of our strongest."

"Is it safe for him to ride with you on patrol if he is that unstable?" The Warlord frowned.

"It will be easier to teach him control with Olivia and Nathanial to help teach and keep an eye on him," Michael said.

"I can take him with me back to Yalleska," the Warlord offered.

"He'll adapt to his new life better if he rides with us, and I'd rather be nearby if Damien loses control," Michael said.

"Very well, I'll accept your judgement. Make sure he has the basics." The Warlord reached out and filled his glass again.

"Of course, Warlord. As you know, we need to show some caution. I'd rather we didn't burn his mind out."

While having more power was a benefit, it also came with disadvantages. While there were few born with greater strength, it seemed their numbers were increasing. No one Michael had spoken to had been able to say why.

"I'll be heading back to Yalleska tomorrow. I want you to do a wide circuit, skirting the Heights through the villages. We have not patrolled them for some time. That should give you some time to train the recruit. Plan to end up in Vallantia," the Warlord instructed, his head turning to catch Michael's eyes. "When you get to Vallantia, get your connections there to investigate the trader rumour."

"Of course, Father, I'll get Ben onto it."

"Task Lukas as well. I want a thorough check into this." The Warlord's jaw clenched, eyes glittering.

"Is there something you aren't telling me, Father?" Michael said carefully. "This isn't the first time this rumour has come up."

"The information has come from several different sources now, and this time it hasn't died off." The Warlord rubbed the back of his neck and shook his head. "I have seen no sign the trade has resumed, but something just seems off."

"Would you rather I go straight to Vallantia?" Michael asked.

"No, Speaker Strafford seemed genuinely shocked and terrified I'd kill him on the spot." A hint of amusement lit the Warlord's eyes. "It's probably nothing, just persistent whispers. I suspect if there was substance to this, your connections in Vallantia would have already reported to us. Just get them to check, anyway. They'll do a more thorough job than any of my Speakers." The Warlord's eyes turned hard. "If it is true, root the filthy trade out and kill it."

"Of course, Father." Michael finished his drink, placing the glass carefully on the low wooden table between them. "The rest of our normal patrol circuit?"

"Send the second band of my louts to complete it. They need the exercise." The Warlord smiled at him.

Michael stood. "Very well. I'd best break the bad news to the other teams, and I'll be on the road tomorrow."

"If you think the lad is progressing well, take the time to outfit him when you get to Vallantia," the Warlord said.

As he left Michael acknowledged the two guards on duty outside the Warlord's door and strode down the hallway. He was relieved, for Olivia's sake, that at least they'd be getting out of Callenhain.

THIRTY

Liliana stood at a window in the inner sanctum, staring down the river towards the suspended bridge that connected their court with the king's. She smiled. Watching for her fellow wives and Ricardo to return from the king's court would not make it happen any sooner. Jaclyn had ordered her to keep to the inner sanctum on their return from the lands of the trader clans. If any learnt that she was with child and sensed she was pregnant with yet another boy at that, it would mean her death. Hers and those of their entire house as soon as the king's wives learnt of it. They already regarded Jaclyn as a threat to their rule, it would be even worse if her standing rose yet again because of another son born to the house.

While she understood Jaclyn's order for her to go into seclusion, Liliana was not that far away from the daggerwife she'd been that she didn't wish she was present and able to protect her family. But she knew the risk, and now she was showing, so, she remained with a squad of the daggerwives, the team she had led until she'd admitted she was pregnant. On the birth of her child, she'd be raised to the rank of primewife, equal to Myra. Until then, she was in between ranks. No longer a daggerwife. Not yet a primewife. She'd gone from one of multiple expendable daggerwives to one of Ricardo's most experienced and best daggerwives to the one they wrapped layers of protection around.

"Come, Lil, they will all relax if you move away from the window."

Liliana turned and smiled at the underwife who'd spoken, embarrassed that she didn't even know the older woman's name. Other than going over the defences, she'd kept to herself. The underwives had made room for her and the daggerwives but kept them separate from their charges. Guarding and the welfare of the children of the house was their province. As, it seemed, was protecting and care of wives like her who were expecting a boy child. Being the one under guard was something she was unaccustomed to. She'd believed she was aware of all the inner working of the court but it had been a shock to her to learn that sleeping quarters within the inner sanctum even existed. Of course, there were very few male children born in Sylanna, and shortly after she'd become a daggerwife of Jaclyn's house, they'd left for war in the trader lands. So this was part of the house she'd never had cause to see.

She looked over at two of her former team members who stood guard in the hallway. In a sign of the threat Jaclyn believed her brother and his wives to be, they would now spend the duration of Liliana's pregnancy in seclusion with her. The underwives had patiently explained it would mean fewer people would know to spread word of her pregnancy. Sighing, she turned back to the window, the silence oddly soothing.

The smile slipped from Liliana's face as she realised she hadn't even heard her own sigh. She stood staring out the window. It was silent. No rustling as the wind blew through the leaves, no lapping of the water in the river below, not even the hum of insects. It was completely silent. Opening her mind to the veil, she closed her eyes, revealing the shimmer of the surrounding net. It glowed in her mind's eye; the thinnest layer of silver-grey hanging in the air like an all-encompassing fog. It was why the silence was so complete: the net absorbed the noise.

Liliana leant closer to the window and switched to her othersight and out of the darkness the glow of a team of daggerwives sprang into her mind. They ran across the walkways, scaled up the sides, jumping expertly from level to level. As the lifeforce of others extinguished where the daggerwives on guard duty would be stationed, the house was under attack. She spun from the window. There was no point in using verbal speech or mindspeech, since with the net in place none around here would hear it. Her hands flashed in battle sign that the house was under attack. It was simple but effective. The smallest ripples in the veil showed the daggerwives checking with their othersight, their posture stiffening as they spotted the thin, almost undulating net that enveloped them all. They wasted no time in leaping forward and slamming the windows shut, dropping the heavy bars across them.

Liliana did not resist as the daggerwives formed around her. They sprinted down the hallway, further into the depths of the house. The inner sanctum was a maze that only long familiarity allowed anyone to traverse it with any speed or accuracy. As they ran, fake walls swung into place and fixed, changing the layout. Other doorways were barred.

Finally, they burst into the nursery. The underwives sprang to their feet. It only took one moment, seeing the daggerwives barricading them into this sanctuary, for them to gather their charges. Unlike in many courts, the underwives of Jaclyn's court were all armed, a result of being in a war zone for years.

A blast of cold washed over Liliana a moment before the wall to the far side splintered, pieces flying inwards. All soundless. The daggerwives and underwives pushed her back behind their protective lines. Liliana bit her lip, feeling torn as she watched the sleeping silks of daggerwives and underwives alike ripple and turn into armour. They were right. It was their duty to protect her and the unborn child, along with the children of the house. Liliana gripped her daggers, placing herself in front of the children, sending soothing emotions to them. With a small thread of power, she coaxed their sleeping silks to harden to afford them a bit more protection.

She glanced at the net in frustration. It would have taken the effort of many daggerwives to gather enough of the veil to raise such a net. There would be a hall filled with unconscious women right now after their exertions. While it took the efforts of many to deploy it and anchor it in place, it would only take one to hold the tether of the net. For the net to come down, they had to take out the person anchoring it. If they were smart, the anchor would not be in the first wave of attackers— they would bury her within their ranks.

Their attackers pause in their headlong rush into the room, shock emanating from them as they recognised they faced daggerwives, not just the underwives they'd expected. Using that shock to their advantage, the daggerwives and underwives launched themselves at the ranks of the invaders.

Liliana kept her attention on the fight, staying in front of the children. The attackers wore black, rather than crimson, yet there was no doubt in her mind that these women were king's daggerwives. A gap in the line of defenders in front of her opened as one underwife fell to her opponent. Liliana lunged, her wicked blades slicing across the attacker's throat as she tried to break through. Liliana along with the children and their protectors retreated again as the line closed once more.

THIRTY-ONE

Jaclyn didn't quite run as she made her way along the suspended wooden bridge that connected her brother's island and her own. It didn't take long, but she sighed with relief as they made their way to the upper walkways to her court, which spanned a dozen of the largest and tallest trees. Their ancient trunks and limbs carried the weight of the court and the network of pathways that stretched between the homes in the upper levels with ease. The faint blue glow thrown by the immature silkspiders was just bright enough to push back the darkness. Her island was inhabited by her people, both upper and lower levels. In these central core islands that housed the ruling families, the islands were close enough for walkways to stretch between the courts. The lower in status someone was, the lower their house, with the collared living at ground level.

As much as she wanted to relax and enjoy being home, she'd almost forgotten the constant pressure here in the Court of a Thousand Islands. By comparison, she hadn't been as on edge while living in their makeshift camp within striking distance of the trader clans. Feeling Ricardo tense next to her, Jaclyn turned to him, then followed his gaze, which was fixed on the windows of their court. That was when she noticed it. The shutters of one window slamming rhythmically, soundlessly against the frame. As she took in her court, she realised it wasn't just one broken window or door. All of them were shattered. Someone, or many someones, had forced their way in. She could see it, but there wasn't so much as a sound coming from any of the broken slats hitting the windowsills. Dread descended on Jaclyn as she stared at the house.

"No, I'm not too late. They're not dead." Jaclyn ruthlessly pushed away the fear that would cripple her if she let it.

She had a job to do, an enemy to find. Jaclyn broke into a run. She drew her blades, Myra, Ricardo, and the daggerwives who'd come with them following her into their home through the broken windows and doors.

They didn't need light. There was enough filtering in from outside for them to skirt their way around the furniture. Jaclyn broadened her mind, reaching out, seeking those who'd invaded her court, but as they'd crossed the threshold of her house, all sound had ceased. She couldn't hear the footfalls of her family around her or even her own breathing. Opening her mind further, the shimmering net of power that had deadened the noise of battle appeared around her. An attack by the Monarch House, no doubt. It was why her brother had been so pleased.

Ricardo nudged her and they burst into a run once more, heading towards the inner sanctum, ignoring those of their own that were fallen, bleeding out or dead on the floor. She didn't bother pulling down the net. It would only give away their approach.

Rounding the corner, the splintered remains of what had been a wall came into view. The silent battle in the inner sanctum was eerie. Liliana stood to the rear in front of the children, with the handful of daggerwives they'd left in the house and the underwives before her. They battled against a group of nearly forty daggerwives with nearly the half that number sprawled with their blood seeping from their mortal injuries into the floorboards. Jaclyn grinned fiercely. The attackers had received a nasty surprise. After years at war, many of the underwives hadn't allowed their fighting skills to deteriorate.

Ricardo's lips pulled back in a soundless snarl as he targeted the enemy who anchored multiple throbbing strands of the veil which fuelled the net. His own ability smashed into the woman, sending her slamming into the wooden beam behind her. As her head crashed into the wall, the net she'd been holding vanished and they fell on those attacking their house from behind. The sounds of battle, clashing blades, and cries rang out.

Jaclyn knew she should stay behind her protective detail, but she pushed aside custom and launched into the fight. She cut down the enemy in front of her without compunction. Ricardo and Myra joined her. As Jaclyn fought her way through their enemies, Liliana lashed out with bloody blades at those who breached the protective ring around her and the children.

Now that the net was down and the sounds of battle were clear, Jaclyn could hear the alarm go out as those on lower levels became aware the house was under attack. Backup would rush to defend the house.

An attack such as this one by daggerwives relied on speed and stealth. Now with their net down and facing an attack from both the front and rear, they became frantic.

No mercy, kill them all, Jaclyn ordered.

As more of their own daggerwives poured into the room, they cut the attackers down. Now that the tide of the battle had turned, the underwives behind the battle lines did their best to shield the view of their charges from the massacre that was occurring.

Jaclyn whirled, then stopped. All the enemies had fallen. The blood dripping from her blades was testament to the fact that she'd been in the thick of this battle.

"Liliana, are you hurt?" Ricardo pushed forward, carefully wrapped his arms around her.

Jaclyn had a moment to take one shuddering breath before Thomas wiggled free of the restraining arms of the underwife who held him and launched himself into her arms.

"Mama."

Jaclyn closed her eyes and hugged him, not wanting to think about the consequences if they hadn't come home when they had. Her eyes rose to see her youngest son, Carlos, in the arms of another underwife. Ricardo reached for the boy and hugged him to his chest.

"Take the children to our inner rooms. Dispose of the bodies, get this mess cleaned up and repair all external damage to the house. Take undamaged doors and shutters from internal rooms if you must. I want the court secure with no sign from the outside that an attack occurred by morning," Jaclyn ordered. "No one outside of our own is to gain access to the court until I say otherwise."

Turning, she walked with Thomas in her arms towards her rooms, knowing from the soft rustle of fabric that the others followed her. By morning, her brother would wonder what happened to his daggerwives. She wouldn't give him the satisfaction of knowing that he'd nearly succeeded.

Now that the battle was over, the children cried. Sinking onto her low bed, she rocked Thomas, soothing his distress.

CHAPTER
THIRTY-TWO

Tarkhan shivered in the wind. Up here, the world offered little protection. Even the grey rocks of the surrounding mountain did little to help. He looked over the array of hide tents spreading out over the mountain plain, aware of the stillness, of being watched. These few were all that remained of his people. This inhospitable mountain range was their only remaining territory. The other clans were dead or absorbed into the Sylannian kingdom. At least the circular tents with their wooden doors, and chimney pumping out smoke from the stove inside, spoke of home and warmth. Tarkhan dismounted and pulled his fur-lined cloak tighter around him. He could even feel the chill on his fingers as his gloves struggled to hold the cold at bay. Without comment, he handed the reins of his horse to one of his tribesmen, waiting barely a moment for Khaliun to join him before they walked across the camp towards the largest tent towards the centre.

As they approached, he noted the two guards who stood outside the door. Neither seemed inclined to move. His annoyance grew, eyes narrowing. It was cold, and he was not in the mood for foolishness. He opened his mouth to order them to move before closing it again as Khaliun spoke.

"Get out of our way or I swear you'll be getting up close and personal with the dirt." Khaliun's hand was on her sword as she strode forward, showing no sign of halting.

He smiled blandly at their faintly panicked expressions as the scrape of her sword sounded harshly. The tent entry opened and Erden came out.

"What is this foolishness? Move, you dunderheads, or Khaliun will make an end of you!" Erden bellowed.

The men were alarmed and muttered an apology as they stepped aside. Khaliun's sword dropped back into her scabbard, and she wrapped Erden in her arms.

"I'm glad you're safe. I was worried about you and Orghana." Khaliun grinned as Erden wrapped her in a bear hug and swung her around.

"You were worried about us?" Erden pulled back slightly. "It was you two riding tail. You're both stubborn. I was beginning to think you'd left your run here too late and the Sylannians had taken you all." Erden reached out with one arm and dragged Tarkhan into a three-way embrace.

"No sign of the Sylannians; we decided it was worth the effort to take time to hide our trail." Tarkhan traded glances with Khaliun.

Erden gestured to some of the tribesmen who'd emerged from their tents, instructing them to help the warriors of Tarkhan and Khaliun's tribe settle in. They turned and took charge of the new arrivals, guiding them to where Tarkhan guessed accommodations had been set up for them.

"Come in from the cold. We have the stove going and more furs to bundle up in." Erden held the door, gesturing for them to proceed him.

They didn't have to be told twice. Tarkhan sighed with

relief as the warmth hit him. The draft from the open wooden door cut off abruptly as Erden closed and secured the entry. Tarkhan wasted no time pulling his gloves off and placing them on a stand near the entry where others had placed their gear. He untied his cloak and hung it up near his gloves. Turning, he saw Erden was assisting Khaliun with her own cloak before guiding her over to sit on a pile of cushions near his own. Tarkhan grinned, doubling up would be one way to keep warm in this appalling place. He greeted other clan leaders and, as Orghana patted a pile of pillows and furs next to where she was sitting, he pulled off his boots, leaving them with the rest and picking his way across the tent to sink with a sigh into the pile of pillows near Orghana.

"This is more luxury than I was expecting." Tarkhan closed his eyes, basking in the glorious heat thrown off the stove in the middle of the tent.

"We took our task to set up a place of sanctuary for our people to retreat to seriously. Given the warriors of Kallith rode out to war over five years ago, we've had plenty of time to get the frames, doors and hides for the tents and provisions up here." Ulagan was solemn.

Tarkhan opened his eyes as Orghana's hand rested lightly on his arm and she passed him a steaming mug. He raised an eyebrow at her.

"Mulled wine. The food is just flat bread with stew." Orghana smiled and placed a steaming bowl of stew with the flat bread on a low table nearby.

"Even though these mountains appear lifeless, our hunters report it has good game," Tuya said.

Tarkhan sipped some wine, appreciating the warmth as it slid down his throat. That had been in short supply since the Sylannians had landed on the shores of the plains and fallen on them with a vengeance.

Khaliun paused long enough before she devoured her stew to ask what he'd been wondering: "Of those who made up the clans of our homeland, it is only those of us of the Kallith with a few stragglers who've survived?"

"Yangir and Narantuya's tribe made it here as well. They're out foraging for supplies," Erden said.

"Has anyone checked the lands on the other side of the mountain? Are they still uninhabited?" Tarkhan's mood lightened as the gathered group of fellow leaders were all smiling and nodding, with an undertone of excitement thrumming through them.

"Yes, we'll go out for a ride tomorrow after you've both rested." Erden grinned.

Tarkhan sighed with relief. That was one wrinkle in their plans. This war they'd been engaged in had been ongoing for years. From the stories their trading caravans came back with, the other side of the Heights had previously held vast tracts of uninhabited land. Enough time had passed since they'd sent a trading caravan this way that it very well could have been claimed by others. Living up here in the harsh environment of the Heights, while possible, was not something he'd contemplated with any favour.

THIRTY-THREE

Damien entered the forest clearing where they were camped for the night, striding towards those who tended the cook pots heating over the fire pits. He leant to one side and, unlocking the ties to the mesh that held the bundle of wood to his back, let it fall onto the small pile to one side of the cooking circle. Walking up to his squad mates on cooking duty, he pulled his satchel over his head and handed it, along with the two waterfowl he'd caught, to Callan, who smiled, accepting the offering. From the aroma wafting across the camp, some others who regularly took on the foraging and hunting duty had had luck with hunting, too. While they had stocked up their supplies in Callenhain, they supplemented meals every night with fresh provender. While he was perfectly capable of hunting more than waterfowl, it would require going further afield. Until Michael trusted he wouldn't run home at the first opportunity, he decided it was best he stayed closer to camp, where his current keepers for the day could monitor him.

"Thanks, these will go well with the meal tonight," Callan said.

"No problems." Damien turned, then halted. "Can I ask you something?"

Callan stopped what he'd been doing with his eyebrows raised and a friendly grin. "Of course. What is it?"

"Are we staying out of villages because of me?"

Damien still couldn't even remember what had happened. They'd entered Callenhain, he'd become confused, then nothing. Even though Olivia hadn't seemed concerned when he'd admitted the memory loss, he couldn't help but worry.

Callan shook his head. "Don't beat yourself up. The Warlord requested we patrol the edges of the Heights. It's sparsely populated here compared to the territory along the river. We'll get to a village tomorrow, all going well."

By his reckoning, it had been nearly a week since they'd left Callenhain, so Damien was not sure if he believed the reason, even if the explanation was plausible.

Since the camp was all in order that left him at a bit of a loss with what he should do between now and dinner. Although he guessed it was a good thing since it meant he was adjusting to his new routine. It had taken him a lot longer than expected to fall into the pattern of his new companions. He'd been relieved to find out he didn't have to get up at the crack of dawn every day to ride out. It was about mid-morning before they all roused and got going for the day. He didn't understand it, particularly since in the brief time they'd ridden in company with the Warlord they all seemed to be up and moving early.

Yet somehow, they seemed to catch up on the road even if they got a later start. It was obvious all these people, his squad mates now, had ridden with each other for a long time. When they made camp in the late afternoon, there were no shouted orders, confusion, or anyone who didn't know the routine—other than him.

He'd caught on slowly. Others would finish their tasks, then come over to help him finish setting up his own sleeping arrangements. Still, he'd finally refined setting up his own camp space, taking his cues from the rest of the band. Without fanfare, he took on the chore of gathering wood for the fires and hunting small animals for fresh meat. And the edible leaves, herbs, and fungi that he collected to complement the evening meals for the self-appointed cooks earned him a grudging approval from everyone, not just those who cooked.

Damien had been so confused when he'd first been claimed by the Warlord. It had taken him some time to work out that the Unwanted did not normally ride with the Warlord. That was the job of the other two warbands. While those around the Warlord had a certain amount of prestige, it became clear they weren't necessarily the best. Not really. He leant that Michael's band was the one that led. It was Michael who was treated with deference, the warleader who everyone listened to. Even the Warlord.

When a group of the Unwanted walked past, everyone noticed them. He'd seen the looks cast their way by the others, heard the whispers. Within the ranks of the Unwanted, they possessed some of the strongest practitioners of the veil, some of the best swordsmen and hunters. They were a close group, and he wondered how long it would take before he really would be considered to be one of them in more than name.

Michael, Olivia, and Nathanial were on the other side of the camp, their heads together, deep in conversation. It made him wonder if they would move on tomorrow. The position of the sun told him he had an hour before it set. He stood, undecided what he should do. Olivia and Nathanial usually partnered him for sword training, but he could see they were both busy.

Finally, he shrugged and walked to one side of the camp. Taking a deep breath, he settled himself, then drew his sword. Picturing opponents, he practiced the strikes and blocks they'd been trying to train him in. He'd been better with the blade than any other of his age in his village. In this company, he was the one that would get them killed. He was the weak link in a well-aligned and functioning fighting unit and it was something he was determined to change. If he was going to be forced to live this life, then he would become one of their best.

Damien didn't know how long he'd been practicing before he realised he was being observed by someone who was close by. Finishing his last sweeping manoeuvre with the sword, ending in a block, he drew himself into a standing position, sword in front of his face, then sheathed it. Finally, he turned and was surprised to see Aiden.

Aiden Olenna of Yalleska, the Warlord's son.

Damien hadn't known what to think since he'd been told who Aiden was. Yet even though there was a part of his brain that urged caution, he paused. Aiden was probably trying to be friendly. At least that was what he thought—he couldn't think of any other reason Aiden would approach him.

"I'm sorry, Aiden. I just decided I'd get some practice in. What do you need?"

"Nothing. You were practicing by yourself and, since Olivia's busy, I thought you could use a little more instruction. You have those moves down. Ready to learn a few more?" Aiden grinned at him.

"Thanks. If you think I'm ready." Despite his reservations, Damien grinned back.

Damien stepped back as Aiden joined him in his improvised training circle. He tried to ignore that their interaction had gained the attention of some of the Unwanted, who drew closer to watch.

"Move back outside the circle and watch with your othersight. You know how to use your othersight, right?"

Damien backed out of the circle, embarrassed that Aiden had needed to ask that question. He concentrated as he switched to his othersight. The world around him was overlain with the patterns of power, tracing from everything around him. The glow of power coming from Aiden made him swallow nervously. Finally, he realised Aiden was obviously waiting for some sort of response.

"Ah, sorry, ready." Damien smiled.

An expression flickered across Aiden's face that he couldn't quite decipher. He watched, fascinated, since he guessed the lesson was going to involve using the veil as well. That was something the others hadn't touched on yet.

"I'm going to run through the moves you were just practicing. However, I'll use the veil as well. These techniques are how we've gained the edge over the Sylannian raiders. It's why we're faster and stronger. So, observe carefully." Aiden looked at him expectantly.

Damien flushed, then withdrew his own blade, flicking it up in front of his face in a much more practiced move than he'd been able to manage so far.

Damien's eyes widened as he watched Aiden with his othersight. The wisps of grey power that drifted and emanated from everything around them suddenly focused and tracked to Aiden as if he was sucking in the veil from around him. As he watched, Aiden glowed. The power seemed to pulse through Aiden's arms and legs, as if he was channelling the veil to various body parts. As interesting as he found it, Damien couldn't think of why Aiden was doing so. Then it occurred to him that the store of energy within Aiden didn't seem to diminish, regardless of how much power he used.

Damien shook himself as he realised Aiden had finished

running through the practice routine. He sheathed his sword in the same smooth motion he'd drawn it and flushed, wondering if Aiden had noticed his hesitation.

"Come, Damien. You can do this." Aiden held out his hand.

Damien smiled uncertainly and walked into the training circle as Aiden moved to stand behind him and, without warning, grabbed his head in a vice-like grip. Damien stiffened in shock. Aiden's mindvoice whispered in his head.

Relax... this is what you need to do.

Damien froze as a series of images and words hammered into his brain. His breath caught as pain lanced through his whole body. His legs buckled, and he fell to the ground. Still, the instructions forced their way into his head and there was nothing he could do to stop the onslaught of images and words, or the pain that accompanied the instructions.

Damien felt a part of his brain pause, like it was disassociated from the rest of him. *Instructions.* The flood of words, feelings, and images were instructions. Right now, he didn't have the capacity to work out what it was Aiden was shoving at him. Although in the future he'd be very careful about allowing anyone else to get behind him, grasp his temples in their hands and invade his head. All he had to work out was how to stop it.

Damn it, Aiden, enough! You'll kill the lad.

Damien fancied that was Michael's voice, and suddenly a mind imposed itself between him and the onslaught. Aiden's hands lost their grip on his head. Pain exploded and Damien toppled forward, the hard ground against his skin before the darkness consumed his vision and he knew nothing more.

THIRTY-FOUR

Jaclyn stood at the large windows, which at this time of morning had a peaceful view out over the water. Her long-layered silks fluttered around her legs as the cool breeze wafted through, or as cool as it got here in the central islands that made up Sylanna. She sighed, wondering if this was the last time she would stand here in her favourite place in her court.

"I wish there was another way."

Ricardo walked into the room behind her and wrapped his arms around her. She rested her head against his chest. The whisper of fabric and soft footfalls told her that some of her fellow wives had also entered the room.

"As do I, but I see no other option," she said.

A wave of remorse washed over her from Ricardo as he moved, and she turned to find he knelt next to her, head bowed.

"I'm sorry. I promised I wouldn't take unnecessary risks with the freedom you grant me." Ricardo paused, his head rose to reveal the pain in his eyes. "But when our children were under attack, I couldn't help myself."

Jaclyn recognised the submissive position. Ricardo was waiting for her to once more claim his mind. To crush his will. She swallowed as the ghost of the past reared in her mind. She would not risk Ricardo or her house. When she'd fled her mother's court, she'd run straight to Ricardo. He was of age and was being introduced to prospective wives. The choice of firstwife was one of the first and last choices a male could make. She'd begged him to accept her.

She sank to her knees and pressed herself against him. "I'll not compel you that way. It is a sickness in our people, sending us to madness and death. As my mother's daughter, I'll not do that to you. To us." Jaclyn meet Ricardo's eyes, her hand brushing aside a lock of his hair. "I should have stayed behind the daggerwives as well, but I did not. Fighting all these years has changed us."

She saw hope in his eyes, mixed with pride and love singing from his mind. Ricardo wrapped his arms around her, tipping his head as he kissed her. The heat and desire rolling from Ricardo as she responded to him. As much as she wished otherwise, it was not her fertile time. It was her husband's duty to mate with one of his wives who could conceive a child. Not one who couldn't, firstwife or otherwise. No matter how enjoyable the experience might be.

"You started changing, defying custom, when you ran from your mother's court all those years ago. I defied custom when I promised you the sanctuary of the mate bond. It's a decision I don't regret." Ricardo's tone was solemn, his lips curving into a soft smile as he gazed at her.

Jaclyn leant against Ricardo as she thought back to the moment that seemed like almost a lifetime ago. A moment in her history that defied centuries of custom. A moment that should not have occurred.

"The first year of my brother's rule, I thought things would be different."

"We all did. Even Samuel."

Jaclyn smiled and pressed her head against his chest. She'd been so young back then, running to save her life. Ricardo was her older brother's friend. He had been about to be mate-bonded to another, but had accepted her plea for him to accept her instead. It had saved her life when her brother and his wives had made their play for the throne.

Her brother's wives weren't happy when they discovered she'd survived. At first Samuel had seemed unconcerned and actively blocked his wives attempts to remedy the oversight, but then, something changed. Samuel changed. Then it had been the mate bond between her and Ricardo that stood like a shield between her and her brother. If they'd killed her, it might very well have taken Ricardo with her. It was one thing to kill the girl child of a mad monarch. Another to kill a rare, pure Sylannian male, of high birth. Of course, as time passed, not even that seemed to hold back her brother's blades.

Content in his arms, it didn't stop her from turning her mind towards the current conflict facing them, rather than the past.

"This fight with the barbarians is different," she said.

It hadn't taken long for her to hear about the campaign against the barbarians. Unlike their war with the traders, the barbarians were on a whole different fighting level. With the losses they'd suffered in this campaign, the other houses had taken it upon themselves to apprise her of their failures. It was this kind of manoeuvring that had prompted her brother to attempt to get rid of her. He was a lot of things, but blind to the political dance of the core houses wasn't one of them.

Yet despite their losses, the Monarch House persisted in trying to expand their territory out to the barbarian lands. Against all logic, the self-styled Warlord who ruled the lands, and those who fought for him, were strong in their use of powers in the "veil"—a term that had taken off among her own people. The power, at least for those who were stronger, appeared like strands of sheer lace, twisting and fluttering in an elemental breeze. The lands claimed by the Warlord had riches, arable land aplenty, and unlike her own people, men. So many men. Their best calculations put the numbers as equal to the female population here in Sylanna. It seemed out of all the others they'd encountered to date, only in their own society were men a rarity. No one, when the Monarch House in her mother's era had ordered the expansion of their territory out into the barbarian lands, would ever have believed that one day not only would they be beaten back, they would lose.

Oh, the campaign had gone as expected to start with in her mother's time. They'd gained valuable farming land and men. Then inexplicably they'd started losing. If anything, it hastened her mother's madness. After her brother had claimed the throne, the most shocking and unbelievable circumstances had occurred, their losses accelerated. Their raiding parties had gone missing, one after the other, time and time again. When survivors finally made it back, they told of a Warlord who'd risen to challenge them. Unbelievably, he'd beaten them back, killed or taken the daggerwives for himself.

At first, they'd assumed the tales were exaggerated. These unorganised, wild barbarians could not possibly fight against them. They couldn't be stronger in using power than they were. At least, that was what her brother and his wives in their arrogance believed. Yet somehow, they were, and still the Monarch House would not withdraw.

That more women were born than men in Sylanna was

something that they'd not realised was an oddity until they started expanding into other territories. As one of the great families of Sylanna, Jaclyn was firstwife in a house of two primes, twenty seconds and more daggerwives than she cared to keep track of. The Monarch House had closer to a hundred secondwives alone, as impractical as that was. With the number of daggerwives her own family housed, most would never share a bed with Ricardo. The bulk of the daggerwives of the Monarch House would go from daggerwife to underwife without ever having the chance to mate with the king to bear a child to the house.

It didn't matter that other lands with easier pickings existed. She'd even won the trader lands for her people in the intervening time, yet still the incursions into the barbarian lands persisted. So, it came to this: the day they ordered her house to go into the barbarian lands to take land, resources and perhaps a few likely specimens for the breeding house, all for the glory of the Monarch House.

This order meant the end of Jaclyn's house. Throwing away their lives over pride for land and space they no longer needed.

"We could call in the sister houses to help."

Jaclyn stiffened. Tracy, one of the daggerwives. She was a sweet enough girl on the surface, but not good at seeing the tactical side of situations. She also suspected the woman was one of her brother's spies. It was Ricardo who spoke, although he didn't so much as turn his head to his daggerwife.

"What, and lead them to their deaths right alongside ours?"

"The Monarch House would not allow our sister houses to join us, Tracy." Bethany, while a daggerwife like Tracy, had a much better grasp of their current position.

The screens being drawn back behind her, and a soft measured footfall with the rustle of fabric gave way to the arrival of one of the other wives. Jaclyn smiled. She'd know Myra anywhere. She'd been elevated to primewife to Ricardo when she'd fallen pregnant and then given birth to the second son born to the house. It was only a year after Jaclyn had given birth to her first son, Thomas, when her house had been newly formed. Her house had been exiled to fight in the trader lands shortly after that. Her youngest son had been conceived and born on foreign soil.

"This latest manoeuvre is political." Myra's voice was soft, but scathing.

She'd obviously overheard enough of the conversation to understand its context. She also couldn't abide fools, and her opinion of Tracy was one that they both shared. Ricardo thankfully shared their apathy towards the woman.

"I don't understand. Surely the Monarch House would approve of any measure that gave us an advantage against the savages," Tracy said.

"This attack isn't about winning. This is a rather expedient way for Samuel to dispose of us." Jaclyn refrained from sighing.

"But why would the Monarch House want that? Jaclyn is a daughter of the Monarch House, sister to the king." Tracy sounded confused.

Jaclyn's eyebrows rose. She couldn't work out if Tracy really was that deluded about the Monarch House or if she was dissembling. Jaclyn pushed the traitor from her mind. She had other things to think about. Although the traitor in their ranks would need to die, doing so now before they left would be pointless. Her brother would just place another in her house who was loyal to him rather than her.

Myra walked across the room, the rustle of fabric giving away the fact that the others made way for her. She came to a halt on the other side of Ricardo.

We will send Liliana and the children on their way to safety this night? Myra's mindvoice was soft and for the two of them alone.

It's time. Before my brother gets impatient and tries again.

When they'd been sent to the trader lands, she, Ricardo and Myra had held their own war council. As a contingency, for the survival of their house, they'd sent a core group of the wives to build a haven in the uninhabited hinterlands at the edge of their own home islands. Now, with Samuel's latest move, they would send Liliana and the children to join them. She could not trust the Monarch House to allow any of hers to survive. Not even the youngest of the girl children.

We could take the Monarch House, Myra said.

No. Jaclyn squeezed her eyes shut, although it did nothing against the memory of the blood spilled that night her brother had taken the throne.

They are showing signs of madness, Ricardo whispered, as if against his will.

No. I remember the madness the night my brother wrested control of the Monarch House. He's not there. Not yet, Jaclyn said.

She was certain the day would come, but it wasn't today. For now, she'd do as the Monarch House ordered.

THIRTY-FIVE

Damien realised he was awake and almost as that realisation hit him, he decided he really didn't want to open his eyes or move. His head pounded, although he couldn't remember what it was he must have done to cause it.

"Kesha, he's awake."

Damien winced as the voice reverberated in his head. It was difficult to be certain, but he thought it was Michael who spoke. Except he couldn't quite work out why Michael would sit near his hammock. As the wood creaked, and the surface under him dipped, he realised he was in a bed. Warm hands placed themselves on his temples, his eyes flared open, and his breath caught. Although he didn't understand why that simple touch made him panic. As light lanced into his eyes, he groaned and squeezed them shut.

It's all right, you're safe. My name is Kesha. I'm a healer. I'm just going to ease your headache.

As the sense of wrongness hit him, an instinctual part of his brain screamed at him. Damien's powers coiled up inside him to respond and strike back at the other person in his mind. Then he became aware that the pounding in his head was receding and his muscles relaxed. All at the will of another. Damien battled with himself to stay calm. Even the knowledge that Kesha was trying to help him did not make it easy to ignore the instinct to push the stranger out of his mind.

This is just my skill. Just try to relax. I'm not trying to hurt you, Kesha said.

It was easy enough for Kesha to tell him to relax, but since he didn't know her and she was in his head, there was the other side of his brain that insisted it was a bad idea.

"Calm down, Damien, you were hurt. Thankfully, we were close to Ardkadia. Kesha is an exceptional healer," Michael said.

Somehow, his warleader's words caused him to relax—or at least try to. At some point, he realised he wasn't in pain anymore. He sighed and opened his eyes. It took a moment for him to realise it wasn't the slip of canvas over his hammock above him, but wooden beams and a thatched ceiling. Damien wondered idly why it seemed important that it was a roof rather than canvas. Then he remembered. One rapid-fire memory hitting the front of his brain after the other. They were in the middle of nowhere. He'd set up his camp, done his chores, then gone to do some training. Then Aiden gave him some instruction. Hands clamped onto his head and a flood of images and instructions being shoved into his mind. Then darkness. He could hear heavy breathing, then realised it was his own. Finally, he rolled his head to the side. He'd been correct, it was Michael who stood nearby. Taking another breath, he turned his attention to the person sitting on the edge of the bed he was lying on.

Kesha.

His mind recognised her, even though this was the first

time he'd set eyes on the woman. Her power differed from his own. Yet she was powerful. He wondered how she wasn't already a member of the Warlord's ranks. Except her people had been better at hiding her, taking her away to hide in the forest until the threat passed, until now. Normally, the villages closest to them would send a runner to warn them a warband was on its way. Damien frowned, wondering how he was privy to that information. Immediately guilt assailed him as he realised he was the one who'd brought Kesha to attention. He felt her sudden shock and the realisation that he was getting more information about her than she wanted. A mind barrier reinserted itself between them and the flow of information cut off.

Damien pushed his confusion aside and focused on Kesha again. She was one of those rare breeds who could heal—not just minor aches and pains, but really heal. They hadn't had such a one in his own village, but Karl, from a neighbouring village, had such a talent and paid them regular visits. Not that Damien had ever needed that kind of attention. The problems he'd had weren't the kind a healer could fix. Karl had travelled from village to village with his own escort whose only job seemed to be to keep him safe. It was a valuable skill that very few had. What he sensed in Kesha was far greater ability than the talent Karl had possessed.

"Thank you. Sorry if I caused you problems." Damien's voice was barely above a whisper.

Her eyes crinkled. "You have nothing to apologise for. It is an unnerving thing to allow another into your mind. Particularly after what you've been through."

Damien stretched and rolled onto his side, but had no inclination to go any further, his eyes settling on Michael.

"What happened?" His eyes narrowed as an image of the

training ring flashed through his mind. "What did Aiden do to me?"

Michael's head ducked, and he took a breath. That unnerved Damien more than anything, and he wished Michael would just come out and tell him what had happened. Michael nodded, as if he could hear his inner monologue. Damien winced as he realised he probably had. He really did need to spend more time working on his mental shields, back in Ranlith he'd thought it was a skill he was good at. As he'd found out, it was as unreliable as his powers. He was suddenly aware that right now it was the healer, Kesha, who was keeping everyone else out of his head.

"He dumped a lifetime's worth of combat training into your head." Michael grabbed a wooden chair and dragged it across the room to the other side of his bed and sat on it.

"Why would he do that? I'm thinking if this was a good way to teach skills, we wouldn't do drills or even schooling like I did in the village," Damian said.

Kesha's hand gently rested on his shoulder. "You are correct. It is not a good way to learn anything. In fact, it nearly killed you. If Michael hadn't intervened and you hadn't been close enough to be brought to me for healing, it might have."

"I'm sorry. I should have been paying closer attention. If I'd known what Aiden intended, I would never have allowed him anywhere near you," Michael said.

Damien closed his eyes, fatigue weighing him down, even though he'd just woken up.

"I think I would have preferred to learn the normal way. It doesn't feel like I know any more than I did before this." Damien alternated his gaze between Kesha and Michael.

Michael shook his head. "It rarely manifests until you need it. So, under attack, you'll suddenly use advanced sword skills that you've never practiced. Maybe. It can't be relied on."

Damien considered what Michael had told him for a moment. "So I'd better not get lazy. I need to learn it all myself."

"It's best, but not today. You need to rest," Michael said.

"I just woke up." Damien protested, even if he didn't feel like it.

"Healing is tiring business. Both for me and for the person being healed." Kesha's hands rested lightly on his forehead.

Now rest, Kesha ordered.

Unable to resist the healer's compulsion, he drifted off into darkness.

THIRTY-SIX

Tarkhan turned from where he stood near the horses with some of the other leaders and grinned at his co-leader Khaliun following Erden out of his tent. At least the two of them had entertained themselves while keeping warm together last night.

"I think when we all resettle, we might want to give consideration to our respective tribes being close together." Orghana's voice rippled with amusement.

Tarkhan grinned. "You could be right. It will make it easier when one or the other of us must track down our co-leader."

Tarkhan mounted, along with the other tribe leaders of the clan. They all waited as Khaliun and Erden swung into their saddles with long, practiced ease. It was cold enough that their breath formed visible plumes as it expelled into the air. The sight made Tarkhan shudder, wondering how long they'd be out in the cold. Although he had to admit it was far more bearable than it would have been. Particularly since those in charge of the stores here in their makeshift camp had provided them with warmer, lined riding gear, along with fur-lined gloves and thick cloaks. While the tops were thin enough that they could still wear their hide protective gear, it was much warmer than their original gear they had from the plains.

Tarkhan was surprised by the easy pace they maintained on their ride to travel to the vantage point, to observe the potential land they would take for their clan. So, he guessed they weren't travelling very far.

"We'll be back in camp by midday," Khaliun reassured him.

Tarkhan didn't need to ask where she'd received her information from. He gathered he'd been leaking enough that she'd caught enough to understand what he'd been thinking. Khaliun was a much stronger mindspeaker than he was. He did not know how she coped with everyone's constant chatter in her head.

"Sorry."

He genuinely wished he had the capability, like she did. Tarkhan had nightmares that one day a stray thought from him would lead to the death of not only his tribe but their entire clan.

"It's not like that, and you are much more controlled when you focus. Which you always are when we go into battle." Khaliun shook her head, a smile touching her lips.

"She's right, as always. You're only leaking now because, after recent events, this is a relaxed ride. The first in quite some time." Erden grinned at him.

"Besides. There isn't anyone around up here besides us." Orghana shrugged.

Tarkhan's face heated as he realised that they'd obviously scanned their surrounds while he'd been reacting like they were going for a casual ride. He shook himself and straightened in his saddle; this wasn't the time to lose track of the situation they were in the middle of. If he didn't focus, he could get their people killed.

Relax, allow others to lift the load for today, Khaliun said.

You've been in the same situation as me, yet you didn't forget to check our surroundings.

I had the night off; a very relaxing evening that had nothing to do with death. I'd warrant you spent the bulk of the night worrying about the fate of not only our tribe, but the Kallith Clan.

Listen to her, Tarkhan, and relax. The rest of us have been here longer, and I fear this respite will be brief. Erden's voice was calm, without even a hint of criticism.

I have outriders out along our path. Relax, my friend. My clan has had months to prepare. There's no one up here but us. Ulagan appeared unconcerned not only in his mind tone but in his saddle as well.

Tarkhan didn't know if he should be embarrassed he'd been projecting that much, or grateful that his fellow leaders had his back. Khaliun and, it seemed, his fellow leaders were familiar with his ways. He'd wrestled with the fate of not only his own tribe, but the entire clan last night. The weight of that responsibility meant he'd had a restless sleep despite his exhaustion.

He took a deep breath and stopped wrestling with himself, reining in his horse to drop back to the middle of the pack. He'd trust the others to take the lead this day; trust the outriders Ulagan had sent out in advance; trust the advice that they were the only ones foolish enough to be up here in the Heights during the onset of winter. He'd do what he hadn't done since he'd been a small boy within his clan: enjoy the ride. Even if it was freezing.

SOMEHOW, letting his mind wander had the effect of them arriving at their destination without him having been aware of the time that had passed or the path they'd taken to get here. Tarkhan shook himself back to the present and dismounted, thankful he was only a moment after the others.

He realised they were at a vantage point that afforded them an admittedly spectacular view over a vast plain. Although one that differed vastly from their own former homeland. He walked to the edge, confident no one below could make out the tiny speck he would seem to be to their eyes. There was the downslope of the mountain, merging from harsh and barren to shrubs dotting the cliffs. Then the land flattened, a vast jungle spread out with clearings and a broad river to one side. Whole swaths of the jungle pushed back to reveal villages and clearings that he guessed were crops. While the land was obviously inhabited, he could see that other than one small cluster of houses, far down a small tributary of the river, the undulating hills that ran off the tall peaks of the Heights had no occupants.

Tarkhan smiled. Those hills were much more pleasant than the Heights where they were currently camped. He could see instantly that while those rolling hills differed from their homeland, the People could thrive there. Herds could roam, crops grow, the clan could continue to wander in this expanse. Better yet, there was a broad section of jungle between the lowland hills and the nearest village, with only a few small tributaries leading back to that main river where the bulk of life seemed to be concentrated.

He and Khaliun shared a smile. He turned his head to the others and nodded his acceptance to the other leaders. For the first time in what seemed like a lifetime, there was hope for his people.

CHAPTER

THIRTY-SEVEN

Michael waited long enough for Damien to drift off to sleep before he spoke.

"His abilities might fluctuate, but he's powerful. Are you sure you can manage if he wakes and panics?" Michael asked.

"It was always that first moment after what happened to him that would have been problematic. He knows me now. I'll be fine," Kesha assured him.

"You weren't here the last time we came through this village," Michael said, keeping his voice low.

"I travel around the surrounding villages to help as many as possible." Kesha smiled.

"You mean you normally get enough early warning that we are coming, and your village ensures you aren't here?" Michael's eyebrows rose.

"Well, that too." Kesha gazed back at him calmly.

"I'm glad, for Damien's sake, you were here this time."

"I judge he would have recovered without my aid to soothe the pounding in his head," Kesha said.

"Although it would have taken much longer, and he probably would have been wishing we'd let him die," Michael said.

"In that, I have no doubt you are correct. Damien is also much better off recovering here, where I can monitor him, than out in the elements. Now go. My patient needs to rest." Kesha fluttered her hands at him, shooing him towards the door.

As Michael walked out of the healer's hut, his gaze tracked across the village and found Aiden. Anger, seething just below carefully enforced shields, reared its head. He could tell by the sudden rise in tension and people making themselves scarce that his shield wasn't all that effective right now. A rumble rolled out with him at its centre. Not even the reaction of the villagers who looked up at the clear blue skies in confusion caused his anger to abate. Aiden, lazing in the middle of their camp, suddenly became aware of his approach and stood, turning to stare at him. Michael was close enough to see the colour drain from Aiden's face as the man suddenly realised he was the object of the anger. The ominous rumble sounded again as the veil reflected what he was feeling. Michael grabbed Aiden and slammed him into a tree trunk. It occurred to him he'd covered a remarkable amount of distance in next to no time, but he dismissed it as something to think of later. His forearm pressed against Aiden's throat with his powers easily shunting aside the feeble attempts by the Warlord's son to fight back. The very air around him was charged, threads of power thickening by the moment in response.

He was aware of Olivia and Nathanial placing themselves between him and a couple of Aiden's people who'd attempted to go to Aiden's assistance. At the dual surge of power and a thud followed by groaning behind him Michael smiled coldly. The rest of his people stood watching, yet none intervened.

"If you ever try your mind-raping game with any of my

people again, I will end your miserable existence," Michael grated.

"I was trying to help," Aiden choked.

"Don't lie, Aiden."

"I was...it was your abilities I shoved into his head." Aiden's gaze darted around the assembled members.

"My powers aren't fluctuating as they were when I was a boy. Never try that little trick on me again, either."

"I didn't know what would happen to you back then. You have your skills. I have mine. I...I really believed I'd perfected the technique this time."

"Stay out of Damien's head. His powers will settle, and I judge he'll be much stronger than you. He won't appreciate your mind games either." Michael shoved Aiden aside. "Get out of my sight."

The scramble behind him and the spurt of fear threaded through with anger and relief signalled Aiden had fled.

There had been a time when Aiden, a few years his senior, had been stronger than he was in both the mental and physical aspects of their talent. Even when the Warlord had first claimed him and called him son, he'd been old enough to understand that Aiden could cause significant problems if he wanted to. So he'd tried to make friends. Before he'd risen through the ranks to command, he'd attempted to find common ground with Aiden. After years of being snubbed and pushed aside, Aiden had suddenly been friendly. It was only much later Michael realised that should have been a tipoff that something was up.

Aiden had taken him by surprise back then, invading his mind, forcing a deep connection between them. Leeching his memories from him. Michael remembered little else of that moment except the fear and pain before darkness had claimed him. There had been no one to intervene on his behalf.

The Warlord told him later they'd found him and Aiden unconscious and close to death on the training grounds of the stronghold. Their minds were in a deep state of shock. The Warlord had dragged a healer from Yalleska village to treat them both. Michael wasn't sure if anyone else had worked out what Aiden had done, or tried to do, but once he'd recovered, and memories of the incident had returned, he understood what his "brother" had intended.

Our brother was always a scheming little bastard, trying to take rather than work hard, Olivia said.

It seems to be a thing with brothers. Michael was disgusted.

They both seem to have some traits in common, but I was thinking of Aiden on this occasion. There was a hint of amusement in Olivia's tone.

I don't for a moment believe Aiden was trying to help, Michael said.

He's been trying to ingratiate himself with Damien of late. Olivia frowned.

Well, the lad is hardly likely to trust him in a hurry after what he's done. Michael allowed his fury to recede to a simmer.

We'll keep a closer eye on Aiden. Nathanial's tone was firm as he and Callan stared in the direction that Aiden had retreated, their eyes hard.

Stick to Damien. Make sure that if he turns to anyone, it is the pair of you. Michael shook his head.

He carefully didn't turn to look where Aiden had scampered off. The risk of his temper getting the better of him was too high. For now, with everyone alert, they would make it their business to keep track of where Aiden was and what he was up to, particularly around their recruit. He smiled. He did not need to count heads to work out that some of them had already made it their business to follow the man.

~

Damien concentrated as he deflected a flurry of blows from Michael. Michael didn't trust anyone else to train opposite Damien now. He'd explained it was dangerous because of what Aiden had done—he could go from bumbling through basic strokes one moment to an expert the next.

Damien's breath caught as strangeness washed over him, and before he could issue a warning, he was shoved aside. An observer in his head. He was drawing in more power than ever, and in a role-reversal, it was suddenly Michael backing up and on the defensive. The speed of their fight increased as Michael stepped up to a different level of swordsmanship, answering his barrage with ease.

Damien gasped and stumbled as that other suddenly faded, and he ended up back in control again, desperately raising his sword to counter Michael's.

"Hold!"

In time with Olivia's command, power wrapped around Damien, hauling him away from Michael's blade. Even so, the sword stopped within a hair of his throat. He fell, landing on his back, staring up at Michael. Tension drained from him and the grip on his sword loosened, although he did not let go as he would have once. Now that he had stopped, he sucked in air. He closed his eyes briefly while he gathered himself, then opened them to find Michael's hand in front of him. He grabbed it and allowed Michael to help him up.

"Thanks. I hate it when that happens. It's like someone has pushed me aside and taken over my mind," Damien growled.

"You'll get there." Michael clapped him on the shoulder. "It probably doesn't seem like it to you but you're already much better. Give yourself time."

Damien was content to walk in silence as they went back

towards the open paved area to the side of the village they'd stopped in. It had readymade fire pits, making it the ideal place for their field kitchen and the natural gathering point. While everyone appeared engaged with other tasks, they'd all been watching his training session with Michael. They always did. Not that it bothered him, he just didn't know what they all were all thinking.

While Aiden had apologised, saying he'd only been trying to help, to speed up his learning, which would be good for all of them, including himself, he wished Aiden hadn't done it. The feeling when that other memory rose in his mind, taking over, was disconcerting. It was usually even worse when it left him. Although he dared not admit it, he feared he'd be driven mad.

Walking over to the pot to one side of the fire, Damien closed his eyes and breathed in the strong, nutty aroma of the kaf. He noticed it was Nathanial who was tending the kitchen that morning and paused, raising his eyebrow.

"Go ahead. It's freshly brewed," Nathanial said.

He suspected the man had watched his training sessions and judged when to have the kaf ready.

Taking a mug from the pile, Damien took a ladle, poured some steaming black liquid into the cup, and handed it to Michael. Michael smiled in appreciation and walked over to sit on a nearby bench. Damien filled one more mug with kaf and a second with water and brought them over to the table, placing the kaf in front of Olivia, who'd fetched them all a small platter of bread, cold meats, cheese and fruits for breakfast.

Damien sipped his water. Then he picked at the food on the platter. He had to eat but he struggled after those memories surged in his head that way. It was always the same. It left him sluggish afterwards, wanting nothing more than to lie back in his hammock and sleep for a few hours. His eyes flicked around his squad mates, who sat quietly, trying to pretend they weren't watching the three of them.

So, when do you think they'll stop waiting for me to go mad?

Michael's and Olivia's eyes flicked up to him and Michael shook his head.

Try to ignore it. The more days that go past without you going psychotic, the less they will worry.

Damien chuckled. *Thanks. I think.* He sobered. *It doesn't help that even I keep wondering when I'm going to go mad.*

Michael's eyes caught his own, conveying sympathy and understanding.

You're strong, and you will recover. Go sleep it off. You'll feel better when you do.

Damien didn't miss the note of command in Michael's tone. He finished his water with one swallow, pushed the plate of bread, cheese and meat towards the others and retreated towards the sleeping area. If Michael had ordered him to sleep, it must mean they were staying here one more night. No matter how much he tried, he couldn't work out the warband's travel pattern. He nearly stopped in his tracks, and he would have, if it were possible, smacked himself on the back of his head.

That was the point.

They didn't follow a pattern. Day after day of travel in succession, then a couple of days in one place, three in another. Riding through one village to spend the night in a rough camp, then stopping in another town. To an outsider, their progress would be hard to predict and report.

It took you long enough. Now go and sleep!

Damien chuckled as he grabbed his tonic and gulped a couple of large mouthfuls. He'd been grateful when he discovered a flask in the bag his mother had packed for him as well as a pouch stuffed with the leaves. The vines that produced the leaves were familiar enough in these parts. In the late afternoon, when he foraged for the evening meal, he gathered more of the herb at the same time. He frowned at the bottle, realising he'd have to find time to brew some more. He usually kept his intake to a minimum during the day since more than a sip would leave him in a state incapable of much except resting, but since they were staying put, for now it would ease the pain in his head and help him sleep. Placing the flask safely back in his saddlebag, he lay back on his hammock, not even taking time to unlace his vest and drag off his boots. He bit his lip against the expected stab of pain that hit first, allowing it to ride over his body, then smiled as a spike of euphoria from his tonic chased the pain away. It soothed his fears and discomforting thoughts away, leaving him feeling like he was floating before the darkness of sleep claimed him.

THIRTY-EIGHT

Jaclyn walked through the darkened, wide-open room towards the balcony with her family. The underwives carried the children in the protective centre, surrounded by the rest. Even here, in their own sprawling home, they would not take risks, not even to will the veil to light their path. If light shone from their windows, any spies would see it. So, they moved with only the glow of moonlight streaming through the shutters. They stole through the house quietly, as if they were in territory at the enemy's heart. Shunning the lift platform, they turned along the balcony and, keeping to the shadows, made their way to the steps down the far end. Jaclyn jumped over the wooden barrier, using just a breath of power to soften her landing on the boat platform below. Hearing a noise, she spun, crouched, daggers drawn. She sprinted towards the ones keeping watch at the end of the jetty.

Aware that Myra and Ricardo ran with her, she closed in on those she guessed were spying for her brother. There was no chance at all that any of those prying eyes would survive this night to report to the king that she had sent the rest of the children of the house to safety. She vowed, if it was at all possible, to survive and reunite her family. Until that day, she had a job to do. Seeing one of those running away turn and dive into the river, Jaclyn sheathed her daggers and increased her pace, then leapt off the end, diving smoothly into the water.

Jaclyn pulled the veil's power to her and used it to push herself forward as she swam after the woman who was trying to flee. The woman, no doubt one of Samuel's lesser wives, spun to face her just before Jaclyn closed on her. Buffeted by the other's feeble power, Jaclyn drew one of her knives while latching onto her adversary with her free hand. Her own power slammed into the woman and they both breached the surface of the river, Jaclyn's powers propelling them out of the water. Jaclyn snarled and hauled the other woman to her. At a surge of energy from Liliana watching from the jetty, Jaclyn grinned as the woman's armour reverted to soft silk. Without waiting, she plunged her dagger into her opponent's abdomen, curving up. The moment where her blade began to penetrate the physical barrier of her opponents armour, the reverberations and pitch of her enemies spidersilk changed to a scream, then cut off abruptly as her knife broke through and pierced her enemy's heart. Her brother's wife gasped, grasping at her hand before her arms dropped away. She slid bonelessly off Jaclyn's blade and back into the depths of the river.

Jaclyn released the power she held enough to slide back into the depths of the river herself, allowing the water to wash away the blood as it slid past her, and swam with easy strokes back to the jetty. Ricardo's hand grasped her own as she reached the edge and he helped haul her back onto the landing.

Myra stood nearby hugging her small son before handing him down to an underwife in the boat. Jaclyn bit her lip and blinked moisture from her eyes as Carlos, her youngest son, was fast asleep in Liliana's arms. The underwife next to Liliana held Thomas. All the others were loaded onto the boat. Jaclyn gathered Thomas into her arms and hugged him fiercely.

Mama, must I go? Thomas whispered, a slight tremor in his mindvoice.

You must be brave, my son. Listen to Liliana and the underwives. Grow up big and strong with your brothers and sisters. Live and defend your family. Jaclyn passed him back to a waiting underwife, who gathered the child to her and stepped down into the centre of the waiting boat.

Jaclyn pulled Liliana into her arms and hugged her, sending a hope out into the veil that this wouldn't be the last time she saw her. She then leant forward and kissed Carlos on the forehead. Although Jaclyn wanted to take him and hug him, she also didn't want to disturb his sleep and potentially make him cry. Jaclyn stepped back and caught the other woman's eye.

"Let the underwives take care of you and our unborn one, Liliana. We give our sons and daughters, the lifeblood of our house, to your care," Jaclyn whispered.

Her fellow wife was still conflicted, understanding she must go but wanting to join her fate with the rest of the family. Ricardo stepped forward and wrapped his own arms around Liliana, and hugged her before gently kissing their sleeping son.

"Go, protect all our children. While they survive, our house survives." Ricardo stepped back to be replaced by Myra.

"Stay alive. All of you, or I swear I will hunt you all in the veil when it is my time," Myra said, handing her son to the waiting arms of an underwife and embraced Liliana.

Liliana turned and stepped onto the boat, taking her own place as they untied the ship from its mooring and pushed it away from the jetty.

A pall of sadness settled on them all as they watched the

boat depart down the river away from their home. Finally, Jaclyn shook herself when the ship with its precious cargo was out of sight. Their stealth would have been for nothing if they were all caught out here on the jetty, staring forlornly down the river.

Hopefully, they would be long gone towards the barbarian lands before her brother worked out his watchers were missing and Jaclyn's family gone. Jaclyn led the way back toward the house, keeping her tread soft, the softly lapping river against the jetty bringing no comfort at all. Together, they walked back into their home, one of the other wives pulling closed the large sliding doors, cutting off the view of the river. None of them really wanted to see it right now.

THIRTY-NINE

Michael wandered along the river, trying to settle his mind. His people had been watchful, a sign he needed to control his temper. Regardless of what happened with Damien, and his genuine anger at Aiden's actions, he shouldn't be this tied up over it. Scanning his surroundings, he opened his mind a little more to those around him. The waves of despair that washed over him, impacting his mood, were not his own. He would have realised it sooner if he hadn't been so self-involved. Pushing aside the emotion that was not his own, he reinstated his mental barriers and took a moment to settle himself. Taking a breath, he finally relaxed his barriers again. This time when the wave of distress rolled over him, it was recognisable as separate from himself. It could be a tricky thing to learn and something those new to higher-level powers struggled with, distinguishing their own emotions from the intense feelings of others.

I can do this, not much further.

The desperate mindvoice continued on in such a vein, a litany urging herself onwards, long before the boat being propelled down one of the minor tributary rivers became visible.

Just around the bend. Keep going. They need me.

A single young villager, who appeared to be on the verge of collapse, was in the boat. She'd obviously been pushing herself. As he checked with his othersight, he could see the spiky red fatigue of her mind and a gift that had been overused. She was going to have a terrible headache when she finally allowed herself to collapse. Only a deep fear for her people kept her pushing forward. He watched for a moment more, then stepped out from the shade, releasing the veil he'd instinctively wrapped around himself to obscure his presence.

He grew more concerned when the woman didn't notice him, her eyes fixed straight ahead, swaying with fatigue. Michael drew in his power. Reaching out, he hauled the boat towards where he stood on the bank. The boat's occupant gasped, reeling as he seized the craft out of her control. Her eyes were wide as she stared up at him, fear emanating from her mind.

Calm down. I will not hurt you. Michael sent soothing emotions at her, trying to calm her panicked mind.

"Invaders, hundreds of them, descending from the Heights." Her voice was low, barely above a whisper.

As the woman toppled, Michael lunged forward, barely catching her as she fell unconscious. Before she passed out, he glimpsed images from her mind that accompanied her whispered words. The villager hadn't been exaggerating. The only thing that was both a relief, and a concern, was that the people she'd seen flooding down from the Heights did not resemble any Sylannian raiders he'd encountered. He wasn't certain who they were, but from the images they were similar to the outland traders. Not that he'd received reports of them visiting the Warlord's domain for years. She might have realised they were familiar if she hadn't panicked. Then again, the sheer numbers streaming down the Heights screamed invasion.

Michael groaned. One extended battle front was enough. Two was not something he cared to contemplate.

Michael gathered the unconscious woman into his arms, and wrapped a small shaft of power around the boat and pulled it further up onto the bank. He turned away from the river and walked a straight line back towards the village. Vines and shrubs pushed aside as he made his own path. It was a shorter distance back, even if he had to exert himself a little, than taking the winding path that mirrored the smaller river's twists and turns.

As he walked out of the tree line, two younger children who'd been playing catch skidded to a halt, their eyes wide as they fixed on the brand-new track leading into the forest. Then they tracked back at him and settled on the woman he carried.

"Her boat is back there on the banks of the smaller river. Do you think you can bring it around to the village jetty?" Michael attempted to keep his voice light.

The boys looked at each other and then back at him before they nodded vigorously.

"Yes, sir!" The brash, skinny blond boy grabbed his friend, and they went pelting through the forest the way he'd come.

Michael smiled, amused despite his concern. While the locals had kept the children close to home when the Unwanted had first descended on their village, they'd moved from fear to curiosity to imitation, with some now playing with wooden sticks after seeing some of his people training. Their parents had some concern at the start, then seemed to relax when their children weren't immediately dragged off in chains.

A group of villagers broke from their conversation as he approached—the unconscious woman in his arms quickly drawing their attention. Michael recognised one of the young men as the healer's brother, who performed a quick assessment, then spun and bolted back towards the village.

"Kesha!"

Michael sighed. He was sure the man's panicked bellow was audible to everyone in the village, and even in the surrounding villages. Those close enough to witness his arrival probably jumped to the assumption he'd caused the girl harm. Not that he could blame them. If he'd been in their shoes, knowing little else but the rumours about the feared warleader, he'd probably be drawn to the same conclusion. It was one of those little details about his reputation. He didn't have to try that hard to appear dangerous. Stories were told about events like this one, and as tales do, they would grow and warp over time, almost beyond recognition, from the circumstance that triggered them.

The door to the healer's hut was open when he got there, courtesy of her brother who had preceded him.

Kesha, her messy blond hair pulled back in a bun, stood in the middle of the living area. She turned from her brother and his garbled warnings. In stark contrast to her brother, she took in Michael's appearance and the unconscious woman he carried calmly. He could see her push her concern aside to concentrate on the immediate problem of the unconscious woman.

"This way."

The direction was hardly necessary. Michael had been to Kesha's healing room multiple times while Damien was recovering enough to move out. Kesha led him to the back of the house, opened the door to her healing room, and gestured him inside. Michael moved past her and placed the woman on the bed. Kesha bustled forward, her fingers loosening the tight-fitting leather vest her patient wore.

"What happened?" Kesha's voice was low and warm. Her grey eyes met his before resting on her patient.

"She's overextended her mind. If I'm any judge, she will have a horrendous headache when she wakes," Michael said, watching as Kesha moved around the bed, placing her hands lightly on the stranger's temples.

Michael switched to his othersight and watched. Those with an affinity for healing manipulated the veil very differently to the way he did himself. He could see she gathered the veil to her, yet it stayed external to her, whereas when he drew on the veil the power flowed into him, seemed to become a part of him. It allowed him to use the energy as effortlessly as he breathed. Others seemed to realise he, and those like him, were different. It was part of what brought out that distrust and fear, even if they couldn't pinpoint exactly what was different. Kesha was perhaps strong enough to see how different he and the members of his warband were, but it didn't mean she understood what the difference meant. Of course, if she ever did, Michael hoped she would fill him in, since he'd like to know too.

Finally, Kesha stirred, her weariness clear. Michael caught her as she swayed, alarmed that yet another woman would collapse on him. He relaxed as Kesha gathered herself, taking a deep breath before straightening and smiled at him.

"Thank you. I'll be fine soon. You are correct. The girl had badly overextended herself. She nearly burnt herself out." Kesha frowned and reached out to draw the curtains closed to darken the room, before pulling a light blanket over her sleeping patient, then shooing him out in front of her.

"Try to keep her here if you can, for her own sake." Michael turned, only to stop when the healer spoke.

"I'm not in the habit of imprisoning people against their will." Kesha's tone was sharp.

Michael could not miss the judgement in Kesha's eyes now that she'd dealt with her patient.

"I understand, healer. She witnessed invaders streaming down from the Heights. It's why she drove herself to the point of collapse. To the brink of death." Michael didn't know why it was important to him this woman understand his motivation, but for some reason he cared. "My people and I need to investigate. She didn't know if her people survived or not. They sent her to get help, to give warning. I think she is the one in her village who is the strongest in the veil and by the looks of her clothing and gear one of their hunters. That combination gave her the best chance of getting here in one piece. It would be kinder if she remained here while I sort this out."

Michael turned away, not taking any satisfaction from the shock and regret on Kesha's face that was followed closely by fear as she understood the implications of invaders somewhere close enough for this stranger to have made it here.

Michael strode out of the healer's hut and across the square to their camp, noting everyone was already gathered and waiting. Unlike the healer, they'd known something was wrong when he'd walked into town with an unconscious woman in his arms. As a hand grabbed his arm, he stopped, glaring at Kesha.

"I'm sorry. I didn't mean to think the worst of you." Kesha's eyes held more understanding right now than he cared to contemplate.

Michael shook his head. "You did, but right now, it doesn't matter."

"Michael, please. Healing like that makes me tired. I really don't think you are the monster everyone says you are. If you were, you wouldn't care enough to bring people here for healing."

Michael stared at her, feeling Kesha's remorse and fatigue.

"The Warlord will pass through here. If you'll take my advice, I suggest you continue your practice of staying out of sight when he does."

"Why, what do you mean?" Kesha asked.

"You're a powerful healer Kesha, don't pretend you don't know. If the Warlord learns about your talent, he will permanently relocate you to the stronghold at Yalleska."

He sensed the healer's confusion but wasted no more time on explanations. Besides he got the distinct impression the pair of heavy-set villagers who stood nearby and seemed to take Kesha's welfare seriously did understand.

"Everyone pack up! I want us on the road out of here before sundown." Michael raised his voice, so it carried easily over their camp.

Michael pushed his impatience at the sight of Aiden off to one side, as he stood with everyone scrambling around him with confusion written all over his face. From previous experience it wouldn't achieve anything to lose his temper. Aiden had obviously picked this moment to be stubborn. While most of his people had made do with their hammocks, Aiden had insisted on dragging out and setting up his tent. Even Damien had made do with a hammock, insisting he was well enough and didn't need a tent, although no one would have begrudged setting one up for him. Michael suspected Damien had been a little embarrassed by all the fuss and he steadfastly ignored Aiden and turned as Olivia approached him.

"The messenger was from an outlying village. Outsiders have appeared, coming down from the Heights," Michael said. "I don't think they are Sylannians."

He shared the images he'd caught from the messenger's mind of the fur-covered strangers.

"Other than that there are far more of them than we usually see, they look like the traders. Although I don't think we have seen them in these parts for years." Olivia was grim. "We'll go on ahead as the advance party?"

"Shouldn't we just wait here for reinforcements to arrive?" Aiden's frown hadn't lifted.

"We'll see what we are facing and devise a plan for when the Warlord joins us," Michael explained.

Nathanial wandered up to him. "I can go and alert the Warlord. If I take Callan with me, between the two of us we can speed up his arrival."

"You're both strongest at that skill. Still, are you sure you don't need your entire squad to share the load?" Olivia asked.

Nathanial shook his head. "No, we can do it. Just make sure you leave enough of a trail for us to follow and there is somewhere for us to collapse for a while when we get to the village that sent the warning of invasion."

Michael smiled tightly. "Fair enough, I trust your judgement. You take Callan and get the Warlord. The rest of us will go on ahead and trust me, you won't miss the path we take."

As Olivia and Nathanial each moved off to make further arrangements, Michael sent the images and directions he'd pulled from the messenger's mind to both of them. Michael was grateful that Olivia and Nathanial were skilled enough to put things in motion without everything being broken down into small steps.

"Isn't that risky?" Aiden asked.

"There is an element of risk, yes." Michael didn't have to hear Aiden's thoughts to know he was desperately trying to work out an excuse for why he should remain behind. Michael knew exactly what the Warlord would think if he remained behind. Obviously, Aiden did as well.

"You think Father will come himself?" Aiden went a little pale at that.

Michael laughed. Clearly, Aiden had worked out what his father's likely reaction would be if he stayed behind in safety.

"Of course he will come. Now pack; my order wasn't optional."

Michael turned his back on Aiden, making it clear that the conversation was over. Two of his men came over, sparing a moment to watch Aiden struggling with his tent. One of them raised his eyebrow but Michael shook his head. It was more than time for Aiden to pull his own weight.

"Rough camp, Warleader?" the older of the two hard-bitten men asked.

"Yes. We'll leave the bulk of the pack animals and supplies here." Michael walked away before he had to hear Aiden's protest about having to camp rough verbalised. Even so, he could feel Aiden's sulky glare at his back.

FORTY

Damien clung to his horse. Exhaustion had been stalking him for what seemed like hours. He gritted his teeth, refusing to utter a complaint. None of them had time for him to admit he was afraid he'd pass out, falling from his horse to be left behind, lost in the underbrush as the others swept on, unaware he was no longer with them.

Draw energy from the veil, Michael said.

Damien stiffened as images from Michael entered his head, then relaxed again as he realised his warleader was simply showing him what he needed to do. Damien steadied his nerves and drew the power into himself. It was as easy as breathing right now. He almost sagged in relief as strength flowed through him. Followed immediately by embarrassment. The last thing Michael needed was to be distracted by his internal monologue.

Thank you. Damien kept his reply brief.

Now that he could think a little clearer, Damien opened his mind just that little further and checked his surroundings with his othersight. All of them in the band were connected to each other. He could feel that thread of power running between them all. He'd witnessed it before, but now he was paying attention, he could hear the low-level hum their energy use caused as they each fed into it. A small trickle of that power flowed from them into the horses. He couldn't work out who in their number controlled that aspect, but it was more than one of them. Under their guidance, the horses seemed to flow, galloping for longer than any horse normally could. Damien groaned as the realisation hit him. It explained how they could sleep in most mornings but still cover a great deal of ground when they rode from place to place.

At their head, he could feel the concentration and energy Michael and Olivia were exerting. The very air around him hummed. Some of it was their own but Damien could see they also drew from their collective power.

He switched his attention to the track they were following, not quite parallel to the river. It was narrow, only allowing them to ride single file. The tree branches seemed to reach out, trying to snag them as they rode past. It was only when a crack of timber resounded and the earth exploded that he realised a solid shield of pure power was clearing their path ahead. Behind them, he would see a new trail forged out of the wilderness with the fighting ranks spreading out behind them. Nathanial and Callan, once they met up with the Warlord, would have no trouble finding and following their path. The path of destruction they left behind them clearly showed where they had travelled.

His position as they rode, right behind Michael and Olivia, gave him pause. It was probably because Nathanial and Callan weren't with them—they had been shadowing him since he'd joined the Unwanted. While he was focusing most of his attention on drawing the veil into himself to keep himself conscious and in the saddle, the other part was channelling energy into the group. He wondered if everyone was as ready to collapse as he was or if they were more accustomed to this energy sharing. As he gazed at the backs of Michael and Olivia ahead of him, he could see not just the thick bands of power flowing into and out of them as they forged the path ahead, but also the fatigue that was bleeding from them.

You can't keep this up, Damien observed.

We can, for as long as we need to, Michael replied.

The village isn't far off, Olivia said.

You aren't the only one who will sleep when we get there, Michael said.

Nathanial and Callan were two of the strongest in the veil, besides Michael and Olivia. Since he'd been with the Unwanted, at least one of them had been nearby. Damien barely restrained a groan as he suddenly realised why.

You don't have to worry. I'm not going to run away and I think I'm too exhausted to get out of control right now, Damien said.

We trust you, Damien, but even your unconscious, veil-fuelled mind can cause considerable damage, Michael said.

Don't worry. It's the gift of being in transition. We've all been through it to one degree or the other, Olivia said.

Now, be quiet and let us concentrate. Michael's amused tone was a counter to his words.

You aren't the only one trying to stay focused, Olivia said.

Powers, now we're sounding like a grumpy old couple. There was an audible groan in Michael's tone.

A scream of timber followed a resounding crack that sent splinters of wood, lumps of dirt and rock flying.

Ooops. Olivia's tone was coloured with embarrassment

What do you mean, ooops? You're meant to be pushing the trees aside out of our way. Not showing off your power to the lad by splin-

tering them into a million pieces and showering everyone with the debris. Michael scolded.

Oh, don't play the innocent. You're not any better. Mock exasperation filled Olivia's mindvoice.

Damien chuckled weakly at the banter between the pair and pulled back to concentrate on staying conscious long enough to get to this village. Now that he wasn't wrestling with himself, simply allowing himself to be a conduit, the rhythm of the veil flowing around him and through him was soothing. Even the occasional explosion of power when Michael or Olivia threw just a little more than they'd meant to just merged into the background. The veil carried him on and swirled around him, making him one with his band mates. An idle part of his mind realised that even he was adding his own power to the collective. His powers might fluctuate, but when they worked, he drew, and shared, more power than the others.

Is this why I was so exhausted? Damien asked.

Yes, sorry, we should have warned you, Michael said.

Damien blinked as he realised his horse had come to a halt. They all had. A small, orderly village spilled out in front of them. All was silent. He couldn't even hear any bird calls. In fact, it had been quiet for quite some time. The village might be still, but there were people here—as heightened as his senses were, he could feel them. There was also an increase in random people's muttering intruding into his head. Unlike previous occasions where he didn't understand what had caused the sudden chaos in his mind, he strengthened his mental shield as the others had been trying to instruct him to do.

The creak of a door opening sounded overloud in the otherwise silent village, as an older woman stepped from the darkness of the doorway into the open. She stood alone, staring at them, somehow dignified as she waited. He could hear her internal monologue as she wondered if they would kill her.

Dismount.

At Michael's command, Damien complied—in part because the connection they all shared urged him off his horse. He smiled weakly as he realised even the simple but impressive moment they all dismounted together, booted feet striking the ground simultaneously, was carefully contrived.

"You sent warning of an invasion, Speaker," Michael said.

The Speaker's eyes widened. "You've come to help?"

"We have. We were in the village up the river when your messenger made it into town."

The Speaker peered at them, and beyond them, her eyes crinkled in amusement.

"I see our only way out isn't the river anymore."

Michael chuckled. "Sorry; from the images your messenger shared, I judged our horses might be useful."

"I take it the barge didn't occur to you?" The Speaker's eyebrows rose.

The silence was deafening for a moment. Damien could feel the tension as they waited for Michael's reply. A raucous peal from a bird, sounding for all the world like laughter, rang across the village and surrounding jungle, causing an explosion of birdsong and insect life to resume. The tension drained from Michael, and he threw his head back and laughed.

"No, Speaker, it didn't, and no one mentioned it," Michael said.

"To be fair, our warleader carried your unconscious messenger into the village to the healer," Olivia said.

"Ah. The others in that village jumped to conclusions thinking you'd harmed the girl and being timid, I take it no one mentioned the barge." The Speaker paused. "She... Is my granddaughter all right?"

"She will be, Speaker. I left her in the healer's care, with instructions to keep her there until we could sort this situation out," Michael replied gravely.

"The invaders haven't moved. I'm afraid we may have panicked a little. Our hunters say they appear similar to the traders who came through the mountain pass years ago. Just a whole heap more of them."

"It's fine. I'd rather you panic and send for us than have a fighting force fall on us from behind while we are already engaged in an ongoing fight elsewhere."

"Please come, rest for the night. My people will show you to where the outsiders are camped tomorrow," the Speaker said.

Gathering his horse's reins, Damien strolled along behind Michael and Olivia as they followed where the Speaker led them without prompting. He paid closer attention to the small collection of ramshackle wooden houses. As he was still open to the veil, he could see the overlay of power that traced lazily, swirling around the buildings. The bulk of the villagers might hide, but it wouldn't have done any good if the warband had intended to harm them. He could sense their energy, sluggish and dull. Still, the size of the village was deceptive. This place was in the middle of nowhere. Before the Unwanted's arrival, it had only been accessible via the river. Yet it sprawled along the length of the water and through pockets of the jungle. Damien realised that even if he could sense the villagers and their whereabouts, could see their energy with his othersight, those who lived here wouldn't have the power to see it. Not the way he could.

It was all a show. You knew, the Warlord knew precisely where I was, Damien said.

You're in transition. Your powers flare whether you will it or no. Michael's mindvoice was calm.

Those in this village do not have the power to hide, but yes, we pinpointed the hut you were in before we rode into Ranlith, Olivia said.

"You're taking invaders on your doorstep remarkably well, Speaker," Michael observed.

Once you stabilise, you'll be able to hide your presence from others a little better. Michael's tone was reassuring.

Damien wondered if he'd ever get any good at such double-talk. He gazed over at Michael, who leant towards the Speaker, listening to her reply, reassurance seeping from his pores. This relaxed man exuding charm, chatting and laughing with the Speaker, was so different to the remote, confident man with an almost tangible threat rolling off him. It was a side of his warleader Damien hadn't seen before.

FORTY-ONE

Michael stood on a hill under the cover of the surrounding forest overlooking the plain where the outsiders were camped. He'd been able to dump Aiden in the village, along with a couple of his people to supervise their camp. Once they'd realised the armed fighters who'd descended on them had come to help, the villagers had been more than accommodating. He'd detailed the villagers to pack only what they could carry themselves, in case they needed to evacuate. He didn't believe it would be necessary, but it wouldn't be the first time he'd misjudged a situation, and he figured it was better to be safe than sorry. The village Speaker, a thin woman with sharp intelligence and a dusting of grey in her otherwise dark hair, had listened carefully and scurried off to organise the villagers.

"They appear to be settling in. Rather than an invading force," Olivia observed.

As he scanned the people below, Michael absently indicated his agreement. While the invaders certainly had large numbers of fighters with them, there were also plenty who were clearly non-combatants. Young children played around the camp. He'd seen a few women who were heavily pregnant and at least a couple of babies being carried in slings, as well as some elderly. There were also signs they were building some permanent structures. There were literally hundreds of what appeared to be hide-covered circular tents of various sizes, sprawling out across the plain below. Despite the situation, he found it fascinating. There was smoke coming from a pipe that jutted out the top of the tents. They even had wooden doors instead of a flap. They were more like circular huts than tents.

"How on earth did they get all those huts down there?" Olivia asked.

"There is clearly a path through the mountains, stable enough for the horses. They are obviously aware of it, even if we aren't."

"They must dismantle, I guess. There's no way they could have built all that this quickly," Olivia said.

"I think our first guess was correct, these are the traders. Even if there is a whole lot more of them," Michael said.

"Reports from the trading families here indicated these people stopped coming our way because of the upheaval here in the Warlord's domain." Olivia said, concern in her eyes.

"We need to know what really caused them to stop. It's unusual for traders to give up markets they have a foothold in." Michael overlayed his actual sight with his othersight, seeing the distinct, mostly low-level use of the veil. "I'd also like to know why they've come back."

"Let's hope it wasn't conflict with Sylanna," Olivia agreed.

There were traces of high-level use of the veil among the outsiders, but not as much as he'd feared. Although the signs were powerful enough to be of concern if they had leant to use their powers in warfare. There were clearly hundreds of these people on the plain below. This was more like a small population had up and moved their entire society.

"I'm hoping it was drought or flooding—something like that rather than war for them to make the trek over the Heights." It was clear from Olivia's tone that she didn't believe that was the case at all.

Michael turned to the members of the Unwanted he'd brought with him, giving out detailed orders for them to scout this area as thoroughly as they could. Regardless of the invaders' intent, the Warlord would not want a potential enemy at their backs while they continued fending off raids from Sylanna. He also wouldn't like that even if these people weren't a threat, whatever they were potentially fleeing clearly was. If these people had found a way over the Heights, others could.

They'd always ignored this approach to their lands thinking the curving mountain range protected their backs. Clearly, they had been wrong.

MICHAEL WAS grateful that while the Unwanted had slept like the dead the night of their arrival, none of them due to the collective use of their power, had pushed themselves too far. As a result, it had given them a week to scout the surrounding countryside and prepare for the Warlord's arrival. In this, some of the local hunters had been of great help. Before the unexpected arrivals, they had roamed the area extensively. Or they had until the discovery of the invaders, after which they had wisely kept their distance. By the time the Warlord had arrived late the night before, Michael had a good grasp of the situation they faced. The Warlord stood beside him at their observation point, with the view of the outsiders sprawling out on the plain.

The villagers, under instruction from their Speaker, had undertaken to feed the warband. They'd eaten well from the produce the villagers usually traded down the river. All of it flavoured with herbs they gathered from the forest and a selection of berries and nuts. In a way, he'd be sad to leave. He'd never eaten so well.

Since their arrival had forged the new road through the thick jungle, plans were afoot in the village to expand their trade. Michael also discovered that some products flowing to the stronghold at Yalleska had come from here.

Like many who found themselves facing off against a hostile force, they didn't seem to care that they were now considered part of the Warlord's domain. They seemed to feel it was a fair trade for the Warlord's fighting forces dealing with the invaders and the new road forged for them with no need to negotiate with other villages or effort on their part. That raised Michael's estimation of the Speaker of this village yet another notch.

"What is your opinion on this, my son?" The Warlord didn't even turn to Aiden.

If he had, he would have seen the dismay on his face. Although Michael had no doubt the Warlord was aware of Aiden's sudden panic as well as he was. Aiden had stayed in the village the entire time and was only seeing what they were facing for the first time now. Just like his father. Aiden stepped forward, moving past his father to stare down into the rolling valley.

Michael swore and, without thinking, grabbed Aiden by the collar of his vest and hauled him back into the sheltering tree line. Aiden landed on his back, his face going bright red. Only the momentary rush of the veil warned Michael of

Aiden's intent to strike at him with it, and he raised his own mental barrier. Aiden's tantrum washed harmlessly off Michael's shield.

"Stop being foolish, Aiden. You stepped past the tree line. If anyone below had been paying attention, you could have given away our presence." The Warlord's expression and voice were neutral as his eyes bore into his son's. "Be grateful I'm standing here, or Michael might have ended your miserable existence for that. Now, answer my question."

Michael watched as Aiden's face went even redder. He pushed away the men who had stepped forward to assist him, and stood. Michael watched as Aiden stepped forward again, although he carefully stayed in cover this time. Michael willed Aiden not to say anything stupid, hoped he'd actually paid attention to the daily briefings. Although he didn't care if Aiden made a fool of himself, he did care if the Warlord ended up in a foul mood. It would make him harder to deal with and manoeuvre.

"I think we should leave these people be." Aiden shrugged. "It will cost us dearly to take them; at least right now, they don't appear to be a threat."

Michael tried not to wince, and while it was difficult to read the Warlord's face, he could tell Aiden's response disappointed him. Again. The Warlord was a lot of things. Many of them despicable. But he did not become *the Warlord* by being tactically stupid.

"Damien. Come here." The Warlord's voice was neutral.

Michael tried not to stiffen as others moved aside to allow Damien a position near the Warlord. He bit back a smile as Damien carefully took a position with Michael between himself and the Warlord.

"Yes, Warlord?" Damien asked.

"Tell me, what do you see below?" The Warlord's voice was calm and low.

Damien's breath was unsteady but to his credit he settled down and turned his gaze to the setting below. It impressed him that Damien took his time, absorbing what he could see. Michael was keenly aware that this was also the first time Damien was setting eyes on the people who'd come down from the Heights. Although in his case, it was because he'd had one of his attacks, with his powers almost completely deserting him after their arrival. Michael had insisted he rest in the camp until the Warlord joined them.

"They seem nomadic or perhaps used to moving with the seasons," Damien said.

The Warlord's eyebrows rose. "What do you mean?"

"The reports of the scouts who've seen them unpack and put up their tents. The speed with which they accomplish it. During the briefing, it reminded me of the trader families who'd come into my village. They'd set up a fair, then pack and move. It was like they'd never been there. My mother used to tell me they were from a faraway place. I don't know if these are the same people, but they remind me of what I was told of them. I was younger then." Damien's voice settled as he spoke, as if he was suddenly on sure footing.

"Very well. What else do you see?" The Warlord smiled, his sharp eyes on Damien.

"There are fighters and hunters. I can see they set sentries, but they clearly have children and elderly with them." Damien, who'd been staring fixedly at the settlement below, finally turned to the Warlord. "I don't have the experience to say if these are invaders, Warlord, but these people, they're not like I'd expect them to be. I'm not sure I'd be happy if they settled next to my home village, though. I think they'd be far more prone to fighting than the average villager back home."

Michael was relieved the Warlord was clearly satisfied with what Damien observed.

"Michael, your advice on what we face below?" The Warlord turned his back on Aiden as he spoke.

Michael turned and took his time to assess the situation below, mind racing, wondering if he could salvage something for Aiden, and drew a blank.

"Granted this seems to have been an orderly exodus, they're well equipped, but these people have all the hall-marks of fleeing their own land. I agree it will cost us to take them if they choose to fight back. But I don't believe we can afford to leave a potential threat to get entrenched. We can't fight on two fronts. Our best bet is to take them while they are unsettled." As he turned to the problem at hand, his mind raced with the possibilities.

"If we just ride down, they will know we are coming," the Warlord said.

"They will. In that, I agree with Aiden. It will potentially cost us to take them." Michael smiled faintly at Aiden's shock that he'd agreed with him. "Unfortunately, they have chosen their position well. They will see us coming no matter what we do. They have sentries keeping watch at all times. Worse, they will have the high ground when we get there, with plenty of time to rouse their people."

"You think they could be strong enough to give us a problem?"

"No, we'll win." Michael went to explain further, only to stop when the Warlord raised his hand.

"Olivia?" The Warlord kept his gaze on the scene below.

Olivia stepped forward on the Warlord's other side. Michael noted his friend was careful not to look in his direc-tion. Not that she needed help in reading the situation they faced. Michael was confident that if he fell in battle one day, Olivia could take over and keep their people alive.

"I fear what these people have fled. They are on a war footing. I don't think they would be if they'd simply migrated because of a flood or a natural occurrence. If they made their way over the Heights to sit at our back door, then whoever they fled could as well," Olivia said.

"Your suggested approach?" the Warlord asked, his lips compressing.

"Aiden is correct in that this may cost us dearly, but like Michael, I do not believe we can afford to leave them here. We fight."

"Or at least give the appearance we are going to…" Damien's eyes widened.

Despite the seriousness of the situation, a small smile spread across Olivia's lips mirroring his own amusement. Damien seemed totally shocked that he'd actually made a comment out loud.

"Go on, I invited you to give me your opinion," the Warlord urged as he regarded his newest recruit.

"I'm not sure how. Sorry, I shouldn't have interrupted." Damien's face flushed. "Perhaps in the early morning? Before the fog rises, it could cover our approach. Allow us to get closer without their sentries being aware."

"We could be here for weeks waiting for a fog thick enough," Aiden interjected, his tone derisive.

"Owen and I used to bring fog sometimes, when hunting." Damien flushed again, then turned pale before flushing again.

Michael caught Olivia's gaze.

I'd warrant it was more Damien than his mentor.

He's already shown a disposition for the elements.

I think we could do this. Although we'd be next to useless if it doesn't work.

"Show me what you did." Michael transferred his gaze to Damien.

Damien's brow creased as he pondered the request. Michael resisted the urge to instruct Damien on what to do. Despite the Warlord and everyone else standing around waiting, it was better for Damien to work through the how of the use of his powers himself. At least when he could. Michael smiled as Damien finally settled and replayed a moment in the past where he'd used fog and enhanced it to his advantage. Michael wasn't sure that Damien knew how much of his personality showed in twisting that hunting skill to their current problem. Not many would think of ways the skills they already had could be used in battle.

Michael took a deep breath, and shared what he'd leant from Damien with Olivia. A complicated mix of communication passed between them in a burst of images and emotions. Following on the heels of her assent, he gazed at the Warlord.

"We can do it, and it might just work." Michael could hear the caution in his own tone.

"Might?" the Warlord asked.

"Might. We can bring fog over the plateau where the invaders are settling in."

"Deaden the sound of the combined forces moving into position," Olivia added.

"Once we engage the mist and the sound-deadening effect, we'll be able to assist the others a little if needed, but we'll have to encompass a large area. The effort will exhaust most of us."

"Even if this doesn't go wrong, the other bands will have to do more heavy lifting once we engage." Olivia turned her gaze on the Warlord.

Michael waited as the Warlord considered them and their

words. The Warlord appraised the members of the Unwanted who stood around them.

"I think you underestimate your abilities. Very well. We will set things in place tomorrow and attack in the early hours of the day after," the Warlord said and then turned, retracing his way back towards the sleepy village.

Thank you for agreeing with me and not making out like I'm a total idiot, Aiden whispered as he turned and followed in his father's footsteps.

Michael traded glances with Olivia, who shrugged. It wasn't like either of them tried to make Aiden appear incompetent. Most of the time, Aiden managed that one all by himself.

FORTY-TWO

Steven tipped his mug before stopping to glower at the remaining dregs. Gulping the last mouthful, he caught the barkeep's eye across the crowded taproom and waggled the empty tankard. Displeasure crossed the stocky innkeeper's face before he poured another drink and passed it to his boy who was working the floor.

Steven frowned and checked out the other patrons in the bar, wondering who had displeased the man. Granted, it was a busy evening. If he was honest, he'd probably be grumpy if he was on that side of the bar rather than this one. Particularly since when the barkeep kicked the rest of them out and they staggered home to their beds, the barman would be stuck cleaning up. Only to repeat the whole thing tomorrow. The barman's lad placed his tankard on the table before him and swiped the empty before retreating to the bar.

Steven scowled as people laughed and joked. Pretending that life was good and they had nothing to concern them all. How soon everyone forgot. He took a gulp from his fresh tankard and placed it back down on the table. As Steven leant forward, some of his drink slopped over the rim and splashed onto the table.

"I tell you, Gareth, this will work. He can't beat us if we all stand together," Steven hissed across at his friend.

"Be realistic. Does anyone here but us want things to change?" Gareth turned, gesturing to the others in the packed bar.

"Lord Rathadon won't have much trouble squashing a rebellion of three," Evan said.

Steven ground his teeth in frustration. "My little brother is not a lord of anything. I'm the eldest. My birthright was to become the next warlord of Vallantia. That was stolen from me."

"Keep your voice down," Gareth hissed at him.

"I have the rightful claim to Vallantia, not the Warlord's appointed sycophant. We three will form the centre of the rebellion, but it will grow. The oppressed will flock to my banner." Steven's lips compressed into a thin line as he ignored Gareth's warning, eyes flashing with pride at the vision of himself victorious in wresting Vallantia from the grip of the oppressors.

Steven jumped as two overly large fists slammed down onto the table. He edged back in his seat as the barman glowered down at them.

"You'll not be talking about starting trouble in my bar. Out with the lot of you." He lifted one hand and pointed it towards the door.

Steven's eyes slid sideways, only just realising the bar had gone still, everyone staring at him. Then he pushed his first reaction of concern aside, annoyed with himself. It was time, more than time, for everyone to stand up for him against the usurper. Steven flushed and lurched to his feet, jabbing the barman in the chest.

"This entire city belongs to my family. I'm the rightful heir. You'll show me some respect."

"Then perhaps instead of whining and causing trouble, you might want to earn it. Now I'm cutting you boys off. Get out." The barman's lip curled.

The smith's over-muscled sons stood and moved to positions behind the innkeeper. One rolled his shoulders and neck, and the other had his hand suggestively on his blade. Steven flushed again, indignant that these commoners would dare to threaten him. That they could possibly imagine they could best him. He'd been taught the sword for as long as he could remember. His overrated upstart of a younger brother wasn't the only one who could be dangerous.

Steven fumbled for his sword, only to have Gareth grab him from one side, Evan the other. As they dragged him across the bar and out the doors, at a bark of laughter from the smith's sons he tried to twist out of their grip. His friends ignored his protests and efforts to break free, propelling him into the still evening outside. Steven stumbled, landing heavily on the cobbles as he suddenly broke free of his friends. He scowled and rolled over, glaring at them both.

"What did you go and do that for?"

"Wasn't it obvious? If Ben didn't reduce us to mush, the twins would have pounded us all into an insignificant mess on the floor," Evan growled.

"They spend all day long swinging hammers in the forge, making and using blades as well. Rumours whisper the twins have a strong affinity for metal." Gareth shuddered. "If they crafted that sword of yours, they could have rendered it back to the useless lump it started as."

"Besides, this is the best bar in town, and we don't want to get thrown out for good," Evan said.

Gareth held out a hand to him.

Steven glared at the offered hand for a moment, then grabbed it, allowing Gareth to help pull him to his feet. He stumbled as he stood, only to be steadied by both Gareth and Evan, who guided him down the road.

"I guess I've had a few too many, but otherwise, I could have taken them," Steven muttered.

"Well, this rebellion of yours will not last long if you keep shooting your mouth off like that. It'll just get us dead," Gareth said.

Steven opened his mouth, about to be outraged, then closed it again equally abruptly and grinned.

"You said us," Steven said, a grin spreading across his lips.

"Not here, Steven. It'll take a bit of organising. We need to plan in secret." Gareth smiled at him tightly.

Steven shot his friends a triumphant look, his eyes shining. This was what should have happened right after the Warlord invaded Vallantia. Finally, the birthright that had been stolen from him would be restored.

FORTY-THREE

The Warlord sat easily on his horse. He could see the growing settlement on the plateau and, unfortunately, not even a hint of fog. Feeling Aiden's impatience, he smiled. His son was about to get a valuable lesson. He'd urged him to grow his relationship with Michael and Olivia. To treat them as his brother and sister. The Warlord had blurred the line long ago, and considered them his children, but Aiden persisted in seeing them as a threat rather than as allies.

He expanded his mind lightly, checking on his people, then further on to the others. Technically, their band leaders should check that their troops were ready, but they were all his. He'd usually leave this task to Michael, but given his warleader was otherwise engaged, he decided he'd best double-check himself. A subtle shift in the veil caught his attention. Even though it was a still night without a hint of a natural breeze, a whisper-like wind rippled around them and swept down onto the plateau, washing up the Heights on the other side of the camp of their target. A slow smile spread across the Warlord's lips as the mist materialised. Slowly gathering, becoming dense enough to mask their presence. He shivered as the moisture hung in the air all around him. As Michael and his Unwanted rode forward, the fog seemed to part and envelop them, obscuring them from regular sight between one step and another.

Start falling into position, Michael ordered.

He didn't take offence. In a tactical movement like this one where they relied on Michael's skill, on the skill of the Unwanted, the combined forces needed to follow the warleader's orders.

As they all urged their horses forward, he winced. The noise they made was distinct, but almost at once he felt the power the Unwanted were exerting intensify. It was like a thick, heavy curtain hung between them and everything around them. Their noise sounded hollow, as if they travelled in a contained room. He could feel the very air around him thrum and pulse with power. Sparks flashed in the fog around them as they rode, indicating none of this was natural. Although he had the feeling the sparks were caused by whatever the Unwanted were doing to deaden the noise of their movement. His skin crawled with the sheer power being utilised, but he couldn't track how or exactly what they were doing—the skill they used was beyond him. This was what Aiden somehow couldn't see. The men and women of the Unwanted were all strong enough to take whatever they wanted. Yet one and all, they fought *for him.*

Get ready. We can't maintain this much longer. Michael's mindvoice was as firm as his spoken one.

It's taking that much effort? the Warlord asked, a hint of concern washing over him.

It is, but no, they have some of significant ability in their camp, Olivia said.

They've just recognised this fog isn't natural. Get ready to fight. There wasn't even a hint of doubt in Michael's words.

We're close enough it shouldn't make much difference, Olivia added.

Power swirled around them, and his horse picked up its pace under the guidance of another mind. The Warlord smiled grimly and drew his blade. A hollow ring heralded the dissipation of the fog between one breath and another. The thundering of their horses, the scraping of blades from scabbards, and the sudden hollering from the camp assaulted him.

Interesting, Michael said.

What is? the Warlord asked.

There's not even a hint of panic in them, Olivia answered.

I'd warrant these people have faced war, Michael observed.

So, they haven't come our way because of flood or famine, the Warlord said grimly.

Does any of that really matter right now? Aiden grumbled.

It increases the likelihood these people have fled a threat that could follow them over those mountains, the Warlord snapped.

He almost sighed as he realised he was on edge. War and killing people was simple. Orchestrating this complicated theatre to avoid killing people—or at least not kill as many— was much harder. This had been Michael's influence over the years, and it yielded much better results. Even if the risk to them, in a lot of ways, was higher.

Focus! The first wave of defenders is on the field! Michael snapped.

The Warlord pulled his attention sharply back to the battle about to unfold in time to see the first wave of defenders from the camp sweep out to meet them. There was a peculiar, somehow familiar, whistling noise over the sounds of battle around.

Arrows! Damien warned.

The Warlord stiffened as a raw thrust of power that could only have come from Damien flew over the battlefield. On the heels of the power usage, flames sprang into existence in the air as the arrows burst into flame. He swore, ducking reflexively expecting the flaming arrows to slam into him, but instead, the cool feather-like caress of flakes brushed his skin. Damien had burnt the first and second flights of arrows to harmless ash.

The Unwanted couldn't keep up their efforts for much longer. The Warlord gritted his teeth. It was time for their next manoeuvre.

Second wave, move! Michael directed.

The Warlord took control of his horse and urged it to take a lead position, allowing Michael and the Unwanted members to peel off and drop back. As planned, they urged their horses into a gallop. Their various units altered their course, converging on each other. The weaving of the horses made their number seem far more formidable and allowed the Unwanted, who'd been spread out across their front to ride around the edges, to come back together and reform. For the defenders, it would seem like they'd materialised out of the mist with overwhelming forces.

Unwanted, form up on me, Michael ordered.

The Warlord didn't have to wait long before his horse's pace slowed in time with those around him, as if guided by another hand. Michael and the Unwanted rode past, forming a line in front of their amassed forces. On that same order, the other bands swept in to take their final positions, falling in beside and behind his personal fighting detail and the line held by the Unwanted, filling out rank after rank of fighters.

He watched, unconcerned, as the defenders swung back around, joined by more of their people from the camp. With an undulating holler, they unleashed another flight of arrows. He barely stopped himself from the instinct to duck as another surge in the veil sounded once again. Cold washed over them, and as he switched to his othersight he caught sight of the power pouring from Damien and a flight of elemental arrows making their way unerringly to meet the arrows from the defenders. As they met, the real arrows shimmered and then burst into flame. Yet another surge of power, this time with the distinct signature of Michael and Olivia at its centre. Lines of energy flared and flowed from every member of the Unwanted to their centre and back again in a loop. All of them seemed to glow and they were not bothering to hide the power they held. He could feel the energy centred on Michael and Olivia as if they were holding back a hammer blow, poised to strike. Peals of thunder sounded; the very air seemed electric. The rumbling all more ominous as the morning had dawned without a single cloud in the sky and the line of the Unwanted closed with the enemy.

The hum of deadly energy increased as Michael's ranks seemed to switch up another gear. Before had been all theatrics. A play in the town square by travelling artisans. Now the shackles that constrained the Unwanted were released.

Normally, by his order, they kept what they could do in check. On this occasion, he was interested to finally see what they could do. Although they'd already exerted themselves, it was a tactic he'd discussed with his warleader on more than one occasion. This way, none would know the Unwanted's full capability until it was too late, although on this occasion, their brief was still to minimise the loss of life.

Bows the enemy carried burst into flames. Some of the invaders were shunted aside, falling from their horses as they were struck with a hammer-fist of power. The front rank of the Unwanted leapt from their mounts, engaging with those they faced on the ground. Even the horses fought, lashing out with their hooves. At first, the melee seemed a chaotic mess. Then Michael leapt from his horse, grabbing hold of one enemy and hauling him from his horse at the same time. They hit the ground and Michael used his momentum to roll to his feet, then reversed his blade and struck the man, driving him to the ground in a boneless heap. The Warlord's othersight told him the man still lived but was unconscious. Even unconscious, power still ran through the enemy, it must have been one of those who'd detected their approach—likely one of the leaders of these people.

Olivia had engaged another invader, a woman who, like the man Michael had engaged, held power. The Warlord smiled as Olivia sparred with her opponent. He could see by the play of swords that she was mostly defending. The woman Olivia faced held power and was good with her sword. Olivia was better on both counts, but she was trying not to kill the invader.

Hearing a buzz that was now familiar, the Warlord didn't even bother to check as yet another flight of arrows headed their way. Before he could even reinforce his own shield, the arrows disintegrated. His gaze tracked unerringly to Damien. The veil cracked again, bolts of energy striking the ground from a cloudless sky as he hauled in power.

Try not to kill them! Michael ordered.

The Warlord felt his eyes widen at the rumbling in the veil. The world around them seemed to pause, then a rolling wave of power lashed out, striking the archers stationed in the safety of the edge of their camp. Every last one of them toppled to the ground.

Olivia's opponent staggered, and half turned towards her companions. Olivia lashed out at that moment, striking her opponent to the ground with a targeted surge of power.

Don't move if you want to live, Olivia said as her blade lashed down, resting on the dazed woman's throat.

Hold! Michael ordered.

Nathanial and Callan, borrowing from the collective power the Unwanted held, exerted themselves, bringing the horses of their opposition to a halt.

There was that moment of stillness before, finally, fear rose from those they opposed.

FORTY-FOUR

Liliana kept her mind open, passively registering those around their party as they passed, awake for any potential threat as they made their way from the central core of islands that made up the heart of the Thousand Islands. Only the original families, the most powerful ones, had home islands here in the inner core. The wives had been cycling through, working in pairs, using their powers to propel their boats through the water faster, to speed them on their way. As one pair exhausted themselves, another pair took their place, to push them faster down the interlinking waterways. They needed to make it from the Thousand Islands without being sighted or the king would have them tracked down and killed. This plan could only work if they disappeared without a trace of the direction they had taken. They hoped by the time the king sent another team to kill them all, they would find an empty court, with no trace of where they'd gone.

Liliana checked her party, particularly those currently on duty propelling their boat, and automatically reassured the children, although all of them except Thomas slept soundly in the arms of the underwives. Thomas was fighting sleep, trying to be brave. He was afraid he might not see his mother again and silent tears tracked down his cheeks as he sat there, trying to follow her last instructions to "defend your family". Liliana's heart broke at the sight. It was such an enormous responsibility for such a young one. However, if Jaclyn fell during the fighting with the barbarians, for their house to have any hope of survival, they would have the job of taking out the Monarch House. With his uncle and cousins out of the way, Thomas would claim the Throne of a Thousand Islands.

As the dawn broke the tree line, the early morning mist started to clear, signalling the tiny creatures to wake and start their morning song. Bird calls sounded across the canopy, and the ever-present daytime hum of insects began in line with the sun as it spread across the islands. The river and islands came to life around them. As peaceful and beautiful as this would be on any other day, she didn't let it distract her. They weren't yet past the boundary that marked the edge of the Thousand Islands, although the minor winding tributaries had widened significantly, giving way to broad expanses between banks. The islands on the outskirts were much further apart, and she could see their destination in the distance, at least their most immediate one.

Mama Lil!

Liliana spun as the warning from Thomas entered her mind, complete with an image of a woman standing on a balcony with a view out over the water, straight towards them. Liliana's heart froze for a moment. Then keeping the action casual Liliana waved as if she'd only just noticed the woman and gently took over their boat, propelling it towards the house where the woman stood. Liliana smiled as they drew close. Two of the daggerwives moved forward to join her. There was nothing to give away their connection to

Jaclyn's house, they wore the plain grey-blue robes of the lower caste. It was unremarkable to see watercraft filled with people going on various tasks. However, she could tell the precise moment when the woman's expression clouded as she noticed all the children. This was not commonplace and something that would be remembered. Liliana wasted no time. She leapt from the boat, drawing more power from the veil as she pushed herself up to the upper deck where the woman stood. Liliana's daggers sprang from their sheaths as she used the veil to spin and lashed out with the wickedly sharp blades that slashed through the woman's throat. Halting her cry of alarm. Liliana raised a shield as the blood sprayed from her victim's throat, catching it in an ethereal net before repelling it into the water. She grabbed the woman as she slumped, hands pressing ineffectually at her throat.

"I'm sorry. You should never have seen us." Liliana watched as the light faded from the woman's eyes.

The daggerwives who'd joined her took the dead woman's body from her, disposing of it in the river. Liliana stood and leapt over the handrail, landing with light feet on the deck. Waiting only a moment for the daggerwives to join them, Liliana took control of the boat once more, propelling them away from the last of the islands at the hinterlands of the Sylannian kingdom towards the shores of the wild lands. She felt a breath of power behind her as two of the underwives worked to cover their final retreat. She turned her gaze back and saw the early morning mist rise behind them, obscuring their path. Liliana smiled and turned her gaze back to their destination. Feeling eyes on her, she sighed, realising the oldest underwife was glaring at her.

"What?" Liliana was irritated, although she guessed what the old one would complain about.

"You risked yourself and your unborn one, Liliana!" The old underwife's voice was scolding.

"I am pregnant, but my blades still work."

"There is a reason Jaclyn and Ricardo detailed some younger ones to come with us. Let those with less to lose take the risks." The old woman's hand reached out as she gently placed it on Liliana's abdomen.

"I'm fine, old one, and so is my child."

Liliana endured the old woman's examination, her powers brushing over her and her unborn child. Finally satisfied, the old woman sat back and, gestured to the seat next to her. Liliana sighed and sat.

"Jaclyn elevated you to Prime early, and there is no sign of harm to your boy, but you must not place yourself at risk again!" The old woman's eyes snapped.

Traditionally, Liliana's elevation to Prime would not have occurred until she'd given birth to a healthy male child to the house. As a consequence, even though her early promotion meant she was the senior wife of the house on this expedition, she still came under the authority of the underwives until she gave birth. Now that the threat had passed, Liliana settled meekly on the bench as the underwife had ordered.

That didn't mean she wouldn't act if necessary to protect her house. However, that wasn't something the underwife needed to know.

FORTY-FIVE

Michael stood his ground with the Unwanted's power swirling around them, waiting to unleash. "Let the woman up," he said.

Olivia backed up a couple of steps from the woman she held at sword point. Surprise flashed across the woman's face. Her eyes flicked across to him, then back to Olivia. The woman kept her eyes on Olivia and slowly climbed to her feet. She wisely left her sword on the ground where it had fallen and raised her hands, palm outwards. Predominantly, it was a mixture of astonishment and confusion emanating from her in almost equal amounts. He simply smiled. He sent a pulse through the veil that connected them and all the Unwanted stepped back from their opponents. Their movement synchronised with each other, which caused the woman's eyes to widen. She kept her eyes on him and licked her lips before she spoke.

While he didn't understand her words, it became clear it was an instruction to her people, who slowly sheathed their weapons and backed off. At least, those capable of it did, his own opponent lay motionless on the ground. The woman stepped in his direction only to freeze as Olivia and the rest of his people reacted, tensing, their weapons raising. Keeping his eyes on the woman, he stepped back and gestured to the unconscious man on the ground.

"Let them tend their wounded," Michael ordered.

His people retreated a little more as those they'd faced off against moments before watched them. They waited on the woman, who spoke haltingly.

"Thank you,"

She turned her head, speaking rapidly to her own people, then moved to the side of her fallen companion. She sighed with relief as she knelt by his side to discover that he was not dead, merely unconscious.

While she was uneasy, the woman finally realised that his people would not slaughter them all. She issued rapid-fire instructions, and her injured countrymen were assisted back to their own lines. As they grew in confidence, more of their people came to help.

They've encountered the sword, and now they see the mercy, the Warlord whispered to him.

Can you feel it? Olivia asked.

They reek of desperation, as if they've lost everything. Michael winced at the pain emanating from not just those they'd fought, but from their camp.

Well, we defeated them, or at least proved we could have if we hadn't held back. Or is it more you sense? the Warlord asked.

More, much more than usual, Olivia replied.

There would typically be some hope threaded through the loss, Michael said.

Finally, a group of men and women walked forward, their empty hands in sight. The woman they'd faced in battle walked a few paces ahead of the others. Michael assessed those in front of them. Other than a few gaps, they appeared to be paired. The woman they'd faced was the strongest in the veil compared to her companions. He guessed she and the man he'd taken out were the two who'd realised the fog had been unnatural.

Interesting. With a couple of exceptions, they are in pairs. One male, one female, dual leaders, do you think? Olivia asked.

It looks that way, Michael agreed.

The tattoos on their faces match up, Olivia said.

Michael inspected the men and woman who stood. Each male and female had a tattoo that matched their partner's, so that standing together the way they were, the mirror images seemed to form a complete pattern spread over the two people.

The Warlord rode forward, a handful of his people who'd ridden closest to him falling back to form a line behind their leader. At this point, they reluctantly ceded the Warlord's safety to Michael and his people

"What brings you to the lands claimed by my people?" The Warlord ensured his voice was just loud enough to carry the distance between the groups, the veil threaded through his words.

"I am Khaliun. We are leaders of the Kallith Clan." The woman's words were halting and slow, as if she considered every word she spoke.

Michael smiled, although it didn't reach his eyes. It was a deliberate tactic to force these people to speak their language, although even now he could hear someone moving up behind him on horseback—a member of the village who spoke at least some of the trader tongue.

The man reeked of fear, clearly not wanting to get closer to these invaders.

"Tell them I didn't ask who they were, only why they are here." The Warlord continued to stare at those in front of them.

Michael watched on as the silence stretched, and the Warlord's irritation grow. The Warlord's jaw clenched and a tic jumped in his temple as the so-called translator stammered. While Michael didn't understand the words the man was using, it was apparent this wouldn't work. Without a means to communicate, they'd be stuck staring at each other across the divide. The few words they had in common, generally used in trade, were insufficient. Either they found another way to communicate or, since they couldn't leave these people sitting at their backs, the Warlord would give the order to kill them.

As far as Michael was concerned, that wasn't desirable since he'd rather find out who these people had fled. He'd also prefer they stood as a defence if the people they feared came over the Heights after them. It was callous of him, but hopefully, these invaders would delay the ones they fled long enough for the Unwanted to get here to face the new threat.

Michael tensed as Khaliun walked forward, almost halving the distance between them, her empty palms up.

"I can… share… talk," Khaliun said.

He could feel the brush of the Warlord's power as he appraised her, considering her offer.

"Damien, let the woman share their language with you." The Warlord jerked his chin towards the woman, his order clear.

"No. I'll do it."

Michael ignored the Warlord's irritation which flared as he turned to glare at him. Michael swung off his horse, handing the reins to Olivia, who took them without comment.

It's a risk I'd rather you didn't take. You are worth far more than the boy, but he's strong enough to do what I've asked, the Warlord snapped.

Aiden meddled with Damien's mind already; he's still recovering. This might send him over the edge, Michael replied calmly.

There was a time when he would have been afraid of angering the Warlord, but that day was long ago.

The Warlord gritted his teeth, as his annoyance at Aiden surged, though he couldn't take Aiden to task right now, in front of this enemy. The Warlord finally signalled his approval with a wave of his hand.

Michael crossed half the distance between their two groups. As he transferred his attention to the woman, he sensed Olivia's shield expand to cover not only herself but the Warlord. Michael took the hint and withdrew his own shield from the Warlord. It wasn't like he'd have been able to maintain that protection once he'd joined minds with the woman anyway.

Khaliun stood waiting, her expression grave, and although she hid the concern from her face, he could feel it through her shields. She went to step forward, her hand outstretched. The ranks of the Unwanted tensed, their power flaring. They no more liked Michael putting himself at risk than the Warlord did. The woman stilled again, obviously feeling the tension at her movement. Michael sent a wave of assent that flowed between him and his opposite number. Khaliun kept her eyes on him, hesitating as her eyes brushed over his weapons.

Michael held up his hand. The woman and her people tensed as he drew his sword.

"Damien." Michael's voice carried a hint of command.

Michael waited until Damien made his way forward and simply passed his sword and daggers to him. Admittedly, it took a few more moments for him to disarm. Thanks to a lifetime of fighting, he had more than a few weapons, and a few hidden ones. The woman's eyes widened, then she smiled faintly. He could feel her amusement. Damien retreated to their own line again when Michael was done.

Michael stepped forward, facing the woman. They stared at

each other for a moment. Michael knelt, resting on his heels, waiting. The woman licked her lips, her eyes taking in their massed ranks over his head. She took a deep breath and sank to her knees, facing Michael.

Michael reached out, placing his hand on one side of the woman's head. The woman mirrored his action, placing her hand on his temple. Other than her ragged breathing, she gave no further sign of nervousness. Damien seemed to have a stronger adverse reaction than the woman, his rising agitation becoming apparent, although given his experience, Michael didn't blame him. A wave of reassurance flowed from Olivia to the lad and Michael turned his regard back to the woman, relaxing his mental shield.

To pass a deep level of understanding to another person, such as language, required a connection to be forged between the two minds. The risk of such a connection was high. In his experience, neither party came out of such a connection unscathed. At worst, they could get lost in each other's minds, and go mad or die. At best, he would learn their language—but to say they would both have a severe headache as a result was an understatement.

FORTY-SIX

Olivia tensed, watching as Michael and the trader woman kneeled on the ground between their two opposing groups. She sensed the moment the two locked minds with each other. Michael stiffened, but otherwise didn't react outwardly. The woman gasped in pain and shuddered as Michael's power flared. Olivia winced in sympathy with them both. That would have been the moment they'd burnt a connection to each other's minds. Transferring knowledge when both minds were linked was much easier, but it was painful and dangerous.

"Should it take this long?" the Warlord asked.

"I don't know." She tore her gaze from her friend briefly as the Warlord came to stand near her. "The longer it goes on, the worse it will be."

As the time drew out with no other movement from the pair, Olivia closed her eyes.

"We need to send fast riders back to fetch Kesha. She has the healer's gift."

The Warlord dragged his eyes from Michael to stare at her. "Michael is strong."

"Even if this doesn't kill him, he will need the healer if you want him to do anything but sleep like the dead. Possibly for half the week." Olivia spoke quietly as she returned her gaze to Michael.

Olivia ruthlessly pushed down her momentary guilt at giving up the healer's existence to the Warlord. Only a moment, though. She'd pick Michael every time if it was between Michael's life and the healer's peaceful existence.

"Do it."

"Nathanial, Callan, Damien, get back as fast as possible. Fetch Kesha. No excuses. Get her here even if you are forced to tie her to the horse to accomplish it." Olivia didn't even bother to turn as she issued her orders.

With the strength of both Callan and Damien to draw on, Nathanial could get to the village the healer called home and back here just after daybreak tomorrow, but it would still be a full day before the healer could get here. They'd be next to useless by the time they got back. She'd have to ensure there was somewhere comfortable for them to collapse. It was why they rarely pushed themselves that far. Having all of them pass out when they stopped was not wise.

Nathanial was just as concerned as she was and didn't need to ask questions. He issued instructions to Callan and Damien. They wasted no time, the hooves of their horses drumming over the ground as they rode back down the rolling hills the way they had come.

Olivia walked towards the kneeling pair, pausing only briefly at movement from the opposing line when they groped for swords that weren't in their accustomed sheaths.

"Don't be foolish. I'm not trying to harm either of them," Olivia said.

While they likely didn't understand her words, it was apparent they read her intent. Their leaders held up their hands, empty of weapons, and spoke to those behind them. Olivia guessed it was an order, since the ranks of the invaders relaxed marginally. Although she noted some were rebellious.

Olivia dismissed them, knowing the troops was keeping their eyes on their opposition. She knelt near the still forms but was careful not to touch either. If she did, they could pull her unwittingly into their minds, resulting in even more confusion.

One of them is approaching you. The Warlord's soft warning sounded in her head.

As a male knelt on the other side and reached out towards his fellow leader Olivia held out her hand.

"No." Olivia shook her head for emphasis.

Wrinkles creased the male's forehead, but he rocked back on his heels without touching either of their respective partners.

"Olivia." She tapped her own chest as she kept her eyes on the man.

"Erden," he said, mimicking her gesture and smiling faintly.

Olivia turned her gaze back to Michael and the woman. Hearing Erden clear his throat, she found him staring at her. He spoke to her, although she didn't understand his words. But as he spoke, he gestured back at his camp, then back at her. She caught images of one of their circular tents being constructed. He pointed at the rising sun and gestured to where they were now. Olivia smiled and dipped her head in acceptance. He turned, speaking to those behind him. Whatever he said caused a flurry of action as some of his people turned and rode back to their own camp.

"I think he's asking permission to construct one of their tents to give Michael and this woman shelter," Olivia said.

"Which you just gave him permission to do," the Warlord acknowledged, then turned to the massed fighters. "Nobody panic."

Olivia chewed her lip, keeping a careful eye on her friend and the woman with her othersight. She could see the veil flaring and throbbing around them both. That was never a good sign, and while she'd never tried to learn a language from another person's mind, she feared this had already taken too long.

"I'm going to try something. If I get trapped, haul me out. Although don't actually touch me, or you might get dragged in as well."

"Are you sure you should do this? I don't want to lose one of you, let alone both," the Warlord said.

Olivia's eyes widened as she sensed the Warlord's concern, not only for Michael but for her. She ducked her head, took a breath, and pushed down her emotions. These rare displays of affection by the Warlord left her confused.

"I'm not sure at all, Father, but I have to try." Her voice was soft, but it carried the distance between them. Finally, he gave his permission.

"Do it, be careful."

Taking a deep breath, she leant forward, tentatively placing her fingertips on Michael's temples. She reared back, falling onto the ground, staring at the blue sky. She was gathered in another's arms and realised it was the Warlord.

Olivia, what happened? Are you all right? he asked.

She winced and, taking a moment, a groan escaped her lips as she leant forward. She shook her head and instantly regretted it as the world spun. Finally, she opened her eyes with the Warlord kneeling near her as he held her in his arms. Michael and the woman were motionless. Erden stood a short distance away with a bunch of his people, staring at her.

"I'm fine. Michael just shoved me away before they could draw me into their madness," she explained.

The Warlord stilled. "Michael is lost?"

"No. Sorry, I shouldn't have put it that way. They're both strong mindspeakers. Their minds are locked together, neither able to give in to the other, no matter the fact that they know one of them needs to. Their unconscious minds fight for supremacy."

"Michael will win that battle." The Warlord sounded certain.

"He will. It will just take a little longer. That he had enough presence of mind to shunt me away from them shows it. Minds are complicated things," Olivia replied.

"What, he didn't need the distraction of you being in his head as well?" The Warlord's eyebrows rose.

Olivia glared at him and then started laughing weakly, seeing the mischievous glint in the Warlord's eyes.

"Probably not." The smile slipped from Olivia's lips as she gazed back at her friend.

She wanted to help Michael, but right now, there wasn't much she could really do but wait.

FORTY-SEVEN

Michael was awake, or at least a part of his mind was aware again, yet he and Khaliun remained bound together. So while the first part of this plan worked, information flowed between them both. Unfortunately, neither of them were in control of this exchange. No matter how much he'd tried to will himself to relax and allow the tribe leader to take charge, his unconscious mind had other ideas. As did hers. She was a powerful mindspeaker and decent at the other talents as well. Michael could not judge how long this battle of wills was taking. It would all be for nothing if they didn't separate from each other.

Khaliun stirred and pain hammered at him as the bond between them flared. If he'd had control of his body right now, he would have groaned in response. His conscious mind had obviously slept at one point, telling him this little transfer of language had gone on for far longer than either wished.

Well, that didn't work, Khaliun said.

In his mind she appeared wearing a long, green, flowing robe, her thick black hair falling around her shoulders. Her eyes were green and seemed to pierce straight through him. Which, in a way, they did. The clothes she had appeared in were not the ones she had been wearing when they'd locked minds. That Khaliun wore hide pants and a top with a fur coat, her long hair bound.

What didn't work? Michael grated, instantly suspicious.

I half hoped we might wake up free of each other if we slept. Khaliun blushed.

Or at least this version of her in his head blushed. As far as he was aware, they both still knelt in the open space between their respective people. He smiled, amused despite himself, before the fleeting smile disappeared from his lips. There was only one thing he could think of to separate them, but he was loath to try it. Right now, it was only their subconscious that battled with each other. He was beginning to fear the only way to separate was for him to join in the battle with that other half of himself. The problem was, he wasn't sure it wouldn't kill her. Besides that, if he struck out at her mind, joined as they were, whatever he did would probably feed back on himself.

Wishful thinking, he commented.

I know. I'm not usually the type. Khaliun sighed.

Our unconscious minds are active. Even when we sleep, Michael said.

The silence stretched between them, although it didn't worry him. He'd never been compelled to fill the silence with needless chatter. He winced and rubbed at his temples. What he perceived of as himself was sheltered in what he fancied was a back corner of his mind. Yet the presence of the bond that bound them could not be ignored. Tiny pinpricks of power lanced his brain as they wrestled for control of what was between them. Unfortunately, it was also the cause of them being locked together this way. At least, until one of them beat the other. He took a deep breath, trying to calm himself. Losing himself to fear and madness wouldn't help the current situation either.

You genuinely see yourself as a fighter. Khaliun's tone was almost absent-minded.

What? Michael blinked, or he would have if all of this wasn't in his head.

You know I wasn't wearing this. Khaliun held up her arms and staring down at her robe.

I had noticed that you'd changed. Michael couldn't help the smile that spread on his lips.

You didn't change, not even for a moment. You see yourself as a warrior.

Michael realised she was correct. He was still wearing his battle leathers, with weapons even though he wasn't currently armed. At least not in reality anyway. His own crest, the sword plunging into the flame, the symbol of the Unwanted, was also right where it should be on his chest.

It is who I am. I've known nothing else since I was a child. Michael shrugged.

Those women, they plague your land as well? Khaliun's mind-voice was soft and laced with pain.

They do. Michael hesitated, he wondered if they were camped out in her mind or his own. Or some no-man's-land in between. *They overran your people and drove you from your home.*

He'd seen the flashes of memory, the images, feelings, and pain. All of which painted a picture of multiple battles against the Sylannians in more numbers than they'd seen in the Warlord's domain. He feared the Sylannians would turn their full attention in this direction now that they were done with the People.

In the end, we decided to try to save those of us who were left, Khaliun said.

When we get out of here, I'll need to know everything you can remember about their tactics. Michael's mood turned grim as he contemplated full-scale warfare.

I have the distinct impression you know more about battle than I do. Despite her sombre tone, she smiled.

Perhaps. Maybe just a little. We've fought the Sylannians, but not in the way you have. They've been minor hit-and-run incursions.

You won those battles, though.

Yes. Most of them.

No. You've won every confrontation you've had with the Sylannians. Even if others that fight for your Warlord have lost a few, Khaliun said.

We've had a lot more practice.

You mean you and everyone who rides with you possess strength in the veil that is breathtaking and frightening all at once? Khaliun's lips quirked briefly before the half-smile fell from her lips. *You all use it to great effect when you fight, utilising your powers as you fight as much as you do your weapons.*

Khaliun cried out and sank to her knees, clutching her head. Michael found he'd closed the distance between them and wrapped his arms around her. While this body of hers that he pulled into his arms wasn't real, it still seemed substantial. Their surroundings changed, now they knelt at the rocky heights of her former homeland, with a outlook over a forest and plains below that stretched out in the distance. Storm clouds gathered, black and ominous. Her black hair whipped as the wind picked up, howling around them, and cracks of lightning stuck with increasing frequency. As darkness descended, a red glow traced through the black clouds in a broken eggshell pattern, bathing them in baleful light. Pain beat at the edges of Michael's mind, but he pushed it aside. He'd be fine.

It hurts. Khaliun's mindvoice had reduced to a whisper.

I know. Fight, hold on to yourself. My people will have worked out that things have gone wrong and sent for a healer. Michael urged.

Guilt assailed him. It was the bond between them. She was strong, but he was stronger. The display around them was the visualisation of the barriers she kept around the inner sanctum of her mind failing.

I can't. End this.

No. I could kill you.

You must, for both our sakes. Tears of pain traced down Khaliun's cheeks.

Michael closed his eyes, acknowledging how hard this decision was. He'd killed for no other reason other than the whim of the Warlord. Wiped out entire villages and left the survivors with nothing to come back from. Most of his life had been filled with conquest and death, yet he'd tried his best to minimise the loss of life in recent years. This woman was in his head. He'd seen the hardship and trauma she'd already lived through these last few years. Right now, at this moment, he cared for her fate.

I'm sorry. Don't die, or I swear I'll follow and haunt you. Michael kissed the top of her head.

You won't, for the sake of both our peoples. They need you and yours. Khaliun was almost fierce, her eyes flashing, although he could see the agony pulsing behind the defiance.

He gathered more power to himself and struck out at her. Her homeland's hills, plains and forest disappeared as he lashed out. Not at the bond that bound them, but at her. As her homeland swept away, it was replaced with thickening dark clouds that flickered with reds and blues. He gritted his teeth against the increasing pain that assaulted his own mind as well. Sheets of lightning flashed across the sky, and some licked down at the ground as darkness and agony consumed them both.

FORTY-EIGHT

Isabella stood at the edge of the commons, staring at the low stone building of the bakery. With Damien gone, collecting the bread now fell to her. The memory of Damien, disappearing along the road behind the bakery out of Ranlith with a horde of armed people, reared in her head again. Isabella swiped at the moisture that welled in her eyes. She'd hidden in the grey place with the cool touch of the veil wrapped around her. There, but not there. Soft and comforting; the power surrounding her with filaments brushing over her skin, through her, as if she was insubstantial. Reality, normal emotions, always seemed to drop away when she was in that place. As did her sense of time.

The veil sang to her, made her feel whole.

Somehow, the curtain that stood between her and everyone else in the real world would sometimes thin. She'd seen Damien's display of power. It had been breathtaking. His power coursed through the energy surrounding her, causing it to crackle and hum. The vibrations through the veil spoke of him and others, strangers with powers like his, like hers. She was familiar with them now, or at least some of them, by how the veil sounded when they used it. It was like a signature. The moments when Damien gave himself up to the Warlord's people, his farewell to their parents and when he rode out of town still hurt. She hadn't realised it then, floating in that place between. Damien's orders to stay in the grey place until he'd left had echoed in her head. She'd watched as he disappeared, an observer of it all, with no attachment or emotion for the events she witnessed.

When she'd emerged, she pushed the grey place from her, returning to the world that everyone existed in. As the thin grey veil of power dropped away, she'd curled up in a tight ball as the pain and loss hammered into her. Damien had given himself up to protect her. He'd always been there, teaching her, sheltering and protecting her mind as her powers had grown beyond their parents' ability. Kept her burgeoning powers from others in the village as long as he could to save her from their fear and hate. She'd seen how some of them had treated him. They did not know how similar her own abilities were becoming to his. He'd done all this for her, even though no one had been there for him. No one could have been. They weren't strong enough. They didn't know what he'd been going through. He'd had to learn alone. Surrounded by a village full of people yet isolated, as if he were the only one of his kind.

Now she was alone.

Isabella drew in a shuddering breath as she drew her attention back to the bakery once more. She hadn't been near the place, near the baker, for months. It had been a chore that Damien had quietly taken on. She'd avoided the task since he'd left, but now her luck had run out. Straightening her shoulders, Isabella walked across the common area, opening herself to the veil just a little, and sighed as the power rushed within her. As it pushed aside the fear, the tension drained from her as if the veil gathered it all and passed it back to that grey place.

Reaching the bakery, Isabella reached out to grab a loaf of bread sitting on the rack, stopping as a hand shot out and grasped her own.

"Isabella, how are you?" the baker asked.

As the veil drained from her Isabella's shock registered. With the contact between them, she could hear what the baker was thinking, what he wanted. Her own perceptions picked up the flickering images from his mind. She stepped back, only to be held with his firm grasp, his fingers kneading her palm as he pulled her back towards him.

Isabella reminded herself to breathe, it sounded ragged and harsh to her own ears. As fast as the veil had fled her moments before, she gasped as it flooded back into her. Her body stiffened, back arching in response to the inrush of power.

Oh, this is what happened to Damien, Isabella whispered.

The words fled out into the veil moments before her awareness splintered with the onslaught of power, thrumming through her at levels she had no conscious ability to grasp, manipulate, or turn off. It was what they called veil sickness. This was much earlier than Damien's attacks had happened, but girls matured earlier than boys, or so her parents had told her.

What had previously always been soft, inviting power wrapped around her suddenly struck her. Blow after blow, racing and sparking along every part of her body. Pain lanced through her. A ragged scream pealed out and she realised, in a small part of her mind that was still working, that the scream was her own.

"Mark! What are you doing? Let go of the girl!"

A snarling voice echoed and bounced around her head as the power within her lashed out. It struck something—no, someone—before the veil drained from her as fast as it had filled her. Isabella's legs buckled. As she slumped, powerful arms caught her. She finally identified the voice that had protested and the one who'd caught her as Owen. She wondered where he'd come from. Isabella hadn't seen him when she'd plucked up the courage to approach the bakery. She would have asked him to get the bread for her if she had. He had been Damien's mentor and protected him. Somehow, she recognised he'd shelter her too. Damien had trusted Owen, so she instinctively did as well. Pain lanced through her mind and her awareness splintered into confusion before darkness claimed her

CHAPTER

FORTY-NINE

D amien was almost numb to the fatigue that haunted him as they rode. While they had travelled fast before, that was nothing to the speed they now travelled at. Once they made it through the small section of winding forest tracks between the invaders and the village that had alerted them, to the trail they'd blasted on their way in, they rode faster. The world around them blurred. The forest was a fleeting ghost image. It reminded him of the grey place he'd found, but he couldn't spare the attention to explore what that meant.

The mind that guided them all was Nathanial. Damien had been struggling to place Nathanial's actual position within the Unwanted. Michael was the undoubted leader and Olivia was obviously his most trusted and second-in-command. But Nathanial was often in company with Michael and Olivia and involved in their decision-making. If Michael or Olivia wanted something done, it was more often than not Nathanial that was trusted to either complete the task or see that others in their number did so.

Concentrate, we can discuss this later if you wish, Nathanial said.

Damien flushed. He'd obviously been leaking again. The command in Nathanial's tone was unmistakable but also held good-natured amusement.

Just stay focused; we're nearly there, Callan said.

Much to Damien's embarrassment, Callan sounded equally amused. After a brief internal struggle with himself, he sighed and let it go. He guessed they'd all been in his place at one point or another, racking their brains to work out the new order they found themselves in. The power thrummed around them, flowing between them all. He allowed it to settle his mind while Nathanial directed its use.

Abruptly, they were at their destination, coming to a halt in the centre of the village. They'd arrived so fast that the villagers stopped and stared. He imagined it appeared as if they'd just appeared in their midst between one breath and the next. One closest to them fell back then turned to run, half tripping over his own feet in his haste to put as much distance between himself and them as he could. Nathanial was off his horse, Callan a step behind and striding to the healer's hut. Damien dismounted and then hesitated, wondering if he was meant to follow or not.

Stay with the horses, Nathanial ordered.

The world seemed as if it was in slow motion, although he was aware it only seemed that way now because of the speed they'd been travelling at to get here. Damien kept his eyes on the door to the healer's hut and wasn't surprised to see Kesha, clutching a leather satchel, bundled out of the cabin between Nathanial and Callan. All signs of the smiling, affable pair vanished from the team to be replaced with two members of the Unwanted, determined to complete their task. Damien was reminded starkly of why people feared the Warlord's people when they rode into town. One of the bigger, heavy-set villagers strode forward, hand on his sword, drawing it. Callan spun, covering the short distance between them in a heartbeat. His blade flashed out at the man's neck so fast it caused the villager to freeze, his face pale.

"I wouldn't," Callan said.

"We will guard the healer's life with our own." Nathanial's words conveyed a promise.

Kesha held a hand up to the man who'd obviously tried to defend her. "I'll be fine."

Reassurance flowed from her to the man. Callan withdrew his blade as Kesha's erstwhile defender relaxed and removed his hand from his sword, although he clearly wasn't happy about the circumstances.

Damien already admired the healer and her abilities, yet at this moment, it went up a notch or two. There was very little fear in this woman. Only an obvious purpose and determination to heal those who needed her. He gathered Nathanial had told her why they'd come for her. It surprised him a little, but he realised it shouldn't have. Even if Olivia had ordered the healer to be tied to her horse if necessary, it probably wasn't the recommended way to get her there. Particularly since they needed her help.

All eyes of those who'd remained out in the village proper were on them as Nathanial assisted Kesha to mount with care and adjusted the stirrups to the correct length for her with practiced ease.

"You've ridden before?" Nathanial asked.

"Yes, of course. I've travelled from village to village in these parts since my abilities matured." Kesha smiled, confidence radiating from her.

"I can strap you to your saddle if you think you'll need it. I warn you, we'll be travelling faster than you've ever done before. Faster than you've ever dreamed was possible," Nathanial said.

"Thank you for the warning. I'll be fine," Kesha said.

"Hang on and try not to fall off, healer," Callan said, his tone a little dry as he swung into his saddle.

Damien waited until Nathanial mounted, giving one last glance around the otherwise motionless village before mounting himself. This time, he didn't need instructions to open himself to the veil and suck in the energy around him before allowing it to flow to Nathanial. Damien kept some of his awareness focused on Kesha, ensuring she didn't fall. Unlike them, she couldn't draw from the veil to renew her strength. In a way, it was a relief, since between sending power to Nathanial and keeping a careful eye on the healer, it was enough to stop his mind from becoming distracted. Once again, his job was simple. The promise of collapsing into a bed once they delivered their charge to Olivia was implied. With a grim smile, he realised on this occasion, he wasn't the only one who'd be collapsing into a deep sleep shortly after they arrived.

FIFTY

"What do you recommend?" the Warlord asked.

"My best judgement is we stay put, get shelter over him and wait for the healer to get here. Both of their minds are showing signs of trauma," Olivia said.

It was the worst possible time to risk losing Michael. The other bands didn't have as much strength as the Unwanted in using the veil, but following Michael's lead meant fewer deaths in the regular teams. Michael was also one of the strongest of them, aside from herself, Nathanial and now Damien—once he settled into his powers. If Damien came out of the other end of transition sound of mind, he'd be even stronger, potentially much more powerful than he was now.

Hearing a sharp intake of breath, she drew her attention back to Michael who reeled backwards, rolling onto the ground away from the woman. Olivia lunged forward, her hands resting on his temples, trying to at least soothe some of the pain coming from him. She took comfort that he was conscious. The woman had slumped immobile on the ground.

Michael's hand shook as he reached out to rest it on Khaliun's temples. He spoke, his voice rough and filled with emotion, his words completely incomprehensible to Olivia.

That part had at least worked—she gathered he was using the language of these people. The man, Erden, sat on the other side of Khaliun and spoke hesitantly to Michael, who shook his head. Erden at least was relieved by whatever it was Michael said to him.

"Please, never ask me to do that again." Michael groaned and rolled over onto his back, his eyes squeezed shut.

"It worked, though. You have their language?" the Warlord asked.

Olivia's irritation spiked and she opened her mouth to scold the Warlord, only to close it again as she sensed the Warlord's personal shield expanding to join hers in shielding Michael's mind. It was rare for Michael to be vulnerable. Despite his words, even rarer for the genuine concern she sensed from the Warlord.

"That and more. They are the Kallith Clan and all that remains of the People. Before war broke out in their lands, they were the ones known here as the traders. We and the Kallith have a common enemy, and the Kallith mean us no harm. I've given my word we do not seek conflict with them." His words were barely a whisper. Michael's eyes flashed to gaze at the Warlord.

"If you've given your word, I'll hold to it as long as they pose no risk to our own," the Warlord acceded.

"I beg your indulgence, Father, but I fear I have no choice but to sleep first." Although he fought it, Michael's eyes closed.

"Rest. The healer is on her way," the Warlord soothed.

Olivia kept control of her expression. The concern from the Warlord for Michael was genuine and she struggled to control her own reactions.

A scrape of blades being drawn from sheaths and the wave of fear coming from not far away caused Olivia to turn. Tribesmen who'd been walking in their direction froze in place, eyes wide, bundles clutched to their chests. She swung her gaze back to their own lines.

"Put your blades away, damn it! I'll tell you if you need to kill someone," Olivia snapped as she didn't even bother to hide her frustration.

Erden gestured to his people, who cautiously edged their way forward. He spoke, and even though she didn't understand the words, she understood his meaning from the images that flickered in his mind. They meant to construct a shelter. She smiled at Erden and indicated agreement.

The tension in her own people persisted as those they had fought edged closer and began setting up a couple of their tents. She gathered there was one for Michael and another for the woman. Although, by the looks of it, they were big enough to house several people comfortably. Erden turned and yelled back at the line of what they'd guessed formed the leadership group of these people, and one of them turned and rode back to their camp. While she watched, a stream of tribesmen came out from their base. They carried furs, cots, stoves, and what appeared like the components of a few more tents, which sprang up like a mini-village as a satellite to their own. Olivia shook her head, trading astonished glances with the Warlord. It seemed they would sleep comfortably, after all.

FIFTY-ONE

Steven had to admit, even if only to himself, now that he was out here on the darkened streets, he was nervous. The idea of meeting in an establishment in the wrong part of town had seemed so daring when Gareth had told him of the meeting venue. Now that he was out here, he'd decided his usual bar had been a much cheerier place to talk about his rebellion. This was a part of Vallantia that he wasn't overly familiar with, or at all if he was being honest. His eyes slid across to Evan again. It honestly surprised him that his friend seemed to know where he was going. The docks were an area frequented by commoners, and if rumours were correct, thieves and other disreputable types roamed these streets and warehouses. Steven grasped the hilt of his sword and tried to shake his uneasy feeling.

"I don't understand why we had to walk. Riding would have been much quicker." Even to his own ears, Steven sounded petulant.

"Because we'd draw attention. We're trying to avoid that, remember?" Evan frowned.

"Right." Steven glanced around the shadowed streets. "Not like we'll run into anyone we know in this district."

"We don't have to do this. We can just turn around and return to the Arms and have another drink." Evan's voice was a low whisper.

Steven's back stiffened. "No, we do. I want my birthright back, and someone has to stand up and fight the tyrant and his thugs."

"One of those thugs is your brother, in case you've forgotten," Evan muttered.

"I can handle my brother," Steven said, turning to stare at Evan, his friend's shoulders hunching as he muttered again under his breath. "I didn't catch that?" Steven glared at Evan.

"I said I doubt it. Damn it, show some sense. Your brother is a killer. If even half the rumours are true, it's a skill he's exceptionally talented at."

Steven stared at Evan's pale face, then laughed. "Oh, come on. We were both trained by the same swordmaster, and you're no slouch with a blade either."

Steven frowned as Evan stopped dead in the middle of the street, disbelief written all over his face. Evan opened and closed his mouth several times before he finally found the words.

"Your brother has been fighting for the Warlord since he was thirteen. By contrast, we've been thrown out of a bar a few times."

Steven opened his mouth to retort then, as they turned the corner, pools of light spilling from an establishment ahead of them, he shut it again. He gathered their destination was the double-storey wooden building with a broad balcony. Mainly since it was the only building lit up along the entire row. It was like a beacon beckoning him towards his future. He pushed Evan's worrying aside. Steven knew Evan; he'd come around.

His longtime friend was always seeing the worst possibility of everything.

"Come on, stop worrying. Gareth seems to be a capable sort. Besides, it's you who introduced me to the man." He slapped Evan on the shoulder, raising his eyebrows.

"I know. Don't come at me later and say I didn't warn you," Evan said.

Steven kept the smile on his face by sheer will alone as he faced the rough men standing on either side of the wooden door. Both wearing equally bored expressions.

"He's expecting you," a burly guard said while the other one opened the door.

Steven frowned at the man as he followed Evan into the rundown poor excuse for a bar. A wet, sticky sound accompanied his steps. Steven shuddered and wondered when the servants last bothered to clean the bar's floor. It certainly wasn't the type of establishment he usually spent his time in. He straightened as those in the room stopped talking at their entrance and turned to stare. Gareth was perched on a stool near the bar and smiled, gesturing them to join him.

"Come, my friends." Gareth poured them a drink from a flask on the bar before gesturing to the people sitting in the taproom. "We were just considering plans."

Steven tried not to pass judgement on the rough assortment of men and women gathered in the bar. They didn't resemble what he had imagined those who would form the core of his rebellion would. They weren't heroic at all, just commoners and not the reputable kind. Still, they had to start somewhere. Steven accepted the goblet of wine and sat up on a stool, Evan taking one on his other side.

"What did you have in mind?" Steven smiled. He liked Gareth's initiative.

Gareth laughed. "I guessed you'd be keen. Tessa here has a

bit of useful information for us. We've worked out how the Warlord's men show up when the Sylannians attack."

A rather homely-looking woman nodded at him but otherwise didn't speak.

"I'd always wondered how they managed it. They couldn't possibly be lucky that many times. Do you think they're in league with the raiders? Staging the raids?" Steven stiffened, eyes flashing as the possibilities ran through his head.

"No, not quite. The Warlord has people with strong mind-speaking skills in some tributaries and smaller islands keeping watch. They send the alert of a coming attack." Gareth's eyes glittered in anticipation.

"Ah, I see." Steven said, trying to think of something he could say to add to the conversation.

"You raise a good point, though, Warlord. What better way than to take down the imposter and his people?" Gareth grabbed the flask and refilled his mug.

"Thank you." Steven drank some wine, trying to figure out what he'd supposedly suggested. He didn't want to ask, though, since Gareth had said it was good.

"We couldn't take the watchers here, of course. It would put the imposter and his people too close to us," Gareth said.

"We could go down the river a ways, doesn't take long. Take out some of them further down. Should keep them right occupied. Long enough, we can start bringing the surrounding villages back under Vallantia's control again." The man who spoke was a pale, skinny redhead with sharp beady eyes.

Steven smiled uncertainly. "We could do that."

"Excellent idea, Warlord. With your permission, we'll get to planning. You'll want to be involved in the assault, of course."

Steven choked on his drink, but agreed as Gareth grinned at him.

"Oh, of course." Steven carefully fixed a smile on his face. "I wouldn't dream of missing it."

"Good, Warlord, I'll detail two of my people, sorry, your people, to escort you safely out of the docks. I'll send word through Evan for our next meeting?" Gareth said.

Steven placed his drink on the bar and stood, smiling. He paused as the gathered band of fellow rebels stared at him. His people. Steven's smile widened. He liked the sound of that. Straightening, he nodded in what he hoped was an authoritative manner.

"I thank you all for your loyalty. Together, we will free Vallantia from the false one who calls himself your Warlord," Steven said, and turned as Gareth gestured for two of the heavily built men who'd stood near the door.

"Escort our warlord back towards the Arms; make sure he gets back there safely," Gareth instructed the two men.

Gareth walked with them towards the door and showed them out. The two men took the lead without comment. Steven saw Evan's pale face and went to ask him what was wrong, but Evan shook his head, nodding towards the two men who guided them through the back streets of the docks. Steven frowned, confused at Evan's attitude, then shrugged off his behaviour. He wasn't about to let Evan ruin his good mood. Tonight had been a significant evening for him and for Vallantia.

FIFTY-TWO

Michael woke to stare at the canvas above him. It took a moment for him to work out that it was real and not something his mind had constructed. A lassitude hung over him and his head still ached, but he was considerably better than he had been when he'd allowed sleep to claim him.

"A few more days and plenty of sleep will see you fully healed." Soft fingers brushed his temples, and a stunning pair of green eyes swum into his view.

It took the barest of moments for his foggy brain to work out that it was the healer, Kesha, who tended him. As her words suddenly made sense, his hand captured her own. His shields rose against her powers.

"Thank you for your care, healer, but I'll sleep later. There are things I must tend to," Michael said, surprised at how rough his voice sounded.

"Even one such as you needs to take time to heal properly, Michael, or you'll feel the worse for wear."

Michael levered himself up, feeling the fatigue that still

hung on him. There were more pressing things he needed to do now—he could do that when this whole mess was settled.

"Please, if you haven't already done so, see to Khaliun. When this negotiation is done, I'll rest for however long you deem necessary." Her brow crease and Michael held up his hand. "With my life no longer in the balance, the Warlord may become impatient. I'm the one who can ease the communication between the clan and him. I'd rather these people not die because I chose to sleep in."

Her lips thinned and he could feel she didn't like it, but she finally conceded and stepped back. Her reaction made him smile. He could sense she was worried for him, which was a novelty outside his ranks. As she stepped back, he rose from the cot, careful not to show the dizziness that assailed him alongside the fatigue.

"How long have I been out?"

"A couple of days. Nathanial, Callan and Damien have been taking turns to watch over you when Olivia has been busy. All three were close to collapse by the time we got here as well," Kesha said, her concern evident.

Michael saw Damien standing by the door, or rather leaning on the frame, trying to make it appear like he was standing upright of his own accord. He doubted the healer was fooled. Fatigue and pain emanated from him in waves, although Michael judged a good sleep would cure him of both.

"Are you all right?" Michael asked.

Damien looked faintly panicked as the healer regarded him. "Yes, I've just had trouble switching off. My wayward powers have decided now is the right time to overcharge."

"You should have said something to Olivia or Nathanial. They would have helped you." Michael frowned and extended his mental barrier, enveloping Damien to cut off the constant stream of the veil he could see charging into his recruit. Damien gasped and bent over double, his hands rising to massage his temples. As Damien straightened, his eyes widened and he stepped back as Kesha reached towards him.

"I'm fine, healer, honestly. It was just a shock when the veil finally stopped charging into me." Damien sighed as Kesha withdrew her hand.

Michael couldn't help the snort of amusement that escaped his lips. Kesha's disapproving eyes swung back to him.

"He's only doing his job, healer. He just needs sleep. I'm sure he'll head off and collapse in a cot somewhere now that I'm conscious." Michael jerked his head at the door.

He shook his head as Damien fled. Although sleep was the most prominent thing on the boy's mind he caught the hint of something else coupled with desire, then dismissed it. A lad his age could think of many things with that emotion. He hadn't missed that his newest recruit had a massive crush on Olivia. Michael grinned, guessing that thing Damien was thinking of was his second-in-command, which would account for that hint of desire.

"What possessed you to link minds with another like you did?" Kesha scolded.

"The Warlord's orders. I figured it was better for me than Damien, given what he's been through."

"Foolishness! I'll deal with your Warlord; he needs to understand he could have killed you," Kesha snapped, her eyes flashing.

Michael's lips twitched, but he considered it was wise to keep his amusement to himself. Kesha was genuinely angry on his behalf. Then he sobered. Michael reached out with his mind, relieved to find Khaliun alive nearby. Seeing Kesha open her mouth to scold him again, he held his hand up.

"I'll be fine. Have you seen Khaliun yet?" Michael asked.

Kesha shook her head. "No. They advised me the tribe had their own healers who were tending to her."

Michael shook his head. "They don't have your talent and, at a guess, she is far more in need of your care than me."

"Try to at least minimise your use of the veil." Kesha sighed.

At the door, Michael paused; catching Kesha's hand, he raised her fingers to brush them with his lips. It was an old gesture filled with meaning, although in this case, since he didn't turn her palm over, that meaning was simply thanks. Michael smiled as Kesha blushed.

"Thank you for your care," he said, meeting her eyes with his own before letting go of her fingers.

He turned, allowing the healer to regain her composure as he led her from his tent to the one pitched next to it. Despite the healer's concern, he hadn't exerted himself much to locate Khaliun since she was so close by. Two burly clansmen who stood at the door to the tent watched his approach with suspicion.

"This is our healer, Kesha; she is here to help heal Khaliun." He spoke their language without having to think about it. At least, after all they had been through, transferring language skills had worked.

Before the two who stood at the door could reply, the door opened. A tall man with long black hair tied back in a knot opened the door. Erden. Michael did not need an introduction. He vaguely remembered having spoken to him briefly before he collapsed. The man's identity could only have come from Khaliun. She'd cared for this man, who'd been prominent in her mind, particularly towards the end. Erden waved off his men and gestured to them both, standing to one side while holding the door.

"Please, come in," Erden said.

Michael noticed his own people take steps in his direction.

"Two of you stay with Kesha and make sure she finds somewhere to sleep after she's done," Michael said. "Forgive me, Kesha. I should report to the Warlord and Olivia and let them know I've recovered."

"Olivia went to rest after she assured herself you would be well just after my arrival," Kesha said.

Michael stood aside as Kesha entered the tent. He was reassured to see Khaliun unconscious but alive on the sleeping cot with another of the clansmen who Michael judged also had a little of the healer's gift. The other man's attention turned to Kesha as she approached, and his eyes widened. He hastily made room for her and Kesha sank onto the cushions near the sleeping cot. Her hands rose and rested on Khaliun's temples, then she sank into a deep trance.

Michael waited long enough for his people to enter and stand out of the way at the side of the tent before he exited and went in search of Olivia. The sun was high in the sky. Wherever Olivia was, the Warlord would be, and he doubted either of them was sleeping right now. No matter what Olivia had told the healer.

FIFTY-THREE

Michael spotted some of his people conveniently nearby. They were trying to make it look like they were deep in conversation and just happened to be standing near his tent, but it did not fool him. The relief that came from them when he walked over to them gave away their reason for loitering. Still, on this occasion, it was helpful.

"Where are the Warlord and Olivia?" Michael asked.

"Over in the clan's camp, Warleader," one of them replied.

Michael considered the distance between where he was standing to where the clan's camp was located. Given that he just wanted to curl back up in his bed and sleep, even after such a small bout of activity, he decided riding was probably a good idea. Not that Kesha needed to know. She'd probably scold him again, and he had the notion she'd do so in front of everyone. He nodded his thanks and, after a quick scan of the camp, spotted the horse line and turned to walk towards it, only to be stopped as a couple of his people pelted past him.

"We'll get your horse ready. Won't be long."

Michael opened his mouth to tell them he could manage,

then closed it again. Even the thought of walking as far as the horse line wasn't so appealing. True to their word, his people were back, leading his horse behind them along with their own. In fact, they'd appeared so quickly he suspected the horses had already been saddled. Michael refrained from commenting; they clearly intended to escort him. He tried to disguise the fact that even mounting was an exhausting exercise, although he doubted those watching him were fooled. Still, they wisely kept their observations to themselves. Two of them took point, the others falling around him in a protective detail. Michael rode silently for a few paces, grateful they rode at a walk.

"So, was it Olivia or the Warlord who gave you orders to watch for me and act as an escort?" Michael asked dryly.

"Both." A chuckle escaped the Unwanted who surrounded him.

The tension in them drained at the exchange, although he could feel their minds ranging for any potential threat to them. Not that he expected they'd find one, but if Olivia found out they'd slacked off and taken their orders lightly, they'd regret it. If the Warlord found out they had disobeyed him, they'd probably end up dead. Fortunately, the distance between their camps wasn't great, and even though he was tired, riding was something his body and muscles were familiar with.

Michael resisted the urge to open his mind to scan the sprawling camp ahead of him but smiled as those in front did so, clearly scanning for the mind signatures they recognised. Even in the middle of this camp filled with hundreds of minds, they would recognise the Warlord and Olivia anywhere.

While he gathered someone in this camp could probably guide them, the Unwanted would rather not give them the impression they needed it. As a general rule, they approached everything they did with a show of strength—not that he believed the clan threatened them, but tension was flowing around this camp.

"They fear for the woman who joined minds with you," the one nearest to him said.

"Their other leaders keep telling them she will be fine, that we are bringing a healer, but the rumour persists that we've taken her prisoner." The woman on his other side kept her eyes scanning their surroundings as she spoke.

Michael realised it had been long enough for a persistent rumour to become problematic. Suddenly, the order for the squad to escort him when he made an appearance made sense. It also explained why negotiations were taking place in the clan's territory.

"I'm not made of glass; let's pick up the pace," Michael ordered.

The entire squad urged their horses into a ground-devouring trot as they made their way through the camp, ignoring the tribesmen who turned to track them as they passed. The eerie silence and eyes as they rode by felt familiar. As did the fear and the thread of anger laced with mistrust. He had to admit if the situation had been reversed and it was him unconscious in the middle of someone else's soldiers, his own people would probably feel the same way. Then again, he couldn't imagine a circumstance where they'd allow that to occur.

Now that he was close up in the camp and his security was being taken care of, he took in his surroundings: the circular hide tents with lazy plumes of smoke twisting and dissipating into the air; the adults and children all bundled up in their furs, and staring. The setting was both foreign and oddly familiar as a result of disconcerting knowledge that was not his own.

As his horse slowed down, he shook himself back to the present, grateful that the battle-trained stallion knew what to do, even if he wasn't paying attention. As they wound their way around the last curve of tents, he found they were in an opening with a ring of circular tents much larger than the others they'd passed. Michael didn't need to use his powers to know that the Warlord and Olivia were inside the one at the centre. He could sense them even without exerting himself. Steeling himself, he dismounted, hand on the saddle to steady himself. Only the knowledge that he'd at least be sitting down as soon as he got inside the tent gave him some reassurance.

He could hear whispers from the people watching. The clan members were shocked that they'd found their way here without guidance, without a single missed turn. On the heels of that shock was fear. Michael handed off the reins of his horse to the closest member of his escort, who took them without comment.

Armed clansmen stood at the entrance to the tent the Warlord and Olivia were in. Not knowing the protocol for entering the tent, Michael shrugged it off and walked towards the door. As the clansmen bristled, hands going to weapons, his people were around him, swords drawn with an ominous rumbling sounding from the veil. Before he could instruct his people to stand down, the wooden door to the tent opened, and a woman came out. Her eyes swept over the scene outside the tent door.

"Stand down." She didn't shout, but her tone held a bite with an undertone of scolding.

Michael glanced at her, then at those guarding the door as their faces reddened and they ducked their heads. He bit back a smile. This woman might not be as strong as Kesha, but those with healing gifts seemed to command a strange ability to make grown men and women feel like little children who'd been caught doing the wrong thing.

Narantuya. The name echoed in his head in another's voice as she held the door for him and gestured him inside.

"Stay here," he said to his escort, before nodding at her. He started walking towards the open door before pausing to look over his shoulder at them. "Don't kill anyone."

The woman stared at him, then over to his people before back at him again. The corners of her eyes crinkled, and she bit her lip. While she didn't shed her emotions like so many, he had the distinct impression she was suddenly as amused as she had been irritated previously. She might not have understood his words, but she clearly recognised the exasperation in his tone.

FIFTY-FOUR

Damien had been at a loss for something to do when he'd woken. The Warlord, Michael, and Olivia were still negotiating with the clans, so he'd fallen back on what was becoming his routine and trained. That probably hadn't been a smart move since his head throbbed in time with his footfalls. Somehow, he was even lousier than before he'd slept. Worse, the smell of food from the cooking pots as he drew near made him feel nauseated. Not that he wanted to go near the healer. She had more important things to do than tend to him.

Images of the conflict they'd been in rose in his mind, as they had when he'd tried to sleep. Damien muffled a groan; he'd hoped the training would exhaust him enough that the memories would disappear. He struggled to understand why they kept plaguing him. It wasn't like he'd killed anyone. His step faltered. At least, he didn't think he had. With the noise of battle, screams, clashing of blades, and the rumbling and crashing of the veil in reaction to their use, it was hard for him to be sure. The sights, smells and images came rushing back.

While it had mostly been a show, it had all been authentic enough for him.

He was still trying to process his feelings about the knowledge that even if he hadn't killed anyone this time, he would eventually, when it occurred to him that they would be staying put for a few more days because of the negotiations.

He walked over to his sleeping area. While the clansmen had erected enough of their strange circular huts for their leadership, the rest of them still camped rough. Damien reached into his saddlebags and withdrew his small flask. Pulling the stopper, he went to take a mouthful of his tonic and sighed as he realised it was empty. Groaning in frustration, he threw it back in his bag and grabbed a small leather pouch. Hands shaking, his fingers fumbled at the knot and took a couple of shaky breaths, trying to settle himself. He attempted the knot again and sighed as it loosened. Flipping the pouch open, he stared inside at the few remnants of dried tiscan leaves. There was barely enough for one mug, but he could have a mouthful and top up his flask. As soon as they left this place, he'd go out hunting and foraging for their evening supplies in their next camp. If they stopped at the village that had called them, it should give him plenty of time to find the vine that produced the leaves he needed for his tonic.

He grabbed a mug from a nearby table, tipping in the remaining leaves from the pouch, then filling the mug from a pitcher of water. He concentrated, sending the thinnest strand of power into the water. In barely a moment, steam curled from the cup. As he raised the mug to his lips, his hands shook badly enough that some liquid slopped over the rim, scalding his hand. Damien cursed softly but sipped the faintly bitter tea, feeling his muscles relax as the liquid rushed down his throat. He glanced back at his bags, where he'd left his flask, as a tremor shook him. It was still daytime, but just this once, he figured it wouldn't matter if he was insensible for a few hours. Pushing down the instant guilt that assaulted him—he rarely did this during the day—he ignored his shaking hands and gulped down the tonic in his mug. Relief instantly washed through him as the brew worked its magic. He'd just consumed enough tonic to last a week, but he pushed his concern aside. Sourcing more would be tomorrow's problem. He gasped as a shaft of pain hit him and gritted his teeth; it was because of the amount he'd consumed and that was why he would typically wait until evening before having his bigger dose. The pain would pass, to be replaced by the euphoria that would chase away his fears and the ache that seemed to be a constant companion of late.

"Damien, what is that?" Nathanial asked.

Damien hadn't even sensed Nathanial approaching him.

"It's just my herbal tonic. It's made from the leaves of a vine, like tea. One of the elders in my village and my mother used to prepare it for me," Damien said.

Nathanial frowned at him and held out his hand. Damien's stomach knotted as he was assailed with the sudden desire to down at the remnants of his tea in the mug. Under Nathanial's steady regard, hand shaking, he handed it over. Nathanial accepted it, raised it and sniffed. His face drained of colour.

"Powers, how did I miss this? No wonder your abilities are so erratic. How long have you been taking this stuff?" Nathanial's eyes flashed.

"What? I don't know, always. They said it helped me with my control. I'm sorry I drank so much. I normally only take a few sips during the day. Save the rest for night-time to help me sleep." Damien found his eyes were on the mug and the remnants of the tea it contained.

"This stuff is tiscan. It is dangerous and highly addictive. Powers, this stuff can kill people like us."

Damien's stomach twisted again, causing him to gasp. He knew he needed to lay down and let the drug take him, rather than fight to hold on. What Nathanial was saying was important, but his mind was foggy, and he struggled to concentrate as finally the euphoria he'd been waiting for hit him. He reached out for the mug, for that last mouthful but Nathanial brushed his hands away before handing it off.

"Aiden, get rid of it," Nathanial ordered.

"Why? Looks like he's enjoying the experience." Aiden chuckled.

"Don't be a fool. It can also cut you off from the veil if consumed in high enough quantities. Get rid of it," Nathanial hissed.

Damien wanted to protest, but found himself herded off to the sleeping area. He was confused, finding it hard to remember why he was trying to fight sleep when he always slept after taking tiscan. It was one of the side effects—one that he liked, even if he hated the pain that preceded it.

As he drifted off, a small part of his mind circled back to what Nathanial had said. The words replayed in his head, yet the words jumbled so he couldn't quite make sense of them.

FIFTY-FIVE

T he heat hit him almost like a physical wall as he walked into the tent's confines behind the Warlord and Olivia. He'd been involved in the negotiations for the last few days, and he was beginning to wish he'd complied with Kesha's opinion that he needed to stay in bed and rest. Although this time, unlike the first time he'd walked into the negotiating tent, he drew on the veil, regulating his body temperature. The furs and pillows scattered around were now familiar and at least comfortable. He sighed at the culprit of the radiating heat smack in the centre of the large tent. For such a small stove, it certainly did a good job. It seemed that none of the Kallith had the strength to control their body temperature, or if they did, they didn't know how to do so.

"Come, Michael, sit." Narantuya grabbed his hand and pulled him down to sit on a pile of cushions next to her.

Michael's eyes widened as he sank into the cushions, uneasy until healing energy pulsed between them.

"My thanks, Narantuya. Please don't overtax yourself on my behalf," Michael said.

"You need more rest." Her concern washed over him.

"I know, Kesha agrees with you."

"Yet you didn't listen?" One elegant eyebrow rose as she regarded him.

"Once this situation is settled, I'll rest for as long as Kesha dictates." His lips twitched.

Michael smiled at the Warlord and Olivia. He could feel both their relief and annoyance that they couldn't understand a word of the conversation that was going on.

What is she saying? the Warlord asked.

Expressing concern for my health.

She is right. You should still be in bed, Olivia said.

You know these negotiations are going better with me attending. Michael shrugged.

Continue to take the lead in negotiations. The sooner we get this done, the sooner we can get home, and you can rest, the Warlord instructed.

Michael accepted the order even though this negotiation was unusual compared with previous experiences. Typically, when the Warlord was present, he was the one who held the prime position in any negotiations. If he was honest, his preference would be to relax back into the cushions and sleep.

I'll double-speak for you both, Michael promised, trading glances with Olivia.

Narantuya gazed between him and the Warlord, assessing them both. She might not have picked up their conversation, but she obviously guessed that they were talking.

"Your Warlord cares for you. Even if he tries to hide the fact behind a stern and unforgiving mask." Narantuya's tone held certainty.

"My Warlord..." Michael paused, then he took the information he'd gained from Khaliun about the clan's idea of family and changed track. "My father isn't the most patient of men."

"He is your father?" The startled question burst from Tarkhan, who was resting easily in his cushions.

Yet again, because of the bond he'd shared with Khaliun, Michael knew this man. He was her co-leader, Tarkhan. It was the man he'd taken out in the brief fight between their people. To his relief, Tarkhan was alive. He hadn't been entirely sure what had happened to him. He usually wouldn't have really cared but there were consequences to sharing minds. The spillover of feelings and emotions that belonged to another was one of them.

"He is not the man who fathered me, but he is the one who raised me," Michael said easily, his eyes holding the Warlord's as he fed the conversation to him and Olivia with mindspeech.

These people have an extended form of family. There are the parents and children, but the care for children extends to the entire tribe. The entire clan is one extended family to them, he explained. *As they grow and know their path, they sometimes swap tribes. That tribe becomes their family. It's why Tarkhan and Khaliun's tribe are renowned fighters within the Kallith Clan.*

Ah, so they didn't randomly birth a bunch of competent fighters in one tribe. Olivia's tone was filled with amusement.

The clan leaders nodded at his explanation, seeming to relax minutely. It was something that made sense to them, as he knew it would. He hoped that little piece of information that suggested they had something in common, something relatable, rather than being totally foreign to them, would ease negotiations, even if only a little. The gathered clan leaders fell silent but were clearly consulting with each other. Michael waited patiently, nearly smiling as the Warlord's irritation notched up another level.

"We had no intention of invading your land." The oldest of the clan leaders, Ulagan, spoke first.

"A war has raged over our ancestral home for years," Tuya said.

"A war we lost, fleeing with the remnants of our people." The pain in that statement was evident in Tarkhan's voice.

"We have sympathy for your people but your appearance caused fear enough on our own for them to call for us, which caused the current situation," Michael said.

Olivia and the Warlord both listened and observed, but neither felt the need to contribute to the conversation at this point. Not that he blamed Olivia. He would have done the same thing if he'd been in her shoes right now. Although he trusted they would interject and tell him if they had insight to offer on any of the points of contention between them and the clans. It was one of the handy things of mindspeech in these situations, they were effectively three people able to act as one. It mollified him somewhat that they were both a little irritated at the circular rehashing of conversations they'd had the day before. All he could do was plough through them and try to get further along.

"I think if the situation had been reversed, I could understand the alarm. I think our own would have sent for aid as well," Ulagan said.

Tarkhan snorted before sobering and holding a placating hand towards his fellow leader.

"You mean they would have if they stopped long enough while running as fast as they could in the opposite direction?" Tarkhan didn't appear at all sorry for his amusement. "Not that I would blame them when faced against such overwhelming odds."

The Warlord's eyes crinkled as Michael passed on the observation, clearly amused.

"I think we can come to a mutually beneficial agreement for both our people," Michael said.

"What do you ask of us?" Tarkhan asked, his amusement banished in an instant.

"No more than you and your people can give. It seems we have a common enemy."

"We can share what we know of them, but I'm not sure it will help. We lost."

"Any knowledge you can share regarding our enemy is of use to us. You can do that and more."

"What else?" Tarkhan asked cautiously.

"You will not like this part."

"I'm sure there will be many parts of this that we won't like. What else?" Tarkhan repeated.

"I'll need you to keep a patrol of your people back up in those mountains guarding the pass you came here on," Michael said.

The leaders conferred each other before Tarkhan shrugged.

"Easily done. It's all right, though. It won't be me up there freezing in those mountains." Tarkhan smirked, clearly not sorry at all for whichever of his people would end up with that particular task.

Do you really think the Sylannians will come at us over the mountains? Olivia asked.

Yes, Michael said.

Why? the Warlord asked curiously.

Because it's what I'd do, Michael replied flatly. *I doubt it has gone unnoticed that a whole clan up and disappeared. They'll be searching for where they went.*

How else would you attack? Olivia prompted, her voice almost a whisper.

If I had the numbers, which I suspect they do. Multiple fronts. Over the mountains, another closer to Callenhain, the other off towards Vallantia.

We'd be spread too thin, Olivia said.

It's why you want these people on board. To cover an attack on this front, the Warlord mused, eyes narrowing as he considered the possibilities.

We're good, but we can't be on three fronts simultaneously. Michael kept his face free of expression.

"If your own people are anything like mine, I'm sure you can come up with some who deserve punishment duty," Michael replied aloud, grinning as Tarkhan rolled his eyes.

"I'd say you have no idea, but I have the funny feeling you do." Tarkhan grinned in return.

"You'll need time to establish yourselves, I'd imagine," Michael said.

"We have supplies with us, and we can live in our tents for some time, but we will need to build more permanent homes and establish crops," Tarkhan said slowly.

"We normally demand tithe, but, in the circumstances, I will waive those. At least for now."

"We thank you," Tarkhan said.

"Along with those guarding the mountain pass, we request some of your fighters to help patrol our lands to prepare for the fight we know is coming," Michael said.

This had been a sticking point they'd been circling around and kept coming back to from different angles. Michael could see the clan leaders didn't want any part of further fighting.

Why is it they have no problem monitoring the mountain pass but won't send some of their fighters with us? Olivia's mindvoice sounded exasperated.

They know we are right about the mountain pass. They don't want their enemy sneaking up behind them any more than we do, Michael said.

I'd wager they are sick of fighting, the Warlord said.

"Perhaps we could revisit our fighters, joining your own"—

Tarkhan drew his gaze from his fellow leaders back to Michael — "when our people are more established?"

Even though he was frustrated by the obvious deflection, Michael was beginning to think he would like Tarkhan. He could understand the clans would want what fighters they had with them until they were more secure and settled in their new home.

"Between our clans, we have enough fighters to send some back up to the Heights and patrol these lands. I fear we don't have enough to send some with you at this point," Ulagan said. His fellow leaders all indicated their agreement.

"How will we get word to you if our garrison finds the Sylannians coming through the pass?" Orghana asked.

Michael almost sighed, recognising the effort to divert the topic back onto safer ground.

"If they come down the Heights following the path you took, can you hold them long enough while some of your people send us the alert?" Michael asked.

"We can. Better if an escape route is in place so we can send the non-combatants to safety." Orghana frowned, turning to the older pair of clan leaders before returning her gaze back at him.

Michael had to admit it made sense. If the parents had the peace of mind to know their children were well back from the fighting line, they could keep their minds on their jobs. It also freed up more of their fighters to do what they were good at instead of playing camp guard.

"I'll leave the road between here and the nearest village for the both of you to sort out. We will, of course, make an introduction between you and their hunters, who will, in turn, make arrangements with their village elder," Michael said.

It will be faster if we blast it through ourselves, Olivia said.

It would, but this way it will give both the clan and the people of the village something to work on together. To get to know each other. We don't need to be constantly hauled back here to settle petty disputes between them.

"We will keep watch here. We can and will hold. You can safely leave this border for us," Tarkhan said.

"Understand we will send at least one of our fighting units this way if the alert goes up, but we are covering a great deal of territory. It may take time, even for us, to get here. Particularly if we are at the other end of the Warlord's domain," Michael replied.

"Perhaps it would be wise if we worked with the hunters who know this land regarding the passage between them and us. We all want to move freely, but we want to hinder the Sylannians if they breach our line or get around it," Tarkhan said.

I'm impressed that his mind is going towards defensive options, Olivia said.

That should be sufficient for now; we can revisit their fighters joining us later. You need your rest. The Warlord wove both order and concern through his tone.

"Very well. We can discuss the details in full later. For now, concentrate on the mountain pass and building a new home for your people. In the Warlord's name, I'll divert the tithe from the nearest village in your direction. It should help tide you over while you get established." Michael stood, indicating negotiations were over, at least for today.

Tarkhan stood as well, the other leaders following his lead. Now that the negotiations for the day were over, concern played across his features.

"Khaliun?" Tarkhan asked.

"She hasn't regained consciousness yet, but our healer is hopeful. Kesha is one of the strongest of her kind I've encountered." Michael ducked his head before meeting the concerned gazes of those opposite him. "I hope, as you do, that she will recover."

The Warlord and Olivia stood smoothly, excusing themselves politely to their hosts before heading towards the door. Michael didn't even bother to hide his fatigue. That was a lost cause.

FIFTY-SIX

Damien cracked his eyes open, then winced, closing them again. It was a marginal improvement. He reached up blindly and placed his forearm against his eyes. He rolled over onto his side, hoping to stop the direct sunlight from hitting his eyes and spearing into the back of his head. Or he tried. Instead, he landed on the ground beside the cot he'd been sleeping in.

He groaned softly. Now it wasn't only his head that hurt. At least he hadn't been in his hammock. Finding thinking a difficult enough proposition, let alone attempting to get up and get back into the sleeping cot, he rolled over. The hard ground was easier to ignore than his head. Nausea rose and sweat broke out all over his body. He shook with uncontrollable tremors.

Voices reverberated and bounced around in his head, making no sense. He curled up and sucked in air as a deep need for his tea clawed at his mind and body. His stomach was tied up in knots. Unable to stop the whimper that he was sure came from his lips, he pressed his palms to his head as his body continued to shake, wishing the pain would go away.

He wasn't sure how long he lay there when hands touched his temples. Damien stiffened instinctively. Then a soothing coolness washed over his brain.

Shhh... sleep. You'll be better when you wake.

The low, restful whisper urged him down into darkness, banishing the sense of wrongness and pain as it did so, and Damien fled into it willingly.

FIFTY-SEVEN

As they rode slowly back into their own makeshift camp from the last round of negotiations, Michael didn't bother to hide his fatigue, keeping to the centre of the escort.

Even though it didn't take long to cover the distance between their respective camps, he was glad to return to their own. At least here, he didn't have to block the undertone of animosity and distrust that had run through the clan's camp. That helped him understand how tired he was. He rarely had a problem blocking out the constant stream of absent-minded, disjointed mutterings and emotions that people unwittingly flung out. For the average person, it wasn't really an issue, but for strong mindspeakers, it was enough to drive you mad if you didn't learn to maintain a good mind shield. With a sigh, he dismounted, passing the reins to a member of the escort who took his horse along with their own off to the horse line.

He was about to walk back to his tent when a large group of his people, Nathanial, among them, alerted him there was an issue. He traded glances with the Warlord and Olivia, unable to keep the groan from escaping his lips.

"Now what?" he muttered.

The Warlord chuckled at his exasperated tone, and Olivia shook her head. All of them altered their course, heading towards whatever problem had occurred now. Aiden sauntered in their direction. Aiden's whole demeanour was far too delighted for whatever was wrong to be a good thing.

"Ah, Warleader, just in time. It appears your latest recruit is an addict." Aiden smiled, although there was no sincerity in it at all.

Nathanial shot a withering look in Aiden's direction, waiting until Michael, along with the Warlord and Olivia had made it to his side before he reported.

"Tiscan. His village elders have been dosing him with the stuff since he was a child." There was no judgement in Nathanial's face, only concern.

"How long have you known?" Michael asked.

"I only found out the other day. You've been busy with the negotiations," Nathanial said without apology.

"How bad?" Michael asked, going down onto one knee near the unconscious form of his recruit.

"Bad enough. I judge Damien's been consuming enough that it would kill a regular person. He threw back almost an entire mug of the stuff without blinking," Nathanial replied.

"Between the tiscan and transition, it would explain some of the erratic nature of his powers," Olivia said, her hand hovering over Damien's temples, her powers questing out to explore their recruit's condition. It did not surprise Michael to see her shake her head.

"Move him to my tent and request Kesha tend him," Michael said.

"No, use mine. You are not sleeping outside," Olivia said.

"I'm that tired I'll sleep anywhere."

"Olivia is right. You'll sleep in the tent," the Warlord countermanded.

Michael opened his mouth to object, then closed it again as the Warlord's eyebrows rose. Finally, he held up his hand, conceding to the order.

"Yes, Warlord." Michael sighed and his eyes swept over those gathered around. "Some of you make up a cot in my tent for Olivia. The thing is big enough for a family to sleep in."

You know I'll be fine out here, Olivia objected.

Of course, he said, *but you might as well have some comfort.*

Nathanial moved to one end of the sleeping cot Damien was in, while Callan went to the other. They picked the whole cot up, using it to carry Damien across the camp to Olivia's tent.

"Rest before you collapse as well," the Warlord said.

Michael was too tired to even bother to protest. He turned and followed along behind Nathanial and Callan as they carried Damien across the camp to the tent opposite his own, before pushing the worry aside. The benefit of having a healer present was that she could ease the cravings Damien would wake up with. The discussion with the lad about how dangerous the stuff could be and the need for him to withdraw from its use could wait until later.

Aiden watched as Michael walked away, carefully keeping his frustration to himself. He patted his vest pocket, reassured to feel the little flask he'd tipped the rest of the tiscan into rather than disposing of it. He didn't know what use it would be. Any more than what purpose he'd put the tiny little mental hook he'd insinuated into Damien's mind to. Michael's people were all so loyal to him. He was sure being able to influence at least one of them without their knowledge would be an asset in the future. He'd been concerned when the healer began treating Damien, but so far, she'd been too busy treating the obvious issues of the fighting knowledge he'd shoved into Damien's head and now his tiscan addiction. She'd missed the little thread he'd placed in Damien's brain. A connection that would allow him to influence the lad without anyone being aware. He watched the people around Damien disperse for a little longer before he turned and stalked across the camp to his father's tent.

"Father, I'd like to speak with you," he called before the Warlord disappeared into his tent.

The Warlord turned and sighed. Aiden's lips thinned but he said nothing as he closed the gap between them. Finally, his father waved him to follow and led the way into his tent. This was yet another thing he found irritating. Michael and Olivia, always his father's favourites, were installed in tents while he made do with a sleeping cot. He smiled insincerely at his father's guards as he passed between them into his father's tent. At least gaining approval before his father disappeared into the tent's confines spared him the games they usually played with him.

"What is it, Aiden?" His father sank into a pile of cushions and gazed up at him. His face was unreadable.

"As much as I've enjoyed riding with Michael and Olivia, I'd like your permission to part company with them as soon as we leave here," Aiden said.

He almost held his breath as his father stared at him, the silence between them stretching.

"No."

"Father, why do you persist..." Heat rose on Aiden's face.

"Michael is not your enemy."

"When will you see he is a risk to you, to both of us?" Aiden's temper snapped.

It horrified a small part of him that he'd displayed his anger at his father. Defiance was not something the Warlord tolerated, not even from him.

"Michael will never betray me. I'm a father to him, more so than the man who helped birth him," the Warlord said smoothly.

"He's not your son," Aiden hissed.

"Put your jealousy aside. You're not a child anymore. I consider Michael just as much my son as you. You will find common ground with your brother." The Warlord deliberately emphasised the word *brother*.

"He and his Unwanted are too powerful. They are loyal to him. Not to you."

"There is a reason I've treated Michael as my son from the moment I took him off his father. I could see the power he would become. That he has become. The Unwanted is indeed a power. They are loyal to Michael, and Michael is loyal to me. They are the shield that stands between me and others of power that might come this way," his father said with infuriating calmness.

"Father—"

"Enough. One way or the other, you will learn. You'll continue to ride with Michael until I say otherwise. Now get out," the Warlord snapped.

Aiden bit back his protest knowing it would fall on deaf ears. Michael was his father's blind spot. He turned and pushed his way out of the tent, ignoring the stares from his father's men at the door. They would have overheard every word of the futile argument he'd just had. Not that it was the first time he'd had this discussion with his father. The animosity between him and Michael wasn't exactly a secret. Ignoring their gaze, he walked over to his sleeping cot and flung himself on it, shutting his eyes, determined to ignore everyone.

FIFTY-EIGHT

Damien sighed and rolled over.

His eyes flared open as it occurred to him that he was comfortable and hadn't fallen out of the narrow cot where he'd gone to sleep. Or he hadn't this time. He distinctly remembered waking earlier and doing so. He found himself staring at a hide canvas above him. He was still trying to work out the comfortable part when laughter sounded nearby.

"We have moved you to Olivia's tent. She's bunking in with Michael," Nathanial said.

Damien turned his head slightly to see Nathanial sitting not far away, comfortably lazing on a pile of cushions and rugs, while Callan was at the small stove in the centre of the hut.

"Sorry to be so much trouble." Damien flushed.

Nathanial shook his head. "You haven't been. I'm sorry I didn't notice the tiscan earlier."

"Besides, if the healer is correct, it's not just the tiscan you've been taking causing you problems. Those damn forced weapons skills are causing you an issue as well. That was Aiden's fault." Callan stood and held out a mug towards him.

Damien contemplated the mug and wondered if he was thirsty enough to move; he ignored the sudden urge that struck him to ask for his tonic. Feeling distinctly lazy, which wasn't usually like him, he pushed himself onto his elbow, even though that seemed like an effort, and reached for the mug.

"Thanks." Damien smiled, took a tentative sip, and then frowned at the sweet taste. His eyebrows raising as his eyes met Callan's.

"Healer said you should be able to manage this, but not to bother trying to get up. She'll be over shortly." Callan's tone was unusually sombre.

Damien sighed, realising Nathanial had told him about his tonic. Even worse, given he'd been moved into Olivia's tent while he was unconscious and was being tended to by the healer, everyone was probably aware of his problem. Embarrassed, he concentrated on keeping his hand steady as he sipped more of the drink. He surprised himself by finishing whatever it was, then handing it back to Callan before slumping back onto his bed. Damien closed his eyes and realised it was restful. Something he rarely experienced. Even when they stopped in a place longer than a day, he was usually up and off hunting, then training, along with the other chores that most of them left for those moments, like washing. It didn't really give much time for actual rest.

He sensed the healer's approach before the door opened as she entered. He turned his head, opening his eyes as she knelt beside his bed.

Let me check the state of your mind, Kesha's low mindvoice whispered to him.

Damien sent his silent assent and found himself lost in eyes that were suddenly compelling, her delicate hands on his temples. It was a strange feeling, her mind lightly fluttering over his own, pausing and probing. Her power, different to his, wrapped around him, protective and comforting. She chased away the images of the battle that plagued him, and he felt unaccountably better afterwards. The chaotic mosaic of images, sights and sounds from the fight seemed to have been separated. When Damien remembered the battle, he knew *what* he'd done instead of being overwhelmed and fearful of what he *might* have done. The battle was suddenly more precise in his head. It was like parts of his mind he hadn't known were agitated had finally been pushed into some sort of order. He wondered if the strange lethargy would lift, and he'd feel like getting up after she was done with him.

It's a compulsion. Yes, you will, but not out of the camp and no training. In this, her mindvoice was firm.

Damien realised with a start that he wouldn't have a choice but to comply. Her words had been laced with her power and settled on him. That also explained why he had no desire to get up when he woke. Then again, he realised if she hadn't taken the choice away, he probably would have had difficulty pushing aside his guilty conscience for being lazy and done both. Kesha's injunction neatly took care of that. Since she'd been rummaging around in his mind, she was obviously aware of that.

Finally, she withdrew slowly and delicately without the sudden wrenching shock it had been when Aiden had been shunted from his mind. He watched calmly as she settled back, relaxing, making no move to rush off. Damien turned his mind inward and found that many of the pressure points he'd learnt to avoid lest it invoke a blinding headache or a blackout had eased. He had no doubt that was because of Kesha's influence.

"Thank you. I thought it was dangerous to enter another person's mind."

"You are most welcome. I only wish it wasn't necessary. What Aiden did was not kind, or, I judge, necessary." Kesha smiled, offsetting the harshness of her last comment. "It is dangerous to join another mind like Michael and Khaliun did. What I just did was different. I will try to explain the difference to you when you are better."

As Kesha went to stand, Damien reached out a hand. "Wait... I wondered..."

Kesha settled back, watching him calmly. "Wondered what?"

"The memories Aiden forced on me. Sometimes they rise, push me aside and take control. Am I going to go mad?" Damien kept his eyes on Kesha.

"I don't believe so; you have made good progress assimilating those memories. Just give yourself time." Kesha's smile faded, her expressing growing troubled. "How long have you been taking tiscan?"

"I don't know, since I was young. I don't remember not taking it," Damien replied.

"I've done what I can to ease your cravings for it, but it will take time. For some, it is highly addictive."

"Is that what caused my headaches?"

"I'm sorry I didn't notice sooner. I was so focused on treating the fallout of Aiden dumping all those memories in your head, I just didn't notice your addiction," Kesha said.

"My mother and the elders used to make it for me. I don't believe they would have if they'd known." Damien vowed that was a minor detail his mother would never find out about.

"For most people, it isn't a problem," Kesha said. "It's commonly used by healers, particularly those with less affinity with the healing arts than I possess, to help relax patients before they begin work."

"I'm just the lucky one?"

His breath caught. Isabella had taken the tonic as well. Not as much as him, since she hadn't suffered any veil sickness yet, but his mother would also push the potion on her. Panic flooded his mind and he struggled to sit up. He had to get back to warn her.

Kesha stroked his forehead with her fingers, and his panic brushed away with the pass of her fingers, the tingling on his skin giving away that she had used her abilities on him. Kesha brushed his temples again, and Damien sighed, the tension draining from him.

"Rest. Allow the work I've done to settle in your mind. I've done what I can to assist you and smooth out the memories that aren't your own, so they aren't as jagged. They were causing you confusion and pain, increasing your desire for tiscan. You were consuming far too much. It may have helped to take the pain away, but it has caused you more problems."

Kesha stood and walked out of the tent with a nod at Nathanial and Callan. Damien gathered she was heading back to check on either the tribeswoman she was tending, or Michael. Taking her instruction seriously, he rolled over, pulling the blanket over himself. He'd contemplate getting up later. Right now, sleep seemed a much better idea. A lassitude settled over him, which he gathered was from the healer meddling in his mind. As far as he was concerned, if it tamed the 'other' that had been shoved into his head, then he'd do precisely as she directed.

FIFTY-NINE

Steven sat in the small trader boat with Gareth and a handpicked group of his people. There was nothing else but the thick jungle around him. The vines from the trees seemed to reach out and try to cling to them as they sailed down the small backwater tributaries. The excitement and the sense of striding towards his destiny when they'd first set off had receded, and even though he didn't want to acknowledge it, he wondered what he was doing. How had things gotten this far? Not that he'd admit it, but he was suddenly terrified of what his brother would do to him. Somehow, he would find out.

Feeling a sharp sting, Steven swore and slapped at the side of his neck. It had never occurred to him that he could be more miserable than he had been, but it seemed he had been wrong. He had no idea where they were or even how far they'd really travelled. This was the first time he'd ever travelled by boat or left Vallantia, but he vowed next time he'd travel in a more civilised manner—overland in a carriage or on his horse.

They'd stop in civilised places with proper beds they could

sleep in. Exhaustion weighed heavily on him. They'd been sleeping in hammocks. If you could really call it sleeping. He'd spent their first few nights picking himself up off the hard ground after being flipped out of his repeatedly. As if falling out of his hammock wasn't bad enough, he'd found that he was being eaten alive by the bloodsuckers which, it seemed, were attracted to him. It was an attraction he could have gone without. Gareth had handed him a pungent-smelling ointment without comment after their first night. It reeked, but it helped keep the bugs away from him.

That was the other thing he wanted. A bath. A hot, steaming bath to soak away the aches and pains. Steven sighed. Clean clothes. He smiled as he imagined how good it would feel. He wanted clean clothes. Gareth had given him strict instructions, with only a tiny bag for personal gear. It was outrageous.

As the boat pulled up on the bank of a deserted stretch of the river, Steven's forlorn hope that they'd stop in a village tonight was dashed. Evan sat silent and withdrawn next to him. They hadn't spoken all day, and Steven had the distinct impression that Evan was unhappy with him. Although on this occasion, he realised he couldn't blame the man. He was disgusted with himself. Next time, he would ask more questions about the logistical side of things. Or better yet, his men could go off and do these uncomfortable missions and just report to him when they got back. As the men in front of him made their way ashore, Steven leant towards Evan.

"Why didn't you stop me?" Steven hissed.

Evan's eyes slid to his own, disbelief written on his face. "I tried."

Steven opened his mouth to retort but stared in astonishment as he was left staring at Evan's back as he abruptly stood and made his way off the boat.

SIXTY

Michael needed a moment to work out what had disturbed his sleep. It wasn't because he was well-rested, or it was time he got up and moving. The startled scream and voices outside sent him surging from his bed. He grabbed his sword, grateful he'd collapsed into the sleeping cot fully clothed, and saw Olivia holding her own sword. Neither of them bothered with the sword belt as they exited the tent door.

Michael automatically sucked in power from around him and threw up a ball, willing it to produce light. It pushed the darkness back to reveal a group of tribesmen facing off against some of his people. Michael's eyes were drawn to Kesha, who stood frozen in the clutches of a tribesman who held a long-bladed knife at her throat.

His focused in on the trail of blood seeping down her neck and the spike of her fear. Energy cracked around him, as his power levels surged. The world around him blurred, and then he was behind the man holding the blade to Kesha's throat. Without pause, his hand shot out, grabbing the man's knife hand, wrenching his arm outward while he drove his own weapon up and through the clansman's body. As the man slumped, life draining from him, Michael wrenched him aside, catching Kesha as she crumpled. Waves of pure anger radiated from him. Hearing surges in the veil, he left the rest of the raiders to his people. He realised he'd collapsed in his bed with his leathers on, and his frustration flared before he ripped a piece of linen from Kesha's skirt and pressed the wad of the fabric against her throat to stem the blood flow.

Michael's eyes flashed to the tribesmen, his voice harsh as he spoke to them in their own language. "No one lays a hand on one under the protection of the Unwanted."

The other tribesmen stood, contained by the Unwanted, when a voice spoke from nearby.

"What have you done?"

Khaliun was leaning against the door frame to her tent. He was about to answer when he realised she was asking her own people. Not him.

"Don't kill them," Olivia ordered, her voice a pool of calm in the storm of emotion around them.

Khaliun pushed herself off the tent's doorframe and crossed the distance to where he knelt with Kesha in his arms. She knelt and brushed her lips on Kesha's temple.

"I'm sorry. This is poor payment for your care. I swear on the lifeblood of my people that I and mine will make up for this blood debt." Khaliun's hand rested on Kesha's trembling shoulder.

"No, leader, they've kept you captive—"

"Enough of this foolishness. Do you honestly believe Erden or any of the other leaders would have left me here alone if I were at risk?" Khaliun snapped.

"But Khaliun, they killed—"

"One of our own raised his blade in anger to one with healer's talent. One who is not a fighter. By the rules of the People, his life was forfeit," Khaliun snapped.

Michael tensed as the thunder of hooves heralded the arrival of more from the direction of the camp of the clan. The number of soldiers gathered increased as they all became alerted to trouble and rolled out of their beds, weapons on display around the camp. The protective cordon growing.

"These people are our allies." Tarkhan's voice sounded from beyond the cordon.

"Let him through," Michael ordered.

Michael watched as his people moved aside, allowing Tarkhan to stride through their ranks. The other man's eyes took in Kesha, still in his arms, and Khaliun, kneeling with them. There was a spark of relief from Tarkhan that his co-leader was up and conscious. The tribe leader's expression closed as he took in the dead tribesman on the ground and the others who stood disarmed under the careful watch of the Unwanted.

"It is our own who are at fault," Khaliun said.

"I came as soon as they alerted me to trouble. I'm sorry I was too late to avert this," Tarkhan said.

"If you bear responsibility for these others, I will cede them to your custody," Michael said, his eyes holding the other man's. "Be warned, if any of yours come against mine again, they will die. Even if it means war between our people."

"I think I have the perfect punishment for them." Tarkhan's tone was sharp as he turned his gaze on his fellow clansmen.

Michael gestured for his own people to release their captives. They warily let go of those they held, but Michael smiled as Nathanial and Callan positioned themselves between him and the clansmen. Still others gathered around the Warlord, who'd appeared at some point. The Warlord's approval clear in his calm demeanour.

"Who was on guard duty? How did they breach our camp?" Michael asked.

"Fetch those who should have prevented this." Olivia glared at some guards who stood staring and snapped, "Now!"

A couple of their people spun and jogged out of sight. It didn't take long before a couple of members presented themselves. Michael didn't recognise either of them but they were members of one of the other units the Warlord had brought with him.

"How did this happen?" Michael was shocked at the calmness in his own tone.

Despite the pool of calm that surrounded him, it had the opposite effect on the two who stood before him. Both men paled.

"I'm sorry, Warleader," a guard whispered.

His eyes tracked over to the dead clansman before returning to the ground in front of him. As if he didn't want to see his fate.

"Your warleader did not ask for your apology," Olivia said, the anger in her voice in stark contrast to his calmness.

"Clansmen have been coming to visit their sick leader from the start. We were told to let them see her. Not to cause trouble," the other said, a note of pleading in the guard's voice.

"It didn't strike you as odd that it is the middle of the night?" Michael asked.

"I... it should have." The man briefly met his eyes before returning to the inspection of his boots.

Michael was about to answer when one of the band leaders finally stepped forward, crossing over to stand beside the two who faced him.

"I'll take responsibility for my people, Warleader, Warlord. It has been standard orders to go softly with the clansmen," the band leader said.

"Your orders have changed. None gain entry but our own at night, except in an emergency. During the day, they will be granted access under escort, and only with one of their tribe leaders with them to act as surety for their behaviour." Michael gazed at Tarkhan, repeating the new instructions in the language of the clans. "I want no more of these misunderstandings."

"I will pass on the new requirement. Under the circumstances, it is understandable. On behalf of my people, I'm sorry this happened," Tarkan said.

"I declared we owe blood debt," Khaliun said, her eyes holding those of her co-leader.

"Blood debt will be honoured. We will join some of our fighting forces with your own to fight those of our mutual enemy who also plague you," Tarkhan conceded.

"On behalf of my people, I acknowledge and accept the payment offered for your blood debt," Michael said formally.

Gathering the veil, Michael stood, Kesha still cradled in his arms, her head resting on his shoulder. He could feel the tremors that still ran through her body, her shock at being attacked. As a healer, Kesha had been sheltered her whole life. It was one thing to deal with the aftermath of violence between people. It was another to be the subject of that violence. Michael thanked Olivia as she opened the tent door for him, and he retreated inside.

CHAPTER
SIXTY-ONE

Kesha pushed her fatigue and that spike of fear aside as she walked out from the tent Khaliun was housed in, satisfied with her work. While her patients still had some way to go, she was relieved rather than deeply saddened. Sometimes she walked out from trying to heal someone knowing that, while she'd done her best, they would die. This time, despite how badly hurt Michael and Khaliun had been and how sick Damien had been, all her patients would live. With Michael, it was like his body was trying its best to heal. As if the addition of her own healing talent helped to point Michael's own powers in the right direction.

People like Michael were different. Although she doubted he was aware how different he and the Unwanted were. They weren't just more powerful than the average person. None of the Unwanted used the veil like ordinary people. She'd discovered the power was actually in them, a living thing running through every section of their body and mind. In Michael, she'd noticed whenever he used the veil, it was power from both within and without. After he was done, the veil seeped back in to replenish what he'd used almost immediately. It was an unusual phenomenon she'd never seen before. Regular people could manipulate the veil a little to do simple things, but it wasn't a part of them. It was a power they could sense, grapple with, and utilise to an extent, but very little of the power lived in the average person's body. Once it was gone, it could take days to replenish.

Khaliun had been an exemplary patient, doing exactly as she'd been told. Damien's condition had been complex and treatment had involved chasing down the cravings that surged in his body and mind for the tiscan he was addicted to. Between combating his addiction, his confusion regarding the recent battle and Aiden's meddling, she'd had her work cut out for her. She could sense the fitful surging of the veil in Damien, a condition she'd always known as veil sickness; however, there was nothing she could do to help. Nathanial assured her it was a condition the Unwanted called transition, and in Damien's case would resolve itself eventually. Where the veil surged through Damien's body, she could see the physical changes it wrought inside him. It was no wonder his attacks caused him such pain. She'd be concerned, but they were changes she'd noted in Michael and the other Unwanted. It was like the veil was moulding Damien into what it wanted him to be.

Not that she'd articulated that to any of the Unwanted. They'd probably laugh at her.

Despite this, Damien followed her instructions and was doing well. Of her three patients, it was Michael she still held the most concern for. Mostly because he refused to rest. Driving himself to broker the peace deal with the clan and check on the welfare of not only the Unwanted, but the other fighters and even her.

She smiled as Nathanial fell beside her as she crossed

between Khaliun and Damien's tents. Despite herself, her unease settled in his presence. One of Michael's people was always with her when she was in the open. No matter where she was going or how far. Even if the one acting as her guard wasn't Nathanial or Callan, she recognised them by the sword-plunging-into-flames crest on their clothing. She'd worked out only the Unwanted sported that branding on their clothing and weapons.

She stopped, turning around in confusion. The space where her own tent had been sitting was bare. Turning, she went to ask where she was meant to sleep when a deep rumbling voice issued orders for the camp to prepare to depart. Kesha stopped dead in her tracks and Nathanial ran into her from behind. His hands reached out, steadying her. Heat flushed her face.

"Sorry," Kesha muttered. "Thank you."

Kesha turned her attention to the one who was issuing orders. She was familiar with that voice. She knew him. Even if she'd only caught a glimpse of him since she'd been in this camp. He'd sat back, watching while Michael pushed himself to settle every dispute that rose instead of resting, as he should have been.

Long ago, her village had spirited her away at the first sign of attack, before the Warlord's arrival. Still, she'd been close enough when the Warlord's deep rumbling voice rolled over her village that dawn. She wasn't likely to forget it. The moment in the early morning light, when her village was under attack by Sylannians and the Warlord rode in and rescued them, was a moment burnt into her brain.

Eyes narrowing, she turned, ignoring the flash of alarm on Nathanial's face. Fatigue forgotten, her lips compressed into a thin line, she marched her way to where the Warlord was issuing orders for everyone to break camp come dawn.

"Do you want Michael to collapse?" Kesha stopped behind

him, hands on her hips, glaring at the broad back of the Warlord.

She ignored the sudden, shocking stillness of Michael's people. Their concern was like a physical thing. These were people who could and would wreak havoc on all around them, stilled by the mere mention of Michael relapsing back into unconsciousness. It was a sign of how important the warleader was to those he led.

The big man turned, his face infused with red. Anger rolled off him in waves that he didn't bother to check. Kesha's anger notched up in response, as she craned her neck to glare up at him. The Warlord paused, then his anger suddenly bled away to be replaced by amusement.

"No, of course not. I care for my people." The Warlord looked down at her. "You would be the healer?"

Kesha nearly sighed and wondered how long it had been since anyone confronted the man and told him he was wrong.

"I would be. The one you nearly killed three more of your men to get here. We will not be leaving here tomorrow. Michael needs the rest you have denied him before I'll allow him to travel." Kesha was aware of the eyes of everyone surrounding them as they watched this confrontation.

"Very well. I'll be guided by your advice." The Warlord smiled down at her, yet there was an edge to it. "Be warned, either Michael comes out of this unharmed and sound of mind, or you die."

Kesha ground her teeth as she bit back the retort she wanted to make to this man in front of her. She'd expected this from the man that everyone called the Warlord. The threat of death unless they did exactly what he wanted. Yet the behaviour of at least some of his people didn't match his harsh declarations. Somehow, she didn't feel threatened. Not like she had when the clansman grabbed her and held the knife at her throat. She knew, logically, that the clansman had been trying to fend off the Unwanted by using her as a hostage but she'd been terrified, with that blade pressed against her throat, biting into her skin, to feel her blood trickling down her neck. While she'd seen blood and death aplenty, it had been a shock to realise a man was dead because he'd laid hands on her. The move he'd believed would save his life was the act that killed him.

"He needs rest before he travels. I'd prefer a couple of days. He's nearer to collapse than he realises." Kesha stared defiantly at this man in front of her.

"You can have one day."

"It must be an easy ride and overnight in the village," Kesha said firmly.

The Warlord stilled, his sharp eyes regarding her. Fire crackling, a mountain breeze rustling the tents and the restless movement of horses were the only sounds. The world around them held its breath.

"I will concede to your knowledge and skill with the healing gift," the Warlord said, his lips twitching.

It was suspiciously like he was trying not to laugh. Kesha frowned.

"Take me to where I can rest for a few hours, Nathanial."

Nathanial, of all the Warlord's people who'd watched the confrontation unfold, showed no shock or even nervousness. Nathanial's eyes danced as he traded glances with the Warlord before he half turned and gestured to one side of the makeshift camp.

"Of course, healer, this way. I've had your tent moved—you're now in the centre of the Unwanted, so you won't be bothered again. Rest all you need; be assured I'll send someone for you should any of your patients need you."

"Oh, it wasn't packed up because we were meant to be leaving?" Kesha asked.

"No, I found out about that at the same time you did. You saved me from having to contradict the Warlord myself or run off to fetch Olivia to do it." Nathanial grinned at her, rolling his eyes. "I probably would have opted to send for Olivia. The Warlord is much more forgiving when Olivia defies him."

Nathanial led her through the camp, away from the Warlord and the rest of his band, who were still staring in shock over the confrontation. She had to resist the urge to stare at Nathanial. He appeared young and inexperienced, even if he was extremely powerful. Yet his manner towards the Warlord just now had signalled that he wasn't the lowly errand boy she'd assumed him to be.

Kesha frowned. All those who bore the sword and flame crest of the Unwanted on their clothing had the same appearance and attitude: young, yet experience and confidence seemed to ooze from them. Not that they hadn't earned their fearsome reputation, but somehow there was something different about them, even beyond what she would expect. When groups of them walked by, people noticed, even members of the other warbands. Just then, with the gaze Nathanial had traded with the Warlord, it was like a much older soul shone from Nathanial's eyes. It was a trait she'd noticed in Michael and Olivia, which she'd dismissed, thinking it seemed that way due to them leading the Unwanted. But sometimes, the Unwanted were uncanny. They all had that appearance. Except for Damien, who was as young as he appeared to be. She glanced over at Nathanial, who walked confidently next to her, leading the way through the camp, and decided she might need to reassess his position in the Unwanted.

SIXTY-TWO

Michael pulled his leathers on, realising he'd lost some weight. He looked down, then reached out, one hand resting on the side of the tent walls as darkness swam around the edges of his vision. Belatedly, he realised maybe he should have followed the healer's instructions and rested more than he had. Yet under the circumstances, he wasn't sure how he could have done so.

The thought of Kesha facing off against the Warlord and winning the argument made him smile. While he knew Nathanial could embellish his version of events occasionally, somehow, it was a vision in his head that he wanted to believe. The image of the petite, delicate healer fronting up to the Warlord was glorious. Then again, when it came to her patients, she had a way with her. Hearing the door open, he turned as Kesha entered and smiled.

"Thank you for your care, Kesha. Recovering without your aid would have been miserable."

Kesha crossed the distance between them and, swatting away his hands, assisted him in buckling on his leather vest.

"You wouldn't have just been miserable. You would have been dead. Never do that again." Her eyes flashed.

Michael nearly stepped back at her intense reaction, then ducked his head, catching one of her hands in his; he lifted her fingers and brushed them lightly with his lips.

"I'm sorry I scared you."

"You are still my patient. Even if you refuse to follow my instructions and rest. Your Warlord insists we need to get moving. It's a short ride, but you must promise me you won't overdo it." Kesha stared at him until he accepted the injunction.

As the door opened again, Michael turned towards it as Olivia walked in. Olivia shook her head and walked over, her eyebrows raising in amusement as Kesha stood there with his weapon belt in one hand and sword in the other, while frowning at his other weapons, confusion written all over her face. Olivia took his weapons belt from her without saying a word and helped him arm. There was no point in hiding the fact that he felt awful from either of them. Olivia knew him better than anyone. Kesha, well, she was an extremely talented healer.

"Not that you have a choice, but do you think you can stay in your saddle long enough to get back to the village?" Olivia asked.

"I'll try my best." He almost stepped back at Olivia's intensity. He could feel she was worried about him.

"I'm not sure that will be good enough," Olivia half muttered under her breath.

"Stop worrying. I'll lay odds that the Warlord will part company with us and head back to the stronghold at Yalleska shortly after reaching our first stop. I promise we'll stay put in the village, and I'll rest up if our good healer demands."

"If it were up to me, you'd rest up here for another couple

of days. Your Warlord would only concede one day, and you spent most of that running around." Kesha said, and she crossed her arms.

Michael decided it was wiser to keep his mouth shut. Particularly since right now, he wasn't sure he could make it back to the village himself. He'd been running on the edge since he'd woken up, sucking in the veil to bolster his energy and stay awake. Even that ability had its limits. It had been a long time since he'd reached the edges of his capacity, but he feared he'd just about made it to that point. It was starting to hurt—fire running through his brain, muscles, every part of him to his fingertips. If it had been one of his people who'd driven themselves this far, he would have ordered them to rest. They were his to protect. Not that it would be a helpful admission right now.

"I'll endure the short ride to the village, even if I collapse when I get there. I'll live." Michael hoped the partial admission would satisfy the pair.

The last thing he needed was for them to go out and confront the Warlord. Again. Despite the outward display of indifference, the Warlord cared. If he truly believed Michael was at risk his father would drag him back to the stronghold for an extended rest. That was the last thing Michael wanted or needed.

"Come on, it's time we got out of here," Olivia said.

"I should see Khaliun before I go." Kesha bit her lip.

"Enough fussing. Khaliun is fine, and you know it. You are coming with us," Olivia said to the other woman, not even a hint of compromise in her.

Michael smiled faintly as Kesha stiffened. "Warlord's orders. I expect, Kesha, you'll be more comfortable riding free than being bound to your horse."

"It's your choice, of course. As Michael has indicated, one

way is more comfortable than the other. Besides that, I feel Michael will need you there when he collapses at the other end." Olivia's voice softened at the last.

"Come, Kesha. You might think if you stay here until we're gone, you'll be able to run back to your village. Without us to intervene, I fear the clans won't allow it and I know you don't want to stay here. Besides, you'd be far more constrained here in a life with the clans than with us. With your talent, you'd be revered but kept hidden. They'd never let you go. No stranger would see you again and live."

"Oh, please, Narantuya and Yangir both have healing talent. They both paid many visits here to sit with Khaliun." Kesha folded her arms against her chest, forehead creased as she seemed to suddenly find her feet fascinating.

"Both are much better fighters than healers. They served as healers to their fighting forces. The clan has all but lost those with the true healing gift to the Sylannians. Of those left, even Narantuya and Yangir will probably find their lives greatly constrained until that circumstance changes."

"I feel your Warlord won't let me go now, either," Kesha said, her eyes shadowed.

"That may be the case," he conceded. "You'd still have more freedom and choice with us than with the clans. We transferred more than a language when I locked minds with Khaliun."

Olivia walked to the door and held it open.

"We will do our best to protect you, Kesha, but your life will be more like it was riding with us than in a cage, albeit a comfortable one, here with the clans."

"You'll just travel more broadly and get to treat more people," Michael added, seeing no point in denying the inevitable.

There were arguments he would win with the Warlord and

ones he wouldn't have a chance of changing his father's mind. He preferred to pick his battles and knowing the Warlord, Kesha's lot had been sealed as soon as he learnt about her. All he could do was try to ensure she rode with them rather than wilting like a flower without sun within the stronghold's walls. Michael gestured at the doorway, stepping aside to allow the healer out first. Kesha shook her head at him as she walked past, but her shoulders straightened, and she held her head up as she walked past them both. Michael traded glances with Olivia, her concern evident. Out of everyone, Olivia understood how dangerous merging his mind with Khaliun's had been. When it went wrong, she'd thought he'd be lost forever. She was aware he'd been siphoning the veil almost constantly to keep his exhaustion at bay, but she kept his counsel anyway. He pulled her in and hugged her, allowing his thanks and apology to flow between them. They'd been together, the two of them, almost from the start. Their lives entangled in a complicated relationship. They cared for each other more than either did for their estranged families. They were family and ultimately, she was one person in this world who would always have his back. Of course, she might smack him over the back of the head afterwards if she thought he was being stupid, but she'd always defend him, as he would her. Michael released her and walked out into the open, finding everyone waiting and Damien holding the reins of his horse. He turned to the Warlord who stood nearby.

"You'll take a back seat and rest for a day or two. Let Olivia do the heavy lifting." The Warlord stared at him.

It seemed the Warlord had listened to Kesha's opinion more closely than she had thought.

"As you command, Father," Michael said, nodding acceptance.

Khaliun stepped forward from the group of clan leaders

that had come to farewell them. She'd only recently relocated back to her own camp. He would have liked the time to sit and discuss what had happened between them, but it was time they left.

"I'm sorry, Michael. I didn't mean for that to happen. Our minds merged there for a time. Your mind dragged me through the whole thing. By the time I realised something was wrong, it was too late." Khaliun was weary, still recovering herself.

"It wasn't your fault. I'm sorry for the loss of the other clans of the People and your homeland. I'm more relieved than you know that you lived through the separation of our minds."

Michael also heard what she didn't say verbally. Her horror at the sections of his own life that she had been dragged through in her turn. She stepped forward, and to Michael's shock, she pulled him in and embraced him.

I'm sorry for the childhood you lost. At least my own nightmares have been as an adult. Her mindvoice was fierce.

For good or ill, we have a connection, you and I. Michael smiled.

Thank you for giving us time to settle our people before coming to aid you in your fight. We will honour the blood debt. Khaliun was solemn.

What happened was a misunderstanding, and the one responsible paid with his life, but I will welcome the warriors of Kallith fighting with us against this scourge of both our people. Michael stepped back and followed her movement as she walked across to Kesha.

Khaliun hugged Kesha, too. "Thank you for your care, Kesha." She pushed the healer away, troubled, shaking her head. "Michael is correct in his assessment of what would happen to you if you stayed among my people. It is not a life and fate you have been brought up with. Go back to your own people, with our thanks."

Kesha ducked her head. "No need for thanks. I wish you well, Khaliun, and I hope we meet again someday."

Michael waited until Kesha mounted before nodding farewell to Khaliun and walking to his horse. Gathering the reins from Damien, he mounted. Olivia's powers swept over him, making one more assessment before she was satisfied.

"We're ready, Warlord," Olivia said.

"Very well." The Warlord's expression was neutral.

Ride!

At Olivia's command, they moved out. Michael allowed himself to drop back until he rode towards the centre. While nothing was said that he overheard, there was a little shuffling, and he found it was Nathanial and Callan who rode to either side of him. Damien had moved up near Olivia. He gathered there had been more orders given to everyone before he'd made an appearance. Michael grinned. It was just as well he'd taken the Warlord's orders that Olivia was in charge in his stride.

Even though the ride from the clan's encampment to the edge of the forest was relatively short, Michael had to admit he was unaccountably glad when their pace slowed to a walk. The path they were on wasn't wide enough to accommodate much more. A more permanent track would be built, but that could be left to the villagers.

The journey back to the nearest village was far longer than he remembered, and only willpower kept him in his saddle. Michael tried to keep the fatigue he was feeling to himself, but he didn't fool Kesha in the slightest. Her feather-like touch had checked on him regularly from the moment they'd started riding. As they rode into the village he hoped the Warlord would honour his agreement that they would stop for the night, but he didn't want to be the one to ask.

"Warlord." Kesha rode forward and pulled up next to the Warlord's mount.

"Yes, healer?" The Warlord had a half-smile on his face as if he still found her somewhat amusing.

"My patient needs to rest. Unless you want him to collapse and hurt himself?"

The Warlord turned to Michael, his mind touching his own, assessing for himself before he turned back to Kesha.

"Very well. Olivia, see that arrangements are made. I think it best if Michael sleeps in one of the village huts tonight rather than a rough camp." The Warlord pulled his horse to a halt in front of the town meeting house and dismounted.

Michael would have been astonished if he hadn't been so tired. Talking with Olivia to determine what was going on was high on his agenda. As Olivia issued rapid orders, Michael dismounted, discreetly steadied by Nathanial on one side. Michael murmured a quiet thanks and leant against his horse, who planted his hooves and snorted, nuzzling him gently.

"Come on, my friend, let's get you into a bed. Think you can make it to the hut on the other side of the meeting hall?" Olivia said.

Michael looked over towards the hut that Olivia gestured to and smiled cynically.

"Well, I guess we'll find out." He turned to grab his saddle bags, only to stop at Olivia's hand on his shoulder.

"Callan will bring them." With that, Olivia and Nathanial not so subtly guided and supported him to the hut, both channelling their own energy to bolster his strength.

That was when Michael remembered the village had a couple of small huts set aside for visitors. Michael remembered thinking it was a nice, if odd, touch. The town was so far out of the way that it was unlikely they'd get too much use. The Speaker had explained that they'd put the huts in primarily for the barge crews. Since they were the last stop for the barge, the cabins gave some of the team who worked on the barge a comfortable place to sleep the night before they went back the next day. As it turned out, with the clans setting up in the hills, there might be more traffic than they'd initially counted on once they established a road between them. Olivia opened the door, and Michael walked into the small one-room hut and collapsed onto the bed against the wall without ceremony.

"I hope we aren't going anywhere for the next few days." Michael groaned and contemplated sitting back up to take his boots off.

"No, we're staying put. Stop channelling the veil and let yourself rest properly. We know you will be fine, but you've scared Kesha." Nathanial knelt and pulled Michael's boots off, placing them to one side. "She thinks you're going to keep pushing yourself until you drop and die."

"Nathanial is right. She doesn't know the worst that will happen is you'll slip into a veil-induced sleep until you've recovered properly and because of the Warlord's orders to keep that little detail about us a secret, we can't reassure her," Olivia scolded, swatting him on the shoulder. "Now sit up before you fall asleep. We need to get your weapons and sword belt off."

Nathanial grinned at him as he groaned dramatically and, grabbing his friend's hand, allowed Olivia and Nathanial to help him back into a sitting position. Michael unbuckled the belt and let it drop onto the bed. Olivia took the weapons and placed them on the small rack nearby while Michael started in on his vest. While he was perfectly capable of sleeping with it on, he figured he might as well be comfortable. Finally, he got it off, and Olivia took it without comment and hung it on a hook as he flopped back onto the bed.

"What's with the Warlord and Kesha?" Michael desperately wanted to sleep, but the Warlord's response to her had been atypical.

Nathanial chuckled. "His mother flashes into his mind when he sees her. She gives him that impression even more when she tells him off. Kesha amuses him, and he finds her useful. So she gets away with behaviour that no one else would dare exhibit."

"His mother?" Michael spluttered.

"I know, hard to believe, right?" Olivia was clearly just as amused as Nathanial.

Neither of them made a move to leave and Michael guessed they were both waiting for Kesha to show up before disappearing. He wondered if they were staying on Kesha's orders or the Warlord's and closed his eyes at last.

SIXTY-THREE

Damien finished setting up his hammock with the thin tarp strung above in case it rained overnight. Not that it mattered overly much. It was warmer down here in the jungle than it had been in the rolling foothills where the Kallith Clan had made their new home.

Olivia's gear still sat in a pile nearby. Neither Olivia nor Nathanial had emerged from the hut they'd disappeared into with Michael. He walked over to her gear and flipping open the side bag, he dragged out the hammock and tarp and, humming to himself, he set to stringing Olivia's bed and shelter for her.

Callan was off by the central fire pit with a spitted beast Damien had snared along the way. His squad mates had been suitably impressed with his skills. Although no one had said anything, Damien had a great deal of work to do in order to repair the damage to his reputation because of his addiction.

"Do we need any more supplies?"

Callan paused and shook his head. "No, we're good with what we managed to get along the way, and the village here has contributed some more from their own supplies. Including restocking us."

He turned towards Nathanial's gear, only to have Callan wave him off.

"Go train. A few villagers will be along to help with the food shortly. I'll set up Nathanial's hammock for him."

Damien flushed again as he sensed what Callan didn't say. His squad mate was aware that despite Kesha's efforts, his skin still crawled. It was a response he recognised now as a symptom of his withdrawal from tiscan. In the past, he would have sipped his tonic to chase away the feeling or downed a couple of good mouthfuls and crawled into his hammock. With Kesha busy tending to Michael, the alternative was to keep himself busy. Training was the only thing that really helped. He wandered a short way from their camp to find a quiet area not too far out of the way. He wasn't sure he trusted himself right now if he spotted a tiscan vine without someone else around to keep him in check.

Training had another benefit. Damien found the more he trained, the more fighting memories stuffed into his head settled, and increasingly they became a part of his own skill and knowledge. Still, occasionally, they reared in his head, pushing him aside. Kesha assured him the sensation would disappear with time.

Taking a deep breath, he drew his blade and ran through one move after the other, increasing his speed as he did so. He started with the basics, before rapidly moving into more complex sword work. Some of which he hadn't learnt himself, yet instinctively the manoeuvres were imbedded deep in his brain as if he'd practiced them his whole life. He'd leant to let that knowledge flow without trying to understand, control, or fight it.

Finally, he drew to the end of his practice session. Damien was aware of observers, but he ignored them. He was used to them by now. Well, he ignored all but one. Olivia was standing on the edge of his training circle.

"Is Michael going to recover?" Damien realised how concerned he was now that he'd finally asked the question.

"He will." Olivia turned and walked with him back to the camp.

"It's disconcerting seeing him still hurt." That was an understatement. He hadn't realised how much he'd relied on Michael until he'd collapsed.

"It is. Michael's always been the strong one. Putting himself between us and harm as much as he could." Olivia placed her hand lightly on his arm, reassurance channelling from her to him. "Honestly, Kesha healed the worst, it's nothing more than exhaustion now. Unlike you he's stubborn. When Kesha ordered bedrest, he did everything but rest. Now the drama with the clans has been resolved he won't budge from that cabin until he's had enough sleep."

"What did that woman do to him?"

"Do you remember when Aiden stuffed fighting skills in your head?" Olivia asked.

"You mean that knowledge I'm still trying to wrangle and stop from driving me mad? Yes, it's why I try to train every day."

"Well, sort of like that, except worse. What you suffered was one way. Aiden to you. With Michael and Khaliun the connection was forged in both directions.Their minds merged. For a time, before they broke free of each other, Michael *was* Khaliun. He wasn't just told what happened. He remembers it as if he lived her pain and loss. Every emotion, the heartbreak and anger over seeing her people rounded up and killed. Their desperate battles and flight with the few of them that survived. When they separated, the bond between their minds recoiled and hurt them both."

"He understood what would happen before he said he'd take my place. He saved me from that?" Guilt flooded Damien.

Olivia shook her head and smiled. "It wasn't your fault. Kesha is one of the strongest of her kind I've ever met. Michael has mostly brought this on himself. Unlike you, he was not an ideal patient."

"That is why the Warlord listens to her, gives her free rein." Damien started walking again.

"Among other things, yes." Olivia clapped him on the shoulder and guided him towards the campfire where the others of their band sat. "How are you coping with your withdrawal symptoms?"

"I'm sorry, I didn't know..." Damien ducked his head.

"Don't be. It's not your fault." Olivia kept her gaze on his without a hint of judgement.

"Training helps with that, too, and Kesha chases the demons away when she has time," he admitted.

"You're not the first to battle with an addiction to tiscan, and I'm afraid you won't be the last. It's not a battle you have to fight alone," Olivia said.

Damien smiled tightly. Determined he'd manage without having to bother Olivia. She had enough on her plate without having to care for him as well.

"If there is anything I can do to help, just ask. I find it helps to stay busy." Damien snorted dismissively, knowing how stupid that was. He was the newest and youngest member of the warband. There wasn't likely much he could do to help Olivia or any of them.

"Just keep doing what you are doing. You are one of the

strongest in the veil we have, and you are assimilating Michael's battle skills better than I think any of us believed you would. We will need you in the coming battle." Olivia pushed him down onto a log and accepted a mug of ale handed to her.

Damien swung to Olivia, feeling like he'd been hit on the head. Callan pushed a mug in his hand for him to grasp it absently.

"Michael's abilities? But it was Aiden who did it. I remember." Damien frowned, suddenly doubting himself.

"Aiden did it to Michael first. It's a nasty habit of his," Olivia said. "He stole those memories."

"How?" Damien was stunned that Aiden had managed to get the better of Michael.

"Michael's powers were fluctuating, much like your own are now. Aiden always favoured mindgifts. He took advantage and forced a connection between their minds," Olivia said. "Like the connection Aiden forged with you, except when Aiden did it all those years ago, Michael was taken by surprise, there was no Kesha and no one to break the mind bond. As best we can work out Michael did it himself."

"Why would Aiden do that?" Damien asked.

"Michael was everything Aiden wasn't. Particularly in strategy and fighting, along with the physical aspects of our powers. It was easier for Aiden to take than to work to improve himself." Olivia's tone was carefully neutral.

"It didn't quite work. Aiden might have Michael's knowledge shoved into his head, but it isn't his own. You are already better," Nathanial said, joining them at the table.

"Why would Aiden risk madness?" Damien asked.

Olivia and Nathanial looked at each other, and Olivia ducked her head as if she was considering his words carefully.

"He didn't know the risks then. None of us did. The consequences of misusing mindgifts can damage both parties. Much of how we use the veil in battle we've made up ourselves." Olivia shrugged.

"Surely others must have—" Damien stopped as Nathanial shook his head.

"You still don't understand, do you?" Nathanial's tone was sombre.

"Understand what?" Damien winced at the frustration in his tone.

"You were not just the strongest in power in your little village. You are one of the strongest in the Warlord's entire domain," Olivia said.

"Of all those who fight for the Warlord, we are the strongest." Nathanial gestured around the camp.

"The Warlord taught Michael and me control, as much as possible. At that time, the Warlord was the strongest in the veil's use that any had seen. Then we trained those who came after. There was no one before us who was stronger that we could learn from," Olivia said.

Damien stared around at the Unwanted. His mind baulking at the implication that all of them were different from the average person.

"I was stronger than anyone in Ranlith, but I just... well... it was because it's a small village. I never dreamed..." Damien trailed off.

Olivia considered him for a moment, then raised her voice. "Everyone relax tonight. We'll be staying here for at least one more night, maybe more."

Damien's mind was spinning. Suddenly, some of those overwhelming memories rearing up in his head made sense. The reason Michael was the only one who had stepped into the training circle with him. Particularly after Aiden had first forced Michael's memories into his head.

Damien's eyes widened in shock. He wondered if that was a

part of why he trusted Michael the way he did. The reason he trusted Olivia implicitly. The pair had been friends and had each other's backs since they were children. Damien shook his head and pushed it all aside. None of it mattered. If he worried about it, the whole thing still had the potential to send him mad. As it was, he'd probably have a headache tomorrow.

SIXTY-FOUR

Michael strode out of the hut he'd been stowed away in and started walking towards where everyone was camped. A quick internal scan had reassured him that he was better than he had been since he'd first regained consciousness. It had taken him two full days of enforced rest to get to this point. Michael smiled as the veil rushed into him. As he absorbed the energy, he could feel it tingling through his body, filaments of power dancing all over him. It made him feel whole, complete. He didn't need to dissemble to anyone about his wellbeing.

"Michael."

Michael changed his path and walked over to the Warlord who was coming out from one of the other visitor huts.

"Warlord," Michael greeted.

"You're sure you are well enough to travel on?"

Michael stood patiently as the Warlord's power brushed over him, a delicate trace of power. The Warlord could be subtle when the occasion warranted it.

"Yes, Father. I feel fine, and Kesha cleared me this morning."

"Good. We'll part ways. It's time you blooded our newest recruit." The Warlord gazed across the camp.

Damien had caught the Warlord's attention. He'd known it was coming, but he still wished Damien had more time to feel like he was one of them.

"Of course. I'll see to it. With your permission, I'll ease him into it. Pick an easy village to take over first," Michael said.

"Good. There should be a couple of excellent prospects before you hit Vallantia. Keep Kesha with you. She's too valuable to leave to rot in her home village."

Michael was about to respond when he was cut off. He almost groaned as he turned to greet the woman marching up to them.

"What? No! You'll have your people return me to my home," Kesha said.

"No, healer, I won't. You can either ride with Michael and perform your healing duties or return with me to spend your days living at my stronghold at Yalleska," the Warlord said as he gazed at Kesha.

"I won't hear of it." Kesha's hands rose to rest on her hips, her eyes narrowing.

Michael intervened. "Kesha, you said you think you need to help Damien some more. To help settle the memories forced into his head and soothe the cravings he suffers because of withdrawal from tiscan."

Kesha swung on him, her eyes widening. "You planned this."

"Hardly. I was unconscious when they sent for you." Michael kept calm. Her anger was understandable, if somewhat risky.

"I can always swing by your village and raze it to the

ground if it will make your decision easier, healer," the Warlord's quiet voice advised.

"You wouldn't." Kesha paled, turning slowly back to face the Warlord.

"You don't know me well at all, Kesha. Now make your choice. You go with Michael, or you come with me." The Warlord's eyes glittered.

"We pass through many villages. You could help many within the Warlord's domain with your talent. You will be safe within the heart of the Unwanted." Michael did his best to soothe the healer's anger. He relaxed as Kesha seemed to wilt.

"I'll go with Michael. I'll go and pack—not that I have much." Kesha turned her back on them and walked back towards her hut.

"Kesha?" Michael called.

She turned to him, her expression closed. "What?"

"Don't climb out the window and run to hide in the forest." Michael ignored her intake of breath and gestured to a couple of his people to accompany her.

"She was going to run?" The anger had bled from the Warlord, and he was now clearly amused.

"Of course she was. Don't worry. I'm used to wrangling new recruits."

"You fear war is coming our way, just as I do, now that Sylanna has finished with the clans," the Warlord observed quietly.

"After what I leant from Khaliun, I know they will. What we've faced from them before were skirmishes from a preoccupied, warlike people." Michael was grim.

"The safest place for the healer, whether or not she knows it, is with you or me," the Warlord said.

"I fear she will learn this herself before too long." Michael shook himself. "When we get to Vallantia, I will see Damien is suitably attired and armed. The healer, too; if she's to ride with us, she should have some protective gear."

The Warlord gave his assent, waving him off. Michael sighed and turned, continuing on his way back to where his people were camped. He needed to discuss the most suitable village to bring into the Warlord's domain. Thankfully, there were several likely contenders that they'd already marked for them to pay a visit to at some point. He'd previously considered them too small to bother about any time soon. They certainly were not a threat to any of them, or particularly valuable. Yet, for Damien's further indoctrination into his new life, they would do.

SIXTY-FIVE

As sweat trickled down his face in the jungle's oppressive heat, Steven's breathing became ragged as he struggled to maintain the pace that the others set. The fact they were going up a steep incline was vaguely offensive. Somehow, he'd always considered these islands flat, uninhabitable places.

Steven smiled bitterly. He'd gotten his wish, in a way. Although travelling overland wasn't proving to be any better than being on the boat had been. Steven jerked backwards, but not soon enough, as a branch snapped into his face. He swore as he stumbled, groping out with one hand and shoving the branch out of his way as he pushed past it. Of course, he hadn't wanted to be walking. He'd expected they would at least be travelling on horseback. If his peers found out he was sweating and slogging away on foot through the wilds like a commoner they'd laugh at him.

The man in front of him turned and impatiently gestured to him to keep silent. Steven's eyes widened in outrage and he grappled with his blade.

"Our quarry is over this hill. We don't want to alert them that we're coming," Gareth whispered to him quietly.

Gareth offered him a hand to drag him up to the top of the hill they'd been climbing. Steven looked at Gareth, a little wide-eyed. He hadn't even noticed that Gareth had somehow made his way back down to him. He'd been up in the lead when he'd last spotted the man. Steven let go of his blade, his lips pressing together in displeasure, and ignored the outstretched hand, struggled the last few steps up to the top, and then stood, sucking in a breath as quietly as he could. It didn't appease him at all that Evan appeared to be coping no better than he did himself. Both of them were unused to this sort of harsh treatment. Steven grabbed the water bottle that Evan handed him and sucked down some water, wishing wistfully that the flask contained something a little harder. When he was done, he drew his attention to the water's edge. To his surprise there was a small makeshift hut on the bank of the river. Steven frowned, wondering what type of person lived out here like this. The small cabin wasn't big enough for more than one person.

"Who is that?" Steven hissed at Gareth.

Gareth grinned tightly. "He's the sentry who sends warning back if the Sylannians pass through here. He's a strong mindspeaker. It's how the false Warlord can beat them every time."

"What are we going to do?" Evan whispered, his eyes strangely fearful.

"We're going to kill him," Gareth said, a cold smile spreading across his lips.

Steven gazed from Gareth, then across at Evan and licked his lips, knowing his eyes were wide. The silence stretched before he could think of a response.

"Why?"

"Because it will keep the false Warlord and his people busy dealing with the Sylannians while we take over Vallantia and the surrounding villages," Gareth said.

"Oh. I see." Steven's smile faltered as he began to hope fervently that there was no one in the cabin. "We'd best get on with it then."

Steven stumbled as Gareth's meaty hand clapped him on the shoulder. Steven watched as the men started descending the slope towards the hut below.

"Couldn't we have sailed here on the boat rather than scramble through the jungle overland?" Steven whispered at Evan.

Evan's face was still red and flushed. "Probably, but whoever is down there might have spotted us."

One of Gareth's women had made her way to the side of the hut and signalled, tapping her forehead.

"Beryl doesn't have a powerful gift, but if she's close enough, she can block a mindspeaker. Let's go, Warlord." Gareth started down the slope after his men.

Steven followed Gareth's lead, wincing as pain shot through his thigh muscles. He flung his arms out as his legs buckled, desperately trying to grab for the branches and tree trunks as he slid to the ground with a yelp. The world blurred as he slid down the slope, his frantic grasping doing nothing to slow his momentum. His breath exploded as he slammed into a boulder at the bottom. Steven wheezed as an all-new sharp pain joined the other assorted aches that had been his constant companion since they started this journey. He ignored the cursing coming from nearby, trusting those of the party already down here had matters well in hand. Breathing seemed a much better thing to concentrate on.

"Warlord, that wasn't quite the entrance I had planned."

Gareth's tone was dry as his head appeared, blocking Steven's view of the sky. Steven grabbed Gareth's outstretched hand, and with a groan as his body protested, allowed Gareth to help him up. A burst of laughter made Steven turn and his back stiffened at the sight of a nondescript commoner being held by his men.

"Warlord? That one? Trust me, that fool isn't the Warlord."

The unpleasant man doubled over with a grunt of pain as one of Gareth's men hit him. Anger and embarrassment rushed through Steven.

"Would you like to do the honours, Warlord?" Gareth asked, eyebrows raised.

Steven was confused for a moment, before following Gareth's gesture back towards the captive. Steven's anger drained and he went cold as he suddenly remembered why they were here. Steven wondered if he was as pale as Evan suddenly was. He became aware of the sudden stillness; he realised everyone was staring at him, waiting for an answer. Mocking laughter rang out, shocking after the silence. Steven's gaze swung back to the sentry, and he scowled. Nodding, he walked forward, drawing his sword from its scabbard. He paused, muttering as the smooth, deadly move he'd been hoping for was ruined as his sword caught on his cloak. Swearing, he wrenched his cloak to one side, stumbling slightly in his effort to untangle himself.

"Oh, you've found a genuine contender here." Amused sarcasm dripped from the man's tone. "Could you possibly have found anyone less competent?"

Steven flushed and screamed; he closed the distance and thrust his sword into the mocking man's stomach. Wrenching his blade free, he stabbed clumsily at the man, again and again, ignoring the wet splatters that rained on his face, hands and clothes in his frenzy. He was filthy anyway; what was a little blood added to the rest? His years of training with the sword he carried were discarded as the only thing he could see and hear was the mocking captive.

CHAPTER

SIXTY-SIX

Damien switched to his othersight; the wispy strands of the veil that came from everything around him sprang into his mind's eye. He frowned and sucked the energy into himself, just as the Unwanted had taught him. Not that he needed to concentrate on drawing on the veil this way, but he was trying to learn how he did it. The one thing the run-in with Aiden had taught him was that doing things automatically was only useful until the intuitive ability fled. He pushed down his doubt. If any of the others had any concerns, it certainly didn't show. Their horses thundered down the dirt road leading into the village. This town had no protection, at least nothing they couldn't efficiently deal with. Damien took a breath. He guessed this is what the Warlord had done to his own village. They rode in, intimidated everyone, and took over. No one had died in Ranlith. He clung to the hope that there wouldn't be any here either. It was a relief, admittedly a small one, that they did not expect him to do any of the talking or threatening. That was Michael's role, with Olivia backing him up. He was just one

378

band member that bolstered their numbers, adding to the perceived threat.

At least, that was what he kept telling himself.

He remembered the fear, anger and uncertainty that had flooded his village when the Warlord's men had arrived in town. Now he was on the other side. Damien suspected this was a village similar to his own, owing no allegiance to any other, with only a loose affiliation with nearby towns for trade purposes. Or so they probably believed.

Before the fall of the Rathadon Warlord, this village had been on the edge of Vallantia's territory. Michael explained to him they just hadn't bothered to ride through this place before now. So this village was much like his own had been: they already belonged to the Warlord whether or not they were aware of it. That was the problem for this place. Like his own, the sight of their successful crops and herds made them an attractive target. He was relieved that there didn't seem to be anyone like himself here in the village. They'd been just on the outskirts of this place for several days now and sensed no overly powerful uses of the veil by anyone. It had shocked him when he realised this band must have been spying on his village for days before they rode in. Spying on him and his power use. The whole entrance had been staged. They'd watched long enough to know who he was and which hut he'd been in. Damien closed his eyes, feeling a momentary pang of regret. If he'd only listened to his parents and elders and limited his veil usage, he might not be in the position he found himself in right now.

You would be. You're in transition, so your power fluctuates regardless of your use.

Damien's eyes widened as Michael spoke to him, and his face heated. He'd obviously been broadcasting again, even though he'd been working hard to not do so. Thankfully there was no sign that any of the others around him picked up his deliberations. It had shocked him to discover he was among the strongest of the Unwanted, even though they all had more knowledge than he did. At least he was when his abilities were functioning properly. Damien frowned. So far, no one in the Unwanted had mentioned the grey place, that place that only he and Isabella seemed to know about. It perplexed him they had known about him, but missed Isabella. Still, on that, he kept his own counsel. There was no expert in everything they could do with the veil. It was a fact he was finding a little disconcerting.

The others didn't seem concerned at all that they had fewer numbers on this occasion. Although he had to admit that if the Unwanted had ridden into his own town without the support of the others, it wouldn't have made much difference to the outcome. It was Michael and his squad mates that did all the real threatening. As far as he could tell, the other bands mostly just stood around offering protection for the Warlord. Although he gathered the others could do the threatening part themselves, it was just that with the Unwanted in play, they let them do what they did best. The Unwanted were intimidating just by their presence alone. It required little effort on their part, and fewer innocent people died when the Unwanted were around. To his shock, the Warlord seemed to be aware of that fact. One or two of them spread across the warbands would still have been a threat. The sheer shock of their combined power on those they faced could not be underestimated.

Relax, Damien, this isn't the first time we've done this. We ride in and take over a place to camp for the night. Michael will take on the village Speaker, Nathanial said.

We know the location of all the villages near our border that we haven't taken into the Warlord's domain yet. We've been at this for years, Callan said.

Unfortunately for this village, it is in our path. It should be an easy one for your second actual attack, Nathanial said.

We're taking this village just, just to test me? Damien asked, feeling his face go pale.

No, don't think that way. This village is prosperous enough; unfortunately for them, we are returning from the Heights plateau. Attacking this village makes sense. It was always going to fall to the Warlord, eventually. Nathanial's mindvoice was laced with reassurance.

Smaller targets like this, we take ourselves, Callan said.

Bigger targets, ones that might pose a threat like the incursion of the Clan or are strategic, are saved for the combined action of multiple warbands, Nathanial explained.

That's when Michael takes command as warleader? Like he did with the Clan?

Correct. Otherwise, we act independently, Nathanial said. *We mix patrolling the Warlord's existing territory with claiming new villages.*

Cheer up. Unless we invade another country like Sylanna, we've almost taken this entire region for the Warlord already, Callan said.

Damien ducked his head. Nathanial seemed to have taken it upon himself to act as a big brother figure whenever Michael and Olivia were otherwise occupied. That was the other thing that perplexed him a little. He hadn't been able to determine why Michael and Olivia, the two most influential of the Warlord's people, had seemed to take a personal interest in him. Damien's abilities continued to be erratic, and even with what Aiden had done, the others were undoubtedly better fighters than him. They both had better things to do than help him settle in.

Damien, calm down. I did not miss your sister, and I take an interest in all my people. Now concentrate, we'll talk later.

Damien stiffened at Michael's exasperated comment. His

horse snorted in response, causing him to force himself to relax. The last thing he needed was for his horse to decide to run off, carrying him with it. Instant fear flooded him with the knowledge that Michael was aware of Isabella's existence.

Relax, we both know. No one else does, or you wouldn't be the only recruit in the Warlord's ranks. Olivia's words were oddly soothing, although, given her comment, Damien's addled mind couldn't work out why.

Lock it down, Damien. We can discuss your sister and the grey place another time. The command in Michael's tone was unmistakable.

Confidence, Damien, your only job is to ooze dangerous confidence, Olivia said, a small pulse of reassurance flowing from her to him.

At Olivia's final instruction, just as they entered the town, Damien took a breath, and deliberately relaxed into his saddle. No one was touching his sister. He'd do whatever he had to, kill whoever he had to, to protect her. Damien remembered how he'd beaten the baker to protect Isabella and he willed that same emotion forward, to seep from his pores, from his eyes. He felt the difference, even in the response from his horse. The skittishness vanished. Her gait firmed as she sensed the importance of this entrance from him and the herd around her.

As they rode into what passed for the main square for this village, Damien found himself fascinated. He watched the belated reactions as parents herded their children inside while what he guessed were the Speaker and elders of this village stepped forward.

Michael left the villagers staring up at him for a moment before he finally dismounted. Olivia, next to him, dismounted but a moment afterwards. That was the signal for the rest of them. They all dismounted in sync with each other, the dust rising from the compacted dirt that made up what passed for a town square as their booted feet hit the ground.

"In the Warlord's name, we'll take shelter this night." Michael's voice was cold with a hint of boredom, riding over the top of the Speaker who'd opened his mouth to speak.

The man flushed as his eyes then took in Olivia, and all of them arrayed behind. Then, unaccountably, the Speaker's back stiffened.

"We'd prefer it if you all rode on. We want no part in the war between your Warlord and the Sylannians." The Speaker's chin rose as he spoke to Michael. It was unfortunate that his voice wavered, betraying his nervousness.

Damien tensed, but Michael threw back his head and laughed.

"Whatever gave you the impression you have a choice in the matter?" The humour bled from Michael. "We will spend the night, and then we will discuss the tribute you will send to Yalleska in the morning. Don't mistake this: the village and everything in it is now the property of the Warlord."

Damien stilled as he became aware of the movement of others. That other imposed memory rose in his mind and he sprang into action, responding to a threat that only one part of him recognised. As a man screamed, drew a hunting dagger, and charged towards Michael and Olivia from behind, Damien's sword was somehow out of its sheath, arcing through the air as he launched himself at the attacker. Damien was peripherally aware that others in the village had started to draw their own weapons, only to freeze as his squad mates responded. While one part of his brain screamed denial, knowing what would happen, the man who'd launched himself at Michael crumpled as Damien's veil-powered sword took him down. As the attacker hit the ground, Damien halted, staring down at the man as he lay with his life bleeding out.

The man would die. It was that analytical part of his brain that possessed that knowledge he'd never leant naturally.

DAMIEN WAS USHERED towards the camping area. He wasn't sure when it had been put up. It was like his mind had gone blank. Exhaustion weighing down on him, and he struggled to grasp the fleeting images and feelings that rose in his brain. Isabella and his resolve to do what he must. Riding into a village. Fear from those he didn't know hammering into him. A man drawing his sword. Screaming echoing through his brain. A blade—the one he carried—dripping with blood. A man on the ground, dying, while he gazed down at him dispassionately.

He'd killed. A man had died by his blade. Tears leaked from Damien's eyes as his mind reacted in horror. At this moment it didn't matter that the man had been a threat. Or that by killing him, it had stilled everyone else in the village and stopped them fighting back. Saving all their lives. It didn't matter that his actions hadn't been conscious, that it had been those abilities stuffed into his head that had surged to the forefront. None of it mattered. It had been his hand holding the blade.

For the first time, he'd taken the life of another.

SIXTY-SEVEN

The Warlord turned from where he was observing the unloading of the first tithe to arrive from the newly acquired territory of Ranlith. He smiled in satisfaction. It might have been a small village they would have otherwise bypassed, but it had proven to be quite profitable. Not only had they added another powerful member to his forces, by the looks of the supplies and livestock below, they were also a pretty lucrative village.

He didn't bother to turn as the door opened behind him.

"Warlord, a man from the Ranlith delegation wishes to speak with you."

The Warlord turned, his eyebrows rising. No one from a newly taken village ever wanted to attract his attention, let alone have an audience with him.

"What does he want?" The Warlord found he was curious despite himself.

"He wouldn't say, Warlord. Only that he had information for you." His guard shrugged.

The Warlord's eyes narrowed. Information. This really was

unusual. While he had informants in the more significant settlements like Vallantia and Callenhain, it was rare for someone from one of the smaller villages to turn informant. To turn traitor to his own. Ranlith was one of those small villages where everyone knew everyone. He considered refusing the request but his interest was piqued.

"Show him in." The Warlord leant against the windowsill, continuing to watch the supplies as they were unloaded.

It didn't take long for his door to open again. He gathered that whoever it was had been just outside under guard. The door closed firmly. The Warlord smiled as two of his men stood guard just inside his door. The third person hesitated, then shuffled forward a few more hesitant steps.

"Who are you?" The Warlord continued to stare out the window.

"I... The baker, Warlord."

The Warlord chuckled. "Your name, baker."

"Oh. Mark, Mark Millar. I'm the baker from Ranlith, Warlord." The silence stretched between them.

Finally, the Warlord turned and stared at the fat, sweating man in the middle of the room. He reeked of nerves. Of course, that wasn't unusual.

"I'm waiting, Mark Millar. What do you want?" The Warlord wasn't usually a patient man, but on this occasion he suspected if he said so much as the word boo, the man would fall over in a dead faint.

"You need all the people with unusual strength in the veil. You said so when you took Damien," Mark stammered.

The Warlord met the man's eyes, noting his face flushing as he said the name Damien. The Warlord regarded his man on the door, raising his eyebrows, feigning ignorance.

"The latest acquisition to the fighting ranks," his guard filled in helpfully.

"What of it?" The Warlord returned his gaze to Mark.

The man seemed to freeze, all except his beady eyes which darted sideways, and he licked his lips as he leant forward and whispered.

"He has a sister. Isabella. Her father keeps her to himself, hidden in the house, away from the rest of us. She's like her brother. Like Damien."

Unfortunately for the baker the Warlord caught the vile whispering in the baker's mind that accompanied his words, along with images of the remarkable young woman who, he gathered, must be the talented Isabella.

He shook his head. "You mean you wanted the girl for yourself, and her father chased you off and won't let you near her?"

Mark straightened. "It was a respectable offer for the girl."

The Warlord laughed. "I'm sure. Get out and go back to your village." The Warlord spoke to his men. "Give Mark Millar, the baker from Ranlith, some money for his troubles and the information he has provided."

The Warlord turned his back as they led the man out, smiling as he returned to his window. So, a sister, hidden away by her family. If nothing else, it would prove good leverage on Damien. On the powerful part, he would reserve judgement. He doubted the baker had the ability to judge what powerful really was. It didn't take long before he observed the fat baker to appear below. The man was huffing from the pace his guards had obviously set to usher him through the stronghold and back down the stairs to the courtyard below. As the baker crossed the courtyard he kept turning nervously over his shoulder, up at the window the Warlord stood at. He was a terrible informant, with several of his counterparts from Ranlith frowning at his odd behaviour as they continued to unload supplies in the yard. He wondered what excuse the man would give for his disappearance. The foul things the baker imagined doing to the girl didn't bode well if he got her alone on his return to the village. If the baker's reaction was anything to go by, the girl was also desirable. Michael and his team would return to Ranlith eventually which meant if the baker acted on his desire, Damien would find out. It was a funny quirk that the more a person desperately told themselves they shouldn't think or say a certain thing, the more they projected their guilty ramblings to others. It would distract not only Damien but the rest of the Unwanted. That was something he couldn't afford to allow to happen. Still, if he was any judge of character—and he'd become quite good at assessing his people over the years—the situation might be enough to push Damien over the tipping point. To make him finally commit to being a member of the Unwanted. As the door opened, he turned from his observation of the courtyard to his guards.

"Do you want us to go back and check for the girl, Warlord?"

"No, not just yet. See if you can find out where Michael and his Unwanted are. When they finally get back to Damien's home village, it might be nice to meet them in Ranlith." The Warlord smiled coldly. "Remind me to arrange for Mark Millar, the baker, to die when we return to Ranlith. Any man that would give one of his own up to me will turn on me in a heartbeat."

Of all the things he was and did, tolerating traitors beyond their usefulness wasn't one of them.

SIXTY-EIGHT

Smoke billowed into the sky above the tree line. Damien's stomach plunged as they picked up their pace on Michael's hand signal. Even he didn't have to be told to prepare to fight, although, given the amount of smoke, he feared that any problems in the village they were approaching were over. Damien didn't know what would be worse: arriving in a destroyed village or having to draw his sword and kill again.

About thirty of his band mates spurred their horses and peeled off from the main pack with Olivia at their head, which explained the series of hand signals he'd seen and was still trying to work out. He wished they'd just use mindspeech. Damien watched as they disappeared on a side track, slowing down his mount as a hand signal from Michael directed. That one he understood. He realised some of them were ones Owen had taught him when they were hunting. Damien made a mental note to ask Nathanial or Callan for more instructions on the ones he didn't know. He'd been told that if anything went wrong and the band separated, where Michael went, he went, unless expressly advised otherwise. It occurred to him they were giving Olivia's group time to circle around to the other side of the village, so they weren't all entering from the same point. That was when it hit him. They probably didn't mindspeak the instruction because Michael feared it was the Sylannian raiders attacking the village. If they had a strong mindspeaker they might have overheard the instructions and, the raiders would have been tipped off that they were incoming. The enemy would hear them anyway, but Damien reasoned there was no need to give them too much warning.

Damien wasn't the only one chafing at the slow pace, even though they all probably realised well before he did why they had slowed. Every moment they delayed their entry to the village, more damage would occur, and more lives would be destroyed.

We're in position, Michael. On your order. Olivia's mindvoice was tense but soft.

Damien realised he'd overheard the tight communication between the pair again. He was one of the few who could. Damien tensed, watching as Michael's hand rose, pumping to show a full attack gallop. At the same time, Michael spoke one word to Olivia.

Attack!

As his nerves threatened to strangle him, Damien ruthlessly pushed his fear aside. If the plumes of smoke were because of an attack by raiders and not just a grain barn burning down, he'd be killing again if they were still there. He took a deep breath. If it was raiders, it was different. Or at least, that was what he tried to tell himself. They were riding in to help the village, not to threaten and intimidate them like they had in the last town. He could feel the excitement thrumming around his squad mates and belatedly started drawing in the veil's power himself. His horse swerved effortlessly as she galloped past Aiden who, right on cue, slowed to position himself at the rear of the warband.

As Michael spurred his mount past the tree line, the herd followed, their hooves thundering across the hard-packed road. Damien had a moment to take in groups of people fighting, before realising it was Sylannians they were fighting and he was right behind Michael. Michael's stallion reared up, lashing out with his hooves. A crack resounded and blood sprayed as they connected with the enemy's skull. Damien's own horse was called a "nag" by the others. She was steady but not trained the same way and was not going to be as useful in a fight. Using the veil, he pushed himself from the saddle to land amid a group of fighters.

Damien only registered that two of his squad mates had landed nearby before his sword blocked a strike from the person he faced off against. Drawing more power to himself, he shunted it at the Sylannian, causing the enemy to stagger back, her eyes widening with shock before narrowing again as she launched a flurry of attacks at him, her flashing blades causing him to step back. He parried his enemy's blade and, drawing the veil into himself, split his power, half repelling the Sylannian's blades while the other half powered his lunge as he drove his blade through his enemy.

There was a moment when they stood, eyes wide, staring at each before the Sylannian's fingers loosened and the blades dropped. Damien used his foot to push his opponent off his sword, immediately sweeping the blade back up to block a blow from another enemy. Damien's eyes flattened and his world narrowed. All concerns, other than the need to survive, forgotten.

DAMIEN SAT on the edge of the pier, leaning on a wooden pole, the rush of the river allowing his mind to idle while he ran a scrap of cloth over his sword. There was a buzz of conversation in the background, which he ignored. The mundane task left his mind free to mull over the fight and his reaction to it. In the previous village, he'd killed one person and struggled to the point that his squad mates had carefully watched over him. The healer had had to weave her mind healing abilities and help him come to terms with his actions. This time, he'd killed more people than he could count. Yet somehow, it wasn't hitting him as hard. Or he didn't think it was. Some of his squad members were nearby, carefully pretending not to be monitoring him.

He remembered during the time of the first attack he had been concerned about Isabella and her safety. As much as he hated to admit it, he would ride into battle and kill again. Michael and Olivia had been right. He would kill to protect those he cared for, somehow that now included his teammates. Strangely, he wasn't even shocked by that revelation. He might not be shocked but it was still an extremely difficult thing to come to terms with. He realised that all the others in his band had been through the same thing he was going through. It was why they watched over him.

Taking a breath, he stood, his lips twitching as he sensed his band members' instant attention, their concern singing in his mind. That, more than anything, told him he was still hyper-aware of everything around him.

Damien realised that was a part of it. The concern of those around him was infecting his own mind. He still struggled to keep up the barriers on his mind that protected him from others. Although he had to admit Callenhain had proven to him there was a big difference between protecting his mind in a small village and a place like Callenhain. Yet even though this place was a similar size to his own, somehow, right now, he was struggling to shut out the concerns and worries of everyone around him. He realised there was also a background need for tiscan. In the past, it probably hadn't been that his barriers had been more effective. It was likely the tiscan had deadened his abilities. When he wasn't preoccupied with other concerns, he had an almost overwhelming desire rush through him. Noticing his hand trembling, he sheathed his sword to hide his response to even the thought of tiscan. He was sure he didn't fool his squad mates, but on this occasion, they would probably put his sudden agitation down to the recent battle.

Like it or not, this was his life now. The killing was a part of it. So it was a life he'd better get used to. Turning away from the river, he sensed the others' calm, which caused him to chuckle. He guessed they'd been concerned that he would use the weapon on himself or them, rather than what he'd actually been doing—cleaning it. Just as the weapons knowledge that Aiden had shoved into his head had demanded.

Damien paused as he spotted Nathanial leaning casually against a nearby fence post and Callan sitting on the steps of what was left of a house that had mostly burnt down.

"Relax, I wasn't going to do anything stupid."

"Good. I wasn't looking forward to trying to take that sword off you. Or rather, trying to stay alive long enough for Michael to come and rescue me." Nathanial grinned, and walked over to slap him on the shoulder.

Callan grinned and joined them as they walked back through the village towards where their own camp was being put up. "Having to dive into the river and fetch you back if you decided that was a way to escape wasn't an idea I was fond of, either."

Damien stopped and made a show of turning back to the

river. "It hadn't even occurred to me, but now that you mention it…"

He went to step in that direction, only to have the pair of them latch onto him. He dissolved into laughter as they grappled with him, dragging him away from the river's edge.

LAUGHTER RANG OUT, as Damien, Nathanial and Callan started wrestling and joking around. Michael sighed with relief that the heavy cloud of darkness had lifted from Damien and he seemed to have come to terms with all the death. Or at least, he had for now. Michael had helped enough new recruits settle into this life to know the Warlord's latest recruit would go through several bouts of depression, shock and horror over the way his life had turned. After all, it wasn't something any sane individual grew up fantasising about.

In some ways, the timing of this attack was perfect. Damien had seen firsthand that at least there was a reason for what they did. The Warlord, despite appearances, really was waging war against those who threatened the existence of all of them. Even if Michael didn't agree with some of what the Warlord did, he acknowledged the need for fighters.

Michael excused himself from the conversation with the survivors regarding their options. They were only rehashing previous discussions. Unlike the last village, these were at least grateful for their arrival.

As Michael crossed the camp to where Damien, Nathanial and Callan were playing around, he could see the survivors tracking his movement and the indulgent smiles from some elders who watched the younger men. Their boisterousness made them all just that little more human, less the monster. Of course, it helped that none here were strong enough in the veil to be recruited to the Warlord's ranks.

Nathanial and Callan noticed his approach, and he jerked his head at them. Both sobered and as Nathanial drew Damien's attention to his approach Damien turned to him while the other two retreated towards their own camp.

"Come on, Damien, let's go for a walk," Michael said.

"I think that is one of the few times you haven't called me lad," Damien said, as he fell into step with him, away from the village towards the edge of the forest.

Michael scanned the surroundings and waved off the men who were about to follow. He couldn't sense anyone in the surrounding forest. On this occasion, he could break his own rules. They walked silently across the town square and into the trees at the edge.

"You're not a lad anymore. Unless I'm mistaken, you've passed your majority." Michael smiled as Damien's head jerked up.

"How did you know that?"

"We make a few enquiries about those we take." Michael's smile faded as he regarded Damien. "I would never give up your sister to the Warlord."

Michael watched as Damien seemed to freeze inside at the mention of his sister, the smile on his lips becoming brittle. Michael knew exactly how Damien felt. He took a deep breath as memory overtook him.

"My sister Nera was as annoying a sister as one could get." Michael ignored the fact that Damien was suddenly staring at him intently. "The Warlord took her, at the same time he took me, except I ended up riding into every war as he expanded his domain, and she ended up in the stronghold at Yalleska."

"He has your sister?"

"Not anymore, she killed herself."

Michael lost himself in memory for a moment, finding Nera's lifeless body in her room in the fortress. He'd snuck in to see her. He'd been worried as she had been growing thinner and paler every time he'd seen her. As it turned out, it had been much too late. Even though the suite they kept her in had been much more pleasant than the cells in the castle's bowels, it was still a cage. A cage she'd wilted in.

"I'm sorry." The whispered words brought him back to the present.

"No need to be. Just believe I will do what I can to protect your sister." Michael willed Damien to understand.

"How can you..." Damien paused, clearly troubled before he continued. "How can you serve the Warlord the way you do?"

"Other than imprison Nera at the stronghold, the Warlord didn't harm her. I had other things to occupy my mind besides what happened at Vallantia. Nera had none of that. She had nothing but time to dwell on the past. While Nera was powerful in the veil, she had a gentle way to her. She wasn't a fighter. At the time, I was grateful she'd been spared the horrors of war. Now I think it would have been better for her if she'd been a more accomplished fighter."

"Nera sounds like Isabella," Damien whispered.

"I know. I will do what I can to protect your sister. Even though I failed to protect my own."

The silence stretched between them for some time while they walked through the forest. Michael was content to allow the time for Damien to process everything.

"You want to know about the grey place?"

"That's not why I called you aside, but yes. I do." Michael didn't see any point in denying his interest. The images he'd caught from Damien's mind about the grey place had been intriguing.

"I don't know how to explain it." Damien bit his lip. "I can show you, I think?"

Michael's eyes widened. Even though the offer was entirely unexpected, he considered the option for a moment. He didn't have to think too hard about what Olivia would say to the proposal. Still, he wasn't Olivia, and she wasn't here to be the voice of reason.

"All right. If it is easier, why don't you show me?" Michael smiled crookedly.

Damien smiled back, although Michael sensed his nervousness peak as Damien's hand grasped his forearm, Michael breathed, not allowing himself to stiffen or show his nervousness. Damien drew in power, and the forest disappeared as it surged. He understood why the tag in Damien's head for this place was the grey world. It was an apt description.

Michael opened his mind, feeling the thick power of the veil all around him. He held out his hand, watching the grey energy play around it. The veil was both impenetrable in some places and almost translucent in others, the lightest touch of mist over water in the early morning. He took a step, shivering as the veil swirled around and through him. The background hum, like the whisper of the wind through leaves and the lapping of water in the river, was soothing. As Michael focused with his othersight, the trees that had been around him one moment came into focus again.

This could be useful. This is how you hid your sister from the Warlord?

I found this place by accident once when I was hiding from the old taskmaster.

Michael grinned. *Literally, it seems.*

A blush rose on Damien's cheeks. *It took me some time before I realised that no one else could access this place except Isabella.*

Keep this little ability of yours to yourself, for now. Michael walked back to Damien, gazing at him until he accepted the order.

As Damien grabbed his arm and drew them back to the real world, Michael left his mind wide open, watching the play of power as Damien did so. This skill was something he intended to experiment with himself.

SIXTY-NINE

Jaclyn ignored her immediate surroundings, secure that her family was watching for any immediate danger. While her body sat in the boat being propelled through the water through back tributaries towards the barbarian lands, her mind was not. Aided by the veil, she sent her awareness questing out. The ever-thinning strands of her power reached out, each filament splitting repeatedly into smaller threads, seeking the minds of those she suspected watched for incoming attackers to report back to the barbarian warlord.

A bright flare of mass consciousness caused her to rock back. A rush of whispered words, making no sense, as if spoken from hundreds of different minds, flooded her awareness. Jaclyn gasped a ragged breath, barely stopping herself from collapsing as she desperately threw her mental barrier back up.

Pull onto the nearest bank.

Jaclyn took a breath, steadying herself before opening her eyes to see the eyes of her family all staring at her. Waiting.

"As you ordered, we are far from the regular entrances used to launch attacks on the barbarians." Myra fixed her eyes on the bank as they pulled up on a seemingly uninhabited stretch of coast.

"You sense them?" Ricardo reached out, steadying her as she stood too suddenly and found her world spinning.

"I'll warrant this embankment isn't that large. There is a large settlement not far away." She allowed the other hands to aid her as she disembarked.

There was no point trying to ignore the fact that her efforts had caused fatigue and disorientation. This wasn't the first time she'd used this skill to search out enemy minds.

Hush, everyone. War footing until further notice. Myra's firm but tight personal communication stilled the chatter that had sprung up.

Jaclyn moved from the boat to land, walking a few steps up the embankment before sinking to her knees, one hand grasping a tree trunk to keep herself from collapsing entirely. She watched as Myra carefully opened her mind and searched their immediate surroundings, double-checking for another presence. As her fellow wife shook her head, Jaclyn rested her cheek against the rough bark. She opened herself, allowing the veil's power to fill her, replacing the energy she'd expelled. Finally, she stood, using the tree to aid her, finding some of her family deployed around, forming a security detail while others hauled their boats up onshore and set to hiding their presence with branches and foliage. She traded glances with both Myra and Ricardo.

Let's go carefully. Be on the lookout for a sentry.

Jaclyn pushed herself from the tree she'd been propping herself up against and walked a winding path through the foliage. Others took the lead, blades lashing out to clear a trail for those who followed. It would have been easier to use power, but any who watched for attackers and that mass of minds she'd sensed not too far away would have picked up their energy use. An explosion of power use where there shouldn't be any would be noticed. Using the manual method only the lookout would be tipped off to the noise of their approach, but with a bit of luck not overly alarmed, since they wouldn't be on the watch for an attack by her people coming overland until it was too late. So, they used the slow, laborious method, clearing their path by hand and blade.

SEVENTY

As they came to the crossroad Michael called a halt. The large, sprawling, multi-storey stone castle that dominated the surrounding lands was a little hard to miss. It was tempting to put off this visit and continue down the road into Vallantia. Michael caught sight of Aiden and sighed. This visit would be difficult enough without Aiden being around to cause further distress and misunderstandings.

"Olivia, take the troops into Vallantia and settle them into our accommodation in town. I'll join you when I'm done—tomorrow, if I can pry myself free." Michael scanned the ranks settling on the two he wanted. "Damien, Kesha, you're with me."

Michael waited long enough for Damien and Kesha to join him, then turned his horse, spurring it into a gallop towards the gates of the Rathadon estate. They clattered through the portcullis into the cobbled courtyard. Michael came to a halt, threw his leg over his horse and dismounted. One of the men ran forward across the cobbled courtyard from the stables, bowing hastily.

"Lord Rathadon, my apologies. No one told us you were coming."

Michael didn't have to look at Damien to know his eyes were wide with astonishment at the honorific.

"I only just rode in. No one would have had time. Take the horses to the stables and separate out two of the better war mounts. My companion needs something better than the nag he is currently riding, and the second"— Michael handed his reins over to the stableman— "needs to protect her rider if needed."

The stableman nodded and one of his assistants came running at his bellow. Breathing heavily, he took the reins of Damien's and Kesha's horses.

Michael turned, smiling thinly as what passed for guards belatedly appear on the doors, and he glanced at Damien and Kesha before he strode towards the stone stairs. A clatter of booted feet made him smile briefly as Kesha and Damien caught up.

"Lord Rathadon?" Damien's whisper was barely loud enough to reach his ears.

"A conceit of the Warlord. My father is now the Speaker of Vallantia. He was a warlord in his day, as were his father and his father before him. I am his youngest son. None but the Warlord is permitted to use the warlord title now. So, when he took me into his fighting ranks, he dropped war from the title and called me lord instead. He insisted these lands were mine to control. He ordered that the Speaker report to me. I report to the Warlord." Michael kept his eyes steady ahead, not altering his expression. He was well aware by now that their approach was being observed.

"This is all yours?" Damien's voice held a hint of awe.

"No. It all belongs to the Warlord. The entire domain does. Never forget it." Michael strode up the stone stairs towards the doors that swung open on his approach, pulling off his gloves as he made his way inside.

"Michael, so you grace us with your presence." The mockery in his brother's tone was clear.

"Of course, Steven, would I miss paying a visit since I'm in town?" Michael didn't even bother to hide the contempt.

"Well, at least some of the company you keep these days is easy on the eye, brother. Why don't you introduce us?" Steven's eyes raked over Kesha.

Michael's expression hardened as Kesha stiffened beside him. "Lay so much as a finger on my healer, and I'll make you wish you were dead."

He continued down the long hallway, guessing his father was in his room at this hour.

"As you command, brother," Steven called after him.

Michael pressed his lips together and clenched his teeth. His brother was going to get himself and probably their parents killed one day.

"Thank you. I think," Kesha whispered.

Michael dipped his head slightly but kept silent as he led the way down the hallway, although he hadn't missed that Damien still rested his hand on his sword. Damien probably wished that Olivia was here right now rather than him.

A servant scurried from the opposite end of the hallway, opening the wooden doors ahead of them. This had once been a large function room before the Warlord had come, before his father had been left crippled. They'd converted it into a suite to save his father the indignity of servants carrying him up and down the stairs. Michael's older brother had expected to be named Speaker of Vallantia, but the Warlord had left his father in place instead; a living, constant reminder of what would happen to them if they defied him. As Damien hesitated at the doorway, Michael turned and waved him in.

"Inform my father that I am here and will speak with him, and prepare three more places for dinner tonight." Michael spoke softly and walked over to the windows with a view of the gardens beyond. They were still well kept, with no sign of the events that had occurred years ago.

"Michael, you should have sent word you were coming." The soft voice held a slight slur.

Michael turned and smiled as his mother entered the sitting room; he watched her cautiously, wondering which version of herself she'd be today. The loving, caring mother or the haughty, controlling mother who kept trying to get into his mind like she did everyone else's.

His mother didn't have control over the use of the veil like he did. That ability came from his Rathadon heritage, but she excelled at mindgifts. As she crossed the space that stood between them and pulled him into a hug, he guessed it was the loving, caring mother. Of all those who feared and hated him, his mother was not one of them—at least, not this version of her, and not in private. Neither was his father. Still, he was conflicted, as always. The little boy in him remembered he loved them, but he didn't entirely trust his mother. He should hate the Warlord for what he'd done. What he'd been turned into. Yet he still remembered all the lessons he'd had growing up before that. It wasn't only the Warlord who'd turned him into a killer.

The Warlord understood Michael's parents had no hold on his loyalty anymore, but there were times it was like he was two people. One the warleader, most feared of all the leaders that rode under the Warlord's banner. The one the Warlord trusted above all others, including his own son, staring dismissively at his parents. The other, deep inside, mere remnants, the small, terrified boy, dragged from his home. The boy who was forced to watch as they tortured his parents for trying to protect him. The boy who'd do anything to protect them, even turning himself into a hardened killer.

For now, he decided he'd just be a son to those that had birthed him, rather than the Warlord who'd raised him.

He pushed his mother back, saddened to see the grey streaks in her otherwise dark hair, although her intense brown eyes still shone with pleasure to see him. The ragged scar down her face and neck was a counterpoint to her beauty. The metal tips of the lash she'd been flogged with, in punishment for Vallantia's defiance, had cut her open, nearly killing her. She still bore the scars on her back as well. The metal tips on the lash and the treatment applied to her wounds after the flogging ensured the disfigurement remained a permanent reminder long after the pain had faded.

The doors to the inner room opened once more, and the servants wheeled his father into the room. He could still walk short distances with the aid of a walking stick and much effort, but the Warlord had ensured he'd never be physically capable of rising in rebellion again by cutting his hamstring and crippling his sword arm and hand. Making sure they had no chance to heal. His leg was left lame and his sword hand in a permanent claw with the fingers frozen and unable to grasp anything.

"Father." One simple word, yet even the conflict in his voice was clear.

The Warlord had had more impact on his life growing up than this man.

"Michael. It's a little early for the tribute payment. Your Warlord sent you on some task, I take it?" Despite the frailty of his body, his father's voice remained firm, yet there was a hint of concern underlying his tone.

"It is, and he did." Michael frowned.

"It's not because of your brother, is it?" His mother's eyes widened slightly.

"No. My latest recruits need outfitting and better horses."

Michael spoke slowly. His gaze flicked between his father and mother. He almost forgot himself and groaned. He knew that look. His brother was always up to something. The only reason the Warlord hadn't had Steven killed was because his utter incompetence meant he was no threat. Michael opened his mouth to question them further when their eyes tracked over to where Damien and Kesha stood pressed up against the wall near the door. Michael had the distinct feeling both were trying to make themselves invisible. With Damien, it was a distinct possibility that he could do so. If it occurred to him.

"Olivia, Nathanial?" his mother asked brightly.

"They continued into town with the rest of my people," Michael said, his irritation rising another notch as he recognised the attempted diversion for what it was.

"Ah, I guess that is why you left them behind this time. Who is this young man and this woman?" His mother turned her attention pointedly over at Damien and Kesha.

"Forgive my rudeness, Mother. This is Damien; he's recently become a member of my warband." Michael bit back his impatience, gesturing at Damien, who stood a little uncomfortable by the doorway.

Damien smiled uncertainly, finding himself under the regard of all of them in the room, muttering something that sounded like, sorry for the intrusion.

Michael's lips twitched in amusement. He didn't need to explain to either of his parents it was the Warlord who insisted he bring at least one of his people with him on these visits, but it was clear Damien did not know why he was present. Michael had a sneaking suspicion his parents had a soft spot for Olivia and Nathanial. It was mutual, since Olivia respected his parents for at least trying to protect their children. Nathanial had known nothing like what others would consider an everyday life or home, since his parents had sold him to the highest bidder to earn a living. Nathanial, like Olivia, appreciated that Michael's parents had cared enough to see their entire world destroyed instead of giving him up.

"This is Kesha; she's a talented healer. One of the strongest I've encountered."

Understanding shone in Kesha's eyes, and something else he couldn't quite define.

"I hope you will allow me to treat you while I am here? I fear your injuries are too old for me to heal completely, but I can perhaps ease some of your pain," Kesha said.

"That is a kind offer, but we're well cared for. I'm sure there are others less fortunate here in Vallantia who could use your strength and talent," his father said.

Kesha bowed her head slightly. "I will, of course, tend as many as I can while I'm here, but I have the strength to relieve your pain if you permit?"

His father's eyes widened at Kesha's claim. He'd seen enough healers in his years to know their limitations reasonably well. As he was about to find out, Kesha was no ordinary healer. If the Warlord couldn't get her to back off from tending those she believed needed her care, his father certainly wasn't about to manage it.

Kesha crossed the room, waving away his father's objections. Placing her hands lightly on his temples, she closed her own eyes and began to work. As fascinating as he always found the process, Michael turned his gaze on his mother, keeping his tone low but firm.

"Quit stalling. What is my dear brother up to now?"

"Nothing—"

As his mother reached for his mind Michael slammed up his mental barriers, ignoring her gasp. "Enough! Your mental games didn't work on me when I was a child. They certainly won't now. What is Steven up to?"

His mother stared at him a moment, eyes wide, before her shoulders straightened and her head rose. All signs of the loving, heartbroken mother disappeared to be replaced by this haughty woman who stared back at him flatly. "I don't know. He's been secretive. You know I have little influence on him when he runs into town or is drunk. Promise me you won't kill him, Michael."

Michael clenched his jaw at the last request, taking a moment to calm the sudden spike of anger the request elicited. This was the side to his mother he had the funny feeling few people ever encountered. But that boy inside him was sure that this side of his mother didn't love him.

"I'd ask you to remember I haven't killed him yet, no matter what he's done. You can't have forgotten the Warlord's methods, Mother. He probably won't order Steven's death if he's gone too far. Just yours, Father's or random people in the city." Michael's voice was low as he stared steadily at her.

"Michael, I'm sorry. I didn't mean it—"

Michael cut his mother off. "You did. You're right; I am the Warlord's creature. As I've said before, I will not seek Steven's death, but I will not allow his foolishness to cause others in Vallantia to suffer in his place."

Michael turned as Kesha sighed, stepping away from his father. He could see by the set of his shoulders that a great deal of tension had drained from him. It was remarkable in such a short time. Kesha hesitated, obviously sensing the conflict between them but clearly not understanding what caused it.

His mother was once more playing her caring, maternal part, pulling this other side back on like a well-worn glove. Kesha frowned, but she'd been lost in her healing trance and missed the entire exchange. Michael filed that little piece of information away.

CHAPTER

SEVENTY-ONE

T he scrape of knives and forks on plates and the clinking of glasses were the only noises in the dining room. Michael did his best to ignore the frosty, difficult silence. After all, this wasn't the first time he'd endured such a dinner. His older brother was unimpressed by his presence, as always. When it came to older brothers, it seemed the Warlord was correct. His actual brother and Aiden had a great deal in common.

Steven was sitting next to Kesha while Michael had found himself on the other side of the table. Steven had shot a triumphant glance in his direction, and he had no doubt his brother had organised the seating arrangements with the servants. Michael just hoped the presence of their parents would curb any inappropriate behaviour.

"So, to what do we owe the pleasure of your company, oh Lord and Master?" Steven was staring at him as the servant refilled his glass.

Michael smiled at the poor girl, who was pale and faintly panicked as she refilled his glass. Of course, him smiling at her

411

caused her eyes to widen in fear, and she only paused long enough to fill his parents' glasses before she fled the dining room.

"I wish I could say it was for the pleasure of your company, brother." Michael smiled, but it didn't reach his eyes.

"Ah, I'm hurt." Insincerity dripped from Steven's voice. "When are you leaving?"

Michael paused before he answered, noting the nervousness displayed in that last question.

"Not any time soon. Some of my people need outfitting." Michael cut a slice of meat, and proceeded to eat it as if he wasn't concerned.

The surge of panic from his brother was unmistakable and Michael repressed a sigh. His mother was correct: Steven was up to something and did not want him in town. That was concerning.

Michael's attention was caught by a wave of unease followed by shock, then closely by anger, from Kesha as she pushed back in her chair, attempting to put herself as far away from Steven as she could.

"I'm sorry, Kesha. I was reaching for my napkin and slipped. Please accept my apologies," Steven said, smiling while his hand rose from under the table to grasp Kesha's shoulder.

Michael stood abruptly and all eyes in the room swung to him as he made his way around the table. He removed his brother's hand from Kesha's shoulder without comment. He feared that if he opened his mouth, matters would deteriorate rapidly into a fight in the dining room. He presented his hand to Kesha, keeping his own body between her and his brother as she rose from her seat. In the sudden silence of the dining room, his boots were the only sound. He walked Kesha around the table and sat her in the chair next to his own so that he was between her and the rest of his family. It caused an imbalance in the table seating, but Michael didn't care at this point. He turned to stare at the servants, his irritation increased, as he barely concealed the anger that burnt within him. That was all it took before they burst into action in the frozen room. They bustled over, picking up Kesha's plate, cutlery and glass, bringing them around the table and setting them before her. Michael waited until they were done before he picked up his wineglass and took a sip, realising it did nothing to ease the simmering anger that bubbled beneath the surface.

"Thank you, Michael," Kesha said quietly.

"I promised to keep you safe. That includes from members of my family."

Her hand rose, resting lightly on his arm, a brief pulse of gratitude passing from her to him. She was out of her depth here in the castle and unsure how to behave or if she'd caused his brother's reaction. Back in her home village and the villages she'd travelled to as a part of her healing duties, she'd always been protected. She feared it left her ill-equipped to deal with situations where things weren't so polite.

Drunken laughter rang out, causing Michael's gaze to turn back to his brother.

"Oh, I get it. She's your plaything and not to be touched. Well, excuse me for touching what is yours, brother. You should be clearer." Steven slouched back in his chair, throwing back the contents of his glass before holding it up impatiently for the servant to refill it again.

Michael gathered his brother had started drinking as soon as he'd shown up with the intention of getting drunk tonight. And being as unpleasant as he could be. With Steven, it was a skill he'd spent years perfecting.

"Stop, just for this once. Curb your tongue."

Steven lurched to his feet, sweeping the plate in front of him from the table. It shattered on the stone floor.

"Such grand advice from the Speaker of Yalleska's lapdog!"

"Enough, Steven! Your brother has no choice in what he is." The crack of his father's walking stick striking the table resounded around the room.

Michael swung his gaze to his father and tried not to let the hurt of those words strike him. This was a well-worn topic of conversation. While had no doubt that his father loved him, the man also meant every word he'd just uttered.

"Oh please, Father, you can't possibly think he's not bedding such a pretty little thing. If she's as talented as you suggest, his Warlord is probably making him breed with her like a prized stallion." Wine spilled from Steven's glass as he gestured to them.

Michael stood, his chair clattering back onto the floor behind him, ignoring his mother's shocked gasp, as he slapped aside her attempts to get into his mind and calm him down. Michael stalked around the table, keeping his eyes on his older brother. As intoxicated as Steven was, his eyes widened as even he realised the approaching threat. As Steven stood and grappled with his sword, Michael was marginally aware that Damien had risen from his own seat as well. The scrape of his sword sounded starkly in the dining room as Damien drew it smoothly from its sheath. Michael smiled grimly, drawing the veil's power to himself, increasing his strength as he stepped into his brother's guard. His knee rose, repeatedly slamming into his brother's abdomen, while he wrenched the sword from Steven's hand. Flinging the blade away, he grasped his brother's shoulders, slamming him into the solid rock wall behind him as the sword skittered and clattered across the floor.

"Yes, brother. I. Am. The Warlord's. Lapdog." Michael snarled out the words and pulled his brother up to face him before slamming him back into the wall behind him again. "His most dangerous one. The stories everyone whispers are true. It's me that the Warlord sends out to subjugate other cities, to crush any rebellion and the raiders from Sylanna. Understand that my pledge to our mother and father has stopped me from killing you all these years. Whatever you are up to, you will stop your activities. Or when I find out, I will return without the Warlord's command and kill you myself."

Michael flung Steven from him, sending him across the room with such force he slammed into the opposite wall and crumpled to the floor with a groan. There was a moment of silence before the doors cracked open and servants, who appeared suspiciously like guards, peeked inside. Michael swung his gaze to them, eyes narrowing.

"Get my brother back to his rooms and let him sleep off his foolishness." Michael turned his back on them, letting them see how unconcerned he was with them entering the dining room. Even though they all bore weapons.

Damien hadn't moved or put away his own sword. His recruit would be between himself and the guards in a moment, if needed. A cold smile touched his lips. Not that he expected the ones who'd entered would ever be stupid enough to attack him. Michael's eyes met his father's and his mother's as they stood together on the other side of the table, fear and recrimination the prominent emotions rolling from them.

Michael turned from them, sat down, picked up his knife and fork, and continued eating his food as if he didn't care. But deep inside, that little boy was weeping; desperately wanting his parents not to hate him. Wishing his mother loved him like she seemed to love his big brother.

CHAPTER
SEVENTY-TWO

The smell assaulted her before the incessant buzzing registered in her mind. Jaclyn halted; the smell was distinctive. Once you'd encountered it, it was something you never forgot. The smell of rotting flesh. Disintegrating, turning to putrid liquid in the heat. Human flesh, to be precise. She didn't gag. After years of war, she'd gotten used to the smell of death. She went to walk forward only to find hands preventing her. She went to object, only to subside to the determined glares that dared her to fight them.

Finally, the daggerwives, reassured that she would stay put, turned and made their way carefully into the clearing with the small hut below. Now that she was concentrating, Jaclyn could see the outline of the dead body slumped on the ground, flesh sloshing from the bones as it liquified and seeped into the soil where it lay. A cloud of insects surrounding it was the cause of the increase of noise, well above the expected background sounds of the forest.

Jaclyn opened her mind to the veil but found no sign of other people except her own. Satisfied, she returned her attention to those inspecting the mess below as two of the dagger-wives came out from their inspection of the small wooden hut.

Seems it was but a single lookout.

There was no need to say the sentry was dead; that much was obvious. It made Jaclyn wonder how the individual had died. She picked her way down the slope, a dark fluttering caught her eye, and she paused. Reaching out with one gloved hand, her fingers brushed the black woollen scrap caught in the tree's bark. Eyes scanning, she saw a bare patch of dirt, leaves, and twigs scraped aside. A sign that something or someone had slid down the slope. She was betting on someone with a scrap of cloth in the tree. Shaking herself, she continued her way down to the small hut.

It doesn't seem big enough for more than one person, Ricardo mused.

Jaclyn agreed, and ignoring the stench, approached the body on the ground. Concentrating, she drew some of her power, placing a barrier around herself. It pushed the black mass of seething insects back as she walked forward. The writhing mass flowing up and over, so thick it nearly blocked out the light. But at least they were on the other side of her barrier. She knelt, careful to do so on a clean patch of earth, inspecting what was left of the dead person. They'd been wearing light leather armour. The undulation of the undershirt spoke of the insects feasting on the body. Jaclyn shifted her eyes back to the leather armour, and observed the multiple cuts that suggested a sword had pierced it.

Finally, she stood and turned her attention to the wooden wall of the hut behind where the body lay. There was a dark stain on the wall that she suspected was blood. She smiled grimly. While she didn't know who'd killed this man, they'd just made her job easier and safer. The presence of the body confirmed her theory of the barbarian warlord's use of sentries.

Jaclyn stood and followed the small trail around the side of the hut to the back. She paused on a small wooden platform, with steps that led to a small inlet with a boat tied to the stump of a tree. Screening vines hid its existence from the casual observer who would pass on the river. While she couldn't see any signs of habitation down the river, she sensed many minds. They weren't that far away. Admittedly being able to sense the presence of others wasn't the same as being able to speak to them but, if the sentry had been a strong enough mindspeaker, he would have been able to send a warning to one of similar skill in the village.

Having seen enough, she turned and walked back the way they'd come. With the lookout dead, regardless of who killed the person, it was time they moved on. Her people formed around her without orders. They followed her lead as they retraced their steps to the boats. They could at least camp back down the river and get a few hours' sleep away from the stink.

SEVENTY-THREE

Michael clattered down the stairs to the courtyard, Kesha by his side and Damien scrambling after them. It was barely dawn, but he had no intention of hanging around longer than he had to. Particularly since he had the perfect excuse this time. It was odd that, for once, he had something to feel grateful to Aiden for. If he hadn't decided it was too much to inflict the Warlord's son on them, he'd be stuck staying with his family for the entire time they were here. As it was, they could all legitimately remain in town. These visits were always challenging and not something he wanted to prolong. It was like a wound, barely healed, had been ripped open all over again. Once more, he'd have to move away from his past, accepting who and what he was now.

The horses waited, saddled and held by the stableman and the stable hands. He smiled. Along with his own there was a new horse each for Damien and Kesha just as he'd requested.

He thanked the stableman as he took the reins and mounted his horse smoothly.

"I cut out two horse that I judged would fit your requirements, Lord Rathadon."

The stableman was an old hand here at the estate, steady and nobody's fool. He suspected the stableman had a firmer grasp of the current situation than his brother.

"My thanks. Damien's mount isn't too temperamental, I hope? I forgot to mention he's only recently started riding." Michael smiled as he turned to watch as Damien mounted and settled himself into the saddle.

"I noticed as much when he rode in. His horse is war-trained but steady. Next season, if he's outgrown her, I'll make sure we have another trained up. Or send word if he needs a new mount sooner."

"I will. Healer Kesha's?" Michael checked on Kesha's horse, satisfied as it stood steady as the healer mounted.

"She's solid, and although not up to your standard, Lord Rathadon, she is war-trained and will keep up with the others. She'll defend Healer Kesha regardless of whether she's mounted, on foot, or unconscious on the ground." He scratched the horse absently as she snorted.

Michael acknowledged the stableman, trying not to chuckle as Damien's mount, sensing her rider's unease, danced sideways. Still, Damien didn't end up flat on his back on the cobbled courtyard with his horse running back to the stables, which showed how far he'd come. The placid mount he'd learnt to ride on was far from the war-trained horse he now rode. Even if it was considered calm compared to his own.

Barely waiting long enough for Damien to gain control of his mount, Michael spurred his horse, leading the way out of the courtyard. Riding away from his family home, Michael didn't turn back. He'd learnt that lesson long ago.

Michael kept the pace until they were well down the

narrow, forested path he favoured and the estate was out of sight. They were hidden by the screening forest before he took pity on his companions and slowed down to a walk. His stallion whinnied. He'd enjoyed the run and would have been perfectly happy to keep going, but he was well-trained and slowed as commanded. Damien's horse slowed more because his own had done so than his rider's skill. Michael's horse was dominant, and Damien's, although battle-trained, was a mare and as such, would follow the stallion's lead, as would Kesha's. Whatever the stableman was being paid, it was not enough.

He sensed Damien scanning their surroundings for signs of anyone else in their vicinity, just as they had trained him to do. He was learning. Michael hoped he had leant even more.

"If I hadn't given myself up, would he have done that to my Speaker? To my father and mother?"

"The Warlord is not the man he was back in those days, but he still won't tolerate disobedience. I doubt even I could sway him if you displease him, and he will probably fall back on behaviour he knows works. He will not lay so much as a fingernail on you—you're too valuable—but he will destroy those you love if you disobey him."

"Yet, you follow the Warlord. He trusts you. He doesn't have to threaten anyone to ensure your loyalty," Damien said.

"I do, and he doesn't. The Warlord, for all his faults, knows it. There is a genuine threat we face. The lives of many people would be worse if it weren't for us. Besides, you can't choose your parents," Michael said softly.

The silence stretched between them as Damien digested the information. There was a lot to take in and unpack on what had happened. Even he was still doing so, even though he'd known all the players involved in this family drama his whole life.

"Your parents don't hate you, despite the public pretence." There was a certainty in Kesha's voice.

"Perhaps, but my mother is not the woman she appears to be and to be honest, I'm closer to the Warlord than I am to them. That isn't something I've shared with them, but I think they're well aware of it. Despite the strain in our relationship, I still don't want anything to happen to them. They are right, though. I am the Warlord's creature. I have been for a very long time." Kesha gasped at his words and Michael smiled at the reassurance she sent him.

"Michael, do not say such things of yourself. You are not the monster you pretend to be." Kesha's voice shook.

"Sometimes it's best if people think I am."

He carefully kept his gaze straight ahead. A small part of him was secretly relieved that this woman who'd seen inside his mind didn't think he was beyond redemption.

"Your brother, though, that wasn't an act. What is he doing?" Damien asked.

"It wasn't. My brother hates me and blames me for everything. I don't know what he's up to, but he's terrified I'll find out whatever it is." Michael found it ironic that if his brother hadn't behaved the way he had, he'd likely have dismissed his mother's concerns.

"Your mother..." Damien stopped, his eyes sliding over to Kesha, then back to him, obviously not sure he should reveal what he'd seen and overheard in the room while Kesha had been busy healing his father.

"Our relationship was strained even before the Warlord happened. She can't seem to help trying to meddle with my mind."

Michael remembered he'd idolised Steven when he was growing up. His mother's intent, when she'd reached out to his mind, had been clear. She'd been trying to turn his mind away from his brother's activities. He would have returned to town, finished their business, and left as soon as it was done if she'd succeeded. Instead, he'd now make it his business to find out what his bitter big brother was up to. Whatever it was, he wanted to stop it before Steven got someone killed.

SEVENTY-FOUR

Michael strode down the cobbled streets, not bothering to pull the hood of his cloak up. Word was already being whispered all over Vallantia that he was in town, and he also had no doubt that everyone marked the fact he'd ridden straight to the estate house, only to return early. Gossip would fly about the cause of the brief visit and what urgent matter had caused him to take to the road as soon as he arrived. Only to stay in town.

He didn't even have to ask around to know where to start digging up information to find out what his brother was up to. The Arms was regarded as one of the better bars in town, at least among those who had money—it was a little expensive for the average working class. The Warlord wasn't the only one with informants in town. Michael was well aware this was the establishment that his brother drank at. The owner of the Arms, Ben, was also one of the few people from his old life that he could visit with impunity. The Warlord had leant of their friendship before Michael had grown up enough to show caution. By the time he had, discretion was too late, so he'd kept calling in on Ben every time he came to town. The Warlord had even bankrolled Ben through discreet channels when he and his wife had set up this bar and had approved when Michael had suggested Ben was the perfect person to head their sentry network. Michael smiled. What better way to hide than in plain sight?

"Surely even your brother isn't stupid enough to hatch whatever he's been up to here?" Olivia asked.

"I wouldn't be so sure about that. Either way, I'll lay odds Ben can point me in the right direction." Michael shrugged.

"Are you sure you don't want me to go to the estate house and beat it out of your brother?" Olivia asked, throwing an exasperated look in his direction.

"I already lost my temper and threw him around. Of course, he was that drunk he might not have remembered this morning."

Michael led the way down the narrow alley, barely wider than his shoulders, to the small nondescript door at the back of the establishment and pushed open the door to the rear kitchen.

Those who sat on stools around the kitchen bench eating breakfast were startled as he entered. Ben turned to his family and muttered a few words about this being business. Olivia smiled and walked past to pull out a stool at the bench as Ben's wife stood and, without ceremony, pulled Michael into her arms, kissing him lightly on the cheek. Michael closed his eyes, taking that moment to accept the genuine welcome and understanding comfort she sent him before she ushered the children out the internal doors with their food. Michael smiled fondly as she disappeared from the kitchen, waiting until the door closed quietly behind Ben's family.

Ben gestured to the seats at the bench and poured them each a kaf without asking, using a small surge of power to push the mugs across the bench to where Michael and Olivia were sitting. Ben was borderline in his abilities. Strong enough to be helpful but weak enough not to be conscripted into one of the Warlord's fighting forces.

"Michael. I was told you were in town." Ben reached with his mind and pushed at two plates, which both slid dutifully across the bench.

Michael smiled and piled his plate with eggs, mushrooms, ham and thick toast from the large platter in the centre. The smell of the food wafted up, causing his stomach to growl. Obligingly, he ate a few mouthfuls as Ben sipped his kaf.

"Glad the rumour mill didn't disappoint." Michael waved at the mountain of food piled on the bench. "You were expecting company?"

"I figured you'd end up here next." Ben's face split into a wide grin.

Olivia swallowed a mouthful of food and shook her head. "We'll be here all day at this rate if you don't get to the point."

"What's my brother been up to?" Michael asked, as he stared at Ben over the rim of his kaf mug.

"Chatter around town is he is trying to gather people to form a rebellion against the Warlord."

"Again?" Michael groaned.

He'd hoped his brother had just been trying to short-change the tithe. Fomenting dissent was enough to get him and everyone here killed. Although this wasn't the first time Steven had tried such a thing, he'd failed miserably on the previous occasions. It would be almost comical if the stakes weren't so high and there wasn't the chance that someone at least half-competent would take advantage of his brother's stupidity. Thankfully, even the Warlord found Steven's efforts amusing—although that wouldn't stop him from destroying those involved if the circumstances warranted it.

Olivia swore. "That numbskull couldn't lead anyone, let alone a rebellion."

"Evan would know more. Those two are always together. I kicked them out of here a couple of months ago when Steven was whining about his birthright and being the rightful heir." Ben continued eating.

"Any outsiders in here that night? Or anyone that doesn't normally come here?" Michael asked.

"Your brother and Evan were with another man that night. Sorry, Michael, it was a busy evening. The bar was packed. The twins might know who your brother's new friend is, they were here that night and close enough to hear the nonsense your brother was spewing. They backed me up when I threw Steven out."

If Ben had believed he might need backup against Steven, it meant his brother must have been in an obnoxious mood that evening.

"Do you know who has the honour of being the Warlord's current informer?" Olivia pushed her now-empty plate aside and picked up her kaf.

"No. Although I guess if an unexplained dead body shows up again, just before you all leave town, I'll know the answer to that question." Ben was entirely unconcerned that they'd think it was him.

Then again, Michael knew full well that he wasn't. They'd played together as kids when he'd been able to escape his lessons and run into town. It was another thing his mother disapproved of. She expressed her displeasure and tried to meddle with his mind and make him forget; she hated that he'd been mixing with commoners. He'd ignored his mother's efforts. Even then, he'd been stronger than her. He and Ben had remained firm friends, but it was apparent his brother had forgotten that, or he doubted Steven would spend so much of his time getting drunk here, no matter how popular the bar was.

"That's the game the Warlord and I play. People run to him, turn traitor to spy on those I love, and then I track them down and kill them. Father hates traitors." Michael smiled crookedly. "Anything else to report?"

"With your brother stirring up trouble, we've all been keeping a low profile. I could arrange to try and get someone into his little group if you like?" Ben raised his eyebrow.

Michael shook his head. "No, I'll not risk exposing you or the network. You're too useful to waste on my brother's stupidity."

"If the Warlord finds out and deals with Steven himself, whoever you sent would end up dead," Olivia said.

"If our people here learn anything interesting, I'll send word through the sentry relay," Ben said.

Ben traded glances with them both as they nodded acceptance. Michael pushed himself back reluctantly and stood. As Ben came around the table, they hugged briefly.

"Don't be alarmed if you find out we are making enquiries while I'm here. It will give some of my people something to do and keep them out of trouble."

"I doubt your people know how to get into trouble." Ben laughed.

"We rarely have much downtime. They'll appreciate it at first, but if we leave them idle for too long..." Olivia rolled her eyes.

"They will find trouble. Trust us, our fighters are very good at both finding and causing trouble."

"You don't want them bored, at least not in the place you call home." Olivia grinned.

"Stay safe, my friend." Michael slapped Ben on the shoulder and headed towards the door, then paused, half turning. "I nearly forgot. The Warlord has heard rumours about traders engaging in the flesh trade. Can you keep your ear to the ground for anything suggesting that nasty practice has started again?"

Ben's eyes widened his expression sober. "Of course."

Michael waved and walked out the door with Olivia a step behind him.

SEVENTY-FIVE

The water barely rippled as Jaclyn slipped over the side of the boat in the stillness before dawn. Using the power she had stored within her, she propelled herself through the water to the village that was still held in the grips of slumber. Although she was hyper-alert, she didn't hear any corresponding surge in the veil to her or her family's efforts. Everyone had followed instructions: drawing in power slowly before they reached this place to launch their attack and holding onto it to use at this moment so that people with access to a higher level of the veil in the village would not be alerted.

Upon reaching the jetty, Jaclyn eased herself onto the wooden structure and ran on light feet towards the still houses. Her team followed her lead and formed around her as she put on a burst of speed and led her group towards some houses to one side of the village, leaving the closer ones to the other teams. As she approached the fence of the house she was targeting, Jaclyn drew power from the stores she held within herself and jumped over the wall, landing only steps from the back door. A quick tap to power confirmed the members of her party who'd sprinted to the back of the house were in place and ready.

Opening the door, she scanned the small dwelling. Now that she was inside she could sense the sluggish power of those who slept within. Slight flares in the veil in her mind's eye were almost indistinguishable from the ambient glow of the eddies and swirls of the strands of power that permeated everything. She tensed as a flare of energy appeared, then relaxed as she recognised the power-draw from one of her team members who'd come through the rear entrance.

Jaclyn continued through the hut towards the faint glow of the veil coming from behind the curtains that hid the residents from her regular sight. Easing herself inside the alcove, she quickly assessed the two sleeping adults. Her eyes flicked to another curtain off to one side, and she left the adults to the team who'd followed her and stole past the end of the sleeping mat. She pushed the heavy drapes aside, staring down at the three children sleeping soundly. Hearing a gasp behind her, suddenly muffled, Jaclyn fell to her knees beside one of the sleeping youngsters and grasped his forehead. His eyes flared open in instant panic.

Hush, no harm will come to you.

Jaclyn sent waves of reassurance to him. Being woken from sleep this way, he was susceptible to suggestion. She smiled as his eyes glazed and he relaxed. A scan of the older boy's mind revealed nothing outstanding, so she turned to the younger one. She brushed his temples with her fingertips and smiled, seeing the signs of the early development of skill awakening within the child. With a mere breath of the veil, a strip of spider silk she had tied to her belt snaked out and wove around the young man's neck. With another whisper of power, the silk hardened into a collar.

Come.

Jaclyn drew the young man with her, noting the husband and the wife had been dealt with by the daggerwives, their minds pushed so deeply into slumber they probably wouldn't wake on their own. This was a raid. Not a conquest. It was their job to come in, grab what they could and leave, taking what they'd secured back to their homeland. It didn't matter if any left here survived.

With the barest push of her mind, she urged her captive into the boat. Tensely, she watched as others of her family returned, each bringing back bounty: food, fabrics, metals and, with a quick head count, three more young males showing early signs of talent. Young men were more pliable than adult males; even so, it had pained her to leave the adult males behind. If they had been attacking this place to keep, the residents would have been of use to them as a workforce, if nothing else. As it was, they had to prioritise.

When Myra and Ricardo return safely onto the boats, she relaxed and pushed away. As some of the braver villagers who'd broken the compulsion to sleep ran towards them, Jaclyn's anger flared. These people hadn't learnt to fear her yet. But they would. With a burst of power, flames erupted, engulfing the huts in the village they'd just raided. It would give the remaining locals something else to think about, particularly if they wished to try and save the occupants who would sleep as they'd been induced to, regardless of the flames.

The screams of the villagers floated over the water to them even as they were almost out of sight. They wasted no energy on stealth now. Jaclyn sat back, exhausted from her outburst of power as the daggerwives propelled them away from the village to return to their camp.

SEVENTY-SIX

Michael didn't have to ask for directions to find the twins. Not because there was only one set of twins in town, Vallantia wasn't that small, but because when someone said "the twins", they meant the smith's sons. As the smithy was on the outskirts of town, he and Olivia went past their inn and picked up two horses to be re-shod and also Damien and Kesha while they were at it. The recruit was still using generic all-purpose blades, which was fine for someone who would never go beyond novice or wouldn't really be riding into battle repeatedly, living and dying by their skill— but not for a member of one of the Warlord's warbands. The errands had the advantage of being necessary and good cover. It was inevitable that the locals would gossip about his visit to the smithy but he didn't want anyone connecting his current excursions with him attempting to track what Steven was up to.

It seemed contradictory, but while he might end up killing his brother one day, it didn't mean he wanted anyone else to do it. If circumstances pushed him to that point, it meant his brother had gone far enough that he really was about to get everyone killed. If others found out and acted first, Steven could die just for being stupid.

"Michael, what is that place?" Damien asked.

Damien and Kesha were staring off to one side. There was only one thing in the direction that could have captivated their attention. Michael traded amused glances with Olivia.

"That would be the place lovingly referred to by locals as the Burrow," Michael said. "Several other names as well, but Burrow is the politest."

Michael stared over at the mishmash of wooden and tin huts, all piled on each other. Some parts of the hovels were painted in garish colours, others not. Rickety ladders and makeshift walkways were strung between the shacks. Nothing seemed to match in the Burrow; like the name suggested, it was like a rabbit warren inside.

"Stay away from there," Olivia advised.

"There are some dangerous people who inhabit that place," Michael said to both Damien and Kesha. "Neither of you have any business going in there."

Damien and Kesha traded glances before they both craned their heads back towards the Burrow. He almost groaned to see that spark of curiosity in Kesha; she seemed more intrigued than anything else.

Remind me to emphasise to those who pull guard duty on these two not to go into the Burrow, Michael said as Olivia rolled her eyes.

It shouldn't need saying; they all know the rules. Worst case, you know Lukas will care for any of our people who end up stumbling into that mess, Olivia said.

If he's there, which is no guarantee. His... Michael paused with a cynical grin, *business takes him all over the domain these days.*

Olivia shrugged. *True, but the uniform of the Unwanted*

should be enough to send even the most undesirable of the residents of the Burrow to track down one of Lukas's people.

Michael was almost relieved when they turned the corner, and the Burrow was hidden from sight. He'd almost forgotten the route between where they were staying in Vallantia and the smithy passed close to what was arguably the worst part of town. As was often the case, things changed rapidly in a matter of blocks, and it wasn't long before they left the outer regions of the poorer quarter behind. The part of town they were headed into was a mixture of two worlds, between the areas frequented by the wealthy and the merchant class. The homes went from simple to extravagant. Although if you compared the places that seemed palatial here to those in the riverside area where the wealthy lived, they paled by comparison. It was yet another sign that life under the Warlord's rule wasn't as bad as some would believe. Vallantia, indeed the entire realm, had more wealth and fewer conflicts than the era before the Warlord laid claim to it by conquest. The two biggest cities of Callenhain and Vallantia had benefitted the most.

As they approached the sprawling stone complex that was the smithy, Michael took note of the expansions that showed how well the business was doing. Before the Warlord took Vallantia, they'd produced the best swords in the Independent Cities with a not-so-coincidental connection to the Warlords of Vallantia. Since the Warlord's reign, they were still known to create the best weaponry, although most of what they made went to the Warlord's warbands. They produced weapons for the locals and the visiting merchant class in between that workload. Michael smiled. He was about to make many of the upper and merchant classes of Vallantia and beyond extremely unhappy.

Michael paused long enough for Damien to tie the horses he led to a rail outside before walking into the smithy. The heat, noise and metallic stench assaulted him as soon as he entered. The Smith was talking to two men who Michael guessed were merchants, and one of his sons was taking to a blade with a hammer over to one side. The twins, Adam and Colin were not only master craftsmen but sword masters in their own right, but still took a hand in every stage of crafting the blades they produced and training those who worked under them in their craft. Had they been born in a different era, with their affinity for metal, they'd be Smith Lords with quite literally an iron-clad hold on everyone around them by fashioning metal collars that only their own kind could control. The twins had never discarded their names and taken the old honorific but if their father had ever been known by any other name other than the Smith, Michael had never heard anyone use it.

The smith turned to Michael as he noted their entrance. The merchants talked on for a moment before realising that the smith wasn't listening to them. They both twisted around to see what had drawn his attention away and froze as recognition kicked in.

"Warlord's business. Get out," Olivia said, her voice flat and commanding.

The men smiled uncertainty at the Smith, stammering that they'd be back later before fleeing. Unfortunately, both men were so busy staring wide-eyed at Michael that one of them ran into Damien. For his part, Damien reacted instantly, pushing the merchant aside and stepping sideways to draw his sword in a smooth motion, using it to track the unfortunate merchant as he landed heavily on the ground. The merchant blanched as the tip of Damien's blade halted at his throat.

"S... sorry, I didn't see you." The merchant scrambled backwards, trying to put distance between himself and Damien.

"Leave," Damien said as he withdrew his blade from the man's throat.

Michael nearly ruined his entire reputation by laughing as the man scrambled to his feet, aided by his companion. They gave a jerky half bow, then both abandoned dignity and ran from the smithy. Damien waited until the door slammed shut behind them, then sheathed his sword. Michael's lips twitched. He gathered Damien was still a little jumpy after Steven had drawn on them the other night.

Michael's eyes flicked over to the smith's apprentices, whose work had slowly stopped as they watched on.

"All right, you lot. Take a break, out the back in the yard," the Smith bellowed at his gawking apprentices.

Michael watched as they put up their tools and headed towards the rear doors. The Smith's sons put down their gear and went to leave with the rest of the workers.

"Not you two." Michael shook his head. "Your father's business is your business."

The twins displayed identical lopsided smiles and nodded simultaneously. Michael could see the mental connection between the two—they'd had that bond as children, and it hadn't faded as they grew up. If anything, it had strengthened, although they were next to useless at communicating with anyone else, but their affinity for metal and talent in making the finest armour and swords was of far more value.

"What is it you need of me, Michael, or is this really the Warlord's business?" The Smith's eyebrow rose enquiringly.

Michael ducked his head, a smile on his lips. The Smith had known him as a child since he'd played with Ben and the twins in the back streets of Vallantia. He was one of the few here in Vallantia who'd never treated him like he'd become a monster about to destroy them all.

"A bit of both, but mostly mine." Michael relaxed now that

the workshop was cleared out. "Damien here is our latest recruit. I'd like you to put the rest of the work aside and outfit him. Blades, fighting leathers, the works. Kesha is our healer; she'll also need better gear than she has."

The smith and the twins turned their gazes on Damien and Kesha, assessing them both, with Adam and Colin retrieving measures from a nearby bench and beginning to measure up their new clients without a word.

"Easily done, although if you want quality, it will still take a couple of weeks. What else? You didn't have us clear the smithy because you need the lad and girl outfitted." The smith was grave.

"I didn't. My brother is up to something. I need to find out what and stop his foolishness before he gets himself and everyone else killed." Michael turned his regard to the twins. "Ben tells me you were both in the bar when Steven was thrown out?"

"We were," Adam and Colin said, echoing each other.

"Notice anyone out of place that night?" It was a long shot. That was a minor detail only Ben was likely to have noticed.

The twins frowned as they continued their task, silent communication passing between them.

"It was filled with the regulars that night, although there was a large contingent of visiting merchants. Place was packed." Adam shook his head. "We didn't notice anyone paying undue attention to your brother."

"Has Steven done more than have a drunken conversation about a rebellion?" Olivia asked.

Colin finished measuring Damien's chest and made a note. "Unfortunately, he has. There's a group of them who meet weekly in the Docklands, although we haven't established where exactly."

"We could probably find out for you where they meet.

Although if we show up, not even Steven will believe we've had a change of heart."

Michael shook his head. "No, don't risk yourselves. Do you know if Lukas is in town?"

Adam shrugged. "We can find out."

"If you could, I don't want to risk being seen running into the Burrow to track him down." Michael couldn't help but grin at the twins over the shared memory of the four of them running into the Burrow on an adventure.

Michael ignored the startled glances thrown at him from Damien and Kesha.

"Not like when we were children." Colin chuckled, eyes dancing. "What do you want of him if he is there?"

"I doubt wherever these conspirators are meeting is a reputable establishment. A little rooftop cover to keep an eye out for strays when we go in might be handy." Michael shook his head. "Also, if he has anyone on the inside of this little mess, I'd advise him to get them out before I go after the group."

"I'd wager he does. Easily done," Colin said gravely. "With Damien and Kesha's fitting, I'm sure we can come up with plenty of reasons to visit you if we hear anything unusual."

Olivia frowned. "I doubt meeting in the Docklands was Steven's idea. It's a little rougher there than he usually frequents."

Adam and Colin snorted in amusement.

Colin grinned. "Just a little. It would be Gareth's influence. His cousins are a little on the shady side and run the docks."

"Steven's other companion in this little adventure, Evan, we know. You don't happen to know where this Gareth lives?" Olivia's eyes narrowed.

"Made it our business to find out." Adam scrawled onto a fresh piece of parchment and handed the address to Olivia.

"How long has my brother been associated with this individual with the shady connections?"

"About three months or so." Adam shrugged. "We believe he got to your brother through a connection with Evan."

"Evan has a gambling habit. We think that is how he knows Gareth," Colin said.

It never ceased to amaze him what fonts of knowledge his old friends were. Their work, Ben in his bar and the twins in the smithy, gave them access to all kinds of knowledge, but it was when the four of them used to run the streets that they'd met Lukas. He was just as successful in his own business as the others were in theirs, but Lukas had his fingers in dealings that ran in the shadows, out of sight of regular people.

Seeing the twins were done with measuring up their newest customers, Michael pulled them both into a rough embrace.

"You two take care of each other and Ben. Do not investigate this further." Michael pulled back and stared at them both.

They both wore identical looks of rebelliousness before they conceded they would stay out of the affair. Unfortunately, Michael didn't believe either of them any more than he had believed Ben. Still, hopefully they would show caution, and if they didn't, he was sure he'd hear about it. Anyone who tackled the twins would come out the worse for the experience. Nodding to Olivia, Damien, and Kesha, he led the way from the smithy.

SEVENTY-SEVEN

Michael kept control of his restlessness with difficulty, sitting in the inn they were housed in, settling accounts of the upcoming shipment of the tithe as if he had no concerns at all. Inside, he was impatient and wanted nothing more than to head out to the address the twins had given him for his brother's new friend, Gareth. Unfortunately, his every move in that part of town would be noticed and reported immediately. He'd rather word didn't get back to Gareth that he was poking around in his affairs.

The door that led to the inner courtyard opened, distracting Michael for a moment, and Damien entered. He walked across to the sideboard and helped himself to a mug of kaf, then settled at a table to the establishment's rear, near a window. Michael felt for his newest recruit. Within reason, the rest of his people could at least go out and explore Vallantia. Unless he had a specific task for them or they were on the protection detail for the inn, their time was their own. Unfortunately, for one battling an addiction to tiscan, Vallantia and all it promised was too much of a temptation. Other than his fittings at the smithy for his new gear, Damien was ordered to stay at the inn. Still, it allowed him to pass messages between Michael and the twins.

Michael turned his attention back to his task. While he might have his own self-imposed restriction, Lukas, who was in town, had no such limitations and passed on his findings to the twins, and they to Damien. For other enquiries, his people could go out and seek the information he needed. In this case, Callan, with two others as support, was checking the area Gareth was said to patronise. What they'd leant about Gareth so far made Michael twitchy. Steven would not typically lower his standards to associate with someone like Gareth. He was too proud of his rank and class.

Hearing the doors, Michael paused again as this time Nathanial walked in. With a sigh of relief, Michael pushed the ledgers aside as Nathanial pulled out the seat opposite him and sat.

"Your information was correct. Evan appears to be gambling his family's fortune away. Not so coincidently, in establishments owned by Gareth's family interests." Nathanial was disgusted.

Michael was not so surprised. They'd been bankrolling Nathanial to attend some of the gambling establishments since it was hard for him to watch Evan from outside the venues, but Nathanial had had a hard childhood and many of the gambling establishments ran other illicit trades behind the gambling. For Nathanial, it was like sliding back into a past life. Not that he would ever seek to return to that life. For Nathanial, unlike many of them, being taken into the Warlord's ranks had been a lifesaver. In the early years it was one of those things that gave Michael pause in his condemnation of the Warlord. He'd started to realise that perhaps the Warlord's actions weren't entirely without merit.

"Do you think Evan's worth leaning on?" Michael sat back in his chair, regarding Nathanial.

"With certainty. No disrespect, but I can't imagine Steven mixing with commoners without someone else's influence. I'm tipping that someone was Evan."

"Or because Steven's convinced in the rise of rebellion, he'll be victorious and become the new warlord." Michael rubbed his face, thinking. "Go get some sleep. If you could keep watch later this afternoon, I have some things to attend to."

"Kesha finally decided to sneak out to treat your father?" Nathanial asked.

"She's getting there. It's her decision, I won't make it for her, but I don't want her going anywhere alone. She doesn't understand how much of a target she is. I particularly don't want Steven cornering her." Michael frowned.

"I better get some sleep then," Nathanial said, his chair scraping as he stood and started walking towards the stairs that led to the upper level before he paused and turned back. With a small quirk of his lips, he withdrew a heavy purse from beneath his cloak and threw it on the table.

"The night's winnings." Nathanial turned once more and headed upstairs to the sleeping facilities.

SEVENTY-EIGHT

Kesha walked into the common room of the inn they were staying in after that one horrible night at the estate house. She sighed with relief that Michael wasn't present. He'd been a fixture in the common room, and if he'd seen her, he would have stopped her. Kesha chewed her lip and pushed aside the instant guilt that assailed her. Michael was only trying to protect her, and after his brother's behaviour at the dinner table, she couldn't say she blamed him. Still, his brother and his parents weren't the same, and Kesha was confident she could help Michael's parents. To achieve that, she needed to go to Michael's ancestral home. Straightening her shoulders, she walked across the common room towards the door that led to a small inner courtyard. Some of Michael's people noticed her entrance almost absently, but none of them paid her any mind.

Relief and a guilty spurt of triumph surged in her as she grabbed the door handle; she'd discovered another door at the back of the courtyard that she could access a laneway at the side of the inn. She could get her horse from the stable and head to the Rathadon family estate.

"Kesha, what are you up to?" Nathanial asked.

Kesha froze and then turned, a smile plastered on her face while internally she swore.

Of all Michael's people other than Olivia, Nathanial was the worst person for her to run into. Kesha was confident she could have bluffed her way past any others if they'd even bothered to question her. It's why she'd picked this time. Michael and Olivia were out, and Nathanial was usually in bed. He'd been up all hours of the night all week on some task for Michael.

"I was just heading out to the courtyard for fresh air." Kesha's smile faltered as his eyebrows rose in response.

"What were you planning after getting that fresh air in the courtyard?" Nathanial asked dryly.

Kesha's cheeks heated. She considered lying to him, but suspected that he'd been waiting for her. Somehow. It was exceedingly difficult to keep things to herself in the company she was in these days. They fascinated the healer in her. Trying to understand how they not only survived but thrived on the veil that quite literally ran through them. So many children, born just like them or with abilities that seemed like theirs, died. They were all so sensitive. Still, despite her fascination, it was cause for frustration at times like this.

"I decided to go out and offer my healing skills." Kesha's mind raced as she kicked herself for not coming up with an appropriate excuse ahead of time. Although she was rather proud of her answer, it was safe enough since she had done so on a few occasions while they had been here, and it wasn't exactly a lie.

Nathanial stared at her for long enough that Kesha ducked her head and fidgeted with the corner of her blouse. Finally, he stood, grabbing his cloak, his face still bland; he gestured towards the front doors.

"Let's go. You know someone must go with you," Nathanial said.

"I didn't want to bother anyone. I'll be fine. No one has tried anything."

"Orders are orders." A smile spread across his lips as she hesitated. "I can either escort you, or we can both wait here for Michael to get back."

Taking a breath, Kesha made an effort to appear confident and turned toward the stables at the side of the building. She stood trying not to display her nerves while Nathanial organised for their horses to be saddled, but Nathanial made no comment and simply waited for direction after they'd mounted.

"Oh, how silly of me, this way," Kesha said.

They rode through the streets heading towards the outer gate. Kesha's tension increased as they approached it. By now Nathanial could obviously tell they weren't heading for the main square or any of the other likely places she'd gone in the past to treat people.

"So, are you going to admit what you are up to?" Nathanial sounded exasperated.

"I... don't know what you mean." Kesha kept her gaze straight ahead as she negotiated her way around some traders and out of the gates.

"We're headed out of town, towards the Rathadon estate." Nathanial's tone was blunt.

"Michael would have stopped me, and I'm certain I can help them," Kesha said.

"Help who?"

"His parents. His father, in particular, lives with so much

pain. I know I can help." Kesha stared at Nathanial, pleading with him to understand.

Nathanial closed his eyes and sighed. "Very well."

They rode in silence for a time. Kesha's eyes slid across to Nathanial several times, although he didn't seem inclined towards small talk. It didn't take long before the walls to the Rathadon castle loomed up ahead of them.

"You guessed I was coming here. Didn't you?" Kesha could hear the accusing note in her voice.

Nathanial smiled. "You leak and have been working your-self up to this all week."

"You think Michael knows?" Kesha's eyes widened.

Nathanial chuckled. "Of course he knows. It's why he kicked me out of bed when he had to leave."

"Why didn't he say anything?"

"He's been waiting to see what you'd do."

"He can be so infuriating." Kesha glared at Nathanial. It wasn't his fault, but she could feel his amusement at her reaction.

"You have constraints like all of us claimed by the Warlord, but if you want to do something, just ask." Nathanial remained calm, seemingly unconcerned by her irritation.

"I don't like to bother any of you."

"It's no bother. We go with you to ensure your safety. Not to make you feel like a prisoner."

"Sometimes I feel like you all treat me like a fragile thing that is about to break," Kesha admitted.

"We don't mean to diminish you. When Michael and Olivia give orders and instructions about what they expect and what will happen if we disobey those orders, well, everyone pays attention if they know what is good for them."

"What is it you are all so afraid of happening?" Kesha frowned.

"Some things in this world aren't very nice. Please, just let us protect you."

As they rode into the cobbled courtyard, Kesha ducked her head, considering Nathanial's words. One of the stable hands walked out and grabbed her reins as she dismounted. She could tell by his body language that while he might not recognise her, he did recognise Nathanial.

"We'll probably be a couple of hours," Nathanial said as he handed over the reins to his horse.

The stable hand nodded shortly and led the horses away towards the stables. Kesha stared across the courtyard towards the doors, taking a deep breath. Raising her head, she crossed the intervening space and walked up the stairs towards the doors. She paused as the doors loomed up, wondering if she should just walk in. Nathanial solved the issue by pushing the large doors open and holding them for her.

"Thank you," Kesha whispered, realising she was just a little intimidated.

She swung around as a scurrying servant finally came bustling out of a side door, half bowing to them.

"My apologies, Nathanial, ma'am, we weren't expecting anyone." He wiped his hands on his trousers, smiling pleasantly.

"No, I'm sorry, it was a last-minute decision. Is Speaker Rathadon in?"

"Of course, ma'am. This way." He led the way down the corridor before turning just before reaching the doors. "May I advise Speaker Rathadon who has come to visit?"

"Healer Kesha," she said with a smile.

"Is there trouble, Nathanial?" the servant asked.

"No, I'm just the muscle following along in case someone gets inappropriate with the good healer." Nathanial shrugged deprecatingly.

The servant hesitated like he didn't believe a word Nathanial had said, but he finally ducked inside the rooms.

"They know who you are," Kesha whispered.

"Of course. I've stayed here before." Nathanial shrugged.

She could hear murmuring for a moment, then the doors finally opened, and they showed her inside. Kesha thanked the servant who motioned them over to where the Speaker and his lady sat near the large floor-to-ceiling windows overlooking the garden.

"Kesha, it's lovely to see you again," the lady said graciously.

"Sorry for intruding, Lady, Speaker Rathadon," Kesha murmured.

"Nathanial, is everything all right with Michael?" Lady Rathadon asked.

"He's fine, Lady Rathadon, just a little busy," Nathanial said.

"When he left abruptly and didn't return, I was worried."

"The Warlord's son, Aiden, rides with us this trip. Michael would not force Aiden's company on either of you. So, we're staying in town this visit."

"After Steven's behaviour..." Lady Rathadon trailed off.

"Steven is always problematic, but Michael does not hold that against either of you. Michael was already out when Healer Kesha decided to visit you. That is the only reason I am her escort on this occasion," Nathanial said, then took a half step back.

Kesha stared at Nathanial, her mouth open. She was becoming just a little suspicious about Nathanial. First there was how he interacted with the Warlord in the Heights, now not only did the servants here know him by name, but the Speaker and lady did as well. She doubted they were aware of the names of all of Michael's people. She was nervous being in such company, yet Nathanial seemed perfectly at ease as if he was used to mixing in such circles. Nathanial simply smiled at her and gestured towards Michael's parents, eyebrows rising. Kesha flushed, and she turned her attention back to her patient.

"Speaker Rathadon, I came to give you another healing session."

"Please, I appreciate the offer, but besides pain relief, there is nothing you can do for these old injuries." The Speaker shook his head.

"Nevertheless, I will do what I can." Kesha turned to the hovering servant. "Speaker Rathadon will probably be more comfortable during his healing session lying in bed. If you could assist him, please?"

The servant bobbed his head after a nod from Lady Rathadon and helped Michael's father to his bedroom despite his protests. Kesha hummed as she followed the servant with Nathanial a step behind her, nervousness banished. In many situations, Kesha was uncomfortable, but when it came to her patients, she was on firm footing and would not take no for an answer.

SEVENTY-NINE

Nathanial watched with his othersight as Kesha worked; he could see her energy levels depleting, yet she kept going, pouring more of herself into her patient. The bright spark that had been Kesha when she'd started was now muddy and sluggish. Feeling a light hand on his arm, he turned as Lady Rathadon came to stand near him, her eyes filled with concern.

"Will she be all right? She's been using her healing ability much longer than any other healers that have tried," Lady Rathadon said.

"I'll push her out of her healer's trance if I have to. I won't let her burn out her mind."

"Can you see what she's trying to do?"

"I can see, but I no more understand what she is attempting than you. It is more than pain relief, though."

"Won't she hurt herself if she doesn't stop?"

Nathanial watched the play of energy around Kesha. She wielded the veil outside of herself, pushing it into Michael's father and manipulating it to do whatever she was attempting.

Yet he could see none of that power going into her to replace the energy she used to manipulate the veil. Her own body was fast depleting its own energy stores.

"Let me try something."

Nathanial frowned, walked forward, and gently placed his hands on Kesha's shoulders. He'd previously shared strength with the members of his warband, but not with a regular person. Without more energy to replace what she was using, just like a regular person, Kesha was exhausting herself. It was why the average person found it easier to close a door with their hand rather than their mind—they would have to wait days for what they used to replenish.

Lowering his barriers, he carefully siphoned energy from himself into Kesha. He sighed with relief as her body reacted, that muddy glow beginning to shine again. He could feel her fatigue lift and, after a startled moment, a pulse of acknowledgement. She might not completely understand what he was doing, but she was aware he was assisting her somehow.

Nathanial kept himself focused, and limited his intake and output of the veil-fuelled energy to a trickle. Kesha was much more fragile than his squad mates, and this way, he could monitor Kesha's fatigue levels. Shadows lengthened in the room, showing the time that was elapsing, and Kesha was wilting, despite the strength he was funnelling into her.

Kesha, enough.

Feeling her stubbornness, Nathanial pressed his lips together and buffeted her mind with his own, shunting her out of her healer's trance. Bracing himself, he cut off the power he'd been feeding her and caught her as she gasped and her legs gave way. Pushing aside his own fatigue, he lifted Kesha into his arms and carried her to the low lounge to one side of the bedroom. He smiled his thanks as Lady Rathadon took a cushion and placed it under her head.

"Nathanial?"

"She'll be fine, ma'am. I judge she needs a moment to catch her breath and will recover after a good night's sleep," Nathanial reassured her.

Now that he didn't have to be as careful, Nathanial opened himself up, relief washing over him as the cool of the veil filled him. It had almost been harder to use less power, requiring more concentration and control.

"I would have been fine, Nathanial," Kesha said.

Nathanial smiled at the hint of reproach in her voice, although he noted she didn't move yet. "I'm sure you would, but you need to get used to utilising the energy I send you in much the same way you probably built up your stamina healing people to begin with. I'll not let you burn yourself out."

"You're as bad as Michael," Kesha grumbled.

Nathanial chuckled. "I'll take that as a compliment."

He watched as she sat up carefully, ready to catch her if she fainted from fatigue now that she was running on her own strength again. She gasped softly; her hand rose and hovered near his temples. Nathanial shivered as a breath of power from her brushed over him.

"You glow. I've never seen you hold that much power before." There was a note equally mixed between awe and concern.

"It's because you've never seen me in battle. I can't sustain myself forever on the veil's power alone; food is preferable, but it will do for now. I'll eat then sleep when we get back to the inn."

"You were channelling me that much energy?" Kesha's eyes widened.

"Not at first. You seemed to get used to the constant supply and increasingly drew more."

Kesha turned towards the bed where her patient still lay

and smiled her thanks at Nathanial, who steadied her as she stood. Crossing the room to the side of the bed once more, she laid her hand on the Speaker's chest when he went to rise.

"Here, grasp my hand," Kesha said, holding out her hand.

Nathanial frowned, watching closely as the Speaker reached out with his ruined arm, his clawed hand resting on Kesha's. While he'd seen Kesha using her powerful healing talent, even he was astonished when her patient's fingers started to move. Tears tracked down Speaker Rathadon's cheek as he watched the movement. Lady Rathadon gasped, her hand rising to her mouth, eyes welling with unshed tears. It was a slight improvement, but those fingers hadn't seen movement since his hand had been crushed, bones broken and ligaments snapped.

"How?" the Speaker asked

"I told you, I'm a healer, and Nathanial kindly lent me his strength. You need to rest; I have more to do." Kesha looked at Nathanial, an unasked question on her lips, and he nodded in response. "Tomorrow morning, I want you to practice moving your hand, perhaps trying to grasp your walking stick with your bad hand."

Kesha turned from the Speaker, only to be engulfed by the lady in a hug.

"Thank you." Lady Rathadon's voice was fierce and heavy with emotion.

"I have no need of thanks, Lady; it is no great thing, just an ability I was born with. I will do what I can for you as well, but I judged Speaker Rathadon's need was greater," Kesha said quietly.

"My scars are of little importance and do nothing to hinder me. Never underplay your abilities. Now I understand why you ride with my son." Lady Rathadon's voice shook.

"I will return when I can, hopefully tomorrow, if Nathanial

is free once more to act as my escort and will consent to be my power source," Kesha said.

Nathanial excused himself to them both and guided Kesha to the door, leaving the couple to contemplate how much improvement Kesha might be able to make in further visits with her healing abilities. Nathanial sensed that she was tired but well pleased with her efforts. That was something he did not begrudge her in the slightest.

CHAPTER

EIGHTY

Michael, along with Olivia and Nathanial by his side, walked down the familiar cobbled streets between their accommodation and the Arms. By night the streets had a different cast, with patches of darkness between the pools of flickering yellow light thrown by the streetlamps. In the houses of those with money to spare, they'd either have their own lamps or, better yet, glow stones. Lower ends of town would be plunged into darkness with the possible exception of low-level lights from the windows of those who lived in such areas. Many couldn't afford lamps, let alone to pay someone like the smith to produce glow stones, so they relied on candles and the glow from the stoves they cooked on, or they went without.

While he and his people could produce their own light in this circumstance, it was a waste of energy. They were used to the darkness, with many a night in camps between towns. They made do with the light thrown by their campfires and, on clear nights, the glow from the stars and moon. If it was an area they were unfamiliar with or had concerns that they might be observed, they doused the cooking fires before nightfall. Besides that, they had their othersight, which brought even the night-time to a whole new life of its own. It allowed them to see in the dark, even if it was a different kind of vision.

Olivia and Nathanial took the lead as they approached and proceeded him into the Arms. His seconds barely pausing before they spotted the man they were after and making their way across the crowded bar. Michael ignored the immediate tension from those in the establishment who not only noticed their arrival but recognised them immediately. It rode like a wave cresting just ahead of their arrival.

Sorry for the disruption, my friend. Michael whispered his apology to Ben, while keeping his eyes fixed on Evan, who sat seemingly oblivious as the pool of silence spread around him. As Michael rounded the table, he drew in a small amount of the veil, then reached out with an unseen hand to pull out the chair and sat. Evan suddenly jerked up from the tankard of ale he'd been lost in, his eyes widening in horror as he lurched upwards. Olivia's and Nathanial's hands clamped onto his shoulders and slammed him back into his seat.

The silence in the bar was complete.

"Evan, tell me what you've done." Michael's tone was flat.

Evan's pudgy chin quivered and he reeked of fear as he stared wide-eyed across the table. His head twisted to either side, eyes rolling at seeing Olivia and Nathanial. His feeble powers reach out, testing the strength of the three of them, only to blanch.

"I, I don't know what you mean," Evan said.

"Yes. You do."

Evan swung around trying to gather support, only to droop as he met staring eyes, with not even a hint of friendship or help. The silence in the tavern seemed to stretch and deepen.

Evan turned his gaze down. He picked up his pitcher, hands visibly shaking as he took a deep gulp.

"I didn't have a choice," Evan whispered, his gaze on the table.

Michael continued to stare unrelentingly at Evan, not saying a word. Waiting for the man to divulge his involvement in his brother scheme.

"I've tried. I tried to divert Steven, but he's obsessed with reclaiming his birthright." Evan's eyes pleaded, but he swallowed, not seeing what he was seeking. "I owe Gareth's family money. He, they wiped it all. Just for being introduced to Steven."

"What's Gareth's role, his family's interest, in this mess?"

"Steven was drunk. It probably would have amounted to nothing. You know what he's like." Evan's eyes pleaded for understanding.

"If I'm aware that Steven is fomenting rebellion again, how long do you think it will take for the Warlord to find out about it? If I don't deal with it, the Warlord most certainly will. What is Gareth's interest?"

Michael noted Evan was even more panicked and had gone pale. His anger spiked as Evan sat there, mute, before the man finally shook himself.

"I don't know. Honestly, I don't, but he urges Steven on," Evan whispered.

"Where do they meet?"

"He'll kill me if I tell you. He's killed others he said were traitors," Evan said.

"I'll kill you if you don't tell me, and I'm right here," Michael grated.

"Put it this way, Evan. Tell us what we need to know, and it sounds like Gareth will not be a problem for you when we're done with him," Olivia prompted.

Evan jerked at Olivia's voice as if he'd forgotten who was behind him. Sweat shone on his forehead as he twisted so he could see Olivia; then, he returned his gaze to the table. Michael could see the man weighing up his chances of survival.

"There's a place in Docklands, right on the pier where all the warehouses start. His family owns it." Evan's shoulders slumped. "Please, I didn't mean it. I tried to talk him out of it."

"When do they meet?" Olivia prompted once again from behind.

"Tomorrow night. Steven and I will meet here first, then go to the meeting place. Gareth is normally there"—Evan's lip started quivering— "about this time. It depends on when we finish our drinks and meal."

Michael hoped the man wouldn't start blubbering. Olivia's lips twitched as she spoke again, although there was none of her amusement clear in her tone.

"How many attend this little conspiracy?"

"It, ch… changes. About thirty or so." Evan swiped at his forehead with his napkin.

"You'll keep Steven here tomorrow night." Michael's anger flared as Evan opened his mouth to protest, before he thought better of it and the words died on his lips. "I don't care how you do it. Neither of you will be anywhere near that meeting."

Nathanial leant forward and whispered in Evan's ear. "If it helps your resolve, you'll probably both end up dead if you don't stay away."

Evan yelped in fear and craned his neck around, almost as if he'd forgotten he had two of Michael's people behind him. Not just one.

"Evan, go home. Stay home until it's time for you to meet Steven tomorrow. Trust that I have people watching you. Don't think of disobeying me," Michael said flatly and motioned with his head towards the door.

Evan nearly fell over in his haste to stand up and all but ran out the doors. A snort of amusement as the doors slammed shut broke the tableau. Michael shook his head as Ben made his way over. Ben placed the pitcher and mugs he was carrying on the table. His gaze travelling over those in the bar caused the conversations to start again. The sudden noise was almost as shocking as the silence had been. Olivia and Nathanial took seats opposite Michael.

"You did that on purpose." Ben's eyebrow rose.

A slow grin spread across Michael's face and he relaxed back into his chair. "I did. The members of the peerage and most of the influential merchants frequent your establishment. A warning was necessary. I have no desire to be forced to wreak the Warlord's vengeance on the citizens of Vallantia."

"Probably overdue. You'll have to deal with the ones involved in this." Ben was troubled.

"It depends on what we find," Michael said carefully.

"Steven and I don't get on. I'm just a publican, no better than the hired help, as far as he's concerned. You know he's all talk and bluster, right? I can't believe he'd do something this stupid without someone goading him on," Ben said.

"I know. Evan is too much of a coward to be influencing this. It's why I said Gareth and I are long overdue for a chat."

"Don't worry, I'll make sure the pair stay here tomorrow, even if I have to tie up your fool of a brother. I haven't forgotten the night the Warlord took Vallantia, even if he has." Ben gestured to a man to come over.

Michael scrutinised the approaching man. By his well-made clothing and money pouch on his thick leather belt, this man was a trader. His dress was good, but not of the gentry. Even how he walked and carried himself screamed wealth, but not of the upper class like Michael's own family or Olivia's. Michael leant back into his chair, his eyebrows rising slightly.

It showed some spine for the man to approach him after their display, even if Ben had called him over. The man was tall with a thin build, as if he'd had a growth spurt as a lad and never fully grown into his height, and his manner was calm and assured. As if he met and talked with dangerous people all the time. Then again, he probably did if Michael was correct about his profession.

"Lord Rathadon, I'm Josh. My father is the head of our trading family. Ben tells me you are interested in Gareth and his family's business?" Josh's voice was low as he kept the conversation between them both. His eyes were calm.

Michael gestured to the seat opposite him.

"What can you tell me?"

Josh sat down, resting his elbows on the table. "There has been talk that his family has been showing off some supplies of fine silks. Testing to see market demand among the upper class. I'm told the silks are such that haven't been seen around here and aren't manufactured here in the Warlord's domain or even the villages that still remain independent."

"Is there talk of where this supply of fine silk is meant to have come from?" Olivia asked.

"It sounds improbable to me, but I'm told they have a small shipment from Sylanna," Josh said.

Michael frowned. "Go on."

"Word is, he and his family have been exploring means and ways to tie up the market and get exclusive rights to trade with Sylanna." Josh's eyes met his own without flinching.

"There are some obvious problems with that strategy." Michael could hear the thread of hardness in his tone.

"Us being one of them. The Warlord will certainly not sanction such trade," Olivia commented.

"Some of Gareth's men were reportedly drunk at a local bar on the docks. They bragged that they took out some sentries so they could slip past your lines to seek out new trade whenever they wanted." Josh pushed his blond hair back from his eyes as he fell silent.

"Thank you for the information, Josh. Is there anything you need?" Michael throttled down his anger at the news the trader had shared.

Josh shook his head and stood. "No, Lord Rathadon. One of the small villages my family used to stop in was raided by Sylanna a few years back. Those people didn't deserve what happened to them. If Gareth's family has made a hole in the sentry line, it's dangerous business that will impact us all."

Michael watched as the man took his leave and walked back to his own table. He turned his gaze to Olivia, then Nathanial, the burning anger, a mirror to his own, reflected back at him from the pair. Michael wondered if his sudden spike of rage was just as apparent to those around him. Taking a breath, he picked up his forgotten glass and downed the contents, nodding to Nathanial as he promptly refilled it for him.

Finally, when he trusted his voice, he spoke. "I think that chat just got upgraded."

"I thought it might," Ben said.

"Make sure you and your people stay well clear. Neither Gareth nor any in his group will walk out of their meeting venue alive tomorrow."

EIGHTY-ONE

Jaclyn watched the daggerwives tear down their makeshift camp. Their latest captives were collared and penned up to one side under a careful guard. When they left this place, there would be very little evidence that anyone had been here. Although it wouldn't stand a thorough inspection, she doubted any of the barbarians would come out this far to check. They'd conducted several successful raids on riverside villages, carefully selected to be small enough that they'd be no threat to her people but with a worthwhile take of resources.

"You know Samuel will order us back here to raid as soon as we get home," Ricardo said quietly from where he stood nearby.

"I know, but he ordered us to raid. We have done so." She shrugged.

"Besides, this brief break from our activities will throw off the barbarians. If even half of what we've been told is true, they aren't all incompetent," Myra said.

"It also gives us a little more time to consider how best to take this land for Sylanna, which my loving brother will also order," Jaclyn said.

"I doubt our heads will spend much more time on our pillows than they did on our last return to the court," Ricardo said.

"They're in a bind really. The only way they can be rid of us long term is to appoint me commander again. Otherwise, we come here, raid as ordered and return promptly to court. If he orders me to take command of an invasion, it gets me out of the way for longer, but it allows us the pick of the houses to assist."

"Enough time to plan and have more of our sister houses withdrawn from the trader lands of the clans to assist," Myra said.

Jaclyn shared identical hard smiles with Myra. One of the only paths they could see for their house's survival was forcing her brother to elevate her to commander. It was a ploy that had benefitted them when he had ordered them to invade the trader lands. Her brother was backing them into a corner. They would force him and his wives into one in return.

With the camp finally cleared, the daggerwives loaded the boats with the prisoners and the other resources they'd gained from the last village. Jaclyn waited as the daggerwives scoured the place one more time then, on their signal, moved forward and took their positions in the boats waiting to take them home.

EIGHTY-TWO

Michael walked through the darkened streets, knowing parties of his people had been on the move in small groups all day. It was all carefully staged so they were in position without too much notice being drawn in their direction. From the description given by Evan, it hadn't taken too much effort for Nathanial and Callan to find the establishment where the conspirators met. He'd had his own input on that, of course. A misspent youth running the streets with his friends meant he was familiar with the docks area much better than someone of his rank and station should have been. Unlike Steven, he'd never been under any illusions. Even back then, he was the youngest son of a warlord. That didn't lead to him believing his station was above anyone else's.

Of course, his life now meant such notions did not constrain him anyway. If his brother knew how at ease he had always been in such places, it would be another thing that lent weight to his brother's disdain and hatred.

Of course, it helped that Michael didn't fear those less

fortunate than himself who generally lived in this area. And even the petty thieves and thugs who called this area of Vallantia home were not as numerous as what passed for the city's gentry believed. Besides, he was a bigger predator than any of them. Even if they didn't recognise him, obscured as he and his party were by darkness, Michael was subtly pushing out with his abilities to thicken the veil and increase their protection from sight.

Turn away. His was the whispering voice that floated out accompanied by a compulsion, causing people to pause and go the other way, while at the same time, a little shove from his mind caused them to forget what had caused them to turn around in the first place.

Those his compulsions didn't work on, and there were a select few, had common sense enough to fade away by themselves. He left them to be tracked, and if necessary dealt with, by Lukas's people, who ran across the rooftops like dark flitting shadows that kept pace with him.

Lukas even had some of his people watching Gareth's family homestead and would deal with any of those who ended up running back there to tell of what they'd seen this night. Those would die before they could tell such a tale. It didn't suit his purpose for anyone to warn away those conspirators he needed to speak to. Not that they encountered that many people; this part of town, near the docks, consisted mainly of warehouses and business premises mostly concerned with shipping and trade. They had little foot traffic, at least at this time of night.

Michael led his group through one of the back alleys and paused at the edge of the Docklands Bar. Pools of light burnt from the windows, showing that there were people within even now. Although given it was a bar, if a somewhat rough one, that probably wasn't unusual. What was unusual on this night was that the establishment was the meeting place for those planning to overthrow the Warlord. The heavy-set men, each with swords at their belts, leaning against either side of the door were unusual.

The premises were owned by Gareth's family, and Michael had been informed they turned away all but their own on the nights the conspirators met. Of course, their usual clientele would have understood to stay away. Or they did as soon as they saw the guards at the door.

Michael widened his mind, the veil showing him where each of his teams was waiting. It had all been timed, so, all going well, his own group would be the last to arrive.

Everyone in position? Michael paused, feeling the affirmative responses from Olivia and Nathanial, who each led their own teams.

Let's get this done. Move!

Michael gathered more of the veil to himself and shaped it in front of his group, pulling the darkness to them as they strode forward, heading towards the doors. They didn't run, but they weren't strolling either. It was obvious the moment the guards on the door spotted their presence through the darkness. The one closest to them tensed, leaning forward and peering at them. Before the man could even alert his fellow guard or draw his weapon, four of Michael's people sprang forward. There was the rush in the veil as each pair drew on their own power. It allowed strength to flow through them, helping them overpower and take down the guards with little effort. Doors slammed as some other groups entered, via other entrances, a moment before his own group did. Nathanial's group leapt from the roof opposite and, with deft surges of power, propelled themselves onto the upper-storey balcony and through the windows. Olivia, on the ground floor, took her team through the rear door.

Michael shoved his power into the large double doors, and they burst open in response. A part of his mind noted that perhaps he'd used too much energy when the doors cracked and splintered, showering those on the inside with wood. One small man who'd been running towards the door, away from the people pouring in through the rear and descending the stairs from the upper levels, skidded to a halt and fell backwards, horror written all over his face as he stared at Michael and his people as they poured into the dilapidated building. The air assaulted Michael's senses as he entered, heavy with sweat, smoke and stale beer. He could almost taste it as he breathed. It was a poor excuse for a pub, but Michael guessed that while this place served what passed for alcohol and food of a sort, it was generally used for other purposes. It took little guesswork to realise the proximity to the river made it remarkably easy to dispose of bodies. Michael scanned the room, ignoring the yells, breaking furniture and clash of steel that all combined to form the familiar sound of battle. Michael's gaze sharpened as he spotted the person he was after: a short, stocky man with dark hair and brown squinty eyes.

Michael ploughed his way through to Gareth, who already had his short blade drawn, half crouching to lunge forward at Michael, obviously no stranger to street brawling. Michael swayed to one side, avoiding the viciously stabbing blade. How Steven had missed who and what this man was, he didn't know. This was not the type of person his brother would usually mix with, and he certainly wouldn't attend a place like this in the heart of the docks.

Still, while Gareth might know how to handle himself with close-quarter fighting, he was in for a shock. Unfortunately for him, Michael was a much better fighter. Michael channelled the veil down his arm as he slammed his fist into his opponent's diaphragm. Gareth instantly doubled over, gasping for breath. In his moment of distraction, Michael hammered his booted foot into Gareth's knee. With an audible crack that sounded around the room, Gareth's leg went from underneath him, and he collapsed. Dropping his dagger, Gareth screamed, rolled over, and grabbed his shattered knee, forgetting the intruders and battle around him.

Gareth screamed again as a couple of Michael's men hauled him unceremoniously up, dumping him into a straight-backed wooden chair.

"So, Gareth, perhaps you'd care to explain this little trading venture and rebellion you are trying to foster?" Michael ignored the others in the room, trusting his people had everything in hand with the other conspirators.

"I don't know what you're—" As one of Michael's men slammed his fist into Gareth's stomach, his words broke off to a scream.

"Let's make one thing clear, Gareth. I know. You haven't been terribly discreet in your endeavours." Michael watched Gareth calmly as the man stared back up at him.

He could see the fleeting emotions across his adversary's face as he tried to figure out exactly how much was known about his plans. Finally, he licked his lips.

"It's just trading. I'm sure we can come up with a split of the profits. Just name your price." Gareth tried to smile, his eyes glinting.

"I haven't found those from Sylanna willing to talk, let alone trade. How ever are you managing it?" Nathanial drawled from where he stood nearby.

Michael kept his face carefully neutral as he noticed the triumph in Gareth's eyes.

"Now, you can't expect me to reveal our trade secrets, but let's just say they aren't all warlike."

"So your men's drunken boasts were true? You've been

killing sentries to break through and make your way to your trading partners in Sylanna?" Nathanial asked.

"Well, the first time, the sentry was already dead."

"The first time?"

"It isn't that hard. They focus most of their attention in the other direction," Gareth said confidently.

"Didn't that leave some villages open to attack?" Nathanial's voice was quiet.

"It's a bit of a waste, but they were only insignificant villages." Gareth shrugged. "It's been easier to conduct business in remote areas. A more permanent solution would be of significant benefit."

"That's why a rebellion occurred to you. Still, you'd need a figurehead to give it a semblance of legitimacy," Nathanial drawled.

"Of course." Gareth grinned.

"Why Steven?" Disbelief rang in Michael's tone.

"Well, you know, he's a bit of a fool." Gareth winced as he leant forward, whispering confidentially.

"I hadn't noticed." Michael's tone was dry, threaded through with a challenging note.

"Oh, he is. You probably aren't here enough to see it, Lord Rathadon. It made him a perfect choice as a figurehead." Gareth's voice dripped with false sincerity. "We could set him up as warlord while we continued our operations and controlled everything. Including him."

"It must have been a shock for your operations that we arrived here early," Olivia commented with a smile, inviting Gareth to join in.

Gareth relaxed back into his chair, chuckling before wincing as the movement hurt his knee. "You could say that! But it may prove mutually beneficial to us all."

"In what way?" Michael asked.

"Well, I'm not sure you realise how loved you are by the people in these parts, Lord Rathadon." Gareth smiled.

"I'd say we have a fairly good idea of what people think," Nathanial commented dryly.

"Honestly, you would be a much better leader, Lord Rathadon. We have the people; we can strike and take back your ancestral lands from the interloper," Gareth said.

Michael shook his head. "I'm afraid you are missing one vital point."

Gareth had a perplexed frown on his face. "I assure you, Lord Rathadon, I've thought of everything. If you are worried about your warlord, he'll soon be too busy with other matters, and it isn't like he cares for the common people whose lives he controls."

"Those insignificant little villages? They belong to the Warlord, so those insignificant people are mine to kill or protect." Michael leant forward, whispering confidentially in Gareth's ear. "So I care. Their lives matter."

As his sword slid into the man's chest, the Unwanted struck, the conspirators all crumpling to the floor, dead before they knew what was happening.

EIGHTY-THREE

Damien stood patiently as Colin fussed with his new fighting leathers, ensuring they fit him just right. He shouldn't have been surprised at how well it fit or that Colin wanted to make sure everything was perfect, given how long it had taken to outfit him. The fact everyone in the workshop had stopped to work solely on his and Kesha's outfitting had also shocked him. He would have been happy with some new leathers bought at the market. After all, how much difference could custom-made gear really make? Or so he'd assumed before this. These fit him perfectly, like a glove.

"Very handsome, Damien," Kesha said.

Kesha sat on the workbench, booted feet swinging. Her eyes sparkled with what looked suspiciously like mischief. They'd outfitted her first before turning on him.

"I'm not sure 'handsome' is what we're going for here," he grumbled.

"You fill out those leathers extremely well." Her eyebrow rose suggestively as her eyes brushed him from head to toe.

"Don't worry, Damien, the ladies might swoon—" Colin cut off as his brother chimed in.

"Or some men, depending on their persuasion," Adam added.

"Of course, but I'm sure you'll terrorise the others," Colin said.

Damien sighed, seeing Kesha's dimples flare and her hand fly to her mouth to ineffectively stifle her laughter. Colin laughed and slapped him on the shoulder good-naturedly.

"Don't worry. These are reinforced and will protect you in a fight much better than your old hunting clothes." Adam took pity on him, although his eyes still danced.

"You'll be able to ride, move and fight without restraint," Colin added.

Adam walked over with his new sword and passed it to him gravely, without fuss. It had taken him some time to be able to tell Colin and Adam apart. Even their minds were interlinked in a way he'd never seen before. Damien smiled, his hand grasping the pommel, which suited his grip perfectly. The part of his memory that came from Michael assessed the blade as perfectly balanced and sized for him. This was a blade of such beauty he expected none but the rich and powerful could typically afford to possess it. Realising he'd been staring at it while Colin and Adam watched, he grinned at the pair and sheathed his new sword.

Colin's lips quirked in amusement, and he handed him a shorter fighting dagger and a matching belt knife.

"This looks too good to cut my food with." Damien chuckled.

"Ha! Michael said a complete fitting. That includes the belt knife," Adam replied.

Damien turned the blade to inspect the other side which bore the symbol of a flame and sword etched into it. The same crest threaded through his vest; it all marked him for what he was now: a member of the Unwanted. He wasn't sure he'd earned it yet. His mood sober, he slid the knife into place on his belt.

"Father personally helped with your weapons and leathers, adding his own special touch," Colin said.

"Your father's touch?"

"In days of old, Father would have been numbered among the Smith Lords," Colin said.

Damien stared. "Your father is a Smith Lord?"

"No. Our great-great-grandfather was a Smith Lord. He was defeated by Michael's great-great-grandfather, the first of the Rathadon warlords." Colin grinned at him.

"Even today, when those with an affinity for metal talk about the Smith, it's our father they mean." Adam shrugged.

"When the Warlord ordered the slave collars destroyed, the smiths had to do it since smiths with an affinity created the filthy things in the first place. Any who disobeyed faced not only the Warlord's justice but, if they survived, were stripped of their abilities by our father," Colin said.

Damien felt his eyes widen. Stories about the Smith Lords were told in tales to children at camp fairs. They were the monsters from their dark era who ruled before the rise of the warlords when people were enslaved and held by metal collars with unique properties tying them to their masters. He'd listened to the stories, but he'd never imagined that one day he'd meet and talk with real, living Smith Lords, even if they didn't call themselves that these days.

"Those blades and the metal laced through your fighting leathers are imbued with the veil," Adam said.

"They won't fight for you or anything. You know the veil doesn't work that way, but the blades, in particular, have been tuned to you specifically," Colin said.

"No one else can use them?" Damien asked.

"They can, but they will be the same as any other fine blade. The veil that inhabits the blade recognises you. For you, those blades are something else again. The veil you channel when fighting will flow through the blades and fighting leathers," Colin said.

"You'll find it much easier to cut through the Sylannians' clothing with our blades. Their silks hold the veil in much the same way our fighting leathers and blades do. Power defeats power," Adam explained, checking to make sure he understood.

A clattering and shouting outside gave a momentary warning before the doors to the smithy burst open. Damien faced the door and the intruders who'd entered, his new sword drawn. Power rushed into him, strength pulsed through him up his arm, and the crest on the blade flared as if it had a life of its own. Power glowed through his fighting leathers, as he'd seen the leathers of the Unwanted when they fought. He could almost feel the veil running through him and the leathers and sword, making both stronger.

The intruders stumbled into the smithy, hands full of crates that crashed to the ground, their eyes wide with shock. After the barest hesitation, they reached for their own swords. The veil swirled around Damien, responding to his heightened tension, then Colin and Adam were between him and the intruders, their hands raised.

"Enough, don't be fools. Continue to draw those weapons, and you'll probably end up dead. Take your hands off your blades." Adam's voice held a note of command as he stared at the intruders.

"Damien, these are some of our suppliers. They aren't a threat," Colin said, speaking calmly.

Damien kept his eyes on the men until they took their

hands off their swords, slowly raising empty palms towards him. Damien allowed the veil to bleed from him and slowly sheathed his own sword.

"You know full well if we shut the doors to the smithy, we have private business." Adam frowned at the men.

"We didn't think. It's been a rough few days," one of the traders said.

The traders leant past Colin and Adam, their gaze assessing although they seemed happy enough to stay where they were with the twins between them and him.

"Why, what's happened?" Adam asked.

"We're fine, but raiders have sacked one of the smaller villages up the river," the man replied. "Some survivors who indicated they had family here in Vallantia are with us, but we couldn't bring everyone."

"We said we'd send word," the trader said, his eyes flicking to Damien once more.

"How far down the river?" Colin asked.

"A couple of days. It was a small village; they didn't stand a chance." The trader's voice caught. "Cavern, if you know it."

"Anything else?" Adam asked.

As the traders shook their heads, Damien thanked the twins and gestured to Kesha, who followed him towards the doors.

"My thanks for your fine work, Colin, Adam. I'll pass this news onto Michael," Damien said.

"Tell Michael we'll inform the Speaker, send teams with carts and supplies, and send someone down the river to check on the sentry network," Adam instructed.

Damien indicated he would pass the message on as requested. Carefully keeping himself between Kesha and the strangers, they walked from the smithy, mounting their horses with no need for discussion. Damien spurred his horse, drawing from the veil as he did so, and mimicked what he'd seen Nathanial and Callan do. He fed energy to his own mount and Kesha's as they thundered down the road back into town. He had more than the traders' words to go on. As they told their tale Damien had caught the fleeting images, feelings and sounds that flowed from the traders. Burnt buildings, dead people on the ground, wailing from the living, the sense of desperation and pain. It was all he needed to urge him on.

Damien paled. He realised he thought—no, he knew—the Unwanted were the ones who could and would help those devastated by this attack. At some point, he'd crossed a line between thinking of the Unwanted as the monster that everyone needed to hide from to thinking of them as the ones that people needed to save them from the monsters.

Michael groaned and leant back against the wall, resting his face in his hands as he contemplated the potential mess Steven was in. He might have dealt with Gareth and some of his people, but Gareth's family was far-reaching and one of the wealthier merchant clans. From what he'd leant, the matriarch of that line had more than one child.

"I don't think my brother is capable of a real rebellion," he said.

"Steven is an idiot, but that won't stop the Warlord if someone halfway competent pushes this little rebellion further." Olivia shook her head, gazing at him steadily.

"I know—" Michael broke off as the doors to the inn opened and Damien and Kesha strode in. Kesha radiated concern while Damien was calm. Almost too calm.

"The twins had visitors while we were there. Traders said a

village down the river has fallen to Sylannian raiders," Damien said.

"How far down the river?" Michael stood.

The band, who had been lazing around the common room, stood and bolted for their sleeping quarters.

"They say it's a smaller village, Cavern, a couple of days' ride back towards Callenhain."

Olivia swore. "If we push ourselves, we can get to Cavern before dusk."

"Then we'd better move. Nathanial, do we have many in town?" Michael asked.

"No, I've just recalled Callan and those out with him. They'll be back directly," Nathanial said.

"Very well, everyone, get ready. We move out within the hour!"

CHAPTER

EIGHTY-FOUR

Steven stood staring out of the large windows of his suite over the forest beyond the castle walls and the road that led to Vallantia's town. He couldn't see his brother and the warband leaving town at a speed only they could manage, but he fancied he could feel it. He should be relieved that Michael was leaving town.

He wasn't.

Eventually, Michael would be back, unless the Sylannian raiders managed to get lucky and kill him in one of their raids. So far, he'd been bitterly disappointed and given up on the vain hope.

"Are you sure they're dead? I mean, all of them?" Steven asked.

"I'm certain," Evan said.

"You think Michael did it?" Steven asked, although he was pretty sure what the answer would be.

"Who else do you think could pull that off?" Evan hissed.

Steven saw disbelief written all over Evan's face. He wanted to be outraged, but, unfortunately, he couldn't be.

479

"How, how does he do this so quickly?"

"There is a reason he's risen in the Warlord's ranks. He's competent." Evan's tone was clipped.

Steven's spine stiffened at the implication that he wasn't, but then slumped as something else occurred to him. Or rather, he circled back to his original concern.

"Do you think he knows about our involvement?" he asked quietly.

"Of course he knows!" Evan snapped.

"But maybe he never got that far? Gareth surely wouldn't have given us up before he died." Steven hated that he sounded desperate even to his own ears.

"You think the delay at the Arms the other night was a coincidence?" Evan snorted in amusement.

"You think the barkeep is on my brother's payroll?"

Steven licked his lips as Evan's mouth fell open, his eyes wide. He wasn't the most perceptive person—that was another thing his little brother seemed to have in bucket loads that he didn't—but he could see his friend was astonished, he just didn't know why.

"You can't be serious, don't you remember?"

"Of course, I remember being delayed at the Arms. That's why I asked," Steven snapped.

"No. When we were young, before the Warlord came and took your brother and sister?"

"Of course I remember that time. What has that got to do with anything?" Steven wished Evan would get to the point.

As the silence stretched between them, Evan stared at him incredulously. Steven was absolutely sure that was the emotion he was picking up. He opened his mouth to demand a response but snapped his mouth shut again when Evan finally answered.

"Michael used to run with Ben and the twins in town. The four of them were best friends, and your brother became more than familiar with the wrong parts of town. It used to drive your mother mad," Evan said.

Steven's face flushed. "They'll pay for this—"

"Don't be foolish; they are your brother's people in town. Everyone knows."

"They told him about us? They forget themselves. We are here, and my brother, their protection, just left town—" Steven stopped as Evan started laughing.

Actually, he didn't just start. His friend was doubled over, and he was almost certain he'd seen tears streaming from the man's eyes. Evan was roaring with laughter to the point that a servant popped her head in to check. Steven smiled weakly and waved the woman out. Evan seemed to give up and slumped onto the ground, clutching his stomach.

"Please, Steven, do you realise they are the reason we make it in and out of town unhindered? They aren't friends with your brother because they need his protection." Evan gazed up at him, the smile slipping from his face. "It was me who gave up Gareth and the meeting place."

"What?" Steven swung around.

"Michael cornered me with his people. He knew." Evan licked his lips. "Gareth wasn't a friend. To either of us."

Steven slid down the wall, hitting the hard stone floor with a thud. He was numb, as if he was caught between outrage, fear, and relief.

"What do you mean?"

"I had a gambling problem," Evan admitted.

"Had?" Steven asked.

"My father cut me off."

"Ah. You could have come to me." Steven sighed.

"I should have. It seemed such a small thing. They said they'd wipe out my debt, give me permanent credit." One of Evan's hands rose as he rested his forehead in the palm of his hand.

"What did they want?"

"It seemed such a small thing." Evan's voice was barely above a whisper.

"Just tell me."

"I just had to introduce Gareth to you. I swear, I didn't realise what they'd try to do." There was a note of pleading in Evan's tone.

"I need a drink." Steven climbed up and tugged the bellpull.

It didn't take long for a servant to arrive. Since his father now lived downstairs and Steven was the only family member residing up here, there were more servants than people to serve, but his father had refused to stand any of them down.

"Bring up a bottle of wine from the cellar," Steven ordered.

"Make that a few; I think we'll need more than one to drown our idiocy," Evan commented.

"Use a trolley." Steven laughed and waved the servant off.

It took so little time for a servant to reappear with a bottle of wine and two glasses that Steven guessed they kept a supply closer to hand than the wine cellars. He reached down and offered his hand to Evan. His expression was sombre; his friend looked up at him before accepting the hand. Steven help haul Evan to his feet and led the way to the couches where the servants had set up the wine and some finger food on a low table between them.

"If Michael wanted us dead, we would be," Evan said firmly.

"I don't think I'll get off that lightly. He was already angry with me after this visit," Steven admitted.

"What else did you do?" Evan groaned.

"I took liberties with his healer."

"You did what?" Evan turned, his eyes wide.

"Did you see the woman? I just groped her a little at the table. How was I to know my brother was partial to her?" Steven said almost desperately.

"Well, I doubt he'd kill you for that infraction. No matter what he thinks of the woman," Evan said cautiously.

"I couldn't get out of bed for days after he was done with me. He guessed, even then, that I was up to something. He said he'd kill me when he found out what it was."

"If he was going to kill you, he already would have. Let's not engage in anything else that could be construed as going against the— um, your brother." Evan kept his eyes firmly on his drink, refusing to meet his eyes.

Steven gulped the rest of the wine in his goblet and poured another, pushing down the anger that automatically flared. Evan had started to say the Warlord. Not his brother, but he got the point. Steven stared into the distance but wasn't really seeing anything, his mind going to that other nagging worry.

"Do you think that village they've gone to rescue was destroyed because of what we did?"

"Hard to be certain. I hadn't been out in the tributaries any more than you had before then. But let's hope Michael never realises we were there and responsible for the sentry's death. He couldn't look the other way for that," Evan said glumly.

Steven appreciated the "we" part. There had been no we in that death; he'd lost his temper and killed the sentry himself. His mood sank even lower as he contemplated the mess he'd gotten himself into, only to be rescued from his own stupidity by his brother. Again.

Steven stared at the wine in his glass; he made terrible choices when drunk. If he was honest with himself, his decisions weren't the best even when sober, but perhaps it was time to cut back. Sighing, he reached for the bottle and topped up his friend's glass before sculling his own and refilling it.

Tomorrow. He promised himself.

He'd think about cutting back on drinking tomorrow.

EIGHTY-FIVE

Damien had been with the Unwanted long enough he was familiar with what was happening this time. His own powers connected to the group, adding to their strength as they rode with a single-minded determination. He just hoped his unpredictable connection to the veil wouldn't choose now to shut down on him. Even if he didn't know where they were going, it was clear the others did. The roads connecting the villages in these parts of the Warlord's domain were much better kept than where he'd grown up. Or even most of the Heights and lowland areas they'd travelled through to get to Vallantia. They didn't follow the river, but he didn't question it. Other travellers took one horrified moment as the warband thundered down on them and scattered out of the way. More than once, there was a flood of relief from travellers as they passed by and kept going. Then, occasionally, worry about why they were in a hurry.

This way is quicker. We'll cut across back to the river soon, Nathanial said.

Damien acknowledged Nathanial's comment and concentrated on the task at hand. Periodically he sent the thinnest thread of the veil seeking back, just the merest breath of power whose touch reassured him that Kesha rode safely at their centre. Of all of them, she was the most vulnerable to attack and they hadn't needed Michael's order to keep her safely at their heart when they rode. Those born like him and the rest of the Unwanted were rare. Ones like Kesha were rarer still.

His world reduced to the rhythmic pounding of hooves, the surging of the veil, and chasing the sun as it descended. Everything was a blur as they rode on until an explosion of colour, burnt orange, pink, red and blue, lit the sky; It heralded dusk would settle on them soon.

As they burst into a small clearing, light was fading from the sky. A pall of smoke lingered on the air as if the wind refused to blow it away. Or had blown it back in to settle over the remnants of what was once a village. To remind those who hid in the wreckage of all they had lost. They didn't need to see the survivors. Each and every one of them could feel the fear emanating from those left alone and abandoned.

An unspoken command raced like lightning, leaping from mind to mind. A puff of dust rose from the ground, bringing Damien's attention back to the fact that they had stopped, and he'd also dismounted. Just as they all had.

"Set up camp and a place for Kesha to treat the injured." Michael's voice was atypically hushed yet carried across the heavy weight of oppression that hung in the very air.

Damien paused, feeling the fear that plucked at him, wanting to go to them and reassure the survivors that they were here to help.

They're scared and hurt. Set up camp, get a fire going, and food on. That will draw in the less timid, Michael whispered in his head.

Sadly, this isn't the first time we've done this, Olivia said.

Damien closed his eyes briefly and reinforced his mental barriers, trying to block out the pain seeming to crash over him in waves.

Here, let me help.

Olivia's soothing light touch brushed over his mind, and a barrier sprang between him and the world. Damien sagged, leaning against his horse in relief. It enabled him the breathing space to re-establish his own shields again.

You feel too much, Damien; it is your strength. Your weakness, Michael said.

Damien couldn't help but chuckle at that observation from Michael, of all people.

As it is yours, Damien replied.

He pushed himself back from his horse, rubbing her neck in appreciation. It amazed him the emanations that flowed between animals and humans. That low, steady, soothing pulse, as if even his horse knew he'd become inexplicably stressed. It was something ordinary people sensed. Animals made them feel better in times of distress. Although they couldn't see, they didn't realise the connection between them and the animal.

He didn't need the urging of his band mates to push himself back and fall into the familiar pattern of setting up camp. It didn't take long. They never really did since their needs didn't lean towards the extravagant, but it was a little different this time since they had set a full tent up for Kesha. They'd also brought their pack animals with them, although they kept their loads light because of their need to get here to render assistance as quickly as possible. He'd been told generally, if they were in a hurry, they left the pack animals behind and retrieved them when whatever emergency they were dealing with was over.

"No, Aiden, set up your hammock like everyone else," Olivia said.

At Olivia's exasperated tone Damien wasn't the only one who was trying to pretend they weren't watching as she took the tent poles off Aiden.

"But she's got one," Aiden spat.

"Kesha is our healer and will need somewhere to treat people." Olivia turned her back on Aiden and started walking away.

Unfortunately for Olivia, the tactic didn't work since Aiden followed her, speaking to her retreating back.

"It's not like anyone is here for her to treat. If she is allowed a tent, I don't understand why I can't have one. You wouldn't make Father sleep in a hammock." Aiden threw his hands up and gestured around the empty wreck of a village.

"You're wrong; there are survivors here. And you are not the Warlord," Michael said.

If that cold tone from Michael had been directed at him, Damien would have backed off instantly. As it was, the disagreement was attracting the attention of the whole band.

"Aiden, come on. I'll help you set up your hammock," Damien said. His eyes widened as he made the offer. He hadn't meant to intervene at all. As Aiden turned to face him, Damien sighed, seeing the closed expression on Aiden's face.

"I don't want to sleep in a hammock," Aiden grumbled.

"I'm sure the survivors hiding from us would be only too glad of a hammock to sleep in," Nathanial interjected.

"How do you know there's anyone here? I can't see anyone," Aiden said.

"Can't you feel them?" Damien asked.

He hoped the increasing darkness hid the dumbfounded expression that would be written all over his face, although it did nothing to mask the disbelief in his tone. Aiden frowned and cocked his head to one side. Damien glanced across at Nathanial, who'd been shepherding Aiden away from Olivia and Michael, and his eyebrow rose. It seemed he wasn't the only one that had caught the undertone emanating from their leaders, their patience running thin.

He's had his own mental barriers so tight he couldn't perceive anything, Nathanial said.

But how could he? I mean, he wouldn't be able to contribute his strength to the group to get here if he held them that tight, Damien said.

Exactly, Michael said.

Damien winced at the cutting tone, but found he couldn't disagree with the sentiment. They all had a job to do, and Aiden was behaving like a child. Regardless of his obstinance, the camp was set up and Aiden ended up with a hammock.

Even Kesha, usually so understanding and tolerant, resorted to ignoring Aiden, who spent the evening glaring in her direction.

I don't know which version of Aiden is worse, Damien said.

What do you mean? Nathanial asked.

Aiden being obnoxious or sulking like a toddler.

Nathanial spluttered, covering his mouth, caught trying not to laugh while he'd been halfway through swallowing a mouthful of food. Damien's lips twitched, and then his grumpy mood evaporated, and he chuckled.

Why are you here?

The laughter died on Damien's lips as the pitiful voice whispered in his head. Michael caught his eye indicating with a gesture he'd caught the comment as well and Damien should reply.

We came to help. Damien sensed the other's hesitation.

You're all equipped like you're ready to kill someone.

It is true. We are fighters. I'm sorry we weren't here to protect you all when your village was raided. We will defend you until help arrives from Vallantia.

I don't think the Sylannian raiders will be back. We have nothing left.

We have food, shelter, and a healer with us if you are injured.

Damien turned slowly as the rustling of leaves and the snap of twigs gave away that the woman had finally revealed herself. Her dark, shoulder-length hair was matted, and a tear traced down her grimy cheek from her brown eyes.

"Healer? Please, the old Trappers, we got them out of their hut, but they are badly burnt. I fear they are beyond help, but please, can you try?" Her voice shook.

Damien stood, then froze, holding his empty hands up as the woman stepped back, a hand pressing against her abdomen. Switching to his othersight, the traces of power around her jumped into focus with the distinct glow of another life, her child. Damien shook himself, wondering how she'd escaped notice. Everyone said the Sylannians took pregnant women, particularly those whose unborn child was male.

"Of course," Damien said.

Michael had stood, placing his hand on Kesha's shoulders, pushing her back down onto the bench.

"I'll not risk you out there. We'll bring your patients to you." His tone was firm, and he stared at her until she acknowledged the order. "Nathanial, Callan, with me."

Damien didn't need to be told he was going with Michael. The woman tensed like she was going to bolt when Michael stood. Then her eyes had fixed on Kesha, clearly guessing from the interaction that she was the healer. A thin strand of veil quested out from her, and Michael immediately stiffened in response.

She doesn't mean any harm. Damien shook his head.

The woman gasped softly, and hope dawned in her eyes.

Then her power faded, breaking apart. The individual little pieces dispelled and joined back into the flow of the veil as it swirled around. Her eyes shied away from Michael, focusing on Damien instead.

I wouldn't hurt one such as her. Please, come.

The woman turned and walked back into the surrounding forest, checking behind her every couple of steps, reassuring herself that they were still following her. Damien was just starting to wonder where they were going when a cave opening seemed to appear out of nowhere, descending into darkness. Damien sent his powers out, but all the layers of earth and rock hindered his ability to sense much of anything. He was only slightly mollified when he sensed that Nathanial, Callan and Michael also drew blanks.

They're smart, Nathanial said.

I doubt they know the cave system hinders our powers. Michael observed.

It's an effective hiding spot away from the river and gives them shelter, Damien said.

If only they'd had time to hide before the Sylannians hit them. There was a hint of sadness in Nathanial's tone.

Damien smiled reassuringly at the woman who stood at the cave entrance, a frown creasing her forehead. Equal parts fear and hope warred within her. Damien sent reassurance towards her and was rewarded as she almost wilted with relief. He gestured for her to lead on, following as she disappeared into the cave's depths.

The air was damp and heavy as they descended into the cave. A ball of light flared, and Damien winced, swearing as he turned to stare at Michael.

"What, you'd all rather stumble around in the dark or get smoked out by that torch?" Michael's eyebrows rose.

"Thank you," the woman said.

Her eyes were wide as she stared at the softly glowing ball of light floating just in front of Michael. She smiled uncertainly and put the torch back on the small stack piled up near the wall.

"We won't hurt you," Damien said.

Her eyes darted to him, then back to Michael before going on to Nathanial and Callan.

"I know who he is. Who you all are," she said, a tremor in her voice.

"Who are we?" Damien asked.

"I know the ones who bear the sword and flame." She stared at Michael again before continuing in a soft voice, "He's the one they call the warleader. You're the Unwanted. The warband everyone fears. The ones the Warlord sends to punish those who disobey his rule."

"Our reputation precedes us. If it helps, the Warlord isn't even aware of your existence." Michael's voice was equally soft, as if he was trying his best not to frighten her.

"If we were sent here to kill you, you'd be dead already," Callan commented.

"We don't always kill everyone we encounter, but Callan is correct, if somewhat undiplomatic." Damien threw an exasperated look at Callan, who shrugged unapologetically. "The Unwanted are also the ones sent in when people desperately need the help only we can give."

The woman hesitated a moment longer before continuing into the cave system. The tunnel they followed seemed to go on long enough that Damien began to wonder if she was leading them in circles before they rounded a bend and entered a large open cavern. Damien paused. There was a handful of young children who stared at them wide-eyed; a few women and older men were all that was left of what had obviously been a small but thriving village. Damien's breath hitched as he caught sight of the unconscious forms that lay on what appeared to be doors repurposed into stretchers to one side of the cavern.

He was across the intervening space, kneeling to one side of the blackened form of an older woman. His hand hovered above her; he'd been about to brush some hair from her forehead only to realise any contact would bring her unbearable agony. Michael had a pained expression on his face. Damien wondered how many times Michael had seen sights such as this before.

"We must get them back to Kesha. Throw shields around them; even a soft breeze will cause them pain." Michael gestured to one of the older men who stepped forward to help, and with Callan on the other end of the door, they carefully picked up the makeshift stretcher.

Damien and Nathanial timed their lift of the old door the woman was lying on, trying to make it as smooth as possible. Drawing in the veil, he ran strength to his arms and legs. Following Michael's example, he drew yet more energy and formed a bubble of power around the badly injured woman.

"Come, all of you. We didn't sense anyone else in these parts, but stay behind us," Michael ordered.

Without waiting for a response, Damien and Nathanial carrying the stretcher between them followed Michael as they retraced their steps back out of the cavern, the blue light of power bobbing along in front of them. The scuffling behind him told of those remaining gathering up the children and following in their wake. It was eerie; other than the footfalls of those who followed them, there was no sound. Not even a whimper from the children.

EIGHTY-SIX

Damien poured kaf into the mugs on a bench they'd salvaged, gesturing for those waiting to help themselves. The handful of survivors from the village had quietly settled where they were told, keeping a wary eye on their rescuers, as if they might suddenly fall on them with drawn blades to end their lives. At Kesha's first sight of the elderly man and woman with their charred skin, she'd directed they be carried into her tent. She'd been trying to heal them all night, with the strength funnelled to her from the warband.

Damien sensed it immediately when the steady pulse of power from Nathanial to the healer faltered. Michael went to stand, and Damien put down the pot, shaking his head.

"Relax, I'll go and check." Damien waited long enough for Michael to nod his acceptance before heading to the healer's tent.

Pulling the flap aside, he ducked in to find Nathanial exhausted and slumped on the ground to one side of Kesha. He was momentary alarmed before Nathanial opened his eyes and grinned weakly.

"Sorry, healer, I'm fine; just as soon as I stopped, my body immediately insisted it needed sleep," Nathanial said.

Kesha was pale with dark circles under her eyes, but otherwise not as exhausted as Nathanial. A number of them had been taking turns to draw energy from the veil and channelling it at Kesha to keep her up and working. She jumped when Damien cleared his throat. She'd been so focused on Nathanial's collapse and her patients that she hadn't even noticed he'd entered.

"Everything all right?" Damien asked.

Nathanial took a deep breath, and then rolled over onto his knees with a groan. He closed his eyes, simply breathing.

"Give me a moment," Nathanial said.

"Nathanial, you should have told me you were about to collapse," Kesha scolded.

"I'll be fine after some sleep. You, however, would have burnt yourself out trying to heal them by yourself, and unlike us, no amount of sleep would have cured you." Nathanial smiled weakly and accepted Damien's hand.

As Damien helped haul Nathanial to his feet he noticed Kesha's patients seemed to sleep peacefully.

"Do you need more?" Damien asked.

"No, they've both stabilised, and the worst of their burns have been healed. They should sleep for the next day while their healing completes."

Damien steadied Nathanial as he staggered and guided him across the camp to his hammock. He waited long enough to ensure Nathanial stayed in the hammock and did not flip out and end up on the ground under it. His friend had been asleep as soon as he relaxed back into his bed.

Retracing his steps, he returned to the healer's tent and ducked inside once more, only to see Kesha, curled up on her side, fast asleep near her patients. Damien grabbed a light blanket and placed it over her. He was about to retreat when his eyes fell on her patients. He remembered their burnt, blackened bodies from the night before and had unconsciously tried not to look at them. The old woman and man lay there, sleeping. Gone was the blackened, dead, and weeping skin. Instead, in its place—while still mottled with pale patches, some pink and others angry red—the skin was healed. He could almost believe they'd just spent too long in the sun or too close to a campfire.

"Powers, how is this possible?" Damien whispered.

He'd known Kesha was strong, but this was astonishing. Granted, she'd had people like Michael, Olivia and Nathanial feeding her power all night long, but he hadn't expected this. He'd seen those who'd survived severe burns. Their skin never recovered, even with a talented healer's support. At most, he'd thought Kesha's healing ability might just be the difference between life and death for the couple.

Damien retreated from the tent before he woke any of those sleeping within. As much as anyone, Kesha deserved some rest now that her work was done.

Damien walked back towards their makeshift communal kitchen, only to find he'd been supplanted by Callan, who just grinned, handing him a kaf with a plate of food before waving him off.

"Thanks," he said.

Damien turned and, at a gesture from Michael, took a seat opposite him. Michael sat quietly while Damien almost inhaled half the mug of kaf before picking up the slice of bread with some cheese and taking a mouthful.

"Kesha has finished healing the elderly couple, I take it?" Michael asked.

"She has. What she can do is remarkable."

"Our kind aren't the only ones getting stronger. It seems those with the healing talent are as well." Michael shrugged.

"Our kind? I guess we are good at killing. I'm not sure it's quite the same." Damien ducked his head.

"That too, but no, that isn't what I meant. It just happens our talent lends itself to war," Michael said.

"Damien, do you remember the village we saved?" Olivia sat on the opposite bench, mug in hand, gazing at him.

Damien frowned. "Of course."

"This would have been their lot if we hadn't been there," Michael said.

"We can't be everywhere, but these people? Well, we can fight against what they can't. They didn't deserve what the Sylannians did to them."

EIGHTY-SEVEN

Damien found his eyes sliding over to the fronds of the tiscan plant that wound up the trunks of trees near his position. The aroma from its leaves wafted over him as the gentle breeze swirled. As faint as it was, he'd recognised it instantly. He pressed his eyes closed as he trembled, a fine sweat breaking out all over his body, stomach churning. It had been months since the debilitating need for tiscan had dominated his awareness. Yet just the sight and smell of it now had thrown him back to when Nathanial had discovered his supply and thrown it away. Back to those terrible days under the healer's careful ministrations as he suffered withdrawal.

Hearing the crunch of stones under boots, Damien sighed with relief. He thanked his replacement and pushed off the tree he'd been leaning on as he was relieved from sentry duty. He walked away, trying not to break out into a run in his endeavour to put distance between himself and the drug he craved. He couldn't just go back to his hammock and plead exhaustion, his fellow band mates would sense there was something up. So he abruptly changed direction and headed towards one side of their encampment, as far away from the tiscan plant as possible. He figured he might as well burn some energy training since it usually helped him settle. As a snarling howl sounded behind him, his sword cleared its scabbard as he spun.

Damien instantly recognised the shape of a giant black cat, fangs displayed as it launched itself through the air. He sucked in the veil, strength running through his body, his blade licking with elemental fire. He swung his sword, realising the leaping cat, with its powerful legs and claws extended to attack him, would be on him the instant before he could strike it. The air exploded out of his lungs as the animal's full weight landed on him as he fell back. In a snap decision, Damien dropped his sword as he drew in the veil and pushed the beast back. The cat snarled as it flew back from him, and slammed into the tree trunk behind. It spun with a howl and bounded back into the forest.

Adrenaline still flooding his body, he slumped back, closing his eyes, and sucked in air. Hearing booted feet drumming in his direction, he opened his eyes to find a hand extended to him.

"Damn, that tree cat was big. Are you all right?" Nathanial asked.

Damien grabbed the proffered hand and allowed Nathanial to help haul him up from the ground.

"Yeah." Damien looked down, grateful for his reinforced fighting leathers. "Remind me to thank the twins when I next see them."

Nathanial shook his head. "I'm not sure they had you fighting one of those monsters in mind when they designed them."

Michael walked over, his eyes on the jungle, then over to

the remains of whatever the cat had been eating. Damien realised with a sudden understanding that he must have interrupted the beast's meal.

Michael turned his head and called back to the camp. "Callan, find a shovel. The locals must have at least one. We'd best bury that body properly."

Damien frowned at Michael, then back towards where the cat had left its meal. Suddenly, what he was seeing became clear. It wasn't a dead animal the tree cat had been gnawing on. The cat had been making lunch from what was an arm. Damien swallowed, fancying he could see a nose and part of a cheek protruding from the ground.

"The graves are too shallow. I hope there aren't too many of these around the village," Nathanial said, almost absently.

"It's not like you to miss game like this." Michael stared at Damien solemnly.

"I was distracted." Shame flooded him. "There's a tiscan vine near the sentry point."

Damien stared morbidly at the half-gnawed arm exposed from its resting place rather than meet Michael's eye. Now it had been pointed out to him, he could see the outline where the body had been buried and the rents in the soil from the cat's claws in pursuit of the flesh it could smell. A quick count of the fresh mounds revealed three shallow graves spread out in this part of the undergrowth. As Callan and Olivia walked over, each with shovels, Damien reached out and took the shovel Olivia had been carrying.

"It looks like it's just these few, but we'd best check," Olivia said.

"Where one predator is after an easy meal, there will be more," Michael agreed.

Leaving the others to determine if there were more graves they'd need to attend to, he, Nathanial, and Callan set to work digging some fresh graves. With the use of the veil to fuel their strength, it wasn't as onerous a task as it would be for others. Although it still consumed some time.

"This chore isn't quite what I had in mind to burn off energy," Damien said.

"How are you coping without tiscan?" Nathanial asked.

Damien put his strength behind his shovel, allowing the monotonous task to calm his mind. "Some days, most days, I still crave the stuff."

"Did you chew any of the leaves?" Nathanial asked.

Damien chuckled, although even to his ears, he couldn't hear any humour. That was one problem with riding with a band filled with equally talented individuals. It was challenging to hide things.

Damien squeezed his eyes shut. "No. But I wanted to."

Damien carefully kept his mind on the task at hand. Combined with the steady pulse of the veil running through him, it helped chase away the sudden nausea that even thinking about tiscan leaves brought on. A fine sweat broke out, prickling all over his skin. In the back of his mind, a traitorous voice whispered that if he just took some of the tiscan, he'd feel better.

"Give yourself time," Callan said.

"You don't get over an addiction like tiscan in a few months," Nathanial said without even a hint of recrimination. "Particularly with the amount you were consuming every day."

"Kesha told me I might never get over it." Damien had to admit the prospect worried him.

"You will. You are stronger than you think," Callan said.

"Going through transition as you are probably isn't helping," Nathanial said.

"What do you mean?" Damien asked.

"Those times you feel like the veil is burning you from the

inside out?" Nathanial paused while Damien nodded. "That's your body reacting to transition. Not withdrawal from tiscan."

Damien didn't know if he quite believed what Nathanial told him. It wasn't like Nathanial would know what tiscan was like, but Damien had to admit he was so messed up himself, he couldn't refute it either. He tried to concentrate on what he was doing rather than the need for tiscan that kept clawing at him. He considered going to see Kesha. She'd told him to see her if things got too bad. Then he dismissed the idea. He couldn't run to the healer to banish cravings from his mind every time he had them. If he became overly reliant on Kesha's healing talent to manage his addiction, he could get out of control with the abilities he was developing. More than anything else, he needed to fight off his own demons.

Damien moved over to where the rotting arm lay exposed above the ground. His skin crawled, although this time, it had nothing to do with his withdrawal from tiscan. Checking over his shoulder, he spotted some villagers who'd gathered to watch them. Unable to think of anything to ease their heartache he went to work with the grisly part of their task: digging up the rotting bodies of the deceased and moving them over to their new graves. This time, he hoped they would be buried far enough underground to deter the predators. Although not only would they be leaving this place, the villagers would as well. So predators near their camp would only be a threat for a short amount of time before they would all be gone, leaving this place for nature to reclaim.

EIGHTY-EIGHT

Michael's gaze took in the party that arrived with Adam at its head, noting that while some of his father's household guards were in the rescue party, his brother was nowhere to be seen. Not that the omission was anything terribly surprising. To be honest, it would have shocked him if Steven had accepted the responsibility of his birthright and come out at the head of the rescue party. This village, while remote and small, was within the old territorial boundaries of Vallantia. Even before the rise of the Warlord.

"Well met, Adam," Michael said.

"This is bad, even for the Sylannians." Adam's expression was grim as he gazed around the devastated, blackened village —or at least, what was left of it, which was next to nothing. Those he'd brought with him to assist were equally shocked. Michael bolstered his shields in response to the devastation he could feel emanating from them.

"There is always some destruction."

"I know; it's just none of the reports I've read detail the Sylannians destroying an entire village." Adam shook his head.

"The raiders normally take out the boats and jetty to avoid pursuit, but you are right; this is new," Michael said.

As the new arrivals started unpacking and setting up their own camp for the night, Michael led Adam over to the table they'd cobbled together from the destroyed buildings. Adam grinned despite the circumstances and held up a bladder he'd been carrying.

"Ben sent some of his new brew." Adam raised his eyebrow.

"Just the one skin?" Michael grinned as mugs suddenly appeared on the table.

"Well, there may be a couple more in the cart. I figured we'd start with this one." Adam gazed around the camp, his smile faltering. "We thought there'd be more survivors; plenty for all to have some."

"You two, why don't you go see if you can find the other skins and share some. Starting with our charges," Michael instructed a couple of his people who were loitering nearby.

"Of course, Michael," one of them said, before turning and walking towards the carts.

"Colin shouldn't be far off," Adam said, pouring ale into the mugs.

Michael absently chilled the contents of the mugs while picking one up and sipping it appreciatively.

"He went to check on the sentry?" Michael didn't really have to ask.

"He left a couple of days before we did," Adam said.

"I fear the sentry is either captured or dead," Olivia said as she slid onto the bench next to Adam, grabbing a mug.

"You haven't been able to contact him?" Adam asked.

Michael shook his head. He went to comment, then paused

as the woman who'd first appeared when they'd shown up approached and stood a short distance off. Michael smiled, sending a subtle thread of reassurance to her.

"What's to become of us?" Her head drooped.

Michael considered her, then beyond her to the small group of survivors who sat not far off. All of them clearly waiting for his response. He guessed the question was prompted by Adam's arrival; with empty carts the remaining villagers could travel in but no sign of building supplies to help them rebuild their village.

"You'll be escorted to Vallantia," Michael said.

"But how will we live? We have nothing left." The woman's lips trembled.

"You will be accommodated by my order until you can make your own way," Michael said calmly.

Her head came up, eyes wide, finally making contact with his own. Michael smiled at her shock and waited patiently for her to find her words.

"You would do that? For us?" Tears welled in the woman's eyes.

"Vallantia is big enough; you should be able to find a new life should you choose to stay on," Michael said, nodding.

"Or, if you have family in another village, we'll arrange for you to travel with traders," Adam added.

"I, we— Thank you," the woman said, her eyes welling with unshed tears as she backed off and returned to her fellow villagers.

As booted feet drummed across the ground, attention turned to the river, as Damien, followed closely by Nathanial and Callan, pelted for the river. The three paused only long enough to divest themselves of their boots and weapons before diving from the bank into the water. Michael snorted in amusement and as Adam glanced at him, eyebrows raised, he felt compelled to explain.

"They just reburied some of the dead."

"The shallow graves had attracted attention," Olivia added.

"That can't have been a pleasant duty," Adam commented.

Damien, Nathanial, and Callan waded out of the river, followed by an inrush of power causing the water to sheet from all three. Their clothes dried in the few steps they took to retrieve their boots and weapons. Adam whistled softly, shaking his head.

"As many times as I've seen you and yours use abilities, it's still astonishing to see feats like that—they don't even look fatigued or like they had to concentrate at all." There was a hint of admiration in Adam's tone.

"We all have our skills; Powers save us all if crafting our weapons is ever left to me," Olivia said.

"To be fair to you, those three are the strongest, besides myself and Olivia," Michael said.

"You set your top people to burial detail?" Adam's eyebrows climbed up to his hairline.

"Damien had to keep himself occupied; the other two assisted." Olivia shrugged.

"It was....easier to keep him distracted while some of the others were detailed to fix the part of the problem we can control," Michael said.

"You take them all in," Adam said quietly.

"Misfits, all of us," Michael said. He appreciated that while Adam was conversant enough with some of the issues that could plague those with high-level abilities, and the less than desirable lives some of the Unwanted lived before they joined the Warlord's service, he dropped the issue rather than persist as many would.

"Perhaps. But you're our misfits, and I think we will need

you all if this indicates the future." Adam gestured at the burnt remains around them and raised his mug.

Michael smiled sadly and raised his mug in return, maintaining eye contact before they all took a sip. Adam sat up, turning expectantly towards the river. Michael didn't have to exert himself; as connected as they were, Adam was always aware of his twin. The small boat with Colin and a handpicked party rounded the river's bend, pulling into the bank.

Michael stood, along with Adam and Olivia, heading down towards the river's edge. They stood a short distance off as Colin and his people, alighted the boat, making their way onshore.

As Colin drew closer, Michael could tell by his grim face that it wasn't good news. Not that he'd really expected anything but the worst. From this distance, he should have been able to reach the sentry and check in with them via the veil. As it was, he couldn't sense them at all, and he'd tried several times since they'd been here.

"Dead; scavengers made quick work of the remains." Colin shook his head in disgust.

"Thank you for checking." Michael turned, leading them all back to their camp.

"Want us to send crews out to check on the rest of the network down the river?" Colin asked.

Michael took a moment, weighing up his options. If Colin and Adam sent people out to check, he could go back to brief the Warlord on this latest attack. Then he dismissed the idea. There wasn't anything the Warlord could do except order more sentries to be put in place, and Michael could do that himself. The Warlord would learn of this eventually, regardless. Even if this attack was a departure from the normal Sylannian raid.

"No, just get these people back to safety and make sure patrols are increased out of Vallantia," Michael instructed.

"We're patrolling along the river ourselves?" Olivia asked.

"Now that the relief party has arrived. We'll continue with our patrol in the morning, then cut into Yalleska to inform the Warlord of this change in the Sylannians' attacks at the other end."

Nathanial, who'd been listening nearby, quietly went about issuing orders to start preparations for an early morning departure. Damien went to assist with packing up. Michael frowned, taking in the dark circles under Damien's eyes and the tremor in his hand he didn't quite manage to hide. He opened his mouth to intervene when Nathanial grabbed Damien by the shoulders and pushed him towards his hammock.

"Not you, you're not well; go sleep it off. I'll send Kesha to help," Nathanial ordered.

Michael nearly smiled as Damien faced a side of Nathanial he hadn't encountered before.

"I'm fine—"

"You're not. Tiscan addiction is not your fault; people who didn't know any better fed it to you from childhood. You don't have to struggle with this alone; we're your team. Let us help." Nathanial stared at Damien until he finally gave up the pretence and went and collapsed into his hammock.

As Kesha came out of her tent, walking across to Damien, alerted that she was needed by one of the others, Nathanial sighed and turned back to his warleader. Michael smiled, poured him a drink, and pushed it to the empty bench space on the other side of the table.

"Did he chew the leaves?" Michael asked.

"No, although he admitted he wanted to. Badly, if his reaction is anything to go by," Nathanial said.

"It's a good sign he resisted, even if he is beating himself up over his body's reaction to being confronted with the stuff again." Michael sipped his drink.

"It is," Nathanial agreed, then frowned as his eyes slid over the remnants of the village. "This may be a far bigger problem."

EIGHTY-NINE

On their winding patrol along the river, they'd encountered a handful of villages, razed to the ground with few survivors. It had been a series of heartbreaking and grim tasks to bury the dead and assist the living to the nearest settlement. They'd fought off the Sylannian raiders a few times before in some villages along their path, but Michael and Olivia suspected there was a different mind behind these new attacks.

Today, however, Damien couldn't help himself: he was filled with anticipation. He was excited and trying to keep it under wraps. Finally, after all their bloody work, their patrol was making their way back to his home village. It seemed like a lifetime had passed since they had torn him away from his family and forced him to join the Warlord's ranks.

Damien couldn't help but be aware the others were concerned; he could feel it, see it in the way they kept a close eye on him and closed ranks around him. He was grateful for their concern and support, but it was unnecessary. While many in his village hadn't liked him, some had even feared him a little, there was no reason why they would reject him. Their worst nightmare because of his presence in the village hadn't happened. It wasn't as if their crops had been burnt, livestock destroyed, villagers killed. None of that had happened. He was the only one who'd paid the price for the Warlord riding into the village that day. Damien closed his eyes against the flood of memories of the things he'd done that assaulted his mind. He'd never believed that he would become what he had. Let alone be good at it. It was something he really wanted to discuss with Owen, who'd be more likely to understand than the others in the village.

The niggling doubt that preyed on his mind was about the other types of attacks. He was reconciled to fighting when he was helping to save lives from Sylanna or other hostile forces. The man he'd killed. The one who'd simply been defending his home from the ones he believed were a threat to their way of life. That death still plagued him. He'd face that situation again. He didn't know if he could bring himself to commit those acts with impunity. To kill on demand from the Warlord.

Michael fell back to ride beside him. They rode together in silence for a while, although his leader wouldn't have dropped back unless he had something to say.

"I remember when we rode out from here. It seems like a lifetime ago." Even to his ears, his voice sounded much older than he was when he'd left his home village.

"It was. You were a naïve boy."

"Now?"

"You're not anymore. No one could be and survive this life."

Sadness hit Damien, that he'd lost forever that boy who chopped wood and hunted for the village supplies. Who yearned for more than the life he had. Still he wouldn't go back to the innocent he'd been, even if he could.

"What does that say about me?" Damien asked.

"It means you know how to survive." Michael's voice was even.

They rode in silence for a moment; Damien smiled as he noticed the others were giving them some distance. There really wasn't much privacy for any of them. They lived together, travelled together, and fought together. When they rode into battle, they depended on each other to survive. It had forged them into a tight-knit group. He was no longer seen as an outsider. Even if there was still that tiny part of him that wasn't sure he really belonged.

"You're concerned." It wasn't a question.

"This visit won't be the welcome home greeting you imagine."

"There's no reason at all for them to reject me. I gave myself up. None of them were hurt because of me, and I'm sure those who feared me are happy I've gone. The villagers will know this visit is temporary." Damien could hear the doubt in his voice and wondered who he was trying to convince.

Damien, if you care for your little sister or your mother and father, keep your distance. Michael's mindvoice held a hint of warning.

They won't...

Do you want the Warlord to know how much you care for them?

He's not here...

Aiden is not his father, but he is still the Warlord's son. If he perceives any gain for himself, he will run to his father with the information. Do you want this?

Damien barely stopped himself from stiffening in shock as Michael sent images into his mind. His father, a powerful man in his prime, screamed in agony as the Warlord severed his hamstrings and crushed the bones in his arm and hand, crippling him. His mother, young and beautiful, was stripped and flogged in the town square with the spike catching the flesh in her face, leaving her scarred for life.

No. Damien could hear the denial in that one word, his mind baulked at the idea such horrors could be inflicted on those he loved if he failed.

It wasn't Michael's father he was seeing crippled. It was his own. The mother being stripped, dragged through the town square and flogged was his own. Isabella was the image of the girl hanging from the rafters of an otherwise comfortable room.

Until the Warlord is absolutely sure he has your undivided loyalty, he won't have any compunction in using your family as a pressure point against you.

What do I do? The joy Damien felt moments before deflated.

Behave the same as you have in every other village. Remember, anyone you show friendship to here could end up paying the price for it.

"Maybe there will be a first time. Just try not to let it get to you too much if things don't go as you expect." Michael spurred his horse up to take his accustomed place.

Damien couldn't escape the conclusion Michael was right. Notwithstanding the death he'd dealt out on order, being told to turn a cold shoulder to his family, to Owen, was one of the most challenging tasks the Unwanted had asked of him.

CHAPTER

NINETY

Damien's eyes widened, and he rode into his home village to see stragglers herding their children indoors. The undercurrent of fear pulsed at him through the veil as he rode in the centre of the band. It was uncommon for him to be in this position; of late, he'd either been towards the front or tail guard. Yet his band mates had closed around him as they entered his home village, pushing him to the centre of the pack.

Still, they couldn't shield him from the whispers from the villagers, the shock and recognition.

Traitor.

He was always going to be a killer!

Damien was careful not to let the hurt and shock show on his face. He tried his best, yet no matter that he told himself this was just the same as all the other villages he'd ridden into as a member of the Warlord's warband, somehow this was different. He hoped he didn't encounter anyone right now that he really cared about. At least, not until he got himself under control. He hadn't expected cheers from his fellow townsfolk, but he hadn't expected hatred and fear. Suddenly Michael's warning held far more importance, and he kept his gaze steadfastly on the back of the rider in front of him. He tried to exude the confident arrogance he'd exhibited while entering other villages.

He thinks he's something special.

Damien's eyes hardened, lips compressing. He spurred his horse forward and speared out to one side, sending out instructions to the rest of his band.

The best campground is this way.

None of them showed the slightest hesitation as they followed his lead to the area to the side of the village. The trees were thin enough to allow camping for visiting trader markets, yet with easy access to the village centre, the river, and the access roads in and out of the village. Damien reined in his horse and swung out of her saddle, handing the reins to a teammate. The only way through this that he could see was to keep to the pattern he'd established with the band. He'd go out with the foragers and hunters to get fresh provisions for the meal. Others would set up his sleeping space for not only him but the others that went out like him.

Gesturing to the small group of hunters in their band, he barely paused before leading them off to the small track that led deeper into the forest. This would provide them with the best hunting opportunity at this hour. It would also keep him out of Aiden's sight and away from the eyes of his former villagers.

If he was truthful, it would also provide less opportunity for him to run into his parents. Although, at a guess, as soon as the village was warned soldiers were approaching, they would have grabbed Isabella and headed indoors. He hoped, unlike him, they had understood the risks inherent to this visit. He hoped they would stay safely hidden inside their home with Isabella until he left.

~

DAMIEN WALKED BACK into the camp, handing over his kill to Callan and his helpers who'd drawn cook duty this evening, and smiled his thanks. Damien didn't have to turn around to know Aiden's eyes were on him, watching. He could feel it. Damien deliberately turned and walked to an open space between their camp and the village's main square, knowing he would be in full sight of most of the village, and started laying out a training circle. This was the other part of his routine; he practiced his sword work. Unlike when he first started, it was a part of the intimidation factor. Now was not the time to ignore that habit. If Michael was correct in his judgement, any change in his routine could lead to horrific consequences for those he loved if he messed up before the Warlord trusted him. Besides he knew Michael had called a town meeting to discuss the tithe. If Michael joined him in this little training exercise, which he normally did, it might reinforce the danger they represented and prevent any of the villagers saying anything stupid.

Damien stepped into his practice circle. The eyes of the villagers were on him; they stopped in their scurrying from one place to another to stare. Some peeled curtains back thinking they were safely out of sight to peer across the square at him. He could sense their attention, regardless. Closing his eyes, he took a deep breath, releasing it slowly, allowing his mind to relax.

Sensing a presence running into the ring and the scrape of a blade being drawn from a scabbard, Damien drew his own sword. It rose to counter his opponent's blade in an assured, smooth motion. He opened his mind to the veil, trusting his powers and the flow of the veil to show him the movement and blade strikes of the other. He'd known it was Michael. No other person would enter the training ring that way. Not since Aiden had shoved weapons training in his head. Not even Aiden, who'd never truly integrated the stolen knowledge into his own abilities. Damien had worked hard to bring that knowledge from the unconscious part of his mind to the forefront. That effort had paid off significantly. Now his band mates didn't stay away from his training session because they feared his descent into madness. They stayed away because he was close to Michael in his skill level. It was clear to him now why the Warlord had taken Michael. Apart from his skills with the veil, he would have been a threat if left in Vallantia. He would have risen to be a leader, a warlord, who could have threatened the power of the Warlord. Instead, the Warlord had turned the loyalty of his old enemy's son to himself.

Damien realised he was at a crossroads of sorts. He could back off from his current course. He could refuse to use his skills to fight against those who threatened his people, or accept it was his duty to put himself between the commoners and the threats they faced.

Damien's attention was drawn sharply back to the clash of blades he was engaged in as he caught the sudden sweep of energy that signified a sword coming straight for his throat.

"Hold!" Olivia's bellow rang out.

Damien froze, experienced enough now to know Olivia wouldn't call an end to the practice bout unless one of them was about to be seriously injured. As always, the one about to be seriously injured was him. While he might have had Michael's sword and war skills shoved into his head, it didn't mean he'd mastered it all. He also hadn't lived it; for him, it was just knowledge stuffed in his mind with minimal real-life experience to base it off.

~

DAMIEN DIDN'T REALISE he'd moved. Not at first. Then he was aware he had his blade drawn and pressed against the insufferable fool of a man's throat as he slammed him against the walls of the meeting house.

"Yes, I'm a traitor to the village. Don't forget, you are one of the ones who advocated giving me up to the Warlord's tender mercies." Damien didn't recognise the menacing hiss coming from his own mouth.

"You were never good at anything but fooling around with blades. You weren't a loss to the village." The quaver in the baker's voice betrayed his fear despite his words.

"Yes, they've turned me into a killer; I'm actually pretty good at it. You might want to remember that little detail next time you open your mouth."

Damien shoved the baker away from him, causing the man to collapse onto the floor. He swept his gaze around the gathered townsfolk. None of them could meet his eyes in the frozen stillness in the room, fear emanating from all of them. The harsh scrape of his sword as he sheathed it caused many of those gathered to jump.

"With your permission, Warleader?"

At Michael's nod, Damien turned and headed for the meeting house doors. A villager standing near them flinched back as he brushed past.

"Damien, lad, they didn't mean anything by it." Owen stood by the door. Of all those here, he was the only one who wasn't scared.

Even though it killed a small part of him inside, Damien

didn't allow his expression to change as he brushed past Owen, ignoring the comment. While the sideways looks and the distrust on the faces of people he'd grown up with hurt, he could tell Owen at least wasn't one of them. Of course, the more they pushed him away, the safer they were. The safer the entire village was, but that knowledge didn't help. His squad mates had been correct when they'd told him the villagers would reject him. He'd been naïve to think otherwise.

Damien clattered down the three steps and strode across the town square, heading to their own camp. As happy and excited as he'd been to be coming back here, now he couldn't wait to leave. After the people he'd killed, the villages they'd taken for the Warlord, he didn't belong anymore.

Callan stared at him gravely as he approached; he reached for a flask and handed it to him. Damien smiled bitterly. Pushing down his anger and hurt, he pulled the stopper off the flask and took a large swallow of the brew it contained. Damien took one more swallow and passed the flask to Callan, who took a swig before handing it back to him.

"Drink. We won't be leaving town at this hour."

Damien took another mouthful. "You were all correct. I am no more wanted here than the rest of you are."

Callan shook his head. "You are one of us now. One of the Unwanted. Wear it as a badge of pride."

Hearing the crunch of stone under boots, Damien passed the flask to Nathanial who had followed him out of the meeting hall.

"We do what we must to stay alive, to protect them all despite them being ungrateful for it. We are your family now; we won't turn our backs on you." Nathanial clapped him on the shoulder and took a drink from the flask himself.

NINETY-ONE

Michael sat against a tree trunk, near the river, concluding it must have been an idyllic, peaceful place to grow up before he'd ridden into town with the Warlord, turning their lives upside down. Michael didn't think he'd have long to wait; he'd been observed as he'd walked out of town alone. Of course, it would be disappointing if the man he needed to speak to didn't follow, but he didn't think he had anything to worry about on that score. These meetings always took some arranging, with one of his men dutifully keeping Aiden occupied, so he didn't notice. Not that it mattered if Aiden went running to the Warlord since he'd already apprised their father he would have this little discussion with Damien's former mentor, but Aiden had a habit of getting in the way at the worst possible times.

Michael smiled, hearing the soft crunch of debris on the forest floor, and expanded his senses. While Owen wasn't exceptionally talented with the veil, he could shield quite well, and he'd already known the man had some mindspeaking capability. What was more surprising was he sensed Owen was an all-rounder; he had a low-level ability across the board. The man was strong, all things considered. Yet just below what they would notice when they'd first come here. Particularly with Damien around, shining like a beacon. Or would have been hard to notice, if he hadn't been throwing his feelings around, muttering away, unwittingly making his feelings plain to anyone who'd been paying attention.

Michael sensed Owen's lifeforce pulsing as he stood, masked by the trunk of an ancient tree. He could hear Owen debating if he should kill the threat to his village, to Damien.

Damien's life will be much worse if you end my miserable existence. Michael didn't add it would be worse because Owen himself would be dead.

While Owen was obviously a skilled hunter and had trained in fighting—Damien had confirmed that Owen was the brain that had set up the defences for the village on the river—he hadn't been fighting a war since he was a child, as Michael had himself. As much as the man's death would pain Damien, if Owen attacked Michael, he would kill him. There was a pause as the man stiffened, then considered his options. Finally, he moved from behind the ancient tree and crossed the intervening space.

Owen stood for a moment before sitting opposite, his expression wary.

"How would his life be worse?" Owen's low voice growled at him.

Michael stared at Owen steadily. "It won't free him. Damien is strong. If I fall, the burden of leading the Unwanted will fall to Olivia, and Damien will have to step up, taking more responsibility sooner."

"Oh, please. He's just a boy, kind and considerate. You promised to protect him. Instead, he's returned just as cold-blooded as the rest of you," Owen snarled.

Anger flashed through Michael. "What do you think our lives are? If we didn't become good at killing, we would die under the blades in the hands of the raiders from Sylanna."

"You said—"

"I said I'd do my best for him, and I have. He'd be dead if I hadn't." Michael let his anger bleed from his eyes as he glared at the other man.

The other man sat for a moment, staring at him. "The Unwanted, you call yourselves that?"

"We do. It helps keep those we love safe. Or as safe as they can be." The stillness at that explanation was palpable.

Michael almost smiled as Owen was at least capable of thinking things through. He decided there was a lot to like about him. Damien's former mentor was one of the few who seemed to be able to process the information he was given and come up with the correct conclusions. Owen's competence explained a great deal about how a simple country boy like Damien could have a good start on his sword skills.

"I shouldn't have tried to intervene when Damien had the run-in with the baker and left the meeting house." Owen's eyes widened, and his face paled.

"You shouldn't have; Aiden was there and noted the interaction."

Pain shadowed Owen's face. "Will it cause issues for him?"

"Only if he makes a mistake and the Warlord wants to punish him. Then you will probably be dragged out and flogged or deliberately crippled in front of him. It will kill him to see another punished for his own failure."

"So the rumours, whispered quietly when you aren't around, are true."

Michael shook his head. "No. The reality is worse. Particularly when you see people's lives and villages destroyed because you didn't get there in time to save them."

After all these years, there was no bitterness or anger, or much of anything. It was just life, and mostly it was the only life he'd ever led. His life before being taken by the Warlord seemed to belong to another.

"How long have you lived this life?" Owen spoke softly.

When Michael looked at the older man, he unexpectedly saw what he interpreted as compassion on his face.

"I've belonged to the Warlord since the fall of Vallantia. I was thirteen."

"You don't belong to that man!"

"Ah, but I do. All of us who ride under his banner do. As does Damien. Don't get me wrong, I no longer fight what I am. I haven't for a very long time, but I will do everything I can to protect those who are mine."

Michael watched Owen quietly as the man struggled to keep his anger under control.

"I came here thinking that killing you would solve a problem, but it won't, will it?" Owen asked quietly.

"No."

"Why would Damien be forced into greater responsibility if you died?"

"He's strong in the veil; I judge he'll end up stronger than any of the others. He also takes to the blade like a natural-born... fighter."

Michael had quickly substituted the word fighter for killer. He doubted Owen would care for the other term, even though it was accurate. Damien might have had a late introduction to the blade and battle, but he was calm, almost dispassionate, and clinical in a fight. Michael wondered how much was actually Damien and how much was because it was his own battle skills that Aiden had shoved into Damien's head. Kesha had confirmed that more than the fighting skill was transferred during the process; some of his experiences, the things that had helped shape him leaked across as well. Aiden had never assimilated it, but it seemed Damien was.

"He always showed an aptitude for such things, but surely he couldn't have developed that fast?" Owen protested, clearly not quite believing what he'd been told.

Michael raised his eyebrow at Owen. "You caught his practice session?"

He'd been aware, when he stepped into Damien's practice session, that Owen had been on the far side of the village square standing in the shade of a tree and had watched the full session.

"I mean, he's good, but it's one thing in practice. In battle..." Owen shrugged.

"Damien has seen battle, quite a bit of it. He's capable. He'll start training as one of my seconds before the year is out." Michael didn't admit it was happening already.

With Damien's ability with the veil and aptitude for the blade and battle it was unavoidable. While the Warlord might not know precisely how strong Damien was, his abilities could not be hidden. Besides the fact that Aiden had been in Damien's head and would have gleaned much from the contact.

"He doesn't deserve this life. He was a good lad," Owen said.

"He still is and no one deserves this life, but it is his anyway. Just keep your head down until we leave."

"I can do that," Owen promised.

Michael considered Owen and could not find a graceful way to insert the question that was foremost in his mind into the conversation. He finally just asked.

"Who were you?"

"What?" Owen's head swung towards him.

"The man who was Damien's mentor, training him with

such skill in the blade, wasn't born and raised in this village. You didn't learn your skill with the sword here in Ranlith."

Owen hesitated then stared off in the distance, his voice when he finally spoke was soft. "I was a member of the household guard in Callenhain back when the Straffords ordered us to throw their daughter, Lady Olivia, out the gates at the Warlord's feet."

Michael stared at the man, shocked. He could feel the pain coming from the older man at the memories the conversation provoked, even after all these years.

"So you left?"

"After what they did, what they ordered me to do. I couldn't do that again." Owen squeezed his eyes shut. "I'd ask her to forgive me for what I did, but nothing could absolve it."

"She doesn't blame you or the guards who threw her out. Her father gave the order, and ultimately she knows the pain others would have suffered if that hadn't been followed."

That the moment had scarred Olivia. Even if she understood more people would have died if she hadn't been thrown out of the gates that day. It still hurt that her family hadn't tried to protect her; no one had. Owen didn't need that fact confirmed to him.

"Tell Damien I'm sorry. I didn't understand." Owen's voice was barely above a whisper.

Michael stood and began walking away before he paused; thinking of the man's pain over his perceived failures, he turned back to Owen. "Whatever you do, make sure his sister, Isabella, stays hidden. None of us will like the consequences should the Warlord learn of her existence."

"What do I do if her powers get out of control, dangerous like Damien's?" Owen asked.

Michael almost smiled as the question was practically

wrung from the man. He turned back to face Damien's former mentor.

"Whatever you do, make sure she isn't given tiscan, the stuff is addictive and will cause more problems than it solves."

"Tiscan, but Damien—"

"I know, it's why I mentioned it. If her powers develop beyond your ability to help her send word. The Smith's sons in Vallantia will be able to reach me. There is another in the village down the river a little way that we took just before your own."

"The reputation of the smiths in Vallantia precedes them, and I know the village you mean. Bad news travels," Owen said, his eyes shadowed.

"A woman, Kara, she's strong in the veil and remains in the village. She's one of mine and will also be able to reach me."

Michael almost smiled as Owen took the time to work through the implications.

"I can do that. I think I'll go on a hunting trip after you leave here. It might be useful to make her acquaintance," Owen said. "Is there anything you'd like her to know?"

"Tell her to keep her eyes, ears, and mind open. There has been a change in the pattern of behaviour of the Sylannians. There have also been traders breaching the lookouts we have in place to serve as an early warning." Michael kept his eyes steady on the other man.

Owen's eyes widened. Michael turned away, satisfied. While Owen might have started the day planning to kill Michael, now he'd shifted track and had a purpose. Protect Isabella and, not so coincidentally, start acting as one of his network of lookouts.

Not that Owen realised that's what he was yet, but he wasn't a stupid man.

NINETY-TWO

Damien packed the last of his gear away, relieved that their stay here in his hometown was nearly over. He'd never dreamed he'd want to be going away. There had only been one regrettable incident with Owen at the meeting house. Other than that, he'd kept to himself. As much as he wanted to see his mother and father and Isabella, he was glad they'd had the sense to stay absent. Even if right now it killed him not to see them.

Hearing incoming horses, Damien spun, his hand going to his sword, and he found himself drawing it and facing the incoming riders without even consciously thinking about it. Damien relaxed marginally as a hand signal from Michael advised them to stand down. Michael sheathed his own blade and turned to Olivia with a face devoid of expression. Damien put away his sword, although he was unsettled and wondered who the incoming riders were.

Or at least he wondered for a moment, before they rounded the bend in the main road approaching the village, and his heart sank. He'd recognise the big stocky man in leathers in the lead anywhere. It was the Warlord. Dust kicked up in the village as they reined in their horses. They were unlikely to be going anywhere this day with the Warlord riding in and sure enough, Olivia issued new orders to unpack the gear he'd just packed up. A bad feeling settled on him. If the Warlord had ridden into town, it could hardly be by happenstance.

"Damien!"

Damien froze, feeling his face drain of colour. He closed his eyes briefly before turning around to face Isabella as she flew into his arms. Nathanial's eyes widened and his face blanched as he looked from him over to where the Warlord was just dismounting from his horse. As Damien shifted his body to mask Isabella from sight, Nathanial and Callan moved their horses subtly.

"Isabella, sorry I've been busy. Since it looks like we'll be delayed, let's go inside so I can see Father and Mother."

Fearing it was too late, but unwilling to wait and find out, Damien walked Isabella back towards their house, desperately hoping that the Warlord had not set eyes on her.

"Well, what have we here? Damien, I didn't know you had a sister. Now be polite and introduce me."

Damien stiffened as the deep voice of the Warlord sounded behind him. Damien closed his eyes, took a steadying breath, and then turned to face the Warlord.

"Warlord, I'm sorry. This is my baby sister, Isabella." Damien's voice was barely a whisper as he tried, he feared in vain, to keep his face blank.

Thankfully Isabella seemed to have finally realised she'd made a mistake and pressed hard against him. The Warlord's eyes raked over his sister and Damien stiffened in automatic response.

"Well, Isabella. How ever could we have missed you the

first time around?" The Warlord smiled, his eyes never leaving hers.

"Warlord, come, leave the child be. Since you are here, I must brief you on some of the recent Sylannian attacks. It appears they may have someone new coordinating their raids." Michael's voice was confident as he placed his hand on the Warlord's arm, interposing himself between the Warlord and Isabella.

As Michael's mention of a new commander captured the Warlord's attention, Damien took the hint. While Michael led the Warlord away, Damien took the opportunity to steer Isabella back home.

Damien stayed calm, at least on the outside, until he guided Isabella inside their family home and shut the door firmly behind him. Once inside, his breath caught in his throat, and the room spun. He squeezed his eyes shut and leant back against the door. Hands pressed against his eyes, he slid down until he hit the floor with a thud.

"Damien, I'm sorry! I just wanted to see you. No one would let me leave the house." Isabella's voice trembled. "Mother!"

The thump of feet signalled his parents running from the back of the house. His mother reached him first, and he leant, unresisting, as she knelt next to him and pulled him into her arms. He wasn't sure how much time passed as she rocked him, stroking the side of his head.

Shhh, everything will be all right, my son.

His mother's soft mindvoice soothed him as if he was a child who'd woken from a nightmare. Except Damien hadn't woken from it. Instead, he'd discovered the nightmare was real.

He knows, Mother. Damien's mindvoice caught.

"Who?"

It was the Warlord who just rode into town.

What does he know? There was a hint of fear in his mother's mindvoice. Damien could tell she dreaded the answer, even though she'd already guessed his response.

Isabella. She came out at just the wrong moment. He knows she exists. He knows she has powers like mine. The crushing weight of responsibility settled on him.

He desperately wanted to keep Isabella safe, yet it was because of him that she was now at risk. Dread descended on him. Her fate would be worse than his. Nothing good would come from the Warlord knowing of her existence.

"I'm sorry."

Damien's eyes flashed open to catch Isabella's. She knelt in front of him with their father's arm around her. Damien shook his head, but did not try to move from his mother's arms.

"Don't be. It's not your fault."

"I don't understand why it was wrong for me to see you. No one will tell me anything!" Isabella threw accusatory looks at their parents.

Damien closed his eyes as he recognised the rebellious complaint in his sister's tone. An echo of his own rebelliousness at restrictions placed on him before the Warlord had ridden into town. She hadn't been informed for her own good. Yet, on this occasion, it had been to her detriment.

"If I make a mistake, the Warlord will punish those I care for. He didn't know you existed until now." Damien kept his gaze steadily on his sister, ignoring that his parents had stiffened.

"Well, what could he do to me? Force me to become a soldier like he did you? That would be stupid. I'm no good with weapons." Isabella was contemptuous.

"Damien, don't…" His father shook his head.

Damien closed his eyes against his father's pleading. He couldn't help but feel his mother stiffen, but she didn't withdraw or object. Damien opened his eyes and stared into his sister's. As he spoke, he shared images, sounds, and feelings with her.

"It's not a life you'd want to live. You'd be forced to learn or die. At best possess some other ability he'd value. Regardless, given how your powers are shaping up, I don't believe he'd allow you to stay here. You'd be a potential threat." The last image Damien shared with Isabella was Nera's dead body. The image Michael had shown him of how he'd last seen his sister, dead in her rooms in the stronghold at Yalleska. Closely followed by the images of what had happened to Michael's parents.

"Damien!" His father's voice was harsh.

The criticism in that one word was only decipherable because he was his father's son, but Damien didn't offer even a hint of apology.

"If Isabella had known why she couldn't see me, she would not have risked you all. Risked herself. She has a right to know." Damien was quite proud that his tone was even, without even a hint of blame.

The age Isabella was at between child and adult was something he understood; he'd been through it not long ago. Damien just wished the consequences for her weren't so high.

"Nera. Who was she?" Isabella's eyes were wide, her voice barely above a whisper.

"Michael's sister. He's the one they call the warleader. The Warlord took them at the fall of Vallantia, much younger than we are now. Nera was strong like him, but not a fighter. The Warlord took her anyway." Damien kept his eyes on Isabella's, grateful he'd been right.

She was calm. Not a hint of panic in her, even though this new information potentially had extreme consequences for her.

"I didn't know." Isabella's voice was barely a whisper. "Will he take me now?"

Damien shook his head. "I don't think so. The Warlord likes to have a threat to enforce obedience, someone to punish if we disobey."

"What should I do?" Isabella's eyes were wide, her face pale, although her voice was steady.

Damien wrestled with his thoughts. Trying to find a way out of their current predicament, but it was too late now. Even if she had been unremarkable, her life would be at risk because of him. Now that the Warlord had seen her, Damien had a sinking feeling he would take Isabella for himself eventually, regardless of his good behaviour.

"Go to Owen. Learn everything he can teach you about protecting yourself. Armed and unarmed." As his mother and father went to protest, Damien's flat stare caused them both to subside.

"What will you do? Will he hurt you for hiding me?" Isabella's lip trembled when she thought of him being hurt as it hadn't when thinking about the risk to herself.

Damien reached out and pulled Isabella into his arms, whispering to her. "No. I'll be fine. Turns out I'm good at fighting—better than good—so I have more value than most. I'll just have to ensure I do everything I can to keep you safe."

"I'm sorry. I didn't mean to make your life harder." Tears spilled from her eyes and traced their way down her cheek.

He brushed them away with his fingers, shaking his head.

"You haven't, not really. In a way, you've just made things a little easier." He smiled sadly. He realised he now had the motivation to do as he was told, even if it was to attack for the sole reason of expanding the Warlord's domain. "One more thing, if you are taking the tonic, stop. It's addictive and poison for the likes of you and me." Damien's mother gasped at that piece of information, her hand flying to her lips.

"But the visiting healer said…" His mother was horrified.

"I don't think he meant harm, but he probably didn't know any better. How could he? All the people like me, who survive and do know the risks of tiscan on our kind, ride for the Warlord." Damien weighed his words trying to ease his mother's guilt at finding out she'd fed her child poison. "I think perhaps for those with low-level abilities it might help, that's all that visiting healer would have known. Kesha our healer would probably know better, perhaps speak to her about it?"

Damien vowed he would do his best to make himself invaluable to the Warlord and never give him so much as a hint of a reason to punish his family. He would commit himself fully to being a member of the Unwanted. Without even the hint of rebellion or hesitation, he would be the killer they wanted him to be.

NINETY-THREE

Samuel waited for the messenger to leave before sinking back onto the pillows of his lounge, his anger barely contained.

"Why won't she have the grace to die as she should?" Samuel's voice hissed.

He'd been full of anticipation of receiving the bad news that his dear sister had died in the barbarian lands, as many other families had before her. Instead, she'd had the gall to succeed where so many others had failed. At first, when he'd received report after report of the failure of the raiding parties, it had incensed him. How dare a bunch of unwashed barbarians not only fight back but have the gall to kill those of fine Sylannian breeding? It was incomprehensible. Then it had become a rather convenient way to get rid of his rivals that went unnoticed by most in the court. Yet Jaclyn had not only lived but also managed to conduct several successful raids without a single loss of life from her own house. The good news was already spreading around the court.

"We must acknowledge her success in court." Fiona's strong fingers kneaded his shoulders.

Samuel flung himself out of his chair, throwing the cushion across the room. He glowered as it fell on the floor and skidded towards one of the shuttered floor-to-ceiling windows. Spinning, Samuel swiped at a vase on a pedestal, sending it to the floor. He grinned, satisfied as it crashed to the ground, the shattered pieces scattering on the floor.

"She was meant to die!"

"You will announce that because of her success, Jaclyn is the perfect person to head the invasion of the barbarians," Fiona said calmly from behind him.

"If I make her commander, she will have her pick of the houses to fight with her. Just like she did in the trader lands." Samuel's irritation flared again.

"The difference, husband, is that the barbarian warlord and his people know how to fight. Her luck will run out, and she will lose." Fiona came up beside him, her hand rising to cup his cheek. "Besides it gets her out of court and her popularity will drop as it did before. Out of sight, out of mind."

"She's manoeuvring me into the position she wants me." Samuel could hear his tone had dropped to a grumble as he stared into Fiona's eyes, struggling to hold on to his anger in the face of her determination that he let it go.

Samuel was aware Fiona was sending a steady stream of soothing emotions to him. Forcing calmness on him. After all these years under the influence of his wives, he had no chance of fighting her will. A small part of his mind recognised that he rarely did these days. Samuel blinked, staring into Fiona's eyes. Clinging to his mood didn't seem so important now as she pulled his head down and kissed him while her hands pulled off his shirt. Samuel knew precisely what she was up to; as all his wives were, Fiona was adept at diverting his attention when she wished.

His focus contracted to Fiona's deep brown eyes, and she pushed aside the barriers on his mind that stood between them. Fiona's delicate touch drew him in, and the issue of his irritatingly competent sister was brushed away as she willed it. It didn't matter that he was the king. He had no more power than his wives allowed him. They would defend him with their lives, even from himself. Samuel gasped softly as Fiona's will rolled over him, cares he'd had but a moment before sliding away. The only thing that existed was Fiona.

He reached up and slipped the silk of her blouse off her shoulders, his eyes drinking her in as it pooled around her waist. Pulling her to him, he kissed her, feeling his desire rise.

"Is it time?"

"Yes, husband, I am fertile; let us have a child together." Fiona's voice was husky as she leant over and kissed him once more before her fingers undid the ties on his pants.

A moment of confusion caused Samuel to pause; he didn't know what he'd been doing the moment before. Then Fiona's hand curled around his cheek, fingers lacing in his hair; she pulled him to her and he found he didn't care. He was fully occupied with his wife. Perhaps they would be lucky and birth another son to his house, proving to all that he and his wives were the leaders of Sylanna by right. Not just a quirk of fate that had meant his first-born child had been a son.

NINETY-FOUR

Damien left his family's home, careful to keep his face blank, his mind churning as he tried to grapple with the consequences of what had just happened. Although he didn't fool the Unwanted.

At movement near him, he didn't bother to turn. It was the Warlord, although the fact that the Warlord was almost upon him before he'd noticed told him how lost in his own world he'd been.

"So, you have a sister, such a pretty little thing." The Warlord's tone held a hint of anticipation.

"I guess, Warlord. She's my little sister, so I can't say I've spent time thinking of her that way." Damien kept his tone light, knowing the Warlord was trying to provoke a reaction from him.

"Well, take it from me. She is quite stunning. I can see why your parents keep her close."

"Isabella isn't of age, yet; people sometimes forget it."

"I can see why; she is quite well-developed." A hint of

desire was evident in the Warlord's tone. Even if the Warlord's, face revealed little.

Damien kept his gaze on the tree line at the edge of the village, battling not to give away how much the Warlord's words were affecting him. By the way the Warlord's eyes glittered, he was failing.

Damien glanced across at Michael, and a bond forged between them, giving him insight into things he hadn't understood. Michael's family had remained untouched since the fall of Vallantia, even though his brother Steven had tried to raise a rebellion against the Warlord several times. Damien realised after the death of his sister that Michael had forged himself into the image of the Warlord's perfect, loyal son. Even more so than his actual son by blood. In return, the Warlord ignored the infractions of his youngest son's birth family. When Michael said he was the Warlord's creature. He meant it.

Damien gave up the pretence of not caring and stared at the Warlord. "I'll ride with the Unwanted, be the perfect killer and more. Just, please, leave Isabella and my parents be."

The Warlord threw his head back with a bark of laughter. "Very well, Damien, just as long as we understand each other. Fail me, and your sister will join me in my home at Yalleska— or perhaps I'll turn her into a perfect little killer."

Damien's face drained of colour, and he turned to walk away. He wasn't sure why his little sister being turned into a killer like him seemed worse. Somehow it just was. There was no response he could make to the threat, other than trying not to show how rattled he was. Then the Warlord spoke once more.

"I'll have to reward the baker here for bringing her existence to my attention."

Damien nearly staggered at the Warlord's words. He stared

at him, wanting to believe he'd misunderstood. Yet he could feel the truth in the Warlord's words.

Damien went cold and spun away, drawing his sword as he strode towards the bakehouse, ignoring the Warlord's harsh laughter that assaulted his ears. But that same laughter, and the scrape of Damien's sword as he drew it from its sheath, attracted the villagers' attention. Damien paid no attention to any of them as they withdrew from his path, their faces clouding with sudden fear. Most of them had made it clear he wasn't welcome but he'd never truly believed that any of them might turn informant, let alone give up anyone, especially a child, to the Warlord.

"Damien, what—"

Damien registered the taskmaster's voice, but he ignored the old man as the baker came out of the bakehouse. The traitor turned, a frown on his face that quickly changed to panic. As he tried to turn and run away, Damien was on him, slamming him against the cold stone walls of the bakehouse.

"You turned informant." Damien barely recognised the harsh tone in his voice.

"What of it!" The baker's face went red as he struggled against Damien's hold.

"You gave up Isabella to him."

"He would have found out about her anyway, and her presence here puts us all at risk." The baker blustered that last as an appeal to the observers, as shocked whispers ran around those brave enough to stay as the confrontation unfolded.

"How much did he pay you?" Damien shook the man and slammed him into the wall again.

"He pays well enough. We all have to survive; you shouldn't be the only one who benefits. We all must work harder because of the tithe." Again, the baker stared around, trying to generate support.

Damien twisted, then hauled the miserable excuse of a man forward, staring straight into his eyes. The baker screamed in pain as he was spitted on Damien's blade. With the veil coursing through him, increasing his strength, Damien twisted his blade viciously as he withdrew it, then cut through the baker's throat with a sharp, fast swing.

Damien stood, eyes cold, as he looked down at the twitching man on the ground. He felt nothing except for the part of his mind that was astonished at how long it took the baker to die. He turned, wiping the blood from his face as he walked back across the quietly horrified village, making a straight line to the Warlord who stood observing his approach.

"That is what you wanted of me, I take it?" Damien's voice was flat, and he stared coldly into the Warlord's eye.

"So. My little cub has teeth." A slow smile spread on the Warlord's lips. "Welcome to the family, son."

Knowing that was all the answer he would get, but sensing the Warlord's satisfaction mingled with his amusement and approval, Damien continued walking back to where he belonged. To his family.

Into the fold of the Unwanted.

THE EMERGENCE SERIES
CONTINUES...

Sacrifice (Emergence, Book Two)

Defiance (Emergence, Book Three)

Find out more by visiting https://www.catherinemwalker.com

About the Author

Catherine M Walker was born in a small country town in Western Australia but now resides in Perth, Western Australia.

Unwanted is the first book in Catherine's second epic fantasy series Emergence.

If you'd like to know more about Catherine's work including following the progress of her new series visit:

https://www.catherinemwalker.com

www.ingramcontent.com/pod-product-compliance
Lightning Source LLC
Chambersburg PA
CBHW060721190726
48285CB00001B/23